THE STRANGLING ON THE STAGE

The local dramatic society provides fertile ground for murder in the brand-new Fethering mystery.

Jude has landed a starring role in the local AmDram Society's production of George Bernard Shaw's The Devil's Disciple. It's an ambitious play, culminating in a dramatic execution scene: a scene that's played for real when one of the actors is found hanging from the stage gallows during rehearsals. A tragic accident – or something more sinister?

THE STRANGLING ON THE STAGE

A Fethering Mystery

Simon Brett

Severn House Large Print
London & New York

This first large print edition published 2014
in Great Britain and the USA by
SEVERN HOUSE PUBLISHERS LTD of
19 Cedar Road, Sutton, Surrey, England, SM2 5DA.
First world regular print edition published 2013 by
Crème de la Crime, an imprint of
Severn House Publishers Ltd., London and New York.

British Library Cataloguing in Publication Data

Brett, Simon author.
  The strangling on the stage.
  1. Seddon, Carole (Fictitious character)--Fiction. 2. Jude
  (Fictitious character : Brett)--Fiction. 3. Fethering
  (England : Imaginary place)--Fiction. 4. Women private
  investigators--England--Fiction. 5. Murder--
  Investigation--Fiction. 6. Shaw, Bernard, 1856-1950
  Devil's disciple--Fiction. 7. Hanging--Fiction.
  8. Detective and mystery stories. 9. Large type books.
  I. Title
  823.9'2-dc23

  ISBN-13: 9780727897169

Severn House Publishers support the Forest Stewardship Council™
[FSC™], the leading international forest certification organisation. All
our titles that are printed on FSC certified paper carry the FSC logo.

MIX
Paper from
responsible sources
FSC
www.fsc.org   FSC® C013056

Printed and bound in Great Britain by
T J International, Padstow, Cornwall.

To
Michael Green
(Author of *The Art of Coarse Acting*),
with admiration

ONE

'And the trouble is,' said Storm Lavelle, 'it's just total murder.'

'What is?' asked Jude.

'My life. Everything.'

Storm Lavelle was stretched out on the treatment table in the front room of Woodside Cottage in the seaside village of Fethering. It was February, cold outside, but snug with the open fire in Jude's front room. The scent of aromatic candles on the mantelpiece mingled with the smell of burning wood.

Storm had in theory come for a healing session, though Jude knew by experience she was basically there to unload the latest aggravations of her life. Which was fair enough. Jude also knew that listening was frequently as effective as any other form of healing.

The irony was that Storm Lavelle also practised as a healer, and she was the ultimate example of where the 'healer, heal thyself' principle broke down. Though very good with her clients, impressing them with her calm and stability, Storm was actually as mad as several

7

container-loads of frogs. Her volatile personality ensured that she skittered from one alternative therapeutic cure-all to another. It was remarkable that she'd stuck with the healing, though it was now only as a practitioner rather than a patient. Storm had long since decided that healing was inadequate to her own needs, and embarked on courses of reflexology, kinesiology, homeopathy, naturopathy and any other 'ologies' or 'opathies' that came to her attention.

She had also dabbled in a wide range of leisure activities. Many of these were fitness-related. Within the previous couple of years Storm had, to Jude's knowledge, tried Aerobics, Aqua Aerobics, Padel Tennis, Pilates and Zumba. She had also taken up macramé, bird watching and bridge, and joined a choir.

None of this worried Jude or stood in the way of the two women's friendship. Her attitude to her fellow human beings reflected a line that had once been quoted to her, the view of someone called Joe Ancis that 'the only normal people are the ones you don't know very well'. And beneath all Storm's traumas and dramas, Jude could recognize an honest, caring person whose only fault – if indeed it was a fault – was to get both too deeply and too shallowly involved with everything.

This applied particularly to Storm Lavelle's love life. As with alternative therapies, she also skittered from relationship to relationship. And in each one she made the same error, believing wholeheartedly that at last, after all of her past failures, she had found the perfect man on whom to lavish all of her affection. Invariably the men, frightened by the intensity of this passion, soon wanted to disengage. And Storm's heart would be broken once again.

It wasn't that she was unattractive, far from it. She was in her forties, some ten years younger than Jude, but unlike her friend, didn't carry a spare ounce of weight anywhere. This was partly due to the cocktail of diets and health fads that she followed, but the traumas of her frequent break-ups also played their part. She had innocent, pained blue eyes and was a natural blonde, though that original colour was very rarely in evidence. Storm was as fickle with new hairstyles as she was with everything else in her life.

That day her hair was cropped short and coloured a striking aubergine. She was dressed in black leggings and a sloppy yellow T-shirt. The precision of her make-up made her look almost like a geisha girl.

Jude sometimes wondered where her friend's name had come from. Surely no parents would actually christen a child 'Storm'? She wouldn't have been surprised to find out that in her younger years Storm had tried out as many names as she had other elements in her life. But she'd stayed with Storm Lavelle for the duration of their friendship.

Jude was giving her a basic relaxing massage, while the more important therapy of Storm unburdening herself continued. Storm would sometimes do a massage for Jude, so in these sessions no money ever changed hands. And whichever one was client or healer, it was still Storm who did most of the talking.

'I told you I'd split up with Paul, didn't I?'

'You didn't actually, but I'd kind of pieced it together from your manner.'

'What is it with men? One moment they're all over you like a rash, then suddenly they go all cold and start mumbling about "needing their own space".'

'Yes.' Jude paused, then decided to say it anyway. It wouldn't be the first time she'd raised the point. 'You don't think, do you, Storm, that it might be because you always go at relationships so full-on, you know, with all guns blazing? Maybe if you started a bit more casually...?'

'I can't be casual about love. I have to follow my heart. I knew when I met Paul that he was absolutely the one for me. And he said the same – he said he'd never met anyone like me.'

Jude reckoned that was probably true, but she didn't voice the thought.

'So how can someone be madly in love with you, saying he's having the best sex with you he's ever had, and then within a couple of weeks say he "needs his own space"?'

'If women knew the answer to that question,

Storm, the relationship between the sexes might be considerably easier.'

'Yes. Do you think men are just differently wired from women?'

'If I did, I wouldn't be the first to have expressed that opinion. But I think there are more similarities than differences between the genders. Everyone, male or female, is afraid of having their personality swamped by another person.'

'And are you saying that's what I do, Jude? Swamp people's personalities?'

'I'm just saying that if you took a more gradual, a slower approach into relationships...'

'But I'm not a gradual person, I'm not a slow person. I have to obey my instincts.'

'Even if those instincts keep pushing you in the wrong direction?'

'What do you mean – "pushing me in the wrong direction"?'

'Well, look, Paul isn't the first man with whom your relationship has ended in much the same way.'

'How can you say that, Jude?'

'From simple observation. Do you want me to name names? Carl, George, Nick, Harry—'

'Those relationships were nothing like what I had with Paul. I knew from the start that Paul was the real thing.'

'I heard you say the same when you first met Carl ... and George ... and Nick ... and—'

'No, I'm sure I never said that with them.'

It wasn't worth arguing the point, though Jude's recollections of Storm's announcement of each new man in her life were extremely accurate.

'Anyway,' Storm announced, as she had so many times before, 'I'm giving up men.'

'In favour of what?'

'Other things. I've wasted so much of my life agonizing over them, it's time I got on with the things that really interest me.'

'And what might they be?' asked Jude, wondering what new fad was about to be revealed.

'Acting,' Storm replied. 'I'm really going to concentrate on my acting.'

Now this was not as foolish an answer as Jude had been expecting. Storm Lavelle was actually rather good at acting. Perhaps the wide variety in her own emotional life had enabled her to see inside the characters of others. Or, then again, like many with a shaky sense of their own identity, maybe she found a security in playing a role, in being a different person.

Jude had been dragged along as support to a selection of West Sussex's church halls where her friend had been appearing with one or other of the local amateur dramatic societies. And though a few of the productions had been a bit ropey, Storm Lavelle had always shone in the not very glittering company. Acting was also a fad that she had stuck with. Whatever else was going on in her life, she was usually involved in rehearsal for some play or other. Jude, whose earlier career as a model had led to a year or two of acting, recognized genuine talent and was sure that her friend had it. Whether Storm also had the temperament and tenacity to pursue the theatre as a full-time career Jude was less certain.

Which prompted her next question. 'Do you mean concentrate on it exclusively? Make it your profession?'

'I wouldn't rule that out,' replied Storm, with a new confidence in her voice. 'I'm certainly going to take it more seriously, concentrate on getting better as an actor.' Jude was amused that the politically correct fashion of not using the word 'actress' had permeated the amateur section of the business.

'My quality is beginning to be recognized,' Storm went on. 'I'm being given better parts. I've just got a really good one with SADOS.'

She pronounced the acronym 'Say-doss', but Jude had to confess that the word meant nothing to her.

'SADOS,' said Storm, 'is the "Smalting Amateur Dramatic and Operatic Society".'

'Ah.'

'They've just held auditions for *The Devil's Disciple* and I've got the part of Judith Anderson.'

Jude had once again to admit ignorance. 'I've heard the title vaguely somewhere, but I'm afraid I don't know anything about it.'

Storm had clearly done her homework. 'It's

one of George Bernard Shaw's earliest plays. Set during the American War of Independence. And it's about this bad American guy called Dick Dudgeon who's going to be hanged by the British because he's been mistaken for the good American pastor called Anthony Anderson...'

'Sounds a bit like *A Tale of Two Cities*.'

'I don't know that play, I'm afraid. But, anyway, Judith is Anthony Anderson's wife and she's really conflicted, because she hates Dick Dudgeon, but at the same time she's very drawn to him.' It didn't sound as if this summary was Storm's own, more as if she were quoting someone. 'And the play's also an attack on puritanism, and reiterates the common theme in Shaw of how people should stand up against convention if they think that convention's wrong. At least,' she concluded, 'that's what Neville thinks.'

'Who's Neville?'

'Neville Prideaux. He's playing General Burgoyne in *The Devil's Disciple*. He's actually quite important in SADOS. Particularly on the Play Selection Committee. He says Shaw's out of fashion, but he doesn't deserve to be. And he thinks that SADOS ought to do more challenging work, not just their usual safe diet of light comedies, Agatha Christies and episodes from television series.'

'Sorry? What do you mean – "episodes from television series"?'

'Oh, it's quite a popular thing now with

14

amdrams. An evening of three episodes of something like *Fawlty Towers* or *Dad's Army*.'

'Yowch!' said Jude, as the ghastly image of local thespians doing their impressions of John Cleese and Arthur Lowe encroached on her imagination.

'Well, Neville says doing them is retrogressive.'

'I would agree with Neville on that.'

'But they are very popular with audiences.'

'Presumably because said audiences know every word of the script off by heart.'

'I think that could be part of it, yes. Anyway, Neville says that SADOS should make a stand against putting on that sort of stuff. He even thought last year's production of *Calendar Girls* was too lightweight. And that's a play about cancer.'

No, it's not, thought Jude. It's a play about women taking their tops off. She was constantly amazed by the British prurient attitude to nudity, which explained the disproportionate success of shows like *Calendar Girls*. It seemed that members of every amateur dramatic society in the country couldn't wait to get their wizened tits out.

But Storm was still continuing her encomium of Neville Prideaux. 'He says there's a wonderful archive of great plays which deserve revival much more than any trivial TV sitcom.'

The devoutness with which Storm was quoting the great Neville Prideaux made Jude

15

wonder if, with Paul out of the way, he was about to be the next recipient of her all-embracing adoration.

She reached for a bottle on her mantelpiece. 'Just finish off the massage with some lavender essential oil. You happy with that?'

'Great,' said Storm, as Jude, with oil rubbed on to her hands, started kneading her friend's shoulders.

'And it's because of Neville's views that you're doing *The Devil's Disciple* – is that right?'

'Exactly. Neville says it would do the people of Smalting good to have their brains engaged by something they see in the theatre.'

'I'm sure it would.'

'Anyway, as I say, I'm delighted to have got the part of Judith Anderson. Though I say it myself, I knew I was the best person in the Society to play it, but I was still very nervous about the audition.'

'Why was that?'

Storm gave a conspiratorial wink. 'Oh, wheels within wheels. There's a lot of politics in SADOS. You see, there's this kind of diva called Elizaveta Dalrymple, who's the widow of Freddie Dalrymple, who's the guy who started the Society, and she's very much its social hub. Holds these little parties on Saturdays that she calls her "drinkies things" and if you're invited to one of those you really know you've arrived in SADOS. Anyway, Elizaveta is kind of used to getting all the major parts in the shows – even ones that she's far too old for. And she's very in with Davina Vere Smith, who's actually directing *The Devil's Disciple*, and with quite a lot of the older members. So I thought there was a real danger that Judith Anderson, who's meant to be – what, thirty? – well, that the part would go to Elizaveta Dalrymple, who's got to be seventy – and that's being generous.'

'But instead you triumphed?'

'Yes. Well, as I said, I was definitely the best person for the part.' In spite of the vagaries and vulnerabilities in other areas of her life, Storm Lavelle was very assured about her acting skills. And indeed it was when witnessing one of her performances that Jude had seen her friend at her most confident. Maybe getting into the professional theatre would be the resolution of Storm's personality problems. Not of course that getting into the professional theatre was an easy thing to be achieved by a woman in her forties.

'And have you actually started rehearsals for the play yet?'

'Read-through on Sunday. Open on the twelfth of May.'

'Wow! Three months' rehearsal. A lot of professional theatres would kill for that amount of time.'

'Maybe, but you forget that we aren't doing it full-time. Most of the cast have day jobs.'

'Yes, of course. I wasn't thinking.'

'So we rehearse Tuesday and Thursday evenings and Sunday afternoons.'

'And how many performances do you do?'

'Just the four. The twelfth of May's a Wednesday, and we go through to the Saturday. SADOS used to open on Tuesdays and throw in a Saturday matinee as well, but they can't get the audiences for that many performances now.'

'Ah.' Jude removed her hands from Storm's body and rubbed the oil off them with a towel. 'That's you done,' she said. 'Unknotted a few of the knots, I hope?'

'Great, as ever. Thank you, Jude.'

'My pleasure. I'm sure I'll soon be asking you to do the same for me. Anyway, good luck with the read-through on Sunday.'

'Yes, I'm a bit nervous about it. Excited too, but at the moment mainly nervous.'

'I'm sure you'll be fine.'

'Oh, I will ... once the read-through actually starts. But, you see, the thing is ... Ritchie Good's playing Dick Dudgeon.'

'Is he?' said Jude, though neither of the names meant anything to her. 'Should I know him?'

'Ritchie Good? Surely you've heard of him?'

'No.'

'Oh, he's a terrific actor. Everyone says he should have done it professionally. He's played star parts with lots of local groups – the Fedborough Thespians, the Clincham Players, the Worthing Rustics – Ritchie's acted with all of

18

them. He even played Hamlet for the Rusting-
ton Barnstormers.'

'Did he?' said Jude, trying to sound appropriately impressed.

'He's really good. Somebody must have
pulled out all the stops to get him for the
SADOS. I suppose it might have been Davina,
though I'd be surprised if she had the clout to
persuade someone like Ritchie Good.'

'Davina?'

'Davina Vere Smith. She's the director. I
said.'

'Yes, I'm sorry.'

'He's incredibly good-looking, Ritchie. Got
quite a following in the amdram world.'

Jude wondered for a moment whether it
would be this new paragon, Ritchie Good,
rather than Neville Prideaux who was about to
be the recipient of Storm Lavelle's full-on
adoration.

Her friend was on the way to the door when
she stopped and said, 'Ooh, one thing, Jude...'

'Yes.'

Storm looked around the cluttered room,
whose furniture was all covered with rugs and
throws. 'I just wondered if you'd still got...?'

A wry smile came to Jude's full lips as she
said, 'You mean the chaise longue?'

'Yes.'

Jude moved across to remove a light-blue
woollen blanket she'd bought in Morocco and
reveal the article under discussion. The chaise

19

longue had come from a little antique shop in Minchinhampton, picked up when she'd been on a trip to the Cotswolds with her second husband. It had been a stage of her life when Jude had been moving away from the husband and towards the idea of becoming a healer. She had thought the chaise longue might possibly do service as a treatment couch, but when she'd got it home she found it to be too low for such a purpose. She had hung on to it, though, and it had moved with her from address to address when other pieces of furniture had been abandoned.

She didn't know how old it was, and the antique dealer who sold the thing to her had been pretty vague on the subject. 'Mid to late Victorian, possibly Edwardian' was as specific as he had got. The base, he said, 'might be mahogany', though Jude thought it was probably a cheaper wood stained to look like mahogany. The upholstery, he felt sure, was not original, but Jude had become quite fond over the years of the purplish flowered print, even though it was usually covered with the Moorish drape. She liked using the chaise longue in the winter months, moving it near the fire, making sure she had an adequate supply of tea, crumpets and books before snuggling under the cover.

Many chaises longues have a supporting arm along one side, but Jude's didn't. And this had proved of great benefit in its life outside Wood-

20

side Cottage.

Because her chaise longue was a much borrowed piece of furniture. And it was always borrowed by the same kind of people – amateur dramatic groups. A chaise longue was so versatile. Any play set in any historical period looked better with a chaise longue as part of its setting. And Jude's armless chaise longue was much loved by directors, because they could set it facing the audience on either the right- or the left-hand side of the stage.

Not even counting the times it had been borrowed before, since Jude came to Fethering her chaise longue had featured in most of the church halls of the area in a variety of thespian endeavours. It had been a shoo-in for a part in *Robert and Elizabeth*, the musical about the poet Browning and his wife, and appeared in more than one stage version of *Pride and Prejudice*. Jude's chaise longue had also taken the stage in *The Winslow Boy*, *Arsenic and Old Lace* (twice) and virtually the entire *oeuvre* of Oscar Wilde. It had even, tarted up in gold foil, provided a suitable surface for the Egyptian queen to be poisoned on by an asp in *Antony and Cleopatra*.

And now, Jude intuited, it might be about to make an appearance in George Bernard Shaw's *The Devil's Disciple*.

So it proved. Storm wondered tentatively whether it might be possible for the SADOS to impose on Jude's generosity to borrow...? The permission was readily given. Jude's sitting room also contained a sofa which could be moved near the fire for the tea, crumpet and book routine, so the chaise longue would not be missed. The only questions really were when would it be needed, and how should it be got to where it needed to be got to.

The answer to the first was as soon as possible, because when Davina Vere Smith was directing she liked to use all the furniture and props right from the beginning of rehearsals. And the chaise longue needed to be got to St Mary's Church Hall in Smalting. Once in situ it could stay there because there was a storeroom the SADOS were allowed to use for their props and things. In fact, they were lucky enough to be able to hold most of their rehearsals in the Hall, which was of course where the performances would take place in May.

'That's very convenient for you,' said Jude. 'So what, will someone come and pick the chaise longue up from here?'

'Yes, that would be good, wouldn't it?' Storm agreed. 'Trouble is, I've only got my Smart car and it'd never fit in there. And Gordon – that's Gordon Blaine, who's in charge of all the backstage stuff for SADOS – well, normally he'd pick it up, but his Land Rover's got some problem that he's busy repairing at the moment and ... You can't think of any way of getting it to St Mary's Hall, can you, Jude?'

'Well, I don't have a car myself.'

'Of no, of course you don't. Sorry, I'd forgotten. But you haven't got a friend, have you? A friend you could ask to...?'

'Yes.' A smile played round Jude's lips. 'Yes, there is someone I could ask.'

TWO

'I've never had any time for amateur dramatics,' announced Carole Seddon. 'Or indeed for the people who indulge in them.'

'I'm not asking you to indulge in anything,' said Jude patiently. 'I'm just asking you to help me deliver a chaise longue.'

'Hm.'

'It's only in Smalting. Early evening Sunday. The whole operation will take maybe an hour of your time.'

Carole looked dubiously at the uncovered chaise longue. 'I'm not sure that'll fit in the Renault.'

'Of course it will. If you put the back seats down.'

'I don't know. It's quite long.'

'That's possibly why it's called a chaise longue.'

'Oh, very funny, Jude,' said Carole without a hint of a smile.

'I happen to know that it will fit in the back of the Renault. It has had such a peripatetic life since I bought it that it has on occasions fitted into the back of virtually every vehicle that's ever been invented – except a Smart car, which would be a squeeze too far. But if you'd rather not do it, just say and I'll get someone else to—'

'Oh, I didn't say I'd rather not do it.' This was classic Carole Seddon. Jude knew her neighbour very well and was used to the obscure processes that had to be gone through in making arrangements with her. Carole may have disapproved of amateur dramatics, but she still had a very strong sense of curiosity. So long as she was accompanied by Jude, the opportunity of invading the stronghold of the Smalting Amateur Dramatic and Operatic Society was not one that she would readily forego. She'd never actually met any amateur thespians. If she were to meet some, they might well provide justification for her prejudice against them.

'So you will do it?'

Carole let out a long-suffering sigh. 'Oh, very well.' Having made that concession, she now deigned to show a faint interest in the SADOS. 'What play is your chaise longue going to feature in?'

'*The Devil's Disciple*.'

'Doesn't mean anything to me.'

'George Bernard Shaw.' Carole's grimace didn't need the support of words. 'Not your

24

favourite, do I detect?'

'I once spent a very long time sitting through *Heartbreak House*. I've known shorter fortnights.'

'Yes, he can be a bit of an old windbag. But there are still some good plays. *Pygmalion*, *Major Barbara*, *Saint Joan* ... they still just about stand up.'

'I'll take your word for it. And what about *The Devil's Disciple* – does that still stand up?'

Jude shook her head. 'Haven't seen it. Never actually heard the title until Storm mentioned it.'

Carole could not restrain herself from saying, 'Is your friend really called "Storm"?'

'Whether she was actually christened it, I don't know. But "Storm" is the name by which she's known.'

'Oh dear. Well, I suppose it goes with the amateur dramatics.'

'Yes,' agreed Jude, suppressing a giggle at the Caroleness of Carole.

'And will the good burghers of Smalting really come out in their thousands to see a minor work of George Bernard Shaw?'

'That,' said Jude, 'remains to be seen. But it doesn't matter a lot to us, because our only involvement in the production will be delivering a chaise longue.'

Little did she realize how wrong that assertion would prove to be.

Following Storm's instructions, relayed by Jude, Carole nosed the Renault into the car park by the church, within walking distance of a fairly new Sainsbury's Local.

The hall next to St Mary's in Smalting was a clone of thousands of other church halls throughout the country. Built in stout red brick towards the end of Victoria's reign, it had over the years hosted innumerable public lectures, wedding receptions, jumble sales, beetle drives, children's parties, Women's Institute coffee mornings and other local events. More recently its space had also accommodated, according to shifting fitness fashions, classes in Aerobics, Swing Aerobics, Pilates and Zumba. The hall, as Carole and Jude had cause to know from the time when they were investigating the discovery of some bones under a beach hut in Smalting, was also the regular venue for the Quiz Nights of the Smalting Beach Hut Association.

Like others of its kind, St Mary's Hall had been in a constant process of refurbishment, though it was never refurbished quite as well as it should have been. The most recent painting of the doors and windows in oxblood red had not been enough to counter the institutional feeling of its cream walls. And nothing seemed to remove the hall's slightly shabby aura or its enduring primary school smell of dampness, disinfectant and dubious drainage.

Storm's instructions to Jude had been exact. If they arrived at six, the read-through of *The*

Devil's Disciple would definitely be over by then. And so it proved. The two women had manhandled the chaise longue out of the Renault, but once they were inside the hall, they were encumbered with help. Storm came swanning across to greet them with a shriek of 'Jude, *darling*!', which made Carole's face look even stonier. For the read-through Storm's hair had undergone another transformation. It was now black, centrally parted and with little curls rather in the manner of Betty Boop. She scattered introductions over Carole and Jude like confetti, far too quickly for the information to be taken in, and organized a couple of men to take the chaise longue into the storeroom.

'Can't thank you enough, Jude darling. We will look after it very well, I promise.'

'I'm sure you will.'

'And now, look, since we've finished the read-through, we were all just about to adjourn to the pub. You will join us, won't you?'

'Well, I don't think—'

Cutting across Carole's words and ignoring the semaphore in her expression, Jude replied, 'Yes, we'd love to.'

They only knew one pub in Smalting, the Crab, and that wasn't really a pub. It was far too poshed-up to be the kind of place that a local could drop in for a pint. It was almost exclusively a restaurant, and the tiny bar area was designed only for people sipping a pre-prandial aperitif.

But fortunately it wasn't the Crab that Storm Lavelle led them to. Almost adjacent to St Mary's Church was a pub called the Cricketers (though why it was called that nobody had ever thought to ask – it was miles from the nearest cricket ground), and it was clear as soon as they walked in that the SADOS members were familiar guests. And welcome guests. The landlord, a perky, bird-like man called Len, seemed to know most of the amateur actors by name. Given the declining numbers of visitors to pubs, the Cricketers was glad of any group who would fall in regularly after rehearsals on a Tuesday, Thursday and Sunday.

Early that particular Sunday evening the amdram crowd seemed to account for most of the pub's clientele. Or maybe, just because they all talked so loudly and flamboyantly, they gave the impression of having taken over the place.

Carole Seddon felt extremely old-fashioned. She hadn't wanted to come to the pub and now she was there all she wanted was to be back in her neat little house, High Tor. Also, although she would never admit to being 'a slave to the television schedules', there was a programme on Sunday nights that she didn't like to miss. About midwives, it combined the unrivalled ingredients of contractions and nuns. Carole sneaked a look at her watch. Only twenty past six. Too early to use the show as an excuse for an early departure. Not of course that she'd ever

28

have revealed the real reason why she wanted to get back.

Jude had moved forward to the bar and just ordered two large glasses of Chilean Chardonnay when she was intercepted by a large man with a ginger beard, whom they'd been vaguely aware of overseeing the transfer of the chaise longue to the storeroom.

'Let me get those,' he said in a voice with a trace of Scottish in it. 'A small thank you to you for sacrificing your furniture to our tender mercies and bringing it over here.'

He thrust a twenty-pound note at the barman and the two women thought they were justified in accepting his generosity. He turned to a young woman also queuing at the bar. 'Let me get you one too, Janie.'

'Oh, you're always buying me drinks.'

'And it's always my pleasure. What're you having?'

'Vodka and coke, please.'

'Your wish is my command. Add a vodka and coke, Len.' The barman nodded. 'And a predictable pint of Guinness for me, please.'

While the bearded man was getting their drinks, the girl introduced herself as 'Janie Trotman'. She was slender, dark, quite pretty, dressed in shiny leggings and a purple hoodie. 'I'm playing Essie,' she volunteered.

'Sorry. I don't know the play,' said Jude.

'It's the only young female part, so I suppose I'm lucky to get it.'

29

'You don't sound too sure about that.'

'Well, I'm certainly not sure about the play. Having just sat through the read-through, it all seems a bit long-winded to me.'

At that moment a short, dumpy woman with improbably red hair bustled across to them. 'Hello, you two look new,' she said to Carole and Jude. 'I'm Mimi Lassiter, Membership Secretary. Also part of the crowd in Act Three, you know, one of the Westerbridge townsfolk.'

'Nice to meet you. I'm Jude. And this is my friend Carole.'

'Ah, good evening. We've got quite a lot of new members in for *The Devil's Disciple*, because it's such a big cast, though Davina has cut the numbers down a bit. And I'm just going round, checking with the newcomers that they are actually members of SADOS. Now I know you're fully paid up, Janie.' The girl nodded. 'The subscription rate for acting members is—'

'Let me stop you there,' said Jude. 'We're nothing to do with the production.'

'No, we certainly aren't,' Carole endorsed.

'Oh?'

'We've just been bearers of a chaise longue which I'm lending to be part of the set.'

Mimi Lassiter looked seriously disappointed. 'So you're not even in the crowd scenes?'

Jude assured her that they weren't.

'And does that mean,' asked Mimi almost pathetically, 'that you don't want to join

SADOS?'

'Certainly not,' replied Carole, as if she'd just been asked to do something very dirty indeed.

'Oh.' Discomfited, the Membership Secretary drifted away.

By now the bearded man had got their drinks which he handed round with old-fashioned gallantry. He introduced himself to Carole and Jude as 'Gordon Blaine – I'm in charge of the heavy backstage stuff for the SADOS – building sets, that kind of thing.'

'Oh yes, Storm mentioned you,' said Jude. 'Your Land Rover's broken down.'

He looked a little affronted by that. 'It's more in a process of refurbishment. I'm putting in a new engine. Haven't quite finished yet. So thanks for the use of your car.'

'It's my car actually,' said Carole tartly.

'Sorry. Then thank *you*,' he said without rancour.

Jude noticed that Janie Trotman was kind of lingering on the edge of their group, as if she wouldn't mind getting away. But maybe she thought, having accepted a drink from Gordon Blaine, she must stay with him for at least a little while.

'Sorry,' he was saying, 'didn't get your names.'

They identified themselves and Jude, to compensate for Carole's frostiness, asked, 'So, Gordon, will you be building the set for *The Devil's Disciple*?'

31

'Oh yes.'

'And designing it too?'

'No, no. I'm not given the name of "design-er",' he replied with careful emphasis. 'Lady over there is "the designer".' He gestured to a thin woman in her thirties, whose short blond hair was dyed almost white. 'I merely interpret the squiggles she puts on the page and turn them into a practical set which won't fall over. And from all accounts, *Disciple* is going to be a real bugger to build.'

'Oh?' said Jude. 'Why? I'm afraid I haven't read the play.'

'Nor have I,' said Gordon with something approaching pride. 'I only arrived at the end of the read-through. I never read the plays we do. Just do as I'm told and get on with whatever I'm instructed to do by the director and the designer.'

'So why is *The Devil's Disciple* going to be such a bugger?' asked Jude, not feeling she was sufficiently part of the SADOS to abbreviate the play's title to *'Disciple'*.

'Well, apparently it's got lots of sets. There's the Dudgeons' house and then the Andersons' house ... which aren't too bad because you can use one basic structure and differentiate the two locations by a bit of set dressing. But then in Act Three there's also the inside of the Town Hall and the outside of the Town Square where the scaffold is set up. Logistical nightmare.'

'So how are you going to manage it?'

32

'Don't worry, I'll manage it,' he replied with almost smug confidence. Jude had readily identified Gordon Blaine's type. He was the kind of man who would build up the difficulties of any task he was given and then apply his miraculous practical skills to succeed in delivering the impossible. In her brief contact with the professional theatre, she had met a good few characters like that, mostly involved in some backstage capacity.

'I think the only way it can be done,' Gordon went on, 'whatever fancy ideas the designer may have, is for me to build a basic box-set structure and then—'

He might clearly have gone on for quite a while had they not been interrupted by the appearance of Storm Lavelle, bringing in her wake a tall, good-looking man in his forties. His long hair flopped apologetically over his brow, and there was an expression of mock-innocence in his blue eyes.

Seeing the man approach, Janie Trotman took the opportunity to detach herself from the group round Gordon Blaine and go to join some of the younger members of the company. Whether this was a pointed avoidance of the newcomer neither Carole nor Jude could not judge.

'Jude!' Storm emoted, loud against the background hubbub. 'I really do want you to meet Ritchie.'

'You haven't properly met my friend Carole who—'

But the introduction was lost as Ritchie Good – it must have been him, there couldn't be two Ritchies in SADOS – took Jude's hand in both of his and said, 'Where have you been hiding all my life?'

It was one of the corniest lines in the world, but she admired the way it was delivered. He imbued the words with a sardonic quality, at the same time sending up their cheesiness and leaving the small possibility that they could be heartfelt.

'I've been hiding all over the place,' Jude replied evenly. 'Currently in Fethering.'

'Oh, lovely Fethering, where the Fether rolls down to the sea,' he said, for no very good reason.

'Ritchie's our Dick Dudgeon,' said Storm enthusiastically. 'He's just done a terrific read-through.'

'Well, you were no slouch yourself, Storm. It's only possible to give a good performance when you're up against other good actors.'

Jude was amused by the solipsism of the compliment. While apparently praising his co-star, he was also putting himself firmly in the category of 'good actors'.

'Well, I thought you were wonderful,' Storm insisted. 'You really *were* Dick Dudgeon. I was nearly tearing up in the last act.'

'Oh,' Ritchie said airily, 'I was just demonstrating a few shabby, manipulative tricks. My performance will get a lot more subtle as we go through the rehearsal process.'

'I'm sure it will,' said Storm devoutly.

Oh dear, thought Jude. She had seen the symptoms in her friend before. It looked as though Ritchie Good was in serious danger of receiving the full impact of Storm Lavelle's adoration. And Jude didn't think it was an encounter that would have a happy outcome.

'Oh, look, there's Elizaveta,' said Ritchie, waving across the bar. 'Must go and say hello to her.'

Storm took Jude's arm. 'You must come and meet Elizaveta too. She is just *so* funny.'

And the three of them swept away. Leaving Carole with Gordon Blaine.

Her nose, susceptible to frequent dislocation, was once again put out of joint. She was taken back to the agony of school dances, where her prettier friends had all been very friendly to her until they'd been swept away by the handsome boys. And she'd been left either pretending that the last thing on her mind was dancing, or stuck with one of the nerdy ones. Like Gordon Blaine.

'There's a little trick I used,' he was saying, 'when I was building the *Midsummer Night's Dream* set for the SADOS. Obvious, but it was surprising how few people thought of it. You see, by hingeing the flats at the back so that they could open up to reveal the cyclorama, and using gauzes for the scenes in the woods, I...'

Carole Seddon's eyes glazed over.

THREE

So I said to the director: "Do you want me to do it *your way*, or do you want me to do it *right*?"'

This was a cue for sycophantic laughter from the group around Elizaveta Dalrymple. Jude had heard the line before – it had been attributed to various Hollywood stars – but clearly the *grand dame* of the SADOS was presenting it as her own coining.

Elizaveta Dalrymple must have been a very beautiful young woman and in her seventies she was still striking. She wore a kaftan-style long dress in fig-coloured linen, which disguised her considerable bulk. Her dyed black hair was swept back from her face and fixed by a comb with a large red artificial flower on it, suggesting the image of a flamenco dancer. Her make-up was skilfully done, though it could not cover the lines on her face – bright red lips and lashes far too luxuriant to have grown out of any human eyelid.

The manner in which she had spoken her line suggested that she had spent rather too much time watching Maggie Smith.

Storm took the natural break given by the

36

laugh as an opportunity to introduce Jude.

'Ah, I didn't notice you at the read-through.' Elizaveta Dalrymple gave the impression that there were a lot of people she didn't regard as worth noticing. 'Presumably you're doing something backstage, are you?'

'No, I'm not involved in the production at all. Just lending my chaise longue for the set.'

'Ah, chaises longues,' said Elizaveta in a voice intended to be thrilling. 'How much fun one has had on chaises longues. A long time ago, of course.' She chuckled fondly. 'And a lot of it actually with Freddie.' She allowed a moment for murmurs of appreciation for SADOS's late founder. 'Who was it who said: "Marriage is the longing for the deep, deep peace of the double-bed after the hurly-burly of the chaise longue?"'

Jude said, 'Mrs Patrick Campbell', because it was something she happened to know, but the pique in Elizaveta Dalrymple's face suggested her question had been rhetorical and not one to be answered by mere chaise longue owners.

To reinforce her disapproval, she turned away from Jude to Storm. 'I thought you did a lovely little reading this afternoon as Judith. And the American accent will come with practice.'

Rather than bridling at being so patronized, Storm smiled meekly, saying, 'Thank you very much, Elizaveta. And your Mrs Dudgeon was wonderful.'

'Yes, it's something when an actor like me

ends up playing a grumpy old woman who dies offstage during Act Two.' The grande dame smiled. 'I'm thinking of it as a character part.' That got a laugh from her coterie of admirers. 'I really wasn't going to do it. I really do keep intending to give up "the business".' You're just an amateur, Jude wanted to scream, acting is not your profession. 'But Davina twisted my arm *once again.*'

Elizaveta Dalrymple turned an expression of mock ruefulness to a dumpy woman with a long blond pigtail, who was dressed in black leggings and a high-collared gold lamé top. This, Jude remembered from the flurry of introductions when she'd joined the group, was Davina Vere Smith.

'Oh, you were dying to do it, Elizaveta,' protested the director of *The Devil's Disciple*. 'There was nothing going to keep you away from this production, away from anything that SADOS does.'

'Don't you believe it, Davina. I really do think there has to come a time when one has to retire gracefully. And I think I've reached that time.' The coterie protested violently at this suggestion. 'I'd rather go at a time of my own choosing than get to the point where I can no longer remember the lines and the old acting skills start to dwindle.'

'That day'll never come,' insisted the most toadyish of the coterie, a young man who had been introduced as Olly Pinto. He was nearly very good-looking, but the size of his shield-like jaw gave him a cartoonish quality. 'Your reading this afternoon showed that you're still at the height of your powers.'

'Oh...' Elizaveta Dalrymple simpered at the compliment. 'And yours was lovely too, Olly. Your Christy's going to be great.'

The young man grimaced. 'It's not much of a part,' he said.

'There are no small parts,' said Elizaveta magisterially, 'only small actors.'

Again she made it sound as if the line was her own, though Jude knew it had been around for years, usually attributed to Stanislavsky. Again Elizaveta Dalrymple received a laugh of approbation from her coterie.

'Well, I think you're going to show that Mrs Dudgeon is far from a small part,' said Olly Pinto, still sucking up.

'I suppose if I can still do something to help out SADOS ... it's what Freddie would have wanted me to do.' Elizaveta Dalrymple left a silence for a few more respectful grunts. Then she turned to the director. 'Were you pleased with the way the read-through went this afternoon, Davina?'

'Yes, pretty good, really. Obviously a few absentees. Three of my soldiers have got flu and my Major Swindon is still off skiing. I suppose, like most amateur productions, I'll be lucky if I get the full company on the first night.'

Elizaveta Dalrymple clearly thought she had been silent for too long. 'I'm determined to have *fun* playing Mrs Dudgeon. And it'll be nice to give my old American accent a little run for its money.'

'It's very good,' said her toady. 'Did you ever live in the States?'

'Good heavens, no,' said Elizaveta on a self-deprecating laugh. 'But I always have had a very good ear. I'm just one of those lucky people who can pick up accents ... like that.' Her eye lingered pityingly on Storm Lavelle. 'Of course, there was a time when I'd have been natural casting for Judith Anderson, but those days are gone...'

Jude couldn't understand why her friend didn't knock the malevolent old woman's block off, but Storm was still listening intently, as though at the feet of a guru. And when Elizaveta said she would invite Storm to one of her 'drinkies things', Jude's friend looked as if she'd just been made a Dame.

'Of course,' Elizaveta Dalrymple went on, 'my American accent was really given a work-out when Freddie and I did *On Golden Pond*. I remember there was someone from Boston in the audience, and he couldn't believe that I hadn't been brought up in the States. He said he'd never heard—'

But her reminiscences were interrupted by the appearance of Len, the Cricketers' landlord, at the edge of their group. 'Department of Lost

Property,' he said, and he held out a star-shaped silver pendant on a silver chain. 'I think it got left here during the pantomime. Someone must've dropped it. So I thought I'd wait till you all came back and see if anyone claims it. Somebody said it might be yours, Elizaveta.'

'Well, yes, I do have one that looks very like that. May I have a look?' The barman handed the necklace across. Elizaveta Dalrymple turned it over to look at the back. 'Yes, this must be mine. It's funny, I hadn't noticed...' She reached up to her neck to find a silver chain around it. She pulled at it and out of the top of her kaftan dress came a silver star, similar in size to the other one. 'Oh no, I've got mine.'

She offered Len's pendant round to her group. 'Anyone claim this? It's not yours, is it, Davina?'

'No,' said the director. 'I don't wear jewellery like that.'

Elizaveta Dalrymple made an elaborate shrug and handed the unclaimed pendant back to Len. 'Be worth asking round the other SADOS members.'

'Yes. And could you mention it at rehearsal?'

'Certainly.'

'I'll keep it behind the bar till someone claims it.' And the landlord drifted away, ready to offer the necklace to other groups.

'Let me know if anyone does claim it,' Elizaveta called after him. Then she turned back to her coterie. 'A rather amusing story about

41

jewellery came out of the production of *When We Are Married* that Freddie and I did. You see, there was someone in the cast who—'

But she was cut off in mid-anecdote by the appearance in their little group of a tall, balding man dressed in black jeans, black shirt and a black leather blouson. In his wake came a pretty but nervous-looking red-haired woman in her forties wearing grey leggings under a heavy off-white jumper.

'Elizaveta,' said the man. 'Lovely reading, as ever. You too, Storm, great stuff.'

'I am duly honoured.' Freddie Dalrymple's widow made a little mock-curtsey. 'To have a compliment from the great George Bernard Shaw expert.'

Jude had recognized the man from Storm's description before introductions were made, and he did indeed prove to be Neville Prideaux.

The woman identified herself as 'Hester Winstone'. She had a glass of orange juice, Neville was drinking red wine.

'And what part are you playing in *The Devil's Disciple*?' asked Jude.

'Oh, nothing,' the woman replied dismissively. 'I'm not important. I'm just the prompter.'

'I've seen amateur productions where the prompter has been *extremely* important. In fact, sometimes I've heard more of the prompter than I have of the actors.'

'Well, that's not the kind of production you'll ever see from SADOS,' said Elizaveta cuttingly.

Jude felt suitably reprimanded. She grinned at Hester Winstone and was rewarded by a little flicker of a smile. But the prompter seemed ill at ease, not quite included in the circle of thespians, but still for some reason needing to be there.

At the arrival of the newcomers, Jude noted that Ritchie Good had detached himself from the circle around Elizaveta Dalrymple and drifted off to chat to another group. She wondered if she was witnessing some masculine territorial ritual. Had Neville Prideaux's appearance threatened Ritchie Good's position as alpha male?

'Well,' Neville said, 'I hope this afternoon's reading has convinced everyone I was right to champion *The Devil's Disciple* ... against considerable opposition.'

The way he looked at Elizaveta Dalrymple as he said this suggested that at least some of that opposition had come from her.

'Oh yes,' she said, 'I think SADOS will probably get away with it.'

'We'll do more than get away with it. It's a very fine play.'

Elizaveta twisted her mouth into a little moue of disagreement. 'I can't help remembering that Freddie always described Shaw as "a left-wing windbag".' Her coterie awarded this a little titter.

'But,' Neville objected, 'we agreed at the Play

43

Selection Committee Meeting that SADOS ought to be doing more challenging work.'

'I'm not arguing with that, Neville love. When Freddie founded the Society, he was determined that we should present material that was "at the forefront of contemporary theatre".'

'And yet it ended up, like every other amdram in the country, doing the usual round of light West End comedies and Agatha Christies.'

'No, I don't think that's fair, Neville.' Clearly nothing that contained the mildest criticism of the hallowed Freddie Dalrymple was fair. Jude also got the impression that Neville and Elizaveta were reanimating an argument which they had visited many times before. 'We have done some very contemporary material,' Elizaveta went on. 'When we did *Shirley Valentine*, that was quite ground-breaking for Smalting – I mean, doing a play based in Liverpool.'

And also one with a socking great part for you in it, thought Jude. The idea of Elizaveta Dalrymple using her 'very good ear' for accents to tackle Scouse was engagingly incongruous.

'I also still think,' the grande dame continued, 'that this time round we should have done *Driving Miss Daisy*.'

And who might have played Miss Daisy? Jude asked herself.

'I mean, that's a play that really tackles serious issues.'

'So does *The Devil's Disciple*,' insisted Neville Prideaux.

'But *Driving Miss Daisy*'s about racial prejudice – anti-Semitism, colour prejudice.'

'Whereas *The Devil's Disciple* is about nothing less than the conflict between Good and Evil. It's also about honour and honesty and bravery and religion and the entire business of being a human being. Anyway, Elizaveta, the other big argument against doing *Driving Miss Daisy* is: where on earth are you going to find a black man in Smalting to play the chauffeur?'

Jude had been aware for a while that Hester Winstone had been trying to attract Neville's attention, and at this moment she interrupted the argument. Looking at her watch, she said, 'Sorry, Neville, I've got to be going.'

'Fine,' he said, without even looking at her. 'See you at the next rehearsal.'

The prompter detached herself from the group. She still looked nervous and unhappy. The next time Jude looked, Hester Winstone was no longer in the pub.

'Well, anyway,' said Elizaveta Dalrymple, as if putting an end to the topic, '*The Devil's Disciple* is the play we're doing and I'm sure the production will be well up to SADOS's high standards.' She vouchsafed a smile to Davina Vere Smith, as if bestowing her blessing on the enterprise. 'I just wonder, though, how many people in Smalting will want to buy tickets...?'

'...and, you see,' Gordon Blaine was still going on to Carole, 'I've worked out a rather cunning way of doing the gallows at the end of the play.'

She looked in desperation around the bar, but saw no prospects of imminent rescue. Jude was still in the middle of the group around the melodramatic old woman with dyed black hair. Ritchie Good, the tall man who had chatted up Jude, was by the pub door in whispered conversation with a red-haired woman who looked as if she was about to leave.

There was no escape as Gordon continued, 'It's important that it looks authentic, but it's also important that the structure would pass a Health and Safety inspection. And Dick Dudgeon has to have the noose actually around his neck so it looks like he's really about to be hanged, so what I'm going to do is to have a break in the noose where the two ends are only joined by Velcro and then the—'

'Oh God,' said a languid approaching voice, 'is Gordon boring you with his technical wizardry?'

The words so exactly mirrored Carole Seddon's thoughts that she couldn't help smiling at their speaker. Even though it was Ritchie Good.

'Carole was actually very interested in what I was saying,' said Gordon Blaine defensively.

'Yes, yes, it was fascinating,' she lied.

'Anyway, I've got things to get on with.' And with that huffy farewell, Gordon moved away from them.

'Looked like you needed rescuing,' said Ritchie.

46

'Thank you very much.'

'And sorry, in all those introductions I didn't get your name...?'

'Carole.'

'Ah. Right.' It never occurred to him that she hadn't taken in his name. 'So...' He took Carole's hand in both of his and said, 'Where have you been hiding all my life?'

FOUR

Having not wanted to go to the Cricketers in the first place, Carole found that an hour and a quarter had passed before she finally managed to extricate Jude and leave the place. Their departure was now quite urgent. In little more than half an hour Carole's saga of convents and placentas would be starting.

The St Mary's Hall car park was in darkness as they came out of the pub, but when they crossed the beam of a sensor an overhead light came on. In spite of the time pressure of her television programme, Carole characteristically said she must put up the back seats of the Renault before they set off. Anything out of place disturbed her, and the car must be returned to its customary configuration. Carole was the kind of woman who had a tendency to clear away her guests' dinner plates almost before they'd finished eating.

While she repositioned the back seats Jude stood waiting. It was a mild evening for February, the first that offered some prospect of spring eventually arriving. She looked around the car park. The range of Mercedes, BMWs and Audis suggested that the members of SADOS didn't have too much to worry about financially.

Out of the corner of her eye Jude caught sight of a movement behind the windscreen of a BMW quite nearby. Looking closer, she recognized the face of Hester Winstone, the *Devil's Disciple*'s prompter.

And the overhead light caught the shine of tears on the woman's cheeks.

Instinctive compassion took Jude towards the car. The closer she got the more sense she had of something being seriously wrong. Hester was slumped a little sideways in the driver's seat and her eyes were closed. Peacefully closed, as though she were asleep.

Jude had no hesitation in snatching open the car door. As she did so, the prompter's arm flopped to the side of her seat.

And from her wrist bright red blood dripped on to the surface of the car park.

FIVE

'I still think we should call the police,' muttered Carole. 'Or at least send for an ambulance.'

'Hester specifically asked me not to,' Jude whispered back. They were in the sitting room of Woodside Cottage and the subject of their conversation had just gone upstairs to the loo.

'Yes, but she's not rational. People who try to kill themselves are by definition not rational.'

'It wasn't a very serious attempt to kill herself. Those nail scissors couldn't have done much damage. The cuts are only surface scratches.'

'Maybe they are this time, but people who do that kind of thing are very likely to try again. Someone in authority should be informed.'

'Carole, I'd rather just talk to Hester for a while, find out what her state of mind really is.'

'Not great, if she's trying to top herself,' said Carole shortly.

'Please. I'd just like to talk to her.'

Jude's words only added to Carole's sense of pique. 'I'd just like to talk to her.' Nothing on the lines of 'We should talk to her.' Not for the first time that evening, Carole felt excluded.

She'd been stuck at the Cricketers with the world's most boring man, Gordon Blaine, while Jude went off with a bunch of people who had, by definition, to be more interesting. Then in the car park her neighbour had overruled her about getting someone from SADOS to look after Hester Winstone. It had also been against Carole's advice that Jude had driven Hester back to Woodside Cottage in the BMW.

To compound these multiple affronts, the business of doing a temporary bandaging job on the would-be suicide in the car park meant that Carole had missed at least half of her chronicle of wimples and waters breaking.

'Very well,' she said huffily to Jude. 'Well, I must go. I've got things to do.'

'The children are off at boarding school,' said Hester Winstone, 'and my husband's away at the moment.'

'Where?' asked Jude.

'He's on a cricket tour in New Zealand.' Jude didn't take much of an interest in the game, but she knew that there seemed to be Test Matches happening somewhere every day right around the world.

'What, watching cricket?'

'No, playing.'

'Really?' That was a surprise. Assuming that Hester Winstone was in her late forties, then her husband might be expected to be the same age or a little older. And though Jude knew that some men continued to play cricket into their fifties and sixties, she didn't expect many to be involved in international tours.

Hester seemed to sense her need for explanation. 'It's a group of them, a kind of ad hoc team called the Subversives. One of the blokes works in the travel industry and he sets up the tours. They've been doing it for years. Some of the players are pushing seventy.'

'How long do the tours last?'

'Oh, never more than a month. Mike will be back next Friday.'

Hester Winstone seemed remarkably together and businesslike for a woman who had within the last two hours slit her wrists. Jude recognized that she was embarrassed and trying to talk about anything except the reason why she had ended up in Woodside Cottage.

'And have you been involved with SADOS for long?'

'Oh no. *Disciple* is the first show I've done with them. No, I just thought, now I've got more time on my hands...'

'Have you done amateur dramatics before?'

'Not really. Well, a certain amount at school, and I started to do a bit at college, but since then ... life's rather taken over ... you know, marriage, children...'

'How many children do you have?'

'Two. Boys, both boarding at Charterhouse. Younger one started in September. Mike was there, so there was never any thought of sending them anywhere else. It's a very good school for sport.'

'Are your boys keen on cricket too?'

'Oh yes,' Hester replied, a note of weariness in her voice. 'And football and tennis and squash.'

'What about you? You do a lot of sport?'

A wrinkling of the lips suggested the answer was no. 'I play a bit of genteel tennis with some friends, that's about the limit of my involvement. Unless, of course, you count the hours I have put in making cricket teas, ferrying Mike and the boys to various matches and tournaments, helping to score in pavilions, shrieking encouragement on chilly touchlines.'

'Sounds like you've served your time.'

'Hm. Maybe.'

Jude was again struck by the incongruity of this normal – even banal – conversation going on with a woman whose right wrist was dressed with a bandage covering the cuts she had inflicted on herself. They weren't very deep, but even so they must reflect some profound malaise within Hester Winstone. But maybe she just came from that class of women who'd been trained from birth to avoid talking about life's unpleasantnesses.

'From what you say,' Jude began cautiously, 'you could be suffering from Empty Nest Syndrome.'

'Oh, I don't believe in Syndromes,' said Hester Winstone dismissively. 'All psychobabble, so far as I'm concerned.'

'Hm,' said Jude gently, 'but, whether it's a Syndrome or not, things aren't right with you, are they?'

'What do you mean?'

'Look, you cut your wrist in the car, didn't you?'

'Oh yes, I just got over-emotional.' She dismissed the incident as if it were some minor social lapse, like sneezing before she'd got her handkerchief to her nose.

'But why did you get over-emotional?'

For a moment Hester Winstone was about to answer, but then she reached for her handbag, saying, 'I must be getting home. Really appreciate your helping me out.'

'I'm sorry,' said Jude firmly, 'but I really don't want you to go home straight away.'

'What do you mean?' She sounded affronted now. 'What business is it of yours?'

'It's my business,' came the calm reply, 'because I found you in your car, having just cut your wrists. And I don't really want you to be on your own until I'm sure you're not about to finish what you started.'

'And what makes you think I'd do that?'

'Because you've done it once.'

'Oh, that was an aberration. As I said, I just got over-emotional.'

'Listen, Hester, I don't have any medical qualifications, but I work as a healer so I do come across a lot of people who've got troubles

53

in their lives. And I'd be failing in my duty to my profession – not to mention in my duty as a human being – if I were just to let you go straight home.'

'But I'm fine.'

'Look, just think how I'd feel if I heard on the local news tomorrow that you'd committed suicide.'

'But I'm not about to commit suicide.'

'That's exactly what someone planning suicide would say.'

Hester Winstone was suddenly on the verge of tears as she said, 'Can't you just leave me alone!'

'No, I really don't think I can.' There was a silence, broken only by Hester's suppressed sobs. 'Look, if you won't agree to talk to me, I'll have no alternative but to call an ambulance.'

'But I don't need an ambulance. You've seen my wrist – it's only a scratch.'

'The fact remains that it's a scratch which you inflicted on yourself. If you were to go home, you'd be on your own, wouldn't you?'

'Yes,' Hester admitted grudgingly.

'Well, is there someone who could come and be with you? A family member? A neighbour?'

'No, there's no one. Anyway, I don't want people knowing about what's happened. If Mike ever got wind it, it would be an absolute disaster.'

'Don't you think you should tell your

husband?'

'No, he wouldn't understand.'

'But surely, if you're unhappy enough to slit your wrists – even if you didn't do it very efficiently – then your husband ought to know.'

'No, he mustn't.'

'So when he comes back next Friday, how are you going to explain the big scar on your wrist?'

'Oh, I've worked that out. I'll say I cut it when I was opening a tin of dog food.'

'And will he believe you?'

'It would never occur to Mike not to believe me.'

'I still think you should tell him what happened.'

'No, Mike's no good with that sort of stuff. It'd confuse him – and upset him.'

'If he's the cause of your unhappiness, then perhaps he needs to be upset.'

'I didn't say he was the cause of it.'

'No. But you haven't said what else is the cause, so I'm just having to make conjectures based on the very small amount of information you have given me.'

'You have no right to make conjectures about my life. I'm going to go.'

'Hester, I'll tell you why I have a right to make conjectures about your life. Because I found you in your car having just cut your wrist. That means, whether you like it or not, I have that information. What I do with that information is up to me. A lot of people would have just rung for an ambulance – or even the police – straight away, regardless of whether you wanted them to or not. Carole and I didn't do that. We brought you back here and tidied you up. And I'm quite happy for no one else to know what happened ... *so long as you persuade me that you're not about to do the same thing again.*'

'What – you're blackmailing me into talking to you?'

'I don't like your choice of word, but if that's what you want to call it, fine. I just want to feel reassured about your mental state.' Hester Winstone was silent. 'Anyway, suppose Carole and I hadn't come into the car park just then...? Would you have cut your wrists some more? Did you want to be discovered there by someone in SADOS?'

The slightest of reactions from the woman suggested Jude might have touched a nerve there. 'I don't know what I was thinking. I wasn't very in control,' Hester mumbled, acknowledging for the first time since Carole had left the two women together that there was something wrong.

'Look, I don't know you,' said Jude. 'I know nothing about your life apart from what you've told me in the last few minutes, but for someone to cut their wrist – however ineffectively – suggests a very deep unhappiness.'

'Maybe,' Hester Winstone conceded.

'Whether that's caused by the state of your marriage, or your boys being away at boarding school or some recent bereavement or a long-term depressive condition or the menopause, I don't know. But if you do want to confide in someone, I have the advantages of not knowing your social circle, so nothing you say will go further than these four walls. I also promise not to be judgemental. And enough people have said it to me that I think I can confidently state I'm a good listener. Not to mention an experienced healer. So if you do want to tell me anything ... well, the ball's in your court.'

Hester twisted her hands together in confusion. 'It's tempting.'

'Then why not give into temptation?'

After a moment the reply came. 'No, I can't. Sorry.'

'Well,' said Jude, 'shall I tell you what I, as an impartial observer of what I saw happen in the Cricketers, think may have caused the sudden deterioration of your mood?'

'You can try. But we were only in the same group of people for a couple of minutes, so you can't have seen much.'

'I had been aware of you in the bar before we were actually introduced. I noticed your body language.'

'God, I didn't know I had any body language.'

'Oh, you did. Hard thing to avoid, body language.'

'And what was mine saying?'

'It was saying you were feeling neglected...'

'Oh?'

'Or possibly rejected.'

'Really? By whom?'

'Neville Prideaux.'

'Oh God.' Hester Winstone's hand shot up to her mouth. 'Was it that obvious? Does that mean everyone in SADOS knows?'

'I wouldn't worry too much about that. From the impression I got of those I met this evening, they're all too preoccupied with themselves to notice what's going on with other people. It was easier for me to observe things as an outsider.'

'So what exactly did you observe? From my body language?'

'You seemed to be trying to engage Neville's attention. He seemed to be very deliberately avoiding eye contact with you, and constantly moving to other groups in the pub, so that you wouldn't get a moment alone with him.'

Hester Winstone was silent. Tears were beginning to well up in her hazel eyes.

'But, as I say, I'm sure nobody else noticed,' Jude reassured her. 'It's just, being introduced to a group of people for the first time, you see things in a detached way ... you know, before you get to know any of them.'

Hester nodded, hoping, but not convinced, that what Jude had said was true.

'So you've got a bit of a history with Neville Prideaux, have you?'

'A very brief history. I hadn't met him a month ago.'

'But you did meet him during the time that your husband's been in New Zealand?'

'Yes,' the woman said wretchedly.

'And he came on to you?'

'It wasn't as obvious as that. Not like Ritchie. He ... Neville ... he kind of took me seriously. At least appeared to take me seriously.'

'You mentioned Ritchie. So he came on to you, did he?'

'Well...'

'He came on to me the minute I was introduced to him,' said Jude.

'Yes, he does that to everyone.' Hester Winstone coloured. 'He's a very attractive man.'

'He certainly thinks he is.'

'But he really is,' Hester insisted, and Jude was forced to admit it was true. Though Ritchie Good's chat-up line had been crass beyond words, Jude had still felt a tug of attraction towards him.

She banished such thoughts from her mind and said, 'One thing I don't quite get is that today was the first rehearsal for *The Devil's Disciple*...?'

'Yes.'

'...and it's only in the last few weeks that both Ritchie and Neville have come on to you...?'

'Well, as I say, with Neville it wasn't so much "coming on".'

'All right. But how did you come to be involved in SADOS before this production started rehearsing?'

'Ah well, it was the end of the panto...'

'Oh?'

'SADOS always do their pantomime at the end of January. And it was round then that Mike went off to New Zealand ... and I was kind of at a loose end, so I got in touch with SADOS to see if there was anything I could do to help out, and they needed some people for front of house during the panto, so that's how I became involved.'

'And were Ritchie and Neville both in the show?'

'Not acting, no. Ritchie just came to see one performance and then he kind of chatted me up in the Cricketers afterwards.'

'And did you mind him chatting you up?'

'No, I was flattered ... just having someone taking some notice of me.'

Jude recognized this as another comment on the state of Hester's marriage, but didn't pursue it. Instead she asked, 'And what about Neville?'

'He wasn't acting in the panto, but he'd written the lyrics for the songs, so he was around quite a lot during the run.'

'And you kind of "got together"?'

Hester Winstone blushed furiously. 'One evening after the show we'd had a few in the Cricketers, and my car was being serviced, so Neville offered to give me a lift home, and I invited him in for a drink and ... I don't think anything would have happened if we hadn't been drinking.'

'And did it happen again?'

'No, just the once. And then suddenly Neville seemed to lose interest. Didn't reply to my texts or calls.'

'And you were hurt because you loved him?'

'I don't know about love. Maybe I convinced myself at the time that was the reason. I don't know. I just felt dreadful. I can't think why I let it happen.'

'You were lonely.'

'Yes, maybe, but that's no excuse, is it? And in my head I've gone through so many scenarios about how I would tell Mike, but that was assuming that Neville still wanted me and ... I don't know. I'm just so confused.'

'From what you say, it sounds as if you've never been unfaithful before.'

'Good Lord, no.' Hester sounded appalled by the very idea. 'And I wouldn't have done, I mean, not unless I thought I actually was, at least at that moment, in love with Neville. And now I feel just so confused. And Mike's back next week, and I'll have to tell him.'

'Why?'

'Well, I can't not, can I?'

'Of course you can,' Jude asserted. 'In my view far too many people rush to tell their partners about their infidelity. In very few cases does it do any good, and in many it destroys a perfectly salvageable relationship.'

'Do you really believe that?' And there was a spark of hope in Hester Winstone's hazel eyes.

'I most certainly do.'

'But when I see Mike, I'm sure I'll just blurt it out.'

'Well, curb the instinct. Don't give him more ammunition with which to criticize you.'

'But I haven't said he does criticize me.'

'I extrapolated that, Hester.'

'Oh, did you?' She sounded a little crushed. And guilty. But also reassured. Jude's recommendation that she shouldn't tell her husband about her lapse had clearly brought her comfort.

'Oh dear, I don't know what to do.' But now Hester sounded weary rather than desperate.

'Well, I'll tell you exactly what you're going to do. You are going to sit here while I open a bottle of wine and pour you a drink. Then I'll cook us some supper. Then I think you should probably stay here the night.'

Hester grimaced. 'Love to, but I've got to get back for the dogs. If they aren't let out ... well, you can imagine what will happen...'

'I think I can. What about the drink and the supper?'

The woman grinned as she replied, 'That'd be wonderful.'

'And when you go back home, you'll be all right, will you?'

'Yes, I'll be fine,' said Hester Winstone.

And Jude believed her.

SIX

The following morning over coffee at High Tor Jude gave Carole an edited version of her conversation with Hester Winstone. Though the woman wasn't a client, their time together had been almost like a therapy session, so Jude kept the details of the infidelity to herself. She just said that Hester was clearly in a bad state, but talking things through had, she hoped, helped. It would have been different if she and Carole were working on a case together. Then she would have recounted everything that had passed between them. But there was no crime involved here, just a cry for help from a very unhappy woman.

Carole, needless to say, couldn't wait to express her views of the SADOS members. 'Really! Who do they think they are? When I was growing up, we had a word for people like that, and it was "show-offs". Can't they see how ridiculous they appear?'

Jude shrugged. 'They're just doing something they enjoy. I don't see there's much harm in it.'

'Well, I'd hate to be involved with a group like that.'

'No problem. No one was rushing to make you join them, were they?'

'No,' Carole conceded.

'Have you ever done any acting?'

'No.' There was a shudder at the very idea.

'Not even at school?'

'Well, I was in a Nativity Play.'

'What part?'

Carole coloured at the recollection as she said, 'I was the Ox.'

'One of the great parts,' said Jude with a grin.

'I've never been so embarrassed in my life. And I think my parents were at least as embarrassed as I was. The Seddons have never been people for putting their heads above the parapet.'

'No, I can believe that,' said Jude.

It was later that afternoon in Woodside Cottage, while she was reading a book about kinesiology written by a friend of hers, that Jude's phone rang. The male voice at the other end was rich, confident and vaguely familiar.

'Is that Jude?'

'Yes.'

'Oh, good, I'm glad I got the right number.'

'Mm.' She still couldn't place him.

'We met yesterday evening in the Cricketers.'

'Oh yes?'

'My name's Ritchie Good.'

'Ah. And to what do I owe the honour of this call?'

64

'I just wanted to talk to you.'

'Well, you seem to have achieved your wish.'

'Mm.' He let a silence dangle between them. 'You made quite an impression on me.'

'I'm flattered. Slightly surprised, because we can't have spoken for more than a couple of minutes.'

'It often doesn't take long.'

Jude groaned. 'That's almost as corny as your "Where have you been hiding all my life" line.'

'At least you remember it.'

'Only for its cheesiness.'

'Touché. Anyway, I was wondering if we could meet for a drink or something.'

'A drink might be all right. I'm not so sure about the "something".'

'Let's start with a drink then...'

Jude didn't really know why she was playing along with him. If she hadn't already decided that Ritchie Good was nothing but an ego on legs, this phone conversation would have convinced her. And yet here she was, responding in kind to his rather elaborate innuendo. Maybe it was just that it had been a long time since she'd flirted with a man. She was still smarting after the end of a pretty serious relationship with a man called Piers Targett, so wasn't looking for anything beyond casual. But having a drink with an attractive bullshitter ... well, there might be worse ways of spending an idle hour.

So she found herself agreeing to meet Ritchie Good at six o'clock in the Crown and Anchor.

* * *

The fact that she had chosen Fethering's only pub as a rendezvous was a measure of how little Jude was anticipating any kind of relationship. Had the assignation been with anyone who really interested her, she would opted for another venue, a place from where the news of her tryst did not immediately go straight round the village. There was security for her in the Crown and Anchor. It put her on her home base, and there'd be people she knew there – Ted Crisp the landlord, his bar manager Zosia and some of the regulars.

Jude also told herself that she might get more information from Ritchie about Hester Winstone and what had reduced her to a suicidal state. The woman had, after all, said that Ritchie had chatted her up. But Jude knew that was really only an excuse. There was also the fact that he was a very attractive man.

He was late. Jude was already installed in an alcove with a large Chilean Chardonnay, and had already heard Ted's Joke of the Day ('Where are the Seychelles?' 'I don't know – where are the Seychelles?' 'On the Seyshore.').

Ritchie Good apologized for his tardiness. 'Sorry, I got held up at work.'

'What do you do?'

'I work in a bank.'

'Oh, are you one of those pariahs of contemporary society who keeps getting whacking bonuses?'

'I wish. No, I work in the Hove branch of HSBC. On the Life Insurance side.'

'Ah.'

'I see you've got a drink.' No suggestion he should buy her another one. Then again she had only had a couple of swallows from the glass. 'I'll get something for myself.'

He came back from the bar with what Jude knew, because she'd overheard him ordering it, was half a pint of shandy. 'Can't drink much,' he said, 'because I'm rehearsing tonight.'

'I thought *The Devil's Disciple* rehearsed on Tuesdays, Thursdays and Sundays.'

'Yes, they do. Tonight isn't for that. I'm playing Benedict in the Fedborough Thespians' *Much Ado*.'

'At the same time as you're doing *The Devil's Disciple*?'

'Yes. Davina knew the deal when she persuaded me to do Dick Dudgeon. The *Much Ado* is on at the end of March, so I'll have to miss a few *Disciple* rehearsals round then.'

'So how long have you been a member of SADOS?'

'The Saddoes?' he said, enjoying the mispronunciation. 'I'm not actually a member.'

'But you have done shows for them before?'

'Oh yes, I've done shows for most of the local amdrams, but I've never been a member of any of them.' He smiled a complacent smile. 'Sooner or later they all need me to help them out.'

'So you audition for all of them in turn, do

you?'

He chuckled. 'I don't do auditions. I get asked to play parts.'

'Is that usual in the world of amateur dramatics?'

'Not usual. But it's how I work. All amdrams have a problem with gender imbalance. There are always more women available. That's why they're always looking for plays with large female casts. Getting enough men's always tough. Getting enough men who can actually act is harder still. So no, I don't audition. I wait till I'm asked to play a part.'

Jude hadn't been aware that there was a star system in amateur dramatics, but clearly there was. And, at least in the Fethering area, Ritchie Good was at the centre of it. The original big fish in a small pond. She almost winced at the conceit of the man.

'Anyway,' he said, 'we don't want to talk about me.' A statement which Jude reckoned might be one hundred per cent inaccurate. He brought the practised focus of his blue eyes on to her brown ones. 'I was really bowled over by meeting you last night, Jude.'

'Were you?'

'Yes, it's not often that I see a woman and just ... pow! You had a big effect on me. I kept waking up in the night thinking of you.'

'Oh yes?'

'Would I lie to you?'

'You really shouldn't set up questions like

68

that for me, Ritchie. They're too tempting.'

'Are you saying you think I would lie to you?'

'I'm damn sure of it.'

'Oh.' He looked a little discomfited. Perhaps his chat-up lines usually got a warmer response. 'Anyway, I thought it would be nice to meet.'

'And here we are – meeting. Is it as nice as you anticipated?'

His face took on the hurt expression of a small boy. 'You're a bit combative, Jude.'

'I wouldn't say that. I just have a finely tuned bullshit detector.'

'Ah. So you reckon I'm a bullshitter?'

'Isn't self-knowledge a wonderful thing?'

'And the possibility doesn't occur to you that I might be sincere?'

'You have it in one.'

'I do find that a bit hurtful,' he said in a voice that was playing for sympathy. 'I'm sorry, it's just that I'm a creature of impulse. I see someone I fancy, I want to get to know that person, find out more about them.'

Jude was silent. She believed his latest statement as little as she had believed his previous ones. Ritchie Good was not, in her estimation, 'a creature of impulse'. She reckoned everything he did was a product of considerable calculation. And she was interested to know the real reason why he had arranged this meeting. His implication that, on first seeing her in the Cricketers, he had experienced a sudden coup de foudre did not convince her.

'So,' she said, taking the conversation on a completely new tack, 'first proper rehearsal for *The Devil's Disciple* tomorrow?'

'Yes.'

'Is it going to be good?'

'Dick Dudgeon's a very good part,' said Ritchie Good. It was the archetypal actor's response. Never mind about the rest of the production, I've got a good part.

'Have you worked with Davina before?'

'Oh yes, a few times. I like her as a director. She's very open to everyone's ideas.'

Jude didn't think she was being over-cynical to translate Ritchie's last sentence as: she listens to my ideas and lets me play the part exactly as I want to.

Time to home in on what she really wanted to ask him. 'I was having a chat with Hester last night...'

'Oh?' There was a slight tension in him, a new alertness at the mention of the name. 'What, in the Cricketers?'

'No, actually after she'd left. We met in the car park.' Which was as much as she wanted to say about the circumstances of their encounter.

'Really? Was she all right?' Which struck Jude as a slightly unusual question from someone who'd been in the same pub with the woman the evening before.

'Oh, fine,' she said, finessing the truth. 'Have you known her long, Ritchie?'

'Met her once before last night. I went to see

70

the SADOS panto a few weeks back. They're always pretty dreadful, but I feel I should go out of loyalty. The trouble is, it's basically knock-about slapstick, but Neville Prideaux insists on writing these dreadfully pretentious lyrics for the songs, and the two elements just don't fit together. You know, his lyrics are all about the cigarettes of hope being stubbed out in the ashtrays of dreams. God knows who he thinks he is – Jacques Brel? But that's how they've always done the panto in recent years, and SADOS are not very good at change. Then again, Neville seems to have an unassailable position in the society. They all seem to think the sun shines out of his every available orifice.'

'What's his background? Was he involved in professional theatre?'

'Good Lord, no. Schoolteacher all his life. At some public school, I can't remember the name. Head of English and in charge of all the drama. Directed every school play, ran the Drama Department like his own private fiefdom, as far as I can gather. And now he's retired, so he's vouchsafing SADOS the benefit of his wisdom and experience.'

The sarcasm in his last words reminded Jude of what she had felt in the Cricketers, that there was considerable rivalry between Ritchie Good and Neville Prideaux, both big beasts in the local amdram circles.

'Anyway,' asked Ritchie, 'do you know Hester well?'

'Met her for the first time yesterday evening.'

'In the Cricketers car park?'

'Well, I'd been introduced to her in the pub, but it was in the car park that I got the chance to talk to her.'

'What about?' Ritchie's urgency was making him drop his guard of nonchalance.

'Oh, this and that,' Jude lied casually. 'The production of *The Devil's Disciple* ... SADOS ... how long she'd been involved ... that kind of thing.'

Ritchie Good nodded, and Jude thought she detected relief in his body language, as he moved on to talk about the play. 'Be interesting to see how *Disciple* goes down in Smalting. Shaw's gone out of fashion, but he does write good parts for actors. Bloody long speeches, mind you. I didn't know the play when Davina asked me to play Dick Dudgeon, but the minute I read it I knew I had to do it. Rather let down the Worthing Rustics, whom I'd vaguely promised that I'd play Higgins in their *Pygmalion*, but I've done the part before, and Dick Dudgeon was much more interesting ... you know, to me as an actor.'

'I'm sure,' said Jude. 'I don't know the play, I'm afraid, but I assume that Dick Dudgeon is the lead part.'

'Yes. Well, Judith's a decent part too.'

'The one Storm Lavelle's playing?'

'Mm. I hadn't met her before the read-through, but she's not a bad little actress. Needs a bit of work on the American accent, but I dare say I can help her out there.'

'And Judith is ... not Dick Dudgeon's wife?'

'No, she's married to the Pastor, Anderson. She starts off hating Dick Dudgeon, but by the end is rather smitten. Davina gave me the choice of playing Anderson or Dudgeon, but there was no contest. Anderson's a goody-goody, whereas Dick's ... well, "The Devil's Disciple". No question Dick Dudgeon is the sexier role.'

'Which I suppose you would regard as type-casting,' suggested Jude slyly.

Although she had intended the remark as satirical, Ritchie took it at face value. 'Yes, very definitely.'

'And who's playing Anderson?'

'Oh, I've forgotten the guy's name, but he's perfectly adequate.' Perhaps, thought Jude, the perfect example of damning with faint praise.

'And is Neville Prideaux in the production?'

'Yes, he's playing General Burgoyne. Only appears in Act Three. Rather a showy part, suits Neville down to the ground.' Clearly no opportunity was going to be missed to have a dig at his rival.

There was a silence. Then Jude, never one to beat about the bush, said, 'I'm still not clear why you wanted to meet me.'

'I told you. You made an instant impression on me. I couldn't not see you again.'

The delivery was as polished as the lines, but once again Jude found them unconvincing. 'And after this meeting, what then...?'

'I hope it's the first of many.' Jude rather doubted whether it would be. 'Why is it,' he protested, 'that people round here are so hidebound? You meet someone you really click with ... and what do you do about it? For most people – nothing. Well, I don't subscribe to that approach. If I meet someone who makes a big impression on me, I want to see more of them, want to get to know them, want to find out whether they're feeling a little bit of what I'm feeling...?'

To someone less full of himself, Jude would have been gentler, but she had no problem saying to Ritchie Good, 'Well, I'm afraid I don't feel anything for you.'

'Oh.' He was clearly taken aback; her reaction was perhaps not one he frequently encountered.

'I mean, I can see you're attractive...'

'Thank you.'

'...and your conversation's quite entertaining...'

He nodded his gratitude.

'...but I can't imagine being in a relationship with you.'

'Why not?'

'I quite like one-to-one relationships.'

'So?'

'Well, I can't see you being very good at concentrating solely on one woman.'

'Try me.'

'No, thanks.' Jude turned the full beam of her brown eyes on him. 'Are you married?'

'Well, yes, but the marriage has—'

'Oh, don't tell me. Which expression were you going to use, Ritchie? "The marriage has been dead for years"? "It's only a marriage in name these days"? "We're more like brother and sister than husband and wife"?'

He looked very disgruntled. 'You've got a nasty cynical streak, Jude.'

'Not normally. Only when I encounter someone who prompts cynicism.'

There was a silence. Then Ritchie asked, 'Is it only now you know I'm married that you've become cynical about me?'

'No, I was cynical about you before that. Mind you, I assumed you were married all along.'

'Why?'

'Your type always are.'

'Hm,' said Ritchie Good, and it was the 'Hm' of a man about to cut his losses. He looked at his watch, swallowed down the remains of his shandy and announced, 'I'd better be off to rehearsal.'

'Right. Oh, one thing...' said Jude as he rose from the table.

'Yes?'

'Where did you get my phone number from?' It was in the directory, but very few people knew under which of her former husbands' surnames it appeared.

'Storm Lavelle gave it to me,' replied Ritchie. And Jude reckoned it was one of the few things he'd said during their encounter that was true.

He hovered for a moment, wanting perhaps to place a farewell kiss on her cheek but unwilling to bend down into the alcove where she still resolutely sat. 'Well, I'll call you,' he said finally.

But Jude very much doubted if he would. And she certainly didn't mind if he didn't.

SEVEN

'But what I still don't know,' she said to Carole, 'is why he really wanted to meet up with me.'

'I thought it was your feminine charms,' came the frosty response. 'I thought you'd "made a great impression" on him.'

'No, that was just flannel. That's how he talks to all women. He's one of those men who never stops trying it on.'

'I believe you. He actually had the nerve to ask me in the Cricketers "where I'd been hiding all his life".'

Jude had to suppress a giggle at the way Carole put the words in quotes. After Ritchie had left, she had phoned her neighbour to come down and join her at the Crown and Anchor for a drink. And that drink, she knew, might well lead to having supper in the pub. She hadn't put the idea forward yet, but she knew it would be greeted by a considerable barrage of disapproval before Carole finally agreed to eat out.

'It still seems odd, though, that he actually wanted to meet me.'

'Not so very odd. You said he's one of those men who never stops trying it on. And if he comes on like that to every woman he meets, maybe he does get the odd one who actually responds.'

'Possibly. He's an attractive man.'

'Huh,' said Carole Seddon as only Carole Seddon could. 'Well, was there anything else he talked about, apart from just chatting you up?'

'He talked a bit about how he is the star of all the local amdrams and they're all falling over themselves to get him to play the leads in their productions. And he talked about *The Devil's Disciple.*'

'Anything else?'

'Well, he did ask about Hester...'

'What about her?'

'He asked if she had been "all right" last night. Which I found rather odd.'

'Why? Obviously he was worried that he'd upset her.'

'But when had he upset her?'

'Just before she went out to the car park.'

'Really?'

'Oh, you probably couldn't see from where you were at the bar.'

'No, I just saw her being cold-shouldered by Neville Prideaux.'

'Well, I saw Ritchie Good stop Hester on the way to the door. He didn't say much, but whatever it was it seemed to upset her. She broke away from him and rushed out of the pub.'

'Oh, really?' said Jude.

And suddenly there were two men whose behaviour towards her might have made Hester Winstone feel suicidal.

Nothing more was heard from anyone to do with SADOS for the next week. Jude was unsurprised to have no call from Storm Lavelle. She knew of old that, once her friend became involved in rehearsals for a play, she hardly noticed what might be happening in the rest of the world. It was only after the performances had finished that Storm would be back on the Woodside Cottage treatment table, bemoaning all the shortcomings of her life.

Jude was also unsurprised to hear nothing more from Ritchie Good. She had had no expectation of hearing back from him again, but his silence once again made her question why he had contacted her so urgently in the first place. If his motive was purely sexual, then perhaps her combative banter had scared him. What he'd thought might be another easy conquest had turned out to be a trickier proposition, so maybe he'd just backed off. But Jude still couldn't help thinking that the important part of their conversation had been his anxiety about Hester Winstone.

Her investigative antennae were alerted by the situation, but she knew there was no case to explore. Hester Winstone, a woman possibly unhappy in her marriage, had made a very unconvincing suicide attempt. It had really been the classic cry for help. Jude doubted whether, after the shock of the first incision, Hester would have had the nerve to make another cut. So there was really nothing to investigate.

For the rest of the week Jude got on with her business of healing, while Carole continued her business of disapproving of most things. And presumably in Saint Mary's Hall in Smalting, on the Tuesday, the Thursday and the Sunday, rehearsals for *The Devil's Disciple* continued in the usual way.

On the following Monday morning Carole came to Woodside Cottage for coffee. By arrangement, of course. Carole was not the kind of person who ever 'dropped in' for coffee – or indeed for anything else. 'Dropping in' on people was the kind of habit that Carole Seddon associated, disparagingly, with 'the North'. Except at times of great urgency, even though she only lived next door, she would never have appeared on Jude's doorstep without having made a preparatory phone call. So the arrangement to meet for coffee that Monday had been made some days before. Carole had an appointment at Fethering Surgery for a blood pressure test – 'just a routine thing, not serious – just something that came up at one of those Well Woman appointments they insist on dragging you along to.'

Carole's health had in fact been remarkably good throughout her life, and retirement from the Home Office had not changed that. She ate sensibly and fairly frugally (except when coerced by Jude into the Crown and Anchor). She drank little (except when coerced by Jude into the Crown and Anchor). And long walks on Fethering Beach with her Labrador Gulliver ensured that she got plenty of exercise and sea air.

But if Carole Seddon were ever to have anything wrong with her, she would certainly not tell anyone. She had a strong animus against people 'who're always going on about their health' or 'imagine that you're interested in their latest operation'. Carole had been brought up not to 'maunder on' about that kind of stuff. Her ideal relationship with the medical profession would be never to have anything to do with any of them. (In fact, at times her ideal relationship with all of mankind would be never to have anything to do with any of them.)

She was not a stupid woman, however, recognizing that growing older one should keep an eye on one's health. So if at a Well Woman appointment she was told she needed to go back to the surgery for a blood pressure test, back to the surgery she would go.

But that didn't stop her from moaning about the experience afterwards. 'You'd think they'd get some system of dealing with appointments in that place,' she said as Jude presented her with a cup of coffee in the jumbled sitting room of Woodside Cottage. 'I'd have been here half an hour ago if those doctors just got vaguely organized. I mean they have all this technology, checking in on a screen when you arrive at the surgery, appointments being flashed up in red lights on another screen, but none of that changes their basic inefficiency. I can't remember a time when I've actually got into an appointment there at the time scheduled.'

'Well, what did the doctor say?'

'Oh, I wasn't even seeing a doctor. Just one of the nurses for the blood pressure test. Nothing important.'

'Are you sure?' asked Jude.

'Yes,' Carole replied, ever more determined not to be one of those people 'who're always going on about their health', and firmly moving the conversation in another direction. 'I noticed as I was walking past Allinstore –' she referred to Fethering's only – and uniquely inefficient – supermarket – 'that they're advertising a new delicatessen counter. If that's as successful as all their other modernization efforts—'

Having dealt with the NHS, Carole's move into a rant about Allinstore was only prevented by the ringing of Woodside Cottage's doorbell. Jude went through to the hall. Carole heard the door being opened and the sound of a masculine voice, but her finely tuned gossip antennae were not up to hearing what was being said. Jude returned to the sitting room with a chubby, balding man, probably round the sixty mark, wearing a blazer with burgundy corduroy trousers and carrying a bottle of champagne. The colour of his face was not a bad match with the trousers.

'Carole, I'd like you to meet Mike Winstone.' In response to her neighbour's puzzled expression, she added the gloss, 'Hester's husband.'

'Oh, hello, how nice to meet you.'

'The pleasure's mutual,' he said in a hearty public school accent. 'And it seems I should be offering you thanks too.'

'What for?'

'I gather you also helped Jude out when Hester threw her little wobbly.'

'Oh. Yes.'

'Sorry about that.' He guffawed. 'Can't be keeping an eye on the better half all the time, can I?'

'Particularly not from New Zealand,' said Jude with some edge.

'What? No, right. She told you I was off, playing cricket, did she?'

'Yes.'

'Ridiculous at my age, isn't it? Just this bunch of old overgrown schoolboys. Call ourselves the Subversives. Old fogeys now, but we have dreams – still waiting for that call from the England selectors, eh?' This again was apparently worthy of a guffaw.

'As you see,' Jude intervened, 'we're having coffee. Would you like a cup or...?'

'Bought you some champers by way of thank-you.' He waved the bottle. 'Still cold, fresh out the fridge. Why don't we crack that open?'

'Well, it's a bit early...' Carole began, but she was overruled by Jude saying:

'What a good idea. I'll get some glasses.'

Left alone together, Mike Winstone favoured Carole with a bonhomous beam. 'You interested in cricket, are you?'

Her recollections of the game came from the very few occasions when she'd watched her son Stephen play while he was at school. Those games only lasted a couple of hours, but they'd still seemed interminable. What watching a full five-day Test Match must be like was too appalling for Carole to contemplate. Thank goodness Stephen had never shown any real aptitude for the game – or indeed for any others – and devoted himself increasingly to his studies.

'No, I'm afraid not,' she replied.

'You're missing a lot, you know, Carole. Very fine game, subtle mix of the very simple and the really quite complex. Lot of women getting interested in it now too, you know, and I must say some of them don't half play a good game.'

Jude returned with the glasses before Carole

was required to amplify her views on cricket. Which was probably just as well.

Mike Winstone expertly removed the foil, wire and cork from the champagne, then filled the three glasses. Passing two to what he referred to as 'the ladies', he raised his own. 'As I say, thanks very much for helping out "her indoors" in her moment of need.'

'Our pleasure,' said Carole.

'So she told you all about it?' asked Jude, a little puzzled because Hester Winstone had so firmly assured her that she wouldn't let her husband know about the suicide attempt. He was, she'd said, 'no good with that sort of stuff'.

'Oh yes,' Mike replied confidently. 'No secrets between Hest and me. Got to tell the truth when you're incarcerated in a marriage – worse luck.' He guffawed again.

'So did she tell you as soon as you got back?'

'Well, we were having a chinwag about everything we'd both been up to while I'd been in the Antipodes and then I notice this dressing on Hest's wrist and I said, "What've you been up to, darling – trying to top yourself?"' This was deemed to merit another huge guffaw.

'And she told you?' asked an incredulous Jude.

'Yes. And I said, "Good heavens, Hest – what a muppet you are!" Because, you know, she's always been scatty, but cutting her wrist when she was opening a tin of dog food ... well, doesn't that just take the biscuit – or should I say "dog biscuit"?' Another rather fine joke, so far as Mike Winstone was concerned.

Jude nodded agreement, at the same time desperately trying to think how to find out the details of the story Hester had told her husband.

Fortunately Mike provided the information himself. 'Anyway, when she told me about cutting herself, of course, I realized it tied in with what happened last Sunday – not yesterday, Sunday before.'

'Ye-es,' said Jude tentatively.

'You see, I'd rung Hest on the landline that evening. Good time from the Antipodes – I'm just getting up about the time she's thinking of bed, but I didn't get any reply. Which I thought at the time was a bit odd ... until Hest explained that she was here with you.'

'Hm.' Jude still wanted a bit more than that ... which Mike again supplied.

'She told me all about what happened in the car park...'

'Really?'

'Yes ... how she'd nipped out early on the Sunday evening to do a bit of shopping...'

'Right.'

'At Sainsbury's.'

'Of course,' said Jude, waiting to see where Hester's fabrication would take them next.

'And how she came over all funny in the car park and fainted or something, and you wondered what had happened.'

You never said a truer word, thought Jude.

'Anyway, I'm so glad you were there. Well, you too, Carole.' He raised his glass again to both of them. 'Very kind of you to take her in, Jude.'

'No problem.' She still hadn't got the complete picture, but Hester Winstone's version of events was becoming clearer.

'Better you than some officious member of the Sainsbury's staff who'd probably have called an ambulance and started God knows what kind of palaver. Poor old thing. Hest must've lost a lot more blood than she thought.'

'Oh?'

'From the cut. For her to have keeled over like that.'

'Ah yes.'

'I've never known her to faint in the ... what? Twenty-five years odd we've been married. Still, it's probably partly her age.'

'Are you talking about the menopause?' asked Carole who, in her view, hadn't said anything for far too long.

'Well, erm...' Mike Winstone coloured. He was clearly not at ease in discussing what he would no doubt have referred to as 'ladies' things'. 'Well, Hest is getting rather scattier than usual.' He raised his glass to them for an unnecessary third time. 'Anyway, this is just to say: thanks enormously.'

'As I say, no problem. Anyone would have done the same.' Jude reckoned she now had the complete text of what Hester Winstone had told her husband. 'You see someone keel over on a cold evening in Sainsbury's car park, you go and help them. It's human nature.'

'Well, I'm glad it was you who did it, anyway. You clearly made quite an impression on Hest.'

'How is she, by the way?'

'Hest? She's right as rain. Scatty as ever, like I said, but fine. Our boys have got an exeat from school this weekend, so she's looking forward to seeing them. Oh, there's never anything wrong with Hest for long. She doesn't let things get to her.'

Jude caught Carole's eye and could see that the same thought was going through both their minds. Namely, that Mike Winstone didn't know his wife at all. So long as he was secure in his cocoon of cricket and general bonhomie, he could keep himself immune from other people's problems.

'She mentioned,' said Carole casually, 'that she's involved in some amateur dramatic group...'

'Oh yes, the "Saddoes".' He used the same pronunciation that Ritchie Good had. And clearly, from the darkening of his expression, he wasn't a great enthusiast of the society. 'Mm, Hest said she'd got time on her hands now the boys are both at Charterhouse and I said, fine, give you a chance to play more tennis, have a serious go at whittling down the old golf handicap. But what does she go and do? Join this bunch of local poseurs in the amdram.'

'You don't sound very keen on the idea.'

'Well, to be quite honest, Carole, I'm not. I mean, I remember at school there was a bunch of boys who spent all their time putting on plays and, quite honestly, they weren't the most interesting specimens. I certainly made many more friends among the sporting types than I did with that lot. I mean, you go on enough minibus trips to cricket matches and football matches with chaps and you really get to know them well. I made some damned good chums through sport, certainly never made any from amongst the drama lot.'

'But presumably they made friends with other people doing drama?' suggested Jude.

'Oh yes, of course they did.' He flipped a limp wrist and said in the voice all schoolboys use to suggest homosexuality, *'Very good friends.'*

Jude made no reaction to this, but said, 'I gather Hester's going to be prompting for the new production of *The Devil's Disciple.'*

'Something like that, yes. I don't remember the name of the play. But no, good for her,' he said without total conviction. 'If that's what Hest wants to do, then I'd be the last one to stand in her way. They say it's important in a marriage for the partners to have different interests. And there's nothing that could be more different from cricket than amateur dramatics!' This was judged to be another guffaw-worthy line.

'You will give Hester our best wishes, won't you?' said Jude.

'Oh, absolutely. Course I will.' He coloured again. 'And, erm, one thing...'

'Yes?'

'I'd appreciate it frightfully if you didn't mention anything to anyone about Hester's, erm ... little lapse.'

Which both Carole and Jude thought was an odd thing for him to say. And which could have suggested Mike Winstone knew more about what had really happened to Hester than he was letting on. And also maybe explained why he had been so keen to talk to Jude and Carole.

EIGHT

'Something really dramatic's happened!'

'Oh yes,' said Jude, not holding her breath. She knew of old that Storm Lavelle was capable of considerable hyperbole. In her priorities 'something really dramatic' could be something that anyone else would have regarded as of very minor significance.

It was the Thursday morning, three days after Mike Winstone's visit to Woodside Cottage.

Jude had been quite surprised to have a call from Storm. Knowing the obsessive concentration her friend brought to amateur dramatics, she hadn't expected to hear anything till after *The Devil's Disciple* had had its last performance.

'It's Elizaveta Dalrymple,' Storm announced.

'What? Is she ill?'

'No, it's worse than that.'

'Why? What's happened?'

'Oh God, it was at rehearsal on Tuesday night.' Storm left a pause, clearly intending to enjoy the narrative she was about to unleash. 'I mean, so far things have been going pretty all right with the production. We've spent the first week just blocking, really, and there hasn't been too much tension. Well, a bit between Davina and Ritchie, because, well, she is the director, but he's pretty firm in his opinions about the way he wants to do things, regardless of what she thinks.'

That chimed in with Jude's recollection of her conversation with Ritchie Good in the Crown and Anchor. Clearly he was one of those actors who regarded directors as minor obstacles in the preordained path of his instinctive genius.

'But, anyway,' Storm went on, 'it's all been fairly amicable, though there's a bit of resentment of Ritchie ... you know, because he's been kind of parachuted into the production, and there are some people who've been members of SADOS for a long time and feel that parts should only go to bona fide members of the society. I mean, Mimi Lassiter obviously, because she's Membership Secretary. But also people like Olly Pinto, who really reckons he should have been playing Dick Dudgeon, because he's kind of served his time in the SADOS, playing supporting parts, and he's thinking it's about time he should get a lead. And he's stuck with being Christy, Dick's brother, who doesn't really have a lot to do, so Olly's still cheesed off about that. But basically everything's been pretty friendly ... until last night.'

Jude didn't say a word, allowing Storm to control the drama of her story in her own way.

'Well, needless to say, it involved Elizaveta.' Jude was not surprised. Clearly the widow of the SADOS' founder thought it her right to be the centre of everything that went on in the society. 'And, you know, she's playing Mrs Dudgeon, Dick Dudgeon's mother. And she's playing it very well. I mean, Mrs Dudgeon is basically a malevolent old bitch...'

'Typecasting,' Jude suggested quietly.

'Well, maybe, yes. But she's only in the first act and she has a bit of a scene with Dick Dudgeon, but not a lot, and anyway a discussion came up on Tuesday night about costume ... and I don't know if you know, but George Bernard Shaw is very specific about what he wants his plays to look like.'

'Oh yes, all those interminably long stage

91

directions.' During her brief acting career, Jude had been in a production of *Caesar and Cleopatra*.

'And anyway, Elizaveta was saying, like, she didn't agree with how Shaw described Mrs Dudgeon, and she thought the character would naturally look rather smarter than the way he wanted her to be. The stage directions don't say much about her actual clothes, just that she's shabby and cantankerous and she wears a shawl over her head. Anyway, Elizaveta was very much against the idea of the shawl.'

'Vanity?'

'I suppose so, Jude. Elizaveta's very proud of her hair.'

'It's certainly a good advertisement for whoever did the dyeing.'

'Yes. And she said everyone in the SADOS' audience recognized her by her hair and if it was covered with a shawl nobody would know it was her playing the part.'

'Don't they have programmes? Couldn't they have looked up the cast list there?'

'Well, yes, you'd have thought so, but no one mentioned that. Anyway, Davina said it wasn't important at that point, we'd got months to sort out the costumes and we should be getting on with rehearsal. But Elizaveta said it was a point of principle and it should be decided right then.'

'Sounds like it was a bit of a power struggle between actor and director.'

'That's exactly what it was. And Davina's

fairly biddable as a director – you know, she doesn't really stand up to people, tends to go with the flow. She was certainly doing that with Ritchie. She'd go along with whatever he suggested.'

'Which no doubt made Elizaveta jealous, and she wanted to be treated the same way?'

'Spot on, Jude. Particularly as she's always been great mates with Davina and she doesn't take kindly to being sort of shut out of things. So, anyway, then Ritchie gets involved. He starts saying that we're wasting valuable rehearsal time ... which is a bit rich coming from him, because most of the interruptions we've had up till that point have been due to him arguing with Davina about how he wants to do things.

'And of course Elizaveta doesn't like this, and then Ritchie makes things worse – quite deliberately, I think – by saying that we shouldn't be spending so much rehearsal time worrying about the play's *minor* characters. Well, that's like a red rag to a bull to Elizaveta. She goes into this great routine about never having been so insulted in her life, and about the fact that she's generously giving of her time to help SADOS out by playing the *minor* role of Mrs Dudgeon. And pretty soon she's listing all of the major roles she's played for the society, even quoting some of the rave reviews she's had from the *Fethering Observer* and the *West Sussex Gazette*. Then she gets started about

Freddie, her ex-husband, and how he started SADOS and how there wouldn't have been any SADOS without him, and how it wasn't the place of "jumped-up actors" who *weren't even members of the society*" to start criticizing the work done by Freddie Dalrymple.'

'And how did Ritchie take all this?'

'Well, by now he's getting pretty annoyed too, and we all kind of realize that what we're witnessing is a scene that's been brewing up since the moment we started rehearsal – that it's a kind of power struggle, Ritchie and Elizaveta fighting over which one of them has more control of Davina. And then it turns out that there's a bit of history between Ritchie and Elizaveta.'

'Really?' Jude thought instantly of the man's habit of coming on to every woman he met. 'Surely not an affair or—?'

'Oh God, no! The history was more between Ritchie's mother and Elizaveta. Apparently his mum was big in local amdram circles, playing lots of major roles, round the time that Freddie Dalrymple was setting up SADOS. And there was some kind of rumpus about Ritchie's mum wanting to join the new society and Elizaveta using her influence with Freddie to keep her out.'

'Elizaveta not wanting a rival for all the leading parts?'

'Exactly. So, anyway, last night at rehearsal the argument between Ritchie and Elizaveta is batting to and fro, kind of over Davina's head, and finally Ritchie loses his temper and says, "Oh, come on, forget all your bloody airs and graces. My mother knew you before you managed to trick Freddie Dalrymple into marrying you – when you were plain Elizabeth Jones, serving behind the counter of the fish and chip shop right here in Smalting!"

'Well, that did it! That really caught the nerve. So there's a lot more from Elizaveta about having never been so insulted in her life. And then she says that, under the circumstances, she can no longer continue in this production of *The Devil's Disciple* – and she walks out!'

'Flouncing, I dare say.'

'Very much so, Jude. Flouncing, slamming doors, completely throwing her toys out of the pram. So suddenly we're without a Mrs Dudgeon.'

'But surely there are lots of people in SADOS who can play it? Amateur dramatic societies may have problems recruiting young men, but there's always a glut of mature women.'

'I know, but the trouble is they're all on Elizaveta Dalrymple's side.'

'What do you mean?'

'The older members of the society are mostly founder members or people who joined in the first few years. They're fiercely loyal to the memory of Freddie Dalrymple. Some of them, I gather, are more ambivalent about Elizaveta. She aced them out of too many good parts for

95

them to support her too much. But once it became known that Ritchie Good had insulted the sainted Freddie...'

'And how did they know this?'

'From Elizaveta, of course. She must have spent the whole day yesterday on the phone to the mature women in the society. And she's persuaded all of them to boycott this production of *The Devil's Disciple*.'

'Ah, has she?'

'Yes. Davina also spent most of yesterday ringing round every woman in the society who was vaguely the right age – and that became more elastic as she got desperate – but Elizaveta had got to every one of them first. The boycott was unbroken.

'And it's not just Mrs Dudgeon she's worried about. Elizaveta's got supporters throughout the society. I mean, Olly Pinto for one. He's playing Christy and he's great mates with Elizaveta. I haven't heard whether he's walked out too, but it wouldn't surprise me.'

'But you're not about to go, are you, Storm?'

'Oh, good heavens, no. Judith's the best part I've ever been offered. No way I'm going to give that up. Anyway, I've always found Elizaveta Dalrymple a bit of a pain. No, I'll see it through.'

'And Ritchie will, presumably?'

'You bet. I wouldn't be surprised if he doesn't think what's happened is a personal triumph.'

'One rival ego removed?'

'Oh, I wouldn't say that. Ritchie hasn't really got a very big ego. When you get to know him, he's actually quite shy. He just has an accurate assessment of his own talents.'

Oh dear, thought Jude. Storm's defensive words might well indicate that Ritchie Good was the next man she was about to throw herself at. And if she did, there was no question that it would end in tears.

'Well,' said Jude, 'exciting times we live in.'

'Yes.' There was a silence. 'So, obviously, there's only one question I have to ask you.'

'What?' came the puzzled reply.

'Davina asked me if I would.'

'Er?'

'Jude, will you step into the breach and play the part of Mrs Dudgeon?'

NINE

'You're absolutely mad,' said Carole. 'What on earth do you want to get involved with that lot for?'

'They're harmless.'

That was greeted by a customized Carole Seddon 'Huh.'

'And they're stuck for someone to play Mrs

Dudgeon. It's not going to take much time out of my life.'

'Not "much time"? Rehearsals three days a week? That sounds like quite a big commitment to me. You wouldn't catch me doing it. I couldn't afford the time.'

For a moment Jude was tempted to ask what her neighbour couldn't afford the time *from*. Although Carole always carried an air of extreme busyness, it was sometimes hard to know what she actually *did* all day ... apart from keeping High Tor antiseptically clean, completing the *Times* crossword and taking Gulliver for long walks on Fethering Beach.

But Jude didn't give voice to her thoughts. The look of distaste on Carole's face suggested that her neighbour's involvement in *The Devil's Disciple* had brought back atavistic fears of 'showing off' and traumatic memories of being The Ox in the School Nativity Play.

'I just thought I could help them out,' said Jude.

Another 'Huh. Well, I still think you're out of your senses. It's one thing lending them your chaise longue. Lending yourself is something else entirely.'

Suspicion appeared in the pale-blue eyes behind the rimless glasses. 'And you're not joining them because of that man?'

'Which man?' asked Jude, though she knew who Carole meant.

'That smooth talker who you met for a drink

last week.'

Jude grinned. 'I can assure you my taking the part has nothing to do with Ritchie Good. If I'm doing it for anyone other than myself, then I'd say it was Storm Lavelle – she's the one who asked me. In fact, thinking about it, I wouldn't be surprised if Ritchie Good is rather annoyed by my arrival in the company.'

'Oh?'

'Because when we met I did prove rather resistant to his charms. He's not used to women reacting like that to him, and I don't think he likes it very much.'

'Huh.'

'Though actually, Carole, there is another reason why I want to be involved in this production.'

'Oh really? What's that?'

'Hester Winstone. I'm still rather worried about her ... particularly since meeting her husband. I'd quite like to keep an eye on Hester.'

'Well, rather you than me, Jude.' Carole positively snorted. 'The day I get involved in amateur dramatics you have my full permission to have me sectioned.'

So it was that Jude took over the part of Mrs Dudgeon in the SADOS' production of *The Devil's Disciple*. She had an early evening healing session booked on the Thursday, so didn't attend her first rehearsal till the Sunday. Sensitive to atmosphere, she could feel the definite air of triumph emanating from Ritchie Good. He was pleased to have seen off Elizaveta Dalrymple.

Nor was he the only one who seemed relieved by the old woman's absence. Davina Vere Smith, despite her reputation as a 'close chum' of Elizaveta, was relaxed and apparently had given up any pretence that she was in charge of the production. She meekly took on board Ritchie's notes and suggestions, even when they applied to performances other than his own. The actor was yet again doing a play on exactly the terms he desired.

Davina accepted all that, but what did annoy her was the regular list of absentees from every rehearsal. Two were involved in a Charity Marathon and one had shingles.

Olly Pinto, self-appointed toady to Elizaveta Dalrymple, did not leave the production, as Storm had suggested he might. But all the time there was something chippy about him, especially in relation to Ritchie Good. He grimaced a lot behind Ritchie's back, and muttered words of dissent at a level that was not quite audible.

Olly also talked a lot about Elizaveta and Freddie Dalrymple. He had been fortunate enough to meet the blessed Freddie just before he died, and reminiscences of the two of them were constantly on his lips. Elizaveta Dalrymple may have walked out of the production, but Olly Pinto ensured that no one in the *Devil's Disciple* company was allowed to forget her.

Able to observe everything at close hand, Jude was again struck by Storm Lavelle's talent. She really was making something of Judith Anderson. Since Jude didn't have her own transport, Storm ferried her to and from rehearsals in her Smart car – Fethering was virtually on the route from Hove. And in the course of those journeys the two women talked a lot – well, to be more accurate, Storm talked and Jude listened a lot. All her friend talked about was the play and how she was approaching the part of Judith Anderson. So far, she seemed too preoccupied with her acting to waste any energy throwing herself at Ritchie Good. Which was a considerable relief.

But Jude did tend to arrive at rehearsals in a state of mental exhaustion from all the listening she'd had to do.

Jude's observations of Hester Winstone at rehearsals were less encouraging. The prompter still seemed very nervous and unhappy. Both Ritchie and Neville Prideaux virtually ignored her and, having met Mike, Jude didn't reckon Hester was getting much support at home either. She tried to be friendly, but her suggestions of going for a drink together at the Cricketers after rehearsals were met with polite refusals. Hester Winstone was continuing to do her job as prompter, but apparently no longer wished to be involved in the social side of SADOS.

And then of course Jude herself had to get

back to the idea of acting. The stuff she had done in the past had arisen directly out of her work as a model. There's an enduring idea amongst agents and producers that someone beautiful enough to be photographed professionally must also be able to act. Though it can work in the cinema where short takes and clever editing can disguise complete lack of talent, the inadequacy of models is more likely to be exposed by a full evening on the stage of a theatre.

But Jude had actually been quite good, she had discovered a genuine aptitude for acting, and she was surprised at how much she enjoyed coming back to it and playing Mrs Dudgeon. Also, in her early twenties she had been cast only for her beauty – in other words in straight roles. She had suspected back then that the actors in character parts were having more fun and, as Mrs Dudgeon, she found that to be true. There was a great freedom to be derived from playing a crotchety old curmudgeon, so different from her own personality.

Jude was unsurprised that Ritchie Good made no further attempt to come on to her, and indeed behaved as if their meeting in the Crown and Anchor had never happened. Any attraction she might have felt towards him quickly dissipated in the course of rehearsals. Seeing what a control freak he was in his discussions with Davina Vere Smith – they had long since ceased to be arguments – Jude was turned off by his egotism.

But she remained intrigued by him. There was something about his personality that didn't ring true, something that had struck her in the Crown and Anchor and had only been reinforced by further acquaintance. His habit of coming on to women was clearly a knee-jerk reaction, but Jude wondered how far he wanted any kind of relationship to develop. Had she proved more amenable when they met in the pub, seemed keener on spending time with him, would they have ended up under her duvet in Woodside Cottage that evening? She somehow doubted it.

Neville Prideaux, Jude could see as she watched him at rehearsals, was a more subtle operator. Jude kept remembering that it was Ritchie who'd chatted up Hester Winstone, but it was Neville who had actually gone to bed with her. He didn't have Ritchie's obvious attractiveness, but maybe he was the more ruthless seducer.

Since his character of General Burgoyne only appeared in Act Three of *The Devil's Disciple*, Neville was not at as many rehearsals as most of the company. As an actor, Jude found him impressive technically, though she wasn't moved by him. But perhaps that was the right way to play General Burgoyne. The right way to play Shaw, anyway. His characters were all, in the view of many playgoers, more like mouthpieces for opinions than people one could engage with on an emotional level.

The impression Neville Prideaux gave out of orderliness and detachment was strengthened by the time Jude spent with him during the inevitable post-rehearsal sessions in the Cricketers. She kept being reminded of Ritchie Good's rather bitchy comments about how, during his days as a schoolmaster, he'd run the drama department like his own 'private fiefdom'. Neville was probably as much of a control freak as Ritchie, but the characteristic manifested itself in different ways. He never took issue with Davina at rehearsals, meekly taking her notes and doing what she told him, but he still contrived to play General Burgoyne exactly the way in which he wanted to play the character.

One evening in the Cricketers Jude was with Neville Prideaux when the subject of Elizaveta Dalrymple's defection came up. 'Have you known her long?' asked Jude. 'Were you with SADOS in the early days?'

'Oh, good heavens, no. I only joined up after I retired ... what, six years ago.'

'And I gather you have some kind of role as the society's dramaturge?'

'It's nothing as formal as that. Nothing official. It's just that there aren't perhaps that many people round SADOS who know a great deal about drama, and having spent my entire career researching and exploring the subject, I do feel I have something to contribute.'

'Well, it's nice to have a hobby in retirement.'

Jude's words had been no more than a bland conversation-filler, but Neville Prideaux reacted to them with some vehemence. 'I hardly have time for hobbies,' he retorted. 'I'm busier since I've been retired than I ever was as a teacher.'

'Oh?'

'I run workshops and drama classes. And then of course there's *my own writing*.'

He spoke of this with some awe, which made Jude feel perhaps she ought to know about something he'd written. Better to confess ignorance, though. 'Sorry, I don't know about your writing ... except Ritchie said you'd written some lyrics for the SADOS' panto. Is that the kind of stuff you do?'

'Oh, good heavens, no. That's just recreational stuff. No, basically I'm a playwright.'

'Ah. Have you written lots of plays?'

'Not as many as I would have wished. There was no time when I was teaching, so I've only really been able to concentrate on it in the last six years.'

'With any success?'

'Oh, I've had some very positive responses,' Neville Prideaux replied. Jude didn't think she was being too cynical to read this answer to her question as a 'No'.

'And,' he went on, 'the SADOS' Play Selection Committee are very keen to do one of my plays next season, but I'm not convinced that

that's a very good idea.'

'Oh? Why not?'

'Well, I just feel a production down here might be too low-key. I think the play would probably benefit from exposure in a larger arena.'

Like the West End? thought Jude. But she didn't ask the question. She was already getting a pretty clear view of the dimensions of Neville Prideaux's ego.

'And what's the play about?' she asked.

'Oh, there are a lot of themes,' he said rather grandly. 'It's set in a school – or apparently set in a school.' Well, that's the only setting you know, thought Jude. 'But obviously the school has considerable symbolic resonance.'

'Obviously,' she echoed, prompting Neville to look at her rather sharply, assessing whether she might be sending him up. Jude's face maintained an expression of total innocence which had proved very useful to her over the years.

'Anyway,' said Neville, 'it's very difficult to talk about one's work – particularly in the drama. A play can only be fully realized and judged when it is acted out in front of an audience.'

Jude nodded agreement. 'And how do you think the current one's going?'

'Play? *The Devil's Disciple*?'

'Yes.'

'Well, I think it gets better in Act Three.' When the character of General Burgoyne comes in, was Jude's thought – i.e. when you're on stage. 'And I think Ritchie's losing a lot of the nuance in Dick Dudgeon's character – particularly in Act One.'

'I thought he was coming across quite strongly.'

'Oh, yes, it's a competent performance, one can't deny that. Ritchie has a few acting tricks and tics to wheel out. But every part he plays is exactly the same. He never gets below the surface of a character.'

'But I thought that was the right way to play Shaw. His characters don't have great emotional depth.'

Neville Prideaux shook his head in sage disagreement. 'That's a very arguable statement, Jude. I mean, yes, GBS is more in the Ben Jonson tradition than the Shakespearean, and he looks forward to Brecht in some ways. His characters are "types" if you like, rather than psychologically complex individuals, but he doesn't go for the full Brechtian *verfremdungseffekt*. I would agree with you, there is emotional distance in Shaw's plays, but there's a high level of psychological engagement too.'

Jude felt she knew what it must have been like to be a sixth former in one of Neville Prideaux's classes.

'And the trouble is,' he continued, 'that Ritchie doesn't get near that psychological engagement. His Dick Dudgeon is nothing more than an assemblage of character tics. But he's not going to change. He doesn't listen to criticism. The only thing someone like Ritchie Good listens to is his own enormous ego.'

Well, it takes one to know one, thought Jude.

A little later on in the pub she was approached by Mimi Lassiter, her hair an even less likely shade of red. 'Now, Jude,' she said, 'now that you're playing Mrs Dudgeon, you can't deny that you're an Acting Member of SADOS.'

'I wouldn't attempt to.'

'So I'm afraid you have to join the society and pay a subscription.'

'I'm very happy to.'

'Everyone who acts in a SADOS production has to be a member.'

'Except Ritchie Good.'

'Hm.' An expression of displeasure crossed the little woman's face. 'Yes, I'm still arguing with Davina about that. Now, as an Acting Member, your subscription will be...'

Jude paid up.

TEN

'Though I say it myself,' announced Gordon Blaine, 'I'm not unpleased with the result. Obviously it did present various engineering challenges, but none I am glad to say that proved beyond my capabilities.'

A month had passed. It was a Sunday at the end of March. They'd reached the stage where Davina would have liked all of the cast to be 'off the book' – in other words, knowing their lines. Some of them had achieved that milestone, others were still fumbling. Hester Winstone was kept busy in her role as prompter.

Jude was a member of the virtuous group; she was 'off the book'. She had been surprised how easy she had found committing Mrs Dudgeon's lines to memory. And of course, given the old lady's early departure from the action, there weren't too many to learn.

Though they usually worked on the stage of St Mary's Hall, on this particular Sunday the rehearsal was taking place in the auditorium. The curtains were firmly closed, but from behind them various thumps, hammerings and muttered curses had been heard in the course of the afternoon. Gordon Blaine was building his gallows.

He'd been hard at work since the Saturday morning. Though all the components of the device had been made in his workshop at home, he was actually assembling them in situ. And, assuming he got it finished in time, the structure was due to be dramatically revealed to the *Devil's Disciple* company at the end of the afternoon's rehearsal.

With this coup de théâtre in prospect, there was around St Mary's Hall an air of excitement mingled with a bit of giggling. Gordon Blaine, the SADOS Mr Fixit, was clearly something of a joke amongst the members, and Jude could understand why. Though it was Carole rather than she who had received the full blast of Gordon's monologue the first evening they had gone to the Cricketers, that did not represent a permanent escape from him. Gordon Blaine was around quite a few rehearsals and he was very even-handed in the distribution of his conversation; he made sure that no one evaded their ration of it. And Jude, being new to the society, had certainly got her share.

The SADOS Sunday rehearsals started at three (so that those who needed to could enjoy their family lunch) and finished on the dot of six. Then everyone rushed to the Cricketers. Maybe this schedule had been established in the time of fixed licensing hours, but it had continued into the era of all-day opening.

That Sunday afternoon, as six o'clock drew nearer, the level of giggliness increased. Davina Vere Smith was facing an uphill battle, trying to get some concentration out of the actors involved in the opening scene. Jude was rock solid on her lines, but Janie Trotman as Essie, along with the actors playing Anderson and Christie, kept breaking down and cracking up with laughter. At about five to six, Davina gave up the unequal struggle and declared the rehearsal over.

As if on cue, Gordon Blaine had then appeared through the curtains to make his announcement. Having duly patted himself on the back for completing his task in the face of insuperable difficulties, he continued for a while talking up his prowess as an engineer.

Jude looked around the assembled company. There was still a level of excitement there, but as Gordon began to speak, the giggles were threatening to take over. Nearly everyone seemed to have stayed for the forthcoming revelation. Glancing round the room, the only significant absentees Jude was aware of were Ritchie Good and Hester Winstone.

The former's disappearance was explained as soon as Gordon Blaine, with an inept attempt at flamboyance, went into the wings to draw back the curtains. Onstage stood a very convincing-looking gallows, beneath which was a small wooden cart. On the cart, with the noose around his neck, stood Ritchie Good. The *Devil's*

111

Disciple company let out a communal half-mocking gasp of appreciation and started a small round of applause.

Stepping back onstage, Gordon Blaine beamed at this appreciation of his talents. 'Thank you,' he said. 'Yes, not a bad bit of work, though I say it myself.'

From behind his back he produced a noose identical to the one hanging from the arm of his gallows. One end was neatly tied in a loop; at the other was a metal ring, clearly designed to hook on to something. Gordon stretched the noose with his hands, demonstrating its strength and solidity. 'Simple piece of equipment, really, isn't it? But very effective for ridding the world of undesirables.' He chuckled a little, indicating that what he'd just said was a Gordon Blaine joke.

'Still, we don't want to have any accidents in our *Devil's Disciple*, do we? Particularly to a fine actor like Ritchie Good. So just in case we have any Health and Safety inspectors in the building, let me give you a demonstration of the means by which, in the use of this apparatus, unpleasant accidents may be avoided.'

He moved ponderously across the stage and took up the T-shaped pulling handle of the wooden cart. 'A few words, did we agree, Ritchie?'

'Yup. Ready when you are.' And the man with the noose around his neck went into Dick Dudgeon mode, though preferring his own words to the ones George Bernard Shaw had written for this dramatic moment. '"It is a far, far better thing that I do now ..." Oops, sorry, wrong play. That's *A Tale of Two Cities*. No, what I want to say to you all is that I've been through everything in my mind over and over again and I've decided –' he gestured to the noose around his neck – 'that this is the best way out.'

There was a ripple of laughter at his melodramatics. Ritchie Good, ever the showman, was enjoying his moment in the spotlight.

'Also I'd like to say that public hangings used to be one of this country's most popular spectator sports, until some wet blanket of a do-gooder decided that they weren't an appropriate divertissement for the Great Unwashed to gawp at. So you're very honoured, ladies and gentlemen, fellow members of SADOS, to have this much-loved entertainment re-created for you, here in St Mary's Hall, Smalting. And with that – let my hanging commence!'

At what was clearly a prearranged cue, Gordon pulled the cart away from beneath his feet. Ritchie Good's hands shot up to grasp the strangling rope around his neck, and for a moment he swung there, choking and kicking out into the nothingness.

The gasp which followed this had no element of irony in it. People rushed forward to the stage.

But before he could be rescued, Ritchie

released his grip on the noose and dropped down to the floor, as neat as an athlete finishing a gymnastic routine. His mocking laughter revealed that the whole thing had been a set-up, and he looked boyishly pleased with the trick he had played on everyone. 'Not bad, is it? Full marks to Gordon!'

Mr Fixit glowed and did a half-bow to acknowledge the rattle of applause. Then he moved across to demonstrate the cunning secret of his handiwork. The noose was no longer a loop, but two parallel pieces of rope. 'Oh, the magic of Velcro,' said Gordon, as he pressed the two ends together and reformed the circle.

'Very clever,' said the sardonic voice of Neville Prideaux, 'but in fact unnecessary. In the text of Shaw's play the cart never gets moved. Dick Dudgeon may have the noose around his neck, but he's in no danger of ever getting hanged. Then he's saved by the arrival of Pastor Anderson.'

Gordon Blaine looked almost pathetically nonplussed at having his moment of triumph diminished. But Ritchie Good came quickly to his rescue. 'Well, speaking as the person who actually has the rope around my neck, may I say I'm very pleased about the sensible precautions Gordon has taken. Accidents do happen. I could black out while I'm up there, or the cart could break or somebody could push it away by mistake. No, thank you very much, but I'm happy to stay with my Velcro rope. And I'm equally happy that General Burgoyne is unable to see through his plan of getting me hanged.'

Though he was talking entirely in terms of *The Devil's Disciple*, Ritchie Good still managed to make his last sentence sound like a criticism of Neville Prideaux, and a point scored in the ongoing rivalry between the two men.

As she watched the action, Jude had been standing next to Mimi Lassiter, who looked seriously shocked by the scene they had just witnessed. 'Are you all right?' asked Jude.

Mimi didn't answer the question, just announced in an appalled voice, 'He said "fellow members of SADOS" – and he hasn't even paid his subscription.'

Clearly she took her duties as Membership Secretary very seriously.

Over by the stage, where the curtains had once again been closed, there was much clapping on the back for Gordon Blaine, along with congratulations on another feat of stagecraft and offers to buy him a drink. He said he and Ritchie would join the others after he'd made a couple of adjustments to his precious gallows.

And the rest of the company, predictably enough, adjourned to the Cricketers.

As Jude crossed the car park towards the pub, she saw Hester Winstone standing by the side of a flash BMW, in heated conversation with someone through the driver's side window.

'I just want to stay and have a drink,' Hester was saying.

'And I just want you to come home.' The voice was recognizably her husband's. 'Look I've already had to rush my Sunday lunch to get you here for the beginning of the bloody re-hearsal. Then I come into the rehearsal room and see some idiot showing off pretending to be hanged – and I see no sign of you. And now you're here and I'd have thought the least you can do is come home now the bally rehearsal's finished.'

'You go home. I'll get a cab.'

'Well, that's a waste of money when I'm here to give you a lift. I'm already stuck with paying the insurance excess on the repairs caused by you pranging your bloody car. On top of that...'

Jude couldn't hear any more of the conver-sation without becoming too overt an eaves-dropper, so she continued her way into the Cricketers.

ELEVEN

The macabre demonstration they had seen had lifted the spirits of the *Devil's Disciple* company. This was partly due to the jokey double act which Gordon and Ritchie had just presented for them, but also to the feeling that they were finally making progress on the production. They were around halfway into their rehearsal schedule, some of the cast were actually 'off the book', and now they were being shown how bits of the set would work. *The Devil's Disciple* was beginning to gather momentum.

Jude had found that sessions in the Cricketers had become considerably more relaxed since the departure of Elizaveta Dalrymple and her cronies. Elizaveta was one of those women who not only needed always to be the centre of attention but who also carried around with her a permanent air of disapproval. And, given her place in SADOS history, though she didn't voice it in so many words, there was an implication of disdain for everything the society had done since the demise of its founding father Freddie Dalrymple. And yet, despite this inevitable decline in standards, Elizaveta Dalrymple had appeared magnanimous enough to offer her services and do what she could for SADOS.

So, without her condescension and prickliness, without everyone kowtowing and worrying about her reaction to things, the atmosphere in the Cricketers after rehearsals had improved considerably. The inevitable glass of Chilean Chardonnay in her hand, Jude found herself looking round quite benignly at her fellow actors. She had come to recognize that most of their flamboyance and ego derived from social awkwardness and, as ever attracted to people by their frailty, she realized that she was getting fond of most of them. To her considerable surprise, she discovered that she was enjoying her involvement in amateur dramatics. She giggled inwardly at the thought of breaking that news to Carole.

Feeling it was her turn to buy a round for the small circle she stood with, Jude looked for the African straw basket which contained her wallet, and realized to her mild irritation that she must have left it in St Mary's Hall.

To joshing cries about 'the Alzheimer's kicking in', Jude left the Cricketers and made her way back to the rehearsal room. The March evening was comfortingly light, finally promising the end of the miserable weather that seemed to have been trickling on forever.

Security at St Mary's Hall was not very sophisticated. The keys were kept behind the bar of the Cricketers and one of Davina Vere

Smith's duties as director was to open the place and lock up at the end of rehearsals. Frequently, because cast members were slow to leave the hall, Davina didn't do the locking up until when she was leaving the pub to go home.

So it proved that Sunday evening. Jude slipped in without difficulty and went through the foyer area to the main hall. She switched on one row of lights and noticed, without thinking much of it, that the stage curtains were almost closed, with just a thin strip of light showing.

The straw bag was exactly where she thought she'd left it, propped against the wall by the trestle table on which the kettle, coffee mugs and biscuit tins were kept.

Jude was about to leave the hall when she thought she should perhaps turn off the stage working lights. Though not obsessive about green issues, she tried whenever possible to save electricity.

There were pass doors on either side, but the simplest route up on to the stage was by the steps in the middle (much used for audience participation when the SADOS did their panto-mimes). Jude stepped up, pushing the curtains aside, in search of the light switches.

But what she saw on stage stopped her in her tracks. The wooden cart had been pushed to one side. From the noose on the gallows dangled the still body of Ritchie Good. His face was congested, his popping blue eyes red-rimmed.

This time he wasn't play-acting.

119

TWELVE

Jude's mobile was in her basket. She knew she should ring the police straight away. But Ritchie Good was unarguably dead, and a few minutes' delay was not, so far as she could see, going to make a lot of difference to the official investigation. She moved closer to the hanging corpse and looked up at the rope tight around his neck.

It was as she suspected. The noose which had strangled Ritchie Good was not the fake one with the Velcro linkage. It was the unbroken one whose strength Gordon Blaine had demonstrated in the run-up to his coup de théâtre.

Jude moved far enough away to see the top of the gallows. Fixed there was a large backward-facing hook, on to which the ring at the end of the noose had been fixed. From it the rope ran through a channel at the beam's end, so that it could dangle in its appropriate position over the cart.

For anyone who knew the structure of the gallows, switching the two nooses would have been a matter of moments. But who on earth could have done it? And how had they persuaded Ritchie Good so helpfully to have stood once again on the cart and placed the noose around his neck?

Though still in a state of shock, Jude found her mind was buzzing with possibilities. She tried to think back over the last half-hour, to remember who had appeared in the Cricketers and in what order. Also who had left the pub, and who hadn't even gone in in the first place.

While these thoughts were scrambling through her mind, Jude became aware of a noise in the empty hall. She heard a low whimpering, sounding like an animal, and yet she knew it to be human. It was coming from the small annex to the side of the stage, which during their productions SADOS used as a Green Room.

She moved softly through and found Hester Winstone collapsed on a chair, incapable of stopping the flow of her tears.

The woman looked up as she heard Jude approaching and said brokenly, 'It's my fault. I'm the reason why he's dead.'

THIRTEEN

Jude would have liked to talk to Hester, to offer comfort, to find out what exactly her words had meant, but they were interrupted by a scream from inside the main hall. Jude rushed through to find an aghast Davina Vere Smith.

The director must have come into St Mary's Hall to lock up, then, just like Jude, have gone to turn the lights off on stage. Where she too had been confronted by the grisly sight of Ritchie Good's dangling body.

Once she had recovered from her initial shock, Davina had no hesitation about ringing the police straight away. Somehow drawn by bad news, a few other SADOS members had drifted over from the Cricketers. The sight of Ritchie's corpse prompted all kinds of emotional displays, making it difficult for Jude to talk privately to the still-weeping Hester Winstone.

And once the police and an ambulance had arrived, such a conversation became impossible. Two uniformed officers came first, but they were quickly calling up plain clothes reinforcements. The paramedics from the ambulance were allowed to confirm that Ritchie Good was dead, but then the police asked them to keep off the stage. Soon after they left St Mary's Hall. Moving the body would happen later, after photographs and other essential procedures.

Jude was struck by how little information the police have when they first arrive at the scene of a crime (or indeed an accident). They'd probably never heard of SADOS; they'd need an explanation of the rehearsal process which had brought everyone to St Mary's Hall. And that was before they started even getting the names of the individuals involved.

But the two officers, later backed up by detectives, showed great patience in their questioning as they began to build up a background to the events of that afternoon. Their job was not made any easier by the histrionic tendencies of the SADOS members. All of them seemed to have something to contribute, and in many cases it was something that placed them centre stage in the day's drama.

Eventually St Mary's Hall was cleared. The police had by then established the identity of the victim. They had also taken names, addresses and contact numbers from everyone present and said that further follow-up questions might be necessary at a later date. The SADOS members were then left in no doubt that it was time for them to leave. Which – with some reluctance, they were enjoying the theatricality of the situation – they did.

They were also forbidden to tell anyone about what they had witnessed in the hall that afternoon. But if the police thought that instruction was likely to be followed, then they had never met anyone involved in amateur dramatics.

Jude was kept till last. As one of the first into the hall after Ritchie Good's death, she was told that a full statement would be required from her. Not straight away – the police needed time to examine the scene of the incident – but the following day, either at her home or the local police station, according to her preference.

'But I'm free to go now, am I?' she asked.

'Yes. You'll get a call in the morning.'

'And...' Jude looked across to where the weeping Hester Winstone was being comforted by a female officer. 'What about...?'

'No, Mrs Winstone won't be leaving straight away,' said the detective.

During the drive back to Fethering in her Smart car Storm Lavelle went into full drama queen mode. 'I mean, it's just such a *shattering* thing to happen. Ritchie's such a good actor, it's such a *waste*! And God knows what's going to happen to *The Devil's Disciple* now.'

Jude was relieved to hear that her friend seemed more worried about the production than heartbroken about Ritchie Good's death. Storm

124

must've been too busy with rehearsals to have any time to start throwing herself at Ritchie.

'What, you mean they're likely to call the whole thing off out of respect for Ritchie?'

'Oh, good Lord, no. The show must go on.' She spoke the words devoutly; they were, after all, the basic principle of amateur dramatics. No matter what disaster might occur during the rehearsal period, *The Devil's Disciple* would still be presented to the paying public in St Mary's Hall on the promised dates.

'No, Jude, Davina'll just juggle the cast around. Presumably Olly Pinto will be boosted up to Dick Dudgeon ... which will please him no end, because he always thought he should have been playing the part in the first place. And, I don't know, one of the boys playing the soldiers will get boosted up to take on Olly's old part of Christy.'

'Will it make a lot of difference to you, playing Judith Anderson to a new Dick Dudgeon?'

'I don't think it will that much, actually. I mean, Ritchie's a very good actor, but you never feel he's really engaging with you onstage. You know, he's thought through how he's going to play his part and that's what he does, regardless of what he's getting back from the rest of the cast. Ritchie's a great technician, but he isn't the kind of actor with whom you can get any kind of emotional roll going. He's very self-contained. It's a bit like having a very cleverly programmed robot on stage with you.'

125

Jude was interested to hear how closely Storm's assessment of Ritchie Good's acting skills matched that of Neville Prideaux. And Storm's was more objective; she wasn't motivated by jealousy.

'What do you think killed him?' asked Jude, in a manner that was meant, but failed, to sound casual.

'Well, obviously, strangulation by the noose round his neck.'

'Yes, but why did it happen?'

'An accident. He and Gordon must've been doing some adjustment to the gallows and unfortunately—'

'Gordon wasn't there. He was in the group that came straight over to the Cricketers at the same time as I did.'

'Oh well, Ritchie may have just been fiddling about with it.'

Storm seemed so remarkably incurious about the circumstances of the death that Jude didn't feel inclined to raise suspicions by asking further questions. Instead she said, 'The police want me to make a statement for them tomorrow. Have you got to do the same?'

'No, they just took my address and mobile number. Said they might be in touch, but didn't make it sound very likely.' There was a silence, then Storm said, 'Hester looked in a pretty bad way, didn't she?'

'Yes. So far as I could work out, she'd found Ritchie's body just before I had. She was in a terrible state of shock.'

'Hm. And she started off pretty neurotic, didn't she?'

'Is that the impression she gave?' asked Jude, surprised at her friend's powers of observation. Then she reminded herself that Storm was also a healer, used to analysing the sufferings of her clients.

'No, on the surface she was fine, but I did get the impression that she was very tense, holding a lot in.'

'Yes, I felt that too.'

'So,' said Storm, 'if Hester doesn't recover, we'll be short of a prompter. And, judging from this afternoon's display, just when her services will be most in demand.'

'Oh, surely there are lots of SADOS members around who could do that?'

'You'd think so, wouldn't you? But a lot of the potential prompters, mature ladies who're unlikely to be cast in plays any more ... well, they're part of the contingent that walked out with Elizaveta Dalrymple.'

'And might they not be lured back?'

'Oh, Good Lord, no. Not until *The Devil's Disciple* boycott is complete. Anyone who breaks through the picket line on that will receive the full blast of Elizaveta's anger.'

'I'm surprised that would worry anyone. I got the impression that she was rather a spent force in the SADOS.'

'A spent force she may be, but there are still a

lot of members terrified of getting the wrong side of her. They might be excluded from the guest list for her famous "drinkies things".'

'Oh dear. Well, maybe Hester will make a full recovery and no replacement prompter will be needed.' But as she said the words, Jude wasn't feeling as positive as she sounded. After all, what Hester Winstone had said to her in the Green Room could have been interpreted as a confession to murder. Whose consequences could make her unavailable for *Devil's Disciple* rehearsals, as well as many other areas of her life.

'Anyway, if Hester is ruled out,' said Storm, 'you wouldn't by any chance have a friend who might step into the breach as prompter, would you?'

Jude could hardly prevent herself from giggling at the thought, as she replied, 'Yes, you know, I think I might.'

FOURTEEN

On the Monday, by arrangement, the police had come to Jude's home to take her statement. She had described to the best of her recollection exactly what she had witnessed the previous day at St Mary's Hall. She had told the truth, but not quite the whole truth, omitting to report Hester Winstone's words about the death being her fault. Jude had glossed over that, saying that Hester was too hysterical to say anything coherent.

Her motives for telling the lie were instinctive and benign. She recognized Hester's mental fragility and didn't want to get her into any more trouble than she already was.

But she decided not to tell her neighbour what she'd done. Perhaps because of her Home Office background, Carole strongly disapproved of lying to the police.

Now that there was a corpse involved, Carole Seddon suddenly found the doings of SADOS a lot more interesting. Her voice was full of suppressed excitement as she asked, 'You say Ritchie Good was hanged, Jude? Was his neck broken?'

'I don't think so.'

'Then it would have been a very painful death.'

'Oh?'

'Humane hangmen usually arrange it so that the force of the drop breaks the victim's neck. Then death – or at least unconsciousness – is more or less instantaneous. If the neck isn't broken, the victim dies slowly of strangulation. It can take ten – or in some cases up to twenty – minutes. Pretty nasty way to go.'

Jude looked at her friend in surprise. 'Is that something you learned at the Home Office? I know there was a lot of back-stabbing there; I didn't know they went in for strangulation too.'

'Ha, ha, very funny. No, it's just information I picked up,' Carole replied airily. She had an increasing interest in the mechanics of crime, and had started filling directories on her laptop with the fruits of her research on the subject. But it was not a hobby she ever talked about, even to Jude.

It was the Tuesday, two days after Ritchie Good's death. They were having coffee at Woodside Cottage. The two women hadn't seen each other for a few days. Carole's daughter-in-law Gaby had been struck down at the weekend by a particularly nasty bout of a sickness bug and Granny had been summoned to the rescue in their house in Fulham. Since Carole absolutely worshipped her granddaughter Lily, this was no hardship for her. And with Gaby confined to bed, she even got over her customary unease at staying anywhere other than High Tor. She had taken Gulliver with her, and she was much entertained by the bonding between dog and granddaughter.

Because of her absence from Fethering till the Tuesday afternoon, this was the first Carole had heard about the death in St Mary's Hall. Jude recognized the sparkle of interest in her pale-blue eyes as she asked, 'So do you reckon that this Ritchie Good person was murdered?'

'I really don't know. It's an odd one. I've been going through the facts, revisualizing everything I saw on Sunday night. And it strikes me there are two major questions that need asking. First, who switched the safe noose with the Velcro joint in it for the real, unbroken one? And, second, why on earth did Ritchie allow the noose to be put around his neck?'

'Are you sure he didn't put it there himself?'

'Why would he do that?'

'To commit suicide. Come on, you saw more of him than I did, Jude. I just exchanged a few words with him in the Cricketers. Did anything he said to you make you think he might have depressive tendencies?'

'Absolutely not. I don't think I've ever met a man so armoured in self-esteem as Ritchie Good. He wouldn't want to deny the world the pleasure of his company. He would have regarded that as a terrible deprivation for everyone else on the planet. No, what happened to him is a complete mystery.'

'Intriguing, though,' said Carole, and behind their rimless glasses there was even more sparkle in her pale-blue eyes.

'Hello, Mike Winstone.' The voice answering Jude's call had its bonhomie firmly fixed in place.

'Hello, it's Jude. Remember, you came round with the champagne to say thank you...?'

'Yes, yes, of course. How the devil are you?'

'Fine, thanks. And you?'

'Never better.'

'I was actually ringing about Hester...'

'Oh yes?' For the first time there was a less welcoming tone in his voice.

'When I last saw her on Sunday she was in a terrible state.'

'Well, she's fine now,' said Mike Winstone curtly.

'But it looked as if she was about to be taken away by the police.'

'She did go with them to the station, where she made a statement and then was allowed to come home.'

'So is she there now? Would it be possible for me to speak to her?'

'No, I'm afraid that wouldn't be possible.'

'But she is there, is she?'

'No. No, she's not.' He spoke as if he had just thought of the answer. 'Hester's gone to stay with a friend.'

And that was all Jude got out of him. Except for the impression that he was lying.

FIFTEEN

A text had gone round to all the *Devil's Disciple* company to say that the Tuesday rehearsal was cancelled. The police were yet to finish their investigations at St Mary's Hall, but there was a hope the SADOS could resume their schedule on the Thursday. They'd receive a confirmatory text from Davina Vere Smith if that proved to be the case.

Jude was not surprised by the cancellation, but it did raise the question of *what* the police were investigating. An accident? Or something more serious? She couldn't get out of her mind what Hester had said in St Mary's Hall after Jude discovered Ritchie Good's body.

If only she could contact Hester ... Partly to find out what had happened to her at the police station, what she'd been asked, what she had told them. But more than that, the healer in Jude was worried by the state in which she had last seen the woman. Though the incident in the car park had been almost too trivial to count as a suicide attempt, it still raised the possibility

133

that, when faced with increased stress, the woman might try again.

Jude hoped the 'friend' that Mike had said Hester was staying with was of the sensitive and nurturing kind. And yet at the same time the suspicion recurred as to whether the 'friend' even existed. Was it just a covering lie from her husband for the fact that Hester was in police custody? Or had she actually been at home with him when he had taken Jude's call?

If so, she didn't think Mike Winstone would necessarily come out very well in the sensitive and nurturing stakes. Jude was seriously worried about Hester.

Later in the day, after she'd had coffee with Carole, she had a call from Davina Vere Smith. 'You got the text, did you?'

'Yes, thanks. Any news yet from the police on whether Thursday's rehearsal's likely to be on?'

'When they were last in touch, things were looking quite hopeful.'

'Good. And how're you going to replace Ritchie?'

'Olly Pinto will be playing Dick Dudgeon.'

'He'll be pleased.'

'What do you mean by that?' asked Davina rather sharply.

'Just that Olly seems to think he should have had the part in the first place.'

'Mm. Maybe you're right. Yes, Olly has served his time in supporting roles. And at least he is a member of SADOS, which is more than Ritchie ever was.' There was an undercurrent of resentment in these words. Jude was reminded once again of Ritchie's outsider status in the society. His behaviour had only been tolerated because of his talent. In the world of amateur dramatics loyalty to an individual group counted for quite a lot. And there was a nit-picking punctiliousness about details like whether someone involved in a production had actually paid his subscription or not.

With this came another thought, that Davina might actually relish working with Olly Pinto more than she did with Ritchie Good. The younger man would probably be more malleable, more inclined to listen to the director's ideas about the play and less likely just to follow his own agenda. Jude wondered how many more members of the *Devil's Disciple* company might regard Ritchie's death as something of a bonus.

'Anyway, Jude, the reason for my call –' oh yes, of course, there must be a reason – 'is that it seems Hester Winstone won't be able to take any further part in the production.'

'Ah. Do you know anything about where she is? Or indeed how she is?'

'No. I spoke to her husband. He said she was staying with a friend.' At least Mike's story was consistent.

'He didn't say any more?'

'No, Jude.'

'Didn't say what was wrong with her?'

'He didn't say that there was anything wrong with her. All he said was that Hester wouldn't be able to continue being our prompter for *The Devil's Disciple*.'

'Ah.'

'And he seemed quite gleeful as he passed on the news.' Jude could picture that. Mike Winstone had always resented his wife's involvement in SADOS. 'Which does put me in a bit of a bind.'

'In what way?'

'Well, it means we haven't got a prompter. And just at this stage of the production, when I'm trying to get everyone off the book ... we need one more than ever.'

'I can see that.'

'And the trouble is that there are plenty of SADOS members who might be happy to take on the role, but they're all friends of Elizaveta's.'

'Ah, yes.'

'And since Elizaveta's boycotting the production – and incidentally being very shirty with me – none of them will help me out. They're all part of her inner circle, you know, the lot who were always going to little "drinkies things" at Elizaveta and Freddie's ... which I used to be, but I've somehow blotted my copybook with Elizaveta. Anyway, if she makes it a three-line whip on the potential prompters, none of them would dare go against her.'

'Mm.'

'But I was talking to Storm Lavelle, who surprisingly now seems to be a fixture at Elizaveta's "drinkies things" –' Jude found herself starting to grin as she realized which way the conversation was heading – 'and she said you had a friend who might be prepared to step into the breach...?'

'Well, I could ask her,' said Jude, suppressing a giggle.

'What – me? Are you asking me to get involved in *amateur dramatics*?' The way the last two words were spoken, they could have been some unhealthy sexual practice.

Jude had gone round to High Tor as soon as she'd ended the call from Davina Vere Smith. She was mischievously intrigued as to how the proposal would be greeted. And her neighbour's reaction did not disappoint.

'I thought,' Carole went on, 'I had made clear my views on *amateur dramatics*.'

'Oh yes, you certainly have. But I thought, you know, helping people out when they're in a bit of a spot...'

'There are people I might help out when they're in a spot, but not people who indulge in *amateur dramatics*.'

'So your answer to taking over as prompter is no?'

'Definitely.'

'That's rather a pity.'

'Why?'

'Well, I thought you might be able to help me on the investigation.'

'The investigation?'

'Into Ritchie Good's death.'

Carole's expression changed instantly from disapproval to alert interest. 'Oh yes, I hadn't thought of that.'

'And, if you were, kind of ... embedded in the production of *The Devil's Disciple* ... well, we'd both be on the spot ... and able to investigate, wouldn't we?'

'That is a thought, yes.' Carole was clearly intrigued. 'You said earlier this afternoon that you didn't know whether it was murder.'

'No, but it's certainly suspicious.'

'Yes.' Carole nodded slowly, but with mounting enthusiasm. 'Suspicious, hm...'

'Well, come on, there is something odd about it. The doctored noose was definitely changed for the real one. I suppose it's possible Ritchie himself might have done that, but it doesn't seem likely.'

'So you reckon someone in the *Devil's Disciple* company did it?'

'Seems the most likely possibility, yes.'

'Hm.' Carole tapped her steepled hands together in front of her mouth as she tried to control her racing thoughts. A spark of excitement had been ignited in her pale-blue eyes. 'Ooh, it's frustrating not to know all the people involved.'

'Well, there's a very good way of getting to know them,' said Jude teasingly.

'What, you mean if I took over from Hester Winstone as prompter?

'Exactly.'

'Oh, I don't think that's for me,' said Carole Seddon, in characteristically wet blanket mode.

It was only half an hour later that the phone rang in High Tor.

'Is that Carole Seddon?'

It was a female voice she didn't recognize. 'Yes,' she replied cautiously.

'Good afternoon. My name's Davina Vere Smith.'

'Oh yes?'

'I gather Jude's asked you about taking over as prompter for the SADOS *Devil's Disciple*.'

'Yes. And I told her I'm afraid I can't do it.'

'I wonder if you could be persuaded.'

'I doubt it,' said Carole.

It was pure curiosity that had made her agree to meet Davina Vere Smith in the Crown and Anchor that evening. Ted Crisp greeted her in his customary lugubrious style. 'On your own, are you? No Jude?'

Carole had been intending to have a soft drink, but Ted had already started pouring a large Chilean Chardonnay, so it seemed churlish to tell him to stop. 'I'm meeting someone.'

'New boyfriend?'

139

'No,' came the chilling reply. Carole knew that Ted's words had reminded both of them of their brief and unlikely affair. The thought that it had happened still gave her a frisson of disbelief ... and excitement.

'Do you know the best way to serve turkey?' asked Ted.

Carole, not expecting a culinary question at that moment, replied that she didn't.

'Join the Turkish army!' said Ted heartily.

It took Carole a moment to register that it was one of his jokes. 'Oh, really,' she said, with annoyance that was only partially feigned.

'Excuse me, are you Carole?'

She turned to face a short woman with blond (almost definitely blonded) hair bunched into a pigtail. She wore grey leggings and a purple cardigan, unbuttoned enough to reveal an extremely well-preserved cleavage. A star-shaped silver pendant hung around her neck.

'Yes. You must be Davina.'

'Mm. I saw you in the Cricketers when you brought over Jude's chaise longue.'

'But we weren't introduced then, were we?'

'No.' Davina pointed to the wine glass Ted Crisp had just placed on the counter. 'Is that yours?'

'Yes.'

'I'll pay for it.'

'Oh, there's no need for you to—'

'Of course I will.' Davina grinned at the landlord. 'And I'll have a large G and T, please.'

140

When they were settled into one of the alcoves, the director said, 'Feels odd to me, being here on a Tuesday.'

'Oh? Why?'

'Tuesdays are always SADOS rehearsal days. But today ... well, did Jude tell you what happened on Sunday?'

'Yes. I was very sorry to hear about it.' A conventional expression of condolence, though even as she said it, Carole wondered why she felt obliged to say the words. She had only met Ritchie Good once and she hadn't taken to him then.

'It was a terrible shock for everyone.' But Davina's response also sounded purely conventional. She didn't appear to feel any grief for her lead actor's demise. 'And it's going to cause a lot of readjustment in my production of *The Devil's Disciple*.'

'I'm sure it will.'

'Which is why I wanted to meet you, Carole.'

'Yes, you said.' The words came out more brusquely than intended.

'Jude thought you'd make a really good prompter.'

'I've no idea whether I would or not. I've never had anything to do with amateur dramatics.' Still a bit frosty.

But Davina Vere Smith persevered. 'I'm sure you'd enjoy it if you did agree to join us. The SADOS are a very friendly bunch.'

Bunch of self-dramatizing poseurs, was

141

Carole's unspoken thought. What she said was, 'As I told Jude, it's really not my sort of thing.'

'Then why did you agree to meet me? If you've already made up your mind to say no?'

It was a good question. Carole was forced to admit to herself that she was more than a little intrigued by the whole SADOS set-up. Particularly now there was an unexplained death in the company. She decided to change the direction of the conversation to a little probing. 'Going back to what happened to your actor on Sunday ... What was his name?' she asked, knowing full well.

'Ritchie Good.'

'Yes. Presumably it was some kind of ghastly accident...?'

'Oh, it must have been, yes. Not that you'd think that from the theories some of the *Devil's Disciple* company are coming up with.'

'You mean some of them think it wasn't an accident?'

'From the texts and phone calls I've had in the last twenty-four hours you'd think they're all auditioning for the part of the detective in an Agatha Christie thriller.'

'Some of them think it was murder?'

'And how!' said Davina Vere Smith.

Which was what persuaded Carole Seddon to take over the role of prompter in the SADOS production of *The Devil's Disciple*.

When Jude was informed of the decision, she

didn't think it was the moment to bring up her neighbour's previous assertion that 'The day I get involved in amateur dramatics you have my full permission to have me sectioned.'

SIXTEEN

It was striking to Jude how little Ritchie Good was mentioned after the Thursday rehearsal following his death. Carole hadn't been there that evening, but she noticed the same once she started attending rehearsals. The Thursday, only four days after the tragedy, had witnessed a lot of emotional outpourings (some of them possibly even genuine), as members of the *Devil's Disciple* company expressed their shock at what had happened.

Very little actual rehearsal got done that evening, which was annoying for the director because prurient interest had ensured that, for the first time, every member of her cast had turned up. But whenever Davina Vere Smith tried to focus their attention on the play, someone else would have hysterics, or go into a routine about how they 'couldn't do the scene without imagining doing it with Ritchie'.

Even Olly Pinto did a big number about how dreadful he felt. This wasn't the way that he had wanted to get the part of Dick Dudgeon. He was going to suffer every time he said one of the lines that rightfully belonged to Ritchie Good. But, nonetheless, he would pull out all the stops to match up to Ritchie's performance. He would do his best 'for Ritchie'. In fact, he asked Davina at one point during that emotional Thursday evening rehearsal whether they could put in the programme the fact that he would be 'dedicating' his performance to 'the memory of Ritchie Good'.

But that was it, really. One evening of un-fettered emotion and then everyone wanted to get on with doing the play. The members of the *Devil's Disciple* company returned to their default preoccupation: themselves. The surface of SADOS had closed over, as if Ritchie Good had never existed.

Not much was said about him during the following Sunday's rehearsal, though they did get the news from Davina that Gordon Blaine had been questioned by the police. At what level this questioning had taken place she did not know, but they'd been to his house rather than taking him to the station. This information caused a surprising lack of discussion amongst the *Devil's Disciple* company. But there was a general view that Gordon's being questioned was logical. After all, he had built the structure which had killed Ritchie Good.

As she was leaving St Mary's Hall at the end of

144

her first rehearsal, that Sunday, Carole was approached by Mimi Lassiter. 'Oh, now you're in the production you must be a member of SADOS.'

'Must I?'

'Yes, nobody can be in a SADOS production if their subscription's not up to date.'

'Unless they're Ritchie Good,' said Carole, who had heard from Jude about his non-membership. Mimi Lassiter's face darkened. 'He wasn't a member, was he?'

The Membership Secretary agreed that he wasn't. 'And look what happened to him,' she said with something like satisfaction.

They were now out in the car park. Carole looked at Mimi Lassiter, dumpy with her dyed red hair. No wedding ring, post-menopausal, archetypal small town spinster. Then she noticed that Mimi was carrying a Burberry raincoat exactly like her own.

Carole took out her car key and unlocked her clean white Renault. As she did so, she realized that parked next to it was the identical model, also white. 'Well, there's a coincidence,' she said.

'Just what I was thinking,' Mimi Lassiter agreed.

'What, you mean ... that one's yours?'

'Yes.'

Carole Seddon felt very uncomfortable. The same Burberry raincoat, the same white Renault. Both post-menopausal. And she'd just mentally condemned Mimi Lassiter as an archetypal spinster. Was that how the denizens of Fethering saw her too?

But Mimi was not to be distracted from her cause. 'Now the subscription of Acting Members is—'

'But I'm not an Acting Member,' Carole objected. Unpleasant memories of the School Nativity Play welled up in her. Ooh, that itchy Ox costume. 'You'll never catch me acting,' she said with some vehemence. 'I am the prompter.'

'Yes, well, that's still covered by Acting Membership. Everyone who's actually involved in the production—'

'Backstage as well?'

'Yes, backstage as well. They're all in the category of Acting Members.'

'Well, it's a misnomer, isn't it?'

'What?'

'Acting Member. Acting Member implies that people in that category actually act. It should be Active Member.'

'I think it's fairly clear that anyone who's involved in—'

'Anyway, what other categories of membership are there?'

'Well, there's Supporters' Membership. That is usually for people who have got too old to continue as Acting Members but are still involved with the society. And then there's Honorary Membership, but that was really only set up for Freddie and Elizaveta ... you know, because they actually started SADOS and there needed to be some recognition of their enormous contribution to the—'

'So how much do I have to pay for an Active Membership?'

'Acting Membership.'

'It really shouldn't be called that,' said Carole.

'Well, it always has been called that!' Mimi Lassiter was very worked up. Clearly she didn't like anyone questioning the way she operated as Membership Secretary. 'And the subscription for Acting Membership is...'

Carole paid up.

Olly Pinto, in the role of Dick Dudgeon, had just asked if Essie knew by what name he was known.

'*Dick*,' replied Janie Trotman, in the role of Essie.

He then told her that he was called something else as well. But before he could say, '*The Devil's Disciple*,' he was interrupted.

'That's wrong,' said Carole. It was the Sunday rehearsal a fortnight after Ritchie Good's death, and she was beginning to feel at ease in her new role of prompter.

'I'm sure it's right,' said Olly Pinto, on the edge of petulance.

'No. You said you were *called* something else as well, whereas what George Bernard Shaw actually wrote did not include the words: *"I am called"*.'

'Well, it means the same thing.'

'It may mean the same thing, but what you said is not the line that Shaw wrote.'

'All right,' said Olly Pinto, well into petulance now. 'I'll take it back to where I ask Essie what they call me.' And he delivered the line that Shaw wrote.

'What?' asked Janie Trotman.

'That was your cue. I was giving you your bloody cue!'

'Keep your hair on. I'm not the one who's cocking up the lines.'

'I am not cocking up the lines! Look, I've taken on the part of Dick Dudgeon at very short notice and I'm doing my best to—'

'All right, all right,' said Janie, who'd heard quite enough of Olly Pinto's moaning. *'Dick.'*

'What?' he asked.

'You gave me my cue. I'm giving you the line that comes next. *Dick.'*

'Well, I didn't know you'd started, did I?'

'All right. Well, I have started. *Dick.'*

Again Olly Pinto tried to get out the line where he mentioned he was called *'The Devil's Disciple'*.

Again Carole interrupted him. 'You said *"as well"*. Shaw actually wrote *"too"*.'

'Oh for God's sake!' snapped Olly Pinto. *'"As well"* – *"too"* – what's the bloody difference? They both mean the same.'

148

'They may mean the same, but George Bernard Shaw chose to write one rather than the other. And the play SADOS is doing is the one written by George Bernard Shaw, not by members of the cast.'

Olly Pinto looked as if he was about to take issue, but decided against it. Hester Winstone had been very timid as a prompter. She wouldn't give the line until one of the actors virtually asked her for it. And she had seemed happy to accept any kind of paraphrase of George Bernard Shaw's words. Whereas with this new one ... blimey, it was like being back at school.

Carole Seddon was surprised to find she was really enjoying her job as prompter. With the text of *The Devil's Disciple* in her hand, she had the advantage over the actors. And even the most flamboyant of them looked pretty silly when they couldn't remember their lines.

Also, although she would never have admitted it to a living soul, she was glad to have the prospect of fewer evenings alone with Gulliver in High Tor, reading or watching television (even about convents and confinements).

Carole and Jude's conviction that they were engaged on an investigation grew weaker and weaker. Whenever they tried raising the subject with members of the cast, asking for their ideas as to who might have switched the two nooses, nobody seemed to be that interested. Getting

The Devil's Disciple on was much more important than Ritchie Good. He was already old gossip.

Despite his problems with the lines, Olly Pinto was really relishing his elevation to the role of Dick Dudgeon. Previously at coffee breaks during rehearsal it had been Ritchie Good round whom the junior members had gathered. Now it was Olly. He wasn't a natural to take on the casual insouciance of an amdram star, but he was getting better at filling the role.

And he mentioned Elizaveta and Freddie Dalrymple and their 'drinkies things' significantly less often. Now he'd got the part that he reckoned had always been his due, he didn't need the imprimatur of their distinguished names. Olly Pinto was now unquestionably the star of *The Devil's Disciple*.

At one point, in the course of that Sunday rehearsal, Jude, returning from the Ladies during a coffee break and passing the Green Room, overheard a snatch of conversation.

'Oh, for heaven's sake, don't start that,' said a peevish voice she identified as Janie Trotman's.

'Come on, I'm not doing any harm. It's just that I do find you stunningly attractive.' It was Olly Pinto's voice, steeped in sincerity.

'Even if that were true, it doesn't give you an excuse to come on to me.'

'Janie, I'm just—'

'Oh, I get it. Now you've got Ritchie's part, you reckon you can take on his personality too, do you?'

'It's not like that.'

'Chat up everything in sight, eh? Get them interested and then drop them like hot cakes? Well, you're not going to succeed with that, Olly. Certainly not with me. For one simple reason. Ritchie *could* get women interested because he was attractive. You can't because you aren't.'

'There's no need to be offensive.' The note of petulance that she'd heard at rehearsal was back in Olly Pinto's voice.

Also he was using that as an exit line. Jude hurried back to the main hall to avoid being caught eavesdropping.

What she had heard was very interesting, though.

Carole had now attended four rehearsals of *The Devil's Disciple*, but she hadn't joined the mass exodus to the Cricketers after any of them. When her neighbour raised the subject, Carole insisted that she was 'not a pub person'. But Jude remembered the very same words being used about the Crown and Anchor in Fethering when they first met. Carole had fairly quickly become something of a 'pub person' there, and Jude reckoned it was only a matter of time before she also became a post-rehearsal regular at the Cricketers. Her natural nosiness would ensure that.

The first Sunday she attended rehearsal

Carole had given Jude a lift in her Renault. Now they were both involved, that seemed to make more sense than having Storm Lavelle go out of her way to pick Jude up. Anyway, there wouldn't be room for three of them in the Smart car. That Sunday Jude had dutifully gone back to Fethering in the Renault immediately after the end of rehearsal, foregoing a drink at the Cricketers. She had wanted to go there, though, not only for the convivial atmosphere, but also in hopes of reactivating the investigation into Ritchie Good's death.

So on the following Tuesday and Thursday Jude travelled from Fethering in the Renault, went to the pub when Carole left and got a lift back home with Storm. Storm was such a chatterbox, particularly when she'd got a few drinks inside her, that she was more than ready to join in conjectures about Ritchie's hanging.

After overhearing the conversation between Janie Trotman and Olly Pinto, there was no way Jude wasn't going to the Cricketers after that Sunday's rehearsal. She hadn't had the chance, with all the *Devil's Disciple* company around, to tell Carole what she had heard, but she was more insistent that her neighbour should come to the pub that evening. Carole once again demurred, though with less conviction than before. Jude reckoned her friend would be a 'pub person' at the Cricketers by the end of the week. But Carole was not to be swayed that evening, so Jude said she'd get a lift back with

Storm.

Though the post-rehearsal SADOS company noisily took over the pub and formed into large groups, it was still possible to have a relatively private conversation with someone at one of the side tables. By good fortune Jude found herself at the bar at the same time as Janie Trotman, and an offer to buy the girl a drink assured her attention. The nearest group of actors centred on Olly Pinto, and Janie seemed unwilling to join them, so Jude had no problem in steering her to a table beside the open fire.

They clinked their glasses, Janie's a vodka and coke, Jude's predictably enough a Chilean Chardonnay. 'Olly seems to be stepping fairly effortlessly into Ritchie's shoes, doesn't he?'

Janie agreed. 'Mind you, he'll never be as good as Ritchie. He hasn't got the same amount of talent. Not nearly.'

'No, but I think he'll be all right.'

'He may be, if he learns his bloody lines.' Janie giggled. 'Mind you, Carole the Dominatrix is keeping him up to his work, isn't she?'

Jude giggled in turn, wondering how Carole would react to the nickname.

'She's quite a hard taskmaster, isn't she?' Janie went on.

'Something of a perfectionist, yes.'

'Where on earth did she come from? I've never seen her round any other SADOS shows.'

'I brought her in.'

'Really?'

'Yes, she's a friend of mine. My next-door neighbour, actually. Why're you looking so surprised?'

'I'm sorry, it's just ... I wouldn't have put you two down as friends. You seem so different. You're so laid back and, well, Carole...'

'Opposites attract,' suggested Jude.

'Maybe.' But Janie didn't sound convinced. 'Hm. Anyway, the surface of the water seems to have closed over Ritchie Good, doesn't it? Like he never existed.'

'I think in some ways that's quite appropriate.'

'How do you mean?' asked Jude.

'Well, there always was something slightly unreal about him.'

Jude found that a very interesting observation; it chimed in with the feeling she had got about Ritchie when they'd met in the Crown and Anchor, that he was going through the motions of life rather than actually living it. She asked Janie to expand on what she had meant.

'The way he used to come on to every woman he met, it never felt spontaneous. It was more like ... I don't know what you'd call it. Learned behaviour, perhaps? Certainly not innate.'

Jude grinned. 'You know the jargon.'

'I've got a degree in psychology,' said Janie.

'And do you use that in your work?'

'Sadly not at the moment. I haven't had a proper job since I left uni. And that was nearly three years ago.'

'I'm sorry.'

'There's nothing I could get round here that'd actually use my qualifications. Unless you reckon that stacking shelves in Lidl gives a unique opportunity to study the patterns of human behaviour.'

'Couldn't you look for something further afield?'

Janie Trotman shook her head ruefully. 'Can't really at the moment. My mother's got Alzheimer's. And my father's desperate that she shouldn't have to go into a home or a hospital. But looking after her is too much for him on his own. So...' She spread her hands wide in a gesture that seemed to encompass the limited possibilities of her life.

'Obviously it won't always be like this. My mother will presumably die at some point. I just hope to God she goes before my father. Otherwise I'll be lumbered full time.' There was no bitterness in her words, just a resignation. What she had described was her current lot in life, and that was all there was to it.

'It's why I keep doing the amateur dramatics,' she explained. 'I enjoy it and it gets me out of the house at least three times a week.'

Jude said again that she was sorry.

'It's all right,' said Janie. 'I'm not after sympathy. My parents looked after me when I couldn't help myself...' She shrugged. 'Some kind of payback seems logical.'

'Are you an only child?'

The girl nodded. 'And I love both my parents ... or perhaps in my mother's case I should say I love what she used to be.' Determined not to succumb to a moment of emotion, she went on briskly, 'Anyway, I've told you about my life. What about you, Jude? What do you do?'

She explained that she was a healer.

'Ah. And it'd be too much to hope for, I suppose, that you might have found a way to heal Alzheimer's?'

'I wish. I can sometimes alleviate distress or panic in a sufferer, but cure ... no.'

Janie grinned wryly. 'I was afraid you'd say that. But at the same time I'm rather relieved you did.'

'Why?'

'Because you don't come across to me like a charlatan.'

'Thank you.'

'I mean, I've looked online endlessly for anything that offers the hope of a cure. And there are plenty of people out there who do just that. If you only buy their patent medication, their dietary supplement ... then hooray, goodbye to Alzheimer's.'

'Did you buy any of them?'

'I'm afraid I did. When my mother started to decline, I was desperate, I'd try anything. Well, I did try one or two things, and they all had one thing in common. They were entirely useless. So, as I say, there are a lot of charlatans out there.'

'I don't doubt it.' Then Jude redirected the conversation. 'Incidentally, did Ritchie Good come on to you?'

'Of course.'

'When he first met you?'

'Yes. Didn't he come on to everyone when he first met them?'

'Certainly did with me. And Carole too, actually.'

'Really?'

'Don't sound so surprised. Carole is a very attractive woman.'

'Yes, I'm sure she is. But there's something a bit ... I don't know, a bit forbidding about her. Like, say a word out of line and she'd cut you down pretty quick. If I were a man, I'd think twice before coming on to Carole.'

'But, as we've established, Ritchie Good came on to *every* woman.'

'Hm.'

'How did you react, Janie?'

'When Ritchie first came on to me? Well, I was flattered, I guess. At that stage I hadn't witnessed him coming on to anyone else, so I thought maybe he was genuinely attracted to me. And then of course he was the star of the show, and he was so much older than me, and ... yes, I was flattered. Also, at the time I was in a rather low state about men.'

'Oh?' Jude smiled sympathetically. 'Relationship just finished?'

Janie nodded. 'Actually, it finished quite a

while ago, but I was still feeling raw. I had quite a lot of boyfriends while I was at uni, but there was this one boy I got together with in my third year, and we kind of stayed together after we'd done our degrees. We had a flat together in Crouch End, but then ... Mummy got ill, and I was having to spend more and more time down here. And, you know, I'd rush up to London for the odd night, but that made me feel guilty and ... Oh, I don't blame him. I don't think I was much fun to be with at the time. Well, we tottered on like that for ... over a year, it was ... and then the inevitable happened.'

'He met someone else?'

'Yup,' replied Janie, trying to make it sound casual, as if the separation was something she had come to terms with. But Jude could tell that she hadn't. 'So, anyway, having an older man, an attractive man coming on to me, telling me I was beautiful, even if he was married, even if he was Ritchie Good ... well, it gave me quite a boost. And yes, I did fall for him a bit.'

'Did anything come of it?'

'Like what? Are you asking whether we went to bed together?'

'Well, yes, I suppose I am.'

'Then the answer's no. But it was odd...'

'Odd in what way?'

'Well, he kind of implied that we would go to bed together. He kept telling me how much he fancied me and trying to persuade me to say yes. And he said he'd book a hotel room for us and ... well, he persuaded me, I guess. I don't know how much I really wanted to, but, you know, it was the prospect of something different happening in my life, something apart from looking after my mother and attending rehearsals for *The Devil's Disciple*.

'So I said yes. And we fixed the date, and Ritchie said he'd booked the hotel room and ... Then the afternoon of that day I had a text from him saying he'd decided he couldn't go through with it.'

'Did he give any reason?'

'He said he'd realized that he was just being selfish and, however much he fancied me, it wouldn't be fair to his wife.'

'And how did he treat you after that, Janie? When you met him at rehearsals? Was he embarrassed?'

'Not a bit of it. He behaved as if nothing had happened between us. I mean, he stopped coming on to me, but he didn't try to avoid me or anything like that. And certainly his confidence wasn't affected. In fact, I would have said he was cockier than ever after that.'

'Pleased that he had avoided the pitfalls of sin?' suggested Jude with some irony.

'I don't think that was it. It was almost as if for him the process was complete. He'd got what he wanted out of his relationship with me. He'd persuaded me to agree to go to bed with him and, having achieved that, he had lost interest.'

What Janie Trotman had said confirmed the impression Jude had got when she and Ritchie met in the Crown and Anchor. She didn't know if there was a word to describe a man who behaved like that, but had it been a woman she would have been called a 'cock-teaser'.

SEVENTEEN

'Is that Jude Nichol?'

She was surprised. So few people ever referred to her by anything other than her first name. It was only on official documentation that she used the surname she had gained from her second marriage.

'Yes,' she replied cautiously.

'It's Detective Inspector Tull,' said the voice from the other end of the phone. 'You remember you gave a statement to me and one of my colleagues after the death of Mr Ritchie Good.'

'Yes, of course I remember.'

'And I said then that I might be in touch with you again in connection with our enquiries.'

'Yes.'

'So here I am, being in touch,' he said with some levity in his voice.

'Right, Inspector. What can I do for you?'

'I just wanted to check a couple of details that

you put in your statement.'

'Fine. Fire away.' But Jude felt a small pang of panic. She had withheld from the police what Hester Winstone had said to her in the Green Room that Sunday night. Maybe, when interviewed, Hester herself had mentioned it and Inspector Tull was about to expose Jude's lie.

'We've now spoken to all of the people who attended the rehearsal that afternoon,' the Inspector began smoothly, 'and they all seem to tell more or less the same story.'

'That's not surprising, is it?'

'Not necessarily, no. And the sequence of events that everyone agrees on is that before the demonstration of his gallows, Gordon Blaine was holding a real noose as opposed to the fake one. Would you go along with that, Mrs Nichol?'

'Please just call me Jude.'

'Very well, Jude.'

'Yes, I would go along with that.'

'Thank you. And then when the stage curtains were drawn back to reveal Mr Good, he had the fake noose around his neck...?'

'Yes.'

'And he was standing on the wooden cart, which Gordon Blaine moved away so that it no longer supported him...?'

'Exactly. And Ritchie then grabbed the noose so that the Velcro didn't give way immediately, and he did a bit of play-acting, as if he was actually being hanged.'

'"Play-acting"?'

'Yes, playing to the gallery, showing off.'

'And to do that would have been in character for Mr Good?'

'Completely.'

'So, after the demonstration, everyone went off to the Cricketers pub opposite St Mary's Hall...?'

'Yes, I'm honestly not certain whether *everyone* went, but most people certainly.'

'And within half an hour you went back to the hall and found Mr Good dead, hanging from the gallows with the real noose round his neck...?'

'As I said in my statement, yes.'

'Yes. So within that half-hour – or however long it was exactly – someone substituted the real noose for the fake one...?'

'They must have done.'

'Mm.' The Inspector was silent for a moment. 'When you went to the Cricketers pub that evening, did you notice any members of the group missing? Or did you see anyone leaving the pub to go back to the hall?'

'I wasn't aware of anyone missing or anyone leaving, but that doesn't mean it didn't happen. You know, I was just having a drink with a bunch of people. I wasn't expecting ever to be cross-examined on the precise events of the evening.'

'No, of course you weren't.' Another silence. 'Well, Jude, you'll be pleased to know that your account tallies more or less exactly with what

162

all the other witnesses have said.'

'Good.'

'Did you know Mr Good well?'

'No, I'd only met him since I became involved in the production.' No need to muddy the waters by mentioning drinks à deux in the Crown and Anchor.

'So you probably didn't know him well enough to have a view on whether or not he might have suicidal tendencies?'

'No. But from what I had seen of him, I would have thought it very unlikely.'

'A lot of suicides are very unlikely.'

Jude agreed. She'd seen plenty of evidence of that in her work as a healer. 'I know. It's often impossible to know what's going on inside another person's mind.'

'Hm.'

'Does that mean, Inspector, that you are thinking Ritchie changed the nooses round himself?'

'It's something we're considering ... along with a lot of other possibilities.' She might have known she would just get the standard evasive answer to a question like that. 'One of the people in your group seemed to think it was the most likely explanation.'

'Oh, who was that?'

'Come on, Jude. You know I won't tell you that.'

'Was it Hester Winstone?'

'Or that.'

'And I suppose you won't tell me if you're about to make an arrest either?'

'How very perceptive of you. Anyway, an arrest implies that a crime has been committed. There seems to be a consensus among the people in your group that Mr Good's death was just an unfortunate accident.'

'Really? No one's mentioned the word "murder"?'

'You're the first.' Once again there was a note of humour in his voice.

'I'm amazed. I would have thought that self-dramatizing lot would have all—'

'You're the first.'

'Well...' She was flabbergasted.

'Anyway, Jude, thank you very much for your time. I think it very unlikely that we will have to trouble you again.'

'Does that mean you've closed the investigation?'

'It means I think it's very unlikely that we will have to trouble you again.'

That was it. Inspector Tull's call did not serve to make Jude feel any more settled. She still felt convinced that Ritchie Good had been murdered, and it was frustrating to have just been talking to someone who undoubtedly knew a great deal about the case. Who had, quite properly, resisted sharing any of that knowledge. Her own investigation seemed to have hit a brick wall.

And she did wish she could contact Hester

Winstone. She'd love to know what the former prompter had said when she was questioned by the police.

Jude had another unexpected call that Monday. It was round five o'clock and she was just tidying up after a healing session with a woman suffering from sciatica. Her efforts had proved efficacious and she felt the usual mix of satisfaction and sheer exhaustion.

'Hello?' she said.

'Is that Jude?' A woman's voice, cultured, precise.

'Yes.'

'My name is Gwenda Good. I'm the widow of Ritchie Good.'

'Oh.' Jude hastened to come out with appropriate expressions of regret and condolence, but the woman cut through them.

'I believe you were the first person to find my late husband's body.'

'One of the first, certainly.' Jude didn't want Hester Winstone's name to come into their conversation unless Gwenda Good introduced it.

'I would very much like to talk to you about what happened to Ritchie.'

'I'd be happy to talk about it. Do you think there was something suspicious about his death?'

'I don't like the word "suspicious". I would prefer to say "unexplained".'

'Very well.'

Jude felt a spark of excitement. She was a great believer in synchronicity. Earlier that day, after her phone call from Inspector Tull, her investigation seemed to have hit a brick wall. Now, out of the blue, she was being offered the chance to speak to the dead man's widow.

'I'm afraid I don't go out much,' said Gwenda Good. 'I wonder if it would be possible for you to visit me at my home?'

'Certainly ... that is, assuming you don't live in the Outer Hebrides.'

If the woman at the other end of the line was amused by this suggestion, she didn't show it. 'I live in Fedborough,' she said.

'Oh, that's fine. I'm only down in Fethering.'

'I knew you couldn't be too far away. We have the same dialling code.'

'Yes. Well, when would be convenient for me to come and see you?'

'Would Wednesday morning be possible? Eleven o'clock.'

So that was agreed. When she put the phone down, Jude was struck by how businesslike and unemotional Gwenda Good had been. She didn't sound like a woman who had just lost a much-loved husband.

EIGHTEEN

Because the character of Mrs Dudgeon only appeared in Act One of *The Devil's Disciple*, Jude was not required for all the play's rehearsals. But Carole, now indispensable as prompter, had to be there every time. And the following day, the Tuesday, was one of those for which her neighbour wasn't called, so Carole drove to Smalting on her own.

Jude had told her about the phone calls from Inspector Tull and Gwenda Good. Though not much information had come out of the first one, Carole was intrigued by what Jude might find out when she visited Ritchie Good's widow. She was also, not to put too fine a point on it, rather jealous. Now she was embedded in the *Devil's Disciple* company as prompter, she wanted to be fully part of any investigating they managed to achieve there.

So she was determined to use her evening at St Mary's Hall without Jude to good effect. To Davina's annoyance, there was a poor turnout that evening, because of a gastric flu bug which was working its way through the *Devil's Disciple* company. Still, Carole found the evening rather enjoyable. She managed to rap most of the surviving cast over the knuckles for paraphrasing George Bernard Shaw's text, and when the cry of 'Anyone for the Cricketers?' went up, Carole conceded that she would join the throng.

She got a strange satisfaction from making that breakthrough on an evening when Jude wasn't there. Next time they were both present, Carole could go to the pub after rehearsal as if she'd been doing it all her life.

Because of the driving, she had been intending to drink something soft. But when Davina Vere Smith said, 'Let me buy you a drink. No prompter should have to work as hard as you had to this evening', her resolve melted away. She asked for a small Chilean Chardonnay, and Davina bought her a large one.

Carole lingered on the periphery of a group in the centre of which Olly Pinto was doing his Ritchie Good 'Life and Soul of the Party' impression, until Neville Prideaux came and joined her. 'Sorry, Carole, we haven't really had a chance to have a proper chat, have we?' he said.

She was glad to have the chance to talk to Neville, though she put herself on her guard. Jude had brought her up to date with everything she knew about the retired teacher, so Carole was wary of appearing to know too much.

'You were certainly kept busy today,' Neville went on.

'I suppose that's the prompter's role.'

'To be busy? Yes. But not *that* busy.'

'Well, I didn't have to prompt you once.'

'No,' he responded rather smugly. 'I felt, since I'm the one who suggested the play, I have to set an example as General Burgoyne.' A complacent smile, then: 'Olly was absolutely hopeless this afternoon, wasn't he?'

'Hopeless on the lines, do you mean, or as an actor?'

'Let's just stick to the lines for the moment, shall we? He was all over the place. You were having to prompt him on virtually every speech.'

'Yes, but of course he has taken the part over at very short notice.' Carole was not just being defensive for the young man; she had spotted an opportunity to steer the conversation back to Ritchie Good's death.

'He's had a couple of weeks. He ought to be more advanced than he is. Olly's always been a bit iffy on lines. I directed him as Algy in *The Importance*, when Elizaveta gave her Lady Bracknell. Oscar Wilde's lines are so beautifully written, you wouldn't think anyone could cock them up. Well, Olly Pinto managed it. He was paraphrasing everything. He's actually not a very good actor either.'

Neville spoke as if sounding the death knell on Olly Pinto's theatrical career.

'Then why does he get big parts in the SADOS?'

'Oh, a couple of reasons. One, the eternal problem of all amateur dramatic societies: not enough men. The gender imbalance is so skewed that a young man with a very small talent can go a long way. And someone with a bit more talent – even a glib, meretricious talent like that possessed by Ritchie Good – can cherry-pick any part he wants.' Even though his rival was no longer on the scene, Neville Prideaux still spoke of Ritchie with considerable venom.

'You said there were two reasons why Olly got good parts...'

'Oh, yes. Well, the other one, of course, is because he's a *creature*. And I use the word in the Shakespearean sense of someone *created* by a more powerful person to whom they are totally subservient.'

'So who fits that role for Olly Pinto?'

'Elizaveta, of course. Elizaveta Dalrymple, undisputed queen of SADOS.'

'I gathered that her right to that title had been disputed.'

'What do you mean, Carole? Oh, that business of her walking out of this production. That won't be forever, I can guarantee you that. SADOS is far too precious to Elizaveta for her really to cut her ties with it.'

'But with regard to Olly, you're saying he owes his success in the society to Elizaveta backing him?'

'Exactly. As I said, he's her *creature*.'

'Or poodle?'

170

'"Creature"'s better,' said Neville definitively. Carole got the feeling that anything he thought of would always be better than anything anyone else thought of. That was why he'd so enjoyed being a schoolteacher, pontificating to small boys who never dared to question his opinions.

'Oh yes,' he went on, 'Olly is very much Elizaveta's creature. Part of the inner circle who spend all their time going for "drinkies" round at her place. She's got a nice house on the seafront at Smalting, and I gather she's been having these little parties for years. She used to co-host them with Freddie and didn't let his death stop her.'

'When did he die, actually?'

'Oh, I suppose about three years ago.'

'What of?'

'Heart attack, I think it was. He had a flat in Worthing where he used to "prepare his productions". He was found there, I believe. Still, he left Elizaveta very well provided for.'

'Oh?'

'Freddie made a lot of money. That's why he could afford an expensive hobby like SADOS.'

'Doing what?'

'You mean how did he make his money? He was a *pensions consultant*.' Neville loaded the words with contempt. 'Nothing even mildly to do with the arts.' Strange, Carole reflected, how Neville seemed to recognize a hierarchy amongst day jobs. To her mind being a schoolteacher wasn't that much more interesting than being a pensions consultant, but to Neville there was evidently a big difference.

'Anyway,' he went on, 'Freddie had sorted out his own pension provisions very carefully indeed. Elizaveta is extremely well-heeled.' He spoke with a degree of resentment. 'It's why she can always afford to be giving her "drinkies things".'

'I've heard about those, but I don't know much detail.'

'Oh, they're part of her power base, those "drinkies" parties. Elizaveta has a level of deviousness in her that makes Machiavelli look like a rank amateur. She's always been one of those manipulators who likes to "colonize" people. If you're not *for* me, you're *against* me, that's her approach to life.'

'Have you ever been to one of her "drinkies things"?'

'Good Lord, no. I can't be bought by a free glass of champagne.' The statement, intended to sound rather magnificent, succeeded in sounding petty.

'But if Olly Pinto is part of this charmed inner circle, then why didn't he join in Elizaveta's boycott of the production?'

'Interesting point, Carole. I wondered that a bit myself. Then I decided it was for one of two reasons.' He clearly liked dividing things into numbered sections, another schoolmasterly trait perhaps. 'Either it was just sheer greed. He saw a socking great part being offered to him, and

172

he thought, "Yes, I'm going to grab that."

'The other possibility – and I think the one I favour – is that Elizaveta encouraged him to take the part.'

'Why would she do that?'

'Because she knows he's not a very good actor. I think what she hoped for first didn't happen – that her walkout would stop the production stone dead in its tracks. Elizaveta's not used to playing small parts, you see. Most productions she's been in for SADOS, if she'd walked out, it really would have been the end. She didn't realize how easy it would be to find another Mrs Dudgeon.'

'I'm sure Jude would be very flattered to hear you say that,' Carole observed drily.

'Sorry, that didn't come out right.' He was quick to come back with a smooth response. 'I mean how easy it would be to find another *and vastly superior* Mrs Dudgeon.'

'Ha-ha. But, Neville, are you saying Elizaveta encouraged Olly to take the part of Dick Dudgeon because she thought he would ruin the production?'

'I wouldn't put it past her. Another reason she might have done it is so that she has a spy in the enemy camp.'

'So that he reports back to her everything that happens during rehearsals for *The Devil's Disciple*?'

'Once again, I wouldn't put it past her. Elizaveta Dalrymple is a woman of remarkable deviousness. She deeply loathed Ritchie Good for what he said to her about her past – particularly because he did it so publicly. She'd want to get her own back.'

'Enough to arrange his hanging?' asked Carole, making the question sound more frivolous than it was.

'Ah. Do I detect I'm with that contingent of the *Devil's Disciple* company who believes we have a murder on our hands?'

'I'd never rule out any possibility.'

'Hm.'

'Do I gather, Neville, that you do rule out that possibility?'

'I think an accident is the more likely scenario. As to murder...' He acted as though he were contemplating the possibility for the first time. 'Well, if it was, we wouldn't lack for suspects, would we? Was there anyone in SADOS whose back Ritchie Good hadn't put up?'

'I don't really know,' Carole lied. Jude had kept her up to date with everything. 'I haven't been with the group for long.'

'No, of course not. Well, someone with an ego the size of Ritchie's doesn't really notice whose sensibilities he's trampling over. I mean, did you hear what he said to cause the big bust-up with Elizaveta?'

'Yes, I got reports of that from Jude.'

'Ah, your pretty friend, yes.' He said this as though he were a great connoisseur of the feminine gender, and Carole felt an atavistic

174

pang from her childhood, the inescapable fact that she would never be known as 'the pretty one'.

Putting such thoughts firmly to one side, she asked, 'And did Ritchie insult you in the same kind of way?'

'No, he laid off me pretty much.' The smug smile reappeared. 'He recognized that I was a lot more intelligent than he was. And at least as good an actor. So he tended to avoid direct confrontation with me.'

'There was no rivalry between you?'

'Good Lord, no. Well, certainly not on my side. I had no reason to be jealous of Ritchie. I suppose he might well have been jealous of me, though.' Again it seemed that this monstrously egotistical thought was a new one to him. 'Yes, he probably was jealous of me.'

'I wondered if there was ever any rivalry between you over women...?'

'Women?'

'Women in the company.'

'How do you mean?' He spoke innocently, but there was a kind of roguishness in his manner too.

'I just wondered whether there might have been any conflict between the two of you over some woman you both fancied...?'

'Unlikely.'

'I mean, Ritchie Good apparently had a habit of coming on to every woman he met. He even came on to me,' confided Carole, blushing slightly.

'I don't think that meant much with him. Just a knee-jerk reaction,' said Neville, unaware of how offensive his remark might be. 'Ritchie was all mouth and no trousers. Glib with the chat, but he didn't follow through.'

'Unlike you...?' Carole suggested rather boldly.

Neville Prideaux smiled a wolfish smile. 'I generally get what I want. And besides, Ritchie was in a different position from me. He was married.'

'And you are not?'

A thin smile answered the question. 'I got divorced when I retired. A wife who is excellent as a house mistress at a boy's public school did not fulfil the requirements I had for the rest of my life. Now I am more of an emotional freelance.'

'What does that mean?'

'I am not looking for anything long term in a relationship. As long as it's still fun, I will keep on with it. Once it ceases to be fun, I end it.'

Carole found that Neville Prideaux's charm was diminishing by the minute. Otherwise she might not have pushed ahead with her next line of questioning. 'I heard someone chatting at rehearsals and saying that you'd had a fling with my predecessor...'

'Sorry?'

'Hester Winstone.'

'Huh.' He looked displeased. 'You can't have

176

any secrets with this lot.' Then he looked defiantly at Carole. 'So what if I did? We're both grown-ups.'

'But I'd heard that Ritchie Good came on to her too.'

'I thought we'd already established that Ritchie came on to anything in a skirt. Why, are you suggesting that Ritchie and I were rivals for Hester's affections, and I murdered him so I could have uncontested access to her?'

This was so close to what Carole had actually been thinking that she had some difficulty making her denial sound convincing.

'Well, I can assure you that wasn't the case. Hester and I shared one night of what could hardly be described as bliss and decided mutually that ours was not going to be *la grande affaire*.'

'Mutually?'

'I decided and told her. She didn't complain. Hester's a very unstable woman.'

Carole didn't disagree. Nor did she think it was the moment to ask Neville whether he thought his behaviour might have contributed to her instability.

'So,' he went on, 'if you're looking for someone who might have murdered Ritchie, I'm afraid you're very much barking up the wrong tree with me.'

'And who do you think might be the right tree?' No harm in asking.

'Well, I actually think you're stuck in a whole

forest full of wrong trees. Because I firmly believe that Ritchie's death was an accident. That probably Gordon Blaine was playing about with his precious mechanism and left the wrong noose in place. But, if I were going to waste my time playing amateur detectives ... I think the question I would ask is: Who has benefited from his death? Who is more relaxed, as if with his decease a huge weight has been lifted off their shoulders?'

'And what would your answer be?'

'Davina Vere Smith.'

NINETEEN

On the Wednesday morning Jude travelled by train for the two stops from Fethering to Fedborough. She felt no guilt in not including Carole in the day's mission. Jude, after all, was the one who had found Ritchie Good's body. Maybe that gave her some obscure right to meet his widow.

On the train she remembered Gwenda saying that she wasn't very mobile, and wondered about her level of disability. But the woman who opened the door of the terraced house in a road off Fedborough High Street showed no overt signs of illness and seemed to move with ease as she hastened to close the front door once her guest was inside. 'Sorry, need to keep out the cold,' she said.

Jude wouldn't have thought it was that cold, even a bit above average temperature for April. She herself was only wearing a cotton jacket over a T-shirt and skirt. The two chiffon scarves wound around her neck were statements of Jude's style rather than for warmth.

And the minute she stepped inside the house, she was glad not to be wearing more. The place was incredibly overheated, but Gwenda Good was wearing a cardigan over a jumper and fleece jogging bottoms. Over this she had on a plastic apron with a Minnie Mouse image on it. Her hands were in yellow Marigold gloves. She wore her greying hair in a thick plait and had unglamorous black-rimmed glasses.

Jude found it very difficult to assess the woman's age, but certainly reckoned she was a lot older than her late husband.

'Very good of you to come,' said Gwenda Good, and led the way into a small sitting room that faced out on to the street. Wooden Venetian blinds were half-closed and two standard lamps were on to compensate for the gloom. One stood over a small table, on which was a bowl of water, dusters and sponges and some small china figurines. Gwenda gestured to them and said, 'Wednesday, that's the day I clean the collection. Oh, do sit down.'

As Jude sat in a leather armchair, she became

aware of the 'collection' referred to. And the scale of it. It was clearly no coincidence that Gwenda had a Minnie Mouse on her apron. Because the image was reduplicated literally hundreds of times throughout the sitting room. Shelves covered the two side walls, and on one of these stood rows of figurines of Minnie Mouse in a variety of costumes and poses, dressed as a ballerina, as Santa Claus, as a tennis player, as a doctor, as a schoolteacher and many more.

A glass-fronted set of shelves was full to bursting of stuffed Minnie Mouse toys, again in a wide range of liveries. Another section featured Minnie Mouse accessories – pencil cases, backpacks, lunch boxes, packs of cards, board games, jigsaws and so on. Above these hung an opened Minnie Mouse umbrella. Jude observed that even the cushion on her chair wore the distinctive image with its spotted red bow. And the two standard lamps had Minnie Mouse shades.

For once she was at a loss for words. She couldn't think of anything nice to say about the aggregation of Minnie Mouses and yet to behave as if she hadn't noticed it would be perverse. She ended up saying, rather limply, 'Well, you've got quite a collection here.'

'Yes, it's not bad,' Gwenda agreed, 'but there's always so much more out there. It's hard work just trying to keep up. EBay's made it easier sourcing the goodies, but you have to keep your eye on the deadlines there, or you could miss something great. And actually,' she said as if admitting some shortcoming, 'most of the stuff I've got here is post-1968.'

'Sorry? Why is that significant?'

'Post-1968 is modern. Pre-1968 is vintage.'

'Ah.'

'And the prices are vintage too. You can spend literally millions if you get into that market.'

Again Jude couldn't think of anything to say. The question she was burning to ask – 'why do you collect it?' – didn't seem appropriate at that moment. So she fell back on a more fitting expression of condolence. 'I'm very sorry about your husband's death.'

'Thank you.' The words were spoken automatically, without much emotion involved. Gwenda had gone back to sit at her table under the standard lamp, and continued with the cleaning process which Jude's arrival had interrupted. She put each figurine in the water, swirled it round and then wiped it down meticulously with a cloth. Those whose hollow interiors were accessible were carefully dried inside with a sponge.

Gwenda appeared almost to have forgotten that there was anyone else in the room. Jude found it a little odd that she hadn't been offered a cup of tea or coffee. After all, Gwenda was the one who had set up the encounter.

The silence was extended while the punctilious figurine-cleaning continued.

Eventually Jude said, 'You wanted to talk to me about your husband...?'

'Oh yes,' said Gwenda, as if being reminded of something she had completely forgotten. She looked a little disgruntled at having her attention taken away from the task in hand. 'You were the one who found him dead – that's right, isn't it?'

'I was the one who raised the alarm, yes,' Jude agreed, again keeping Hester Winstone's name out of it.

'And he was dead when you found him, not dying?'

'He was definitely dead.'

'And I gather just before that he'd been taking part in a demonstration of how the gallows worked.'

'That's right. He was part of a set-up with Gordon.'

'Gordon?'

'Yes. Gordon Blaine. He'd designed and built the gallows.'

'Ah. I don't know the names of any of the people Ritchie did his acting with.' She said this as if it would have been rather bizarre for her to have known them.

'Did you go and see any of the shows?'

'No.' Gwenda sounded surprised that the question needed asking. 'I couldn't, could I?'

This was such a peculiar statement that Jude immediately asked, 'Why couldn't you?'

'Well, for obvious reasons.' Which didn't do much to clarify the situation.

'What do you mean by—?'

But Gwenda was not about to offer explanations. 'Ritchie didn't talk about any of that,' she said. 'Except the women, of course.'

'The women?'

Once again Gwenda just moved on. 'From what you saw of Ritchie's body, would you say his death looked accidental?'

'It seems most likely that it was an accident, yes,' Jude replied cautiously. 'That is, if it wasn't suicide. Do you know whether your husband ever had any suicidal thoughts?'

'Good heavens, no. Ritchie had a very happy life. He liked his work at the bank. He enjoyed his play-acting. And then of course we had a very happy marriage.'

Jude knew it was impossible ever to look inside a marriage and see what's going on, but she would have loved to know how Gwenda Good defined 'happy'. She said, 'You must have been very upset when you got the news of his death.'

'Why?' Again the strangest of responses.

'Well, because your happy marriage was over.'

'It had run its course,' said the widow without sentiment. 'That was when it was destined to end. There's no point in getting upset over things that are preordained.'

This sounded like part of some spiritual

package, so Jude said, 'It must be a comfort for you to have your faith.'

'I don't have any faith,' said Gwenda. 'Just a knowledge that everything that happens is pre-ordained.'

'By whom?'

'Oh, I don't know that.'

This was becoming one of the most bizarre conversations Jude had ever participated in, and yet Ritchie Good's widow did not sound at all unhinged. Everything she said seemed to be entirely logical, at least to her.

Jude had heard that Ritchie Good's funeral had taken place the week before and assumed that, since the body had been released, the police investigation into the death had ended. So she asked, 'Was there a good turnout for your husband's funeral?'

'I believe so, yes.'

'You *believe so*?'

'Well, obviously I couldn't be there.'

'Why obviously?'

'I can't leave the house,' replied Gwenda, as if this were something that everyone in the world knew.

'Do you mean you are agoraphobic?'

The woman dismissed the word with a shrug. 'I'm not too bothered what people call it. I have no interest in psychobabble. I just don't leave the house.' This was spoken without any anxiety or self-pity, as a simple statement of fact. Not leaving the house seemed very normal

184

to her.

'Not even to go to the shops?'

'I have everything delivered. I order online. What with that and eBay, I spend quite a lot of time on the laptop.' Again this was made to sound like the most natural thing in the world.

'A few minutes ago,' said Jude, 'you said that Ritchie didn't talk about his amateur dramatics, but he did talk about "the women"...'

'Yes.'

'Do you mind if I ask what you meant by that?'

'Not at all.' Gwenda seemed pleased that the matter had been raised. 'The thing is, Ritchie was a very attractive man...'

Jude was tempted to say, *Well, he certainly thought so*, but restrained herself.

'...and so, obviously, he had lots of women throwing themselves at him.' Gwenda looked straight at Jude for the first time in their conversation. 'Did you throw yourself at him?'

'Hardly.' Throwing herself at men was not Jude's style, though she couldn't deny the initial attraction she had felt for Ritchie Good.

'No, he didn't mention you.'

'Are you implying by that that he mentioned others?'

'Oh yes. Ritchie told me everything. There are a lot of unattached women in amateur dramatic societies, and quite a lot of them came on to him.'

'Don't you think he did some of the "coming

on"?' Jude couldn't forget his automatic 'Where have you been hiding all my life?'

'Oh no. He told me all about it. A lot of the women were very brazen. They would seek him out and try to get him on his own. Ritchie didn't give them any encouragement. And then most of them would quite shamelessly try to get him to go to bed with them.'

Jude, remembering how Janie Trotman had described her involvement with Ritchie Good, thought she could see a pattern emerging. She waited for more from Gwenda.

'And then of course at that point he had to disappoint them. He had to point out that he was happily married. To me.' There was huge complacency in the way she said these words.

And to Jude it all made perfect sense, explaining the gut feeling that she had had when alone in the Crown and Anchor with Ritchie. He was, as she'd thought after her chat with Janie, the male equivalent of a cock-teaser. He would come on to women, chat them up, get them to the point where they would agree to go to bed with him, before suddenly announcing that he couldn't go through with it because of his undying loyalty to his wife.

That was how he got his kicks. And then he would add the refinement of telling Gwenda exactly what had happened – or at least his version of what had happened. And their marriage would be strengthened. In fact, Jude suspected, Ritchie's descriptions of his skirmishes with other women were the dynamo of his relationship with Gwenda. As she had frequently thought before, human imagination can hardly cope with the variety of what goes on inside marriages.

Gwenda Good was still smiling smugly as she dried off a figurine of Minnie Mouse as cheerleader. She didn't seem to feel the need to initiate further conversation.

So, after a lengthy silence, Jude said, 'I'm still not quite clear why you asked me here. Have we talked about what you wanted to talk about?'

'Oh yes,' said Gwenda blandly.

'Well, could you tell me what it was?'

'Of course. I just wanted to know that you agreed Ritchie's death was an accident.'

A part of Jude wondered why that question couldn't have been asked on the telephone. But a more substantial part of her wouldn't have missed the morning she'd just experienced for the world.

'Why was that important to you, Gwenda?'

'Because of the Life Insurance. I didn't want there to be any delay on the Life Insurance, and that could have happened if there was any doubt about the circumstances of his death.'

'Yes, I suppose there could have been.'

'And if there were a question of suicide the cover could be invalid.'

'Well, I just asked you about that, and you said there was no chance that Ritchie would ever have committed suicide.'

'Oh yes, I know that. But I wondered if anyone had been spreading contrary rumours around.'

'From everything that I've heard discussed at rehearsals, nobody seems to think there was any question of suicide.'

'Oh, good.' The smug smile grew broader. 'Ritchie worked in Life Insurance, you see. And so he himself was very well insured. He used to say to me quite often – it was one of our little jokes – "I'd be a lot more valuable to you dead than I am while I'm alive."'

And Gwenda Good laughed. 'So I think when it all comes through,' she said, 'I'll be allowing myself a real splurge on eBay for more of my precious Minnies.'

TWENTY

As she travelled back on the train to Fethering, Jude went over in her mind the conversation she had just shared. And the more she thought about it, the more bizarre it seemed. Through her work as a healer, Jude had come across mental illness in many forms, but she had never met anyone who behaved like Gwenda. And indeed she wondered whether 'mental illness' was the right diagnosis. Though undoubtedly agoraphobic, the woman did not seem distressed at any level. But there was something definitely odd about her.

The glee with which she'd talked about the Life Insurance windfall about to come her way made Jude wonder for a moment whether Gwenda could have had a hand in her husband's death. Killing someone for their insurance is one of the oldest plotlines in the history of crime (and in its fictional version).

On the other hand, if the woman really never left the house, she couldn't have arranged the murder without the help of an accomplice. The more Jude thought about it, the less likely it seemed that Gwenda had been involved.

Still, she had plenty of news to share with Carole so, on her way back from Fethering Station, she called at High Tor to invite her neighbour round for coffee. And, once inside Woodside Cottage, because it was so near lunchtime, opening a bottle of Chilean Chardonnay seemed simpler than the palaver of making coffee.

After the exchange of their news, Carole asked, 'What do you think of Neville's idea that Davina had a motive to kill Ritchie?'

'Well, he's certainly right that she's more relaxed without him around. He totally destroyed her confidence as a director. She just kowtowed to him, whereas with Olly as Dick

Dudgeon, she orders him about all over the place.'

'And, of course, after you, she was the first one into St Mary's Hall to discover Ritchie's body. Maybe she was checking up that her little ploy had worked.'

'Possible.' Sceptically, Jude screwed up her face. 'Doesn't seem likely, though. And your mentioning that reminds me that Hester Winstone was also present. She was in the hall before I got there.'

'Alone with Ritchie – alive or dead. And tell me again, Jude, what was it exactly that Hester said?'

'"It's my fault. I'm the reason why he's dead."'

'Which could be an admission that she had killed him.'

'It could ... except for the fact that the police released her after interviewing her. I can't imagine Hester was in a robust enough emotional state to lie convincingly, so she must have provided an explanation for her presence in St Mary's Hall that let her off the hook.'

Carole sighed. 'It's a pity we can't contact Hester. I think she could provide answers to many of the questions that are troubling us.'

'I agree. I tried ringing her home again yesterday. Once again the phone was answered by Mike, not very pleased to hear from me. Once again he said Hester was "staying with a friend".'

'Do you think that's true?'

Jude shrugged. 'Could be. No way of finding out.'

'I think we should keep an eye on Davina at rehearsal tomorrow night. See if she gives anything away.'

'What, like confessing that she murdered Ritchie? I don't think it's very likely she'd provide chapter and verse on—'

'Don't be trivial, Jude. You know what I mean.'

'Well, yes, I do, but—'

Jude was again interrupted, this time by the phone ringing. She answered it, and heard an elocuted female voice ask, 'Is that Jude?'

'Yes.'

'How nice to hear you. This is Elizaveta Dalrymple.'

'Oh.' That was a surprise.

'I gather I have to congratulate you, Jude.'

'On what?'

'On taking over from me as Mrs Dudgeon and, from all accounts, being rather splendid in the part.'

'Well, I'm doing my best.'

'I'm sure you are. And also I gather you've got a friend of yours involved too, in the role of prompter. Carole Seddon, isn't that right?'

'Yes, it is.' For someone who was boycotting the production of *The Devil's Disciple*, Elizaveta Dalrymple seemed very well informed about it. Jude wondered who was reporting back to her. Olly Pinto seemed the most likely candidate.

'Anyway,' said Elizaveta, 'I was wondering whether you – and your friend Carole – might be free on Saturday evening...?'

'Well...'

'It's just for a little "drinkies thing" at my place. Totally informal. Say about six o'clock...? Would you be free?'

'Well, I know I am. I'm not sure about Carole.' At the mention of her name Carole looked puzzled. 'But actually she's here. I'll ask her.'

'Oh, she's there?' said Elizaveta. 'I didn't realize you two cohabited.'

'No, we don't. We—'

'Don't worry. Your secret's safe with me.'

Jude suppressed a giggle. It wasn't the moment to put Elizaveta right, to say no, in fact she and Carole were not a lesbian couple. She wondered whether the misapprehension would lead to interesting misunderstandings on the Saturday night. That is, assuming Carole was free.

Jude looked across at her neighbour and said that they were being invited for 'drinkies' at Elizaveta Dalrymple's. And was able to relay the glad news to their hostess that Carole Seddon would be able to come too.

'Interesting,' said Carole when Jude had put the phone down.

'I agree.'

'Neville Prideaux told me that these "drinkies" sessions of Elizaveta's have been going on
for years. Something she started when the
much-adored Freddie was around. He described
them as part of her "power base".'

'So why have we been invited?'

'Well, Jude, I'm sure it's not just for the
charm of our personalities. According to Neville, Elizaveta Dalrymple always has an ulterior
motive.'

'So we just have to find out what it is.'

'Yes,' agreed Carole. 'We do.'

They were both at rehearsal on the Thursday
evening and, as agreed, they kept a watching
brief on Davina Vere Smith. It was undeniable
that since the death of Ritchie Good she had
relaxed considerably in her directorial role. And
she enjoyed having Olly Pinto as a punchbag.

He still wasn't on top of Dick Dudgeon's
lines, so Carole was once again kept busy as
prompter. And the further he got into rehearsal
for his leading role, the more clearly his in-
adequacies as an actor were exposed. He just
didn't convince on stage. While he should have
been projecting the sardonic insouciance of
Shaw's anti-hero, he looked insecure, uncertain
not only about his lines but also in his whole
demeanour.

Increasingly Carole wondered if what Neville
Prideaux had suggested might be right. That, in
spite of her boycott, Elizaveta Dalrymple had

193

encouraged Olly to take part because she knew he would ruin the production.

There was one confrontation during that evening's rehearsal which caused Carole and Jude to exchange covert looks. Davina Vere Smith was working on a scene in Act Two, the first time Dick Dudgeon and Judith Anderson are left alone together. Storm Lavelle, who by then had her words indelibly fixed on the interior of her cranium, was being very patient as Olly Pinto stumbled and paraphrased, as ever. And even when he got the lines right, he managed to get the intonations wrong.

Each time they had to go back on the scene, the tension in Davina increased. Eventfully, she could stand it no more and burst out, 'Oh, for God's sake, Olly! Don't you have any idea of the basics of acting?'

'Yes, of course I do. I'm just used to working with more sympathetic directors.'

'Oh, are you? Well, let me tell you, I can be a very sympathetic director when the talent of the people involved justifies my sympathy. Come back, Ritchie Good – all is forgiven!'

'You weren't sympathetic to Ritchie,' objected Olly. 'You were just afraid of him.'

'I was certainly not afraid of him.'

'Yes, you were. You never argued with him. Whatever he suggested, whatever he wanted to do, you just went along with it.'

'That was because I trusted him. Because I'd worked with him many times before on other

194

productions and I respected his instincts. I knew he was a good actor, and it was worth putting up with a few disadvantages – like his ego, for instance – because a really good performance would emerge at the end of the process. Why else do you think I put such effort into persuading him to be in the production?'

It was at this moment that Carole and Jude exchanged looks. Somehow they'd both thought that Ritchie Good had been foisted on to Davina Vere Smith by the power brokers of SADOS. But if it was she who had brought him into the *Devil's Disciple* company, that rather changed their views on the situation.

The last thing Davina would have wanted would be to lose her original Dick Dudgeon.

Jude had a call the following morning from a friend she hadn't heard anything of for a long time. They had first met when Isabel, known universally as 'Belle', worked as a nurse in one of the big London hospitals. It had been on a course about healing. Belle, increasingly disillusioned by the shortcomings and iniquities of the NHS, had a growing interest in alternative therapies, but she found there was still a scepticism about them amongst the more traditional medical practitioners. Her ambition was to see the alternative integrated with the professional.

The two women had seen a lot of each other when, both between marriages, they had lived in London, but since Jude had moved to Fethering their contact had reduced to the occasional phone call. So when Belle rang on that Friday morning in April they had a lot of catching up to do.

They checked up first on each other's love lives. Both were currently unattached, Belle's second marriage having come to 'as sticky an end as the first one – God, men are bastards'. She asked whether her friend had had any recent 'skirmishes' but, normally very open to her intimates about such matters, Jude didn't mention her recent involvement with a real tennis enthusiast called Piers Targett. Even though months had passed since she had last seen him, it still hurt.

'Anyway, what about work?' she asked.

'Big changes,' said Belle. 'I've left the NHS.'

'Really?'

'Yes, it was just getting so dispiriting. They kept bringing in new schedules. I wasn't being allowed to spend the kind of time with patients that I wanted to. I was leaving every shift feeling totally frustrated by the fact that I hadn't achieved as much as I wanted to.

'Anyway, the one good thing that came out of my second divorce was that I got a bit of money from the bastard. Not much, but enough for me to take some time out from being employed, so I gave in my notice at the hospital.'

'Not early retirement?'

'God, no.' Belle was about the same age as Jude. 'I like to think I've got a few more useful years in me. But I took the opportunity to do a couple of courses. Like the healing one when we first met, though I've decided I haven't really got what it takes to be a healer.'

'I thought you were very good.'

'I was OK, but I hadn't got the magic. Not like you have.'

Jude did not demur at the compliment. She knew, when it came to healing, she was blessed with a gift, and she was no believer in false modesty.

'So,' Belle went on, 'I thought I should concentrate on a more practical kind of therapy. I did a course in reflexology, which I found very interesting, but I still didn't think it was quite for me. And then I did a course in kinesiology.'

Whereas when Storm Lavelle talked about going on courses, Jude suspected a level of faddishness in her, she never doubted the complete seriousness of Belle.

'Funny you should mention that. I'm getting very interested in kinesiology,' she said. 'Been reading up about it. I think it really works.'

'Me too.' The enthusiasm grew in Belle's voice. 'No, the further I got into the subject, the more I realized it fitted me like a glove.'

'So have you put a shingle on your door and set up on your own as a kinesiologist?'

'No, I'm not quite ready for that yet. And when my money from the bastard ran out, I needed a regular income, so I got another nursing job.'

'Not back in the NHS?'

'By no means. Private sector. In a convalescent home. I've been there for five months. And I've been intending to ring you all that time, but I've got waylaid by, you know, starting the job, and getting my new house – well, old house but new to me – vaguely habitable. But the reason I wanted to ring you is that we're practically neighbours.'

'What?'

'The home where I'm working is in Clincham...'

'Wow!'

'...and I'm living in a little village called Weldisham.'

'Oh, goodness me. Just up on the edge of the Downs. It's lovely up there.' Jude remembered when she and Carole had investigated some human bones discovered in a barn near Weldisham. 'Well, since you're so close, we absolutely must meet up.'

'I agree. That's why I was ringing.'

'But tell me first about this convalescent home where you're working. Are you enjoying it?'

'Best job I've ever had. I've been so caught up in it that's another reason why I haven't phoned you. It's a big house just on the outskirts of Clincham, lovely setting, great views looking up towards Goodwood and the Downs. Called Casements. And the patients are, well, what you'd expect – people recovering from operations, a bit of respite care, some who're just run down or have had breakdowns, a few terminal cases. But the doctor who runs it is the kind I've been looking for all my life.'

'You don't mean in the sense of a potential Husband Number Three?'

'Certainly not. Rob is very happily married, I'm glad to say. He's a qualified doctor, but he's really found his métier as director of Casements. What's more, he's the perfect boss for me because he does genuinely believe in mixing traditional and alternative therapies.'

'So you get to do a bit of kinesiology?'

'Yes. Which is great. Rob also has people who come in to do reiki and acupuncture. I mean, none of it's forced on the patients. And of course I do the normal everyday nursing stuff as well. But if any of the patients want to have a go with me on the kinesiology, well, they can. And I must say I've had some really encouraging results. Really think I've helped some of them. I no longer leave work feeling dissatisfied.'

'That sounds brilliant. Well, look, come on, diaries at the ready. Let's sort out a time when we can meet up. Presumably if you're in Weldisham three miles up a country lane, you must have a car. There's a very nice pub here in Fethering called the Crown and Anchor.'

'There's also a nice one in Weldisham called the Hare and Hounds.'

'Yes, I know it.' Jude and Carole had spent

quite a bit of time there when they'd been in-vestigating the death on the Downs.

'Oh, before I forget, Jude ... there was another reason why I phoned you today.'

'Really?'

'Yes. Your name came up yesterday when I was talking to one of the patients here.'

'Oh? Who was it?'

'Her name's Hester Winstone.'

TWENTY-ONE

'Staying with a friend.' Yes, thought Jude, that's exactly how a man like Mike Winstone would explain away his wife's absence. In his shallow world of cricketing heartiness there was no room for uncomfortable realities like mental illness. Belle told her that Hester had been in Casements almost from the moment she had been released by the police after questioning about Ritchie Good's death. She was under the care of a psychiatrist, but she had also accepted Belle's offer of some kinesiology treatment. It was during one of their sessions that Jude's name had come up. 'She was very kind to me,' Hester Winstone had said.

According to Belle, Hester wasn't isolated at Casements. Though she had breakfast in her room, she ate other meals communally with the other patients. She was on a heavy dose of anti-depressants, and she was given sleeping pills at night. Belle said she was not a difficult patient. She seemed very withdrawn and, yes, in a state of shock.

Jude had then given a brief outline of the events in Smalting that had led to Ritchie Good's death, and Belle said, hearing that, she wasn't surprised at the state Hester was in. 'So do you think she actually witnessed him dying?'

'I think so. But I can't be sure. I'd really love to talk to Hester about that.'

'Well, why don't you?'

'What do you mean?'

'Come and visit her at Casements.'

'Could I do that?'

'Why not?'

'I thought perhaps she wasn't allowed visitors.'

'Not so far as I know. Her husband comes to visit her twice a week. Regular as clockwork. Two o'clock on Wednesdays and Saturdays.'

'Have you met him, Belle?'

'No, I haven't.'

'So you don't think there'd be any problem if I were to visit her?'

'I wouldn't think so. I'll check with Rob if you like. I think he'd welcome your coming. I think he'd also welcome it if you tried a bit of healing on her.'

'That's a thought. Would you mind asking him, though?'

'No problem. I'll be going in after lunch. My shift starts at two. I'll ask Rob and phone you back.'

'Well, if it's OK, maybe I could come and see Hester this afternoon?'

'I can see no reason why not,' said Belle.

As it turned out she must have phoned her boss straight after their call ended, because she rang back within five minutes, offering to pick Jude up in Fethering at one-thirty and drive her to Casements.

It was good to see Belle again. Jude always found that, whatever time had elapsed since their last meeting, they could pick up together as if they'd only met the day before. But they didn't talk a lot on the journey to Clincham. Jude was preoccupied with her forthcoming encounter with Hester Winstone and, as she did before a healing session, was focusing her energies. Belle knew her well enough to respect the silence between them.

Casements was a large house set back from the road some miles outside Clincham in the Midhurst direction. Its name clearly derived from its large number of windows, all criss-crossed with lead latticework. It looked more like a country house than a hospital.

As she brought her Toyota Yaris to a halt in the staff car park, Belle said, 'I'd like you to meet Rob. I told him you were a healer.'

'Fine.'

The door off the main hall to the Director's Office was open, which seemed to typify the air of relaxed warmth around Casements. Rob himself reinforced that impression. A tall man in his forties, he dressed more casually than the average GP, but there was a shrewdness in his blue eyes which suggested he was aware of everything that was going on around him.

'My friend Jude,' said Belle as they stood in the doorway.

'Great to meet you.' Rob's handshake was firm and welcoming. 'I hear you're a healer.'

'Yes.'

'I can't claim to understand how it works, but I have a great respect for your profession.' Jude wondered how Carole would have reacted to hearing what she did described as a 'profession', as Rob went on, 'And I've seen some remarkable results from the work of healers.'

Jude grinned. 'I can't claim that I know how it works either. But I know *when* it works.'

'Sounds good enough to me. As Belle's probably said, we use a lot of alternative therapies here – though actually I prefer to call them *complementary* therapies. Medical knowledge is improving all the time, but there are still too many things we are clueless about when it comes to curing them. So I'm in favour of trying anything – short of downright charlatanism – that might work.'

'Sounds a good approach to me,' said Jude.

'Were you thinking of trying any healing with Hester this afternoon?'

'Only with your permission. She's your patient, not mine. I don't want to do anything that might clash with the treatment she's already receiving.'

'I don't see how healing could do that,' said Rob. 'Mixing therapies is not like mixing medications. No, if you think you can help her – and Hester herself doesn't object – you have my permission to use your healing powers on her.'

'I'll see how she feels about it ... if the moment comes up. But thank you.'

'And I wish you good luck.'

'Oh?'

'The psychiatrist who's working with Hester is finding it hard work. Not that she doesn't cooperate. She's very polite, very accommodating, but there's a whole lot of stuff she's holding in, things she won't talk about.'

'But she's not pretending there's nothing wrong with her?'

'No, she recognizes there's something wrong. She seems almost relieved to be here. But in terms of getting her better ... Well, until she opens up a bit about what's really traumatized her, it's uphill work.'

'I'll see if I can get her talking, though I'm really just here as a friend, not in any professional capacity.'

'I understand that. Anyway, let me know how you get on with her. Drop in here when you're leaving.'

'Of course.'

'There have been quite a few cases in the past where I've thought healing might have some effect.' Rob focused his blue eyes on her. 'I wonder, Jude, would you mind my contacting you if something similar were to come up in the future?'

'I'd certainly be up for having a go. Can't guarantee results, I'm afraid. You never can with healing.'

'You never can with a lot of traditional medicine,' said Rob, smiling.

Hester Winstone's room was at the back of Casements, with latticework windows looking up towards the gentle undulations of the South Downs. It was comfortably furnished, more like an upmarket hotel room than anything to do with a hospital.

And the manner of Hester's greeting to Jude was more suited to a hotel guest than a patient. She was smartly dressed in a tartan skirt and pink cashmere jumper. Her red hair was neatly gathered at the back in a black slide and she was wearing more make-up than she had when attending SADOS rehearsals.

Belle had gone ahead to check that Hester felt up to the visit, and the patient was prepared for Jude's appearance. Which meant that she must have agreed to their meeting. Her behaviour was that of a well-brought-up hostess, offering her visitor tea or coffee. 'The staff are very good at catering for our every need.'

Jude opted for tea, thinking that having a drink might extend the length of her stay. There were a great many things she wanted to ask, but she recognized that she had to be gentle and circumspect in her approach. Beneath Hester's brittle politeness, Jude knew there was a lot of pain, and she did not want to be responsible for aggravating that pain. Given Mike Winstone's unwillingness to have anything potentially unpleasant in his life, having his wife hospital-ized (even if it was covered up by the bland lie about 'staying with a friend') must have meant there was something seriously wrong with her.

But in their first few exchanges the woman's mask of middle-class gentility did not crack at all. The only discordant sign was a slight detachment in her manner. Her eyes were not glazed, but they looked distant. She behaved like some skilfully constructed and very correct automaton. Jude presumed this was the effect of her medication.

Their polite surface conversation had almost run out before the welcome interruption of a neatly uniformed woman with tea and biscuits. Hester's expert hostess manner seemed to wel-come the rituals of pouring and passing the cup.

Having taken a sip of tea and a bite of biscuit,

Jude felt she could risk moving the conversation away from pleasantries. 'All's going well with *The Devil's Disciple*,' she said. 'If they knew I was seeing you today, I'm sure lots of the company would have sent good wishes.'

'That's very nice of them.' Since no actual good wishes had been sent, this comment sounded slightly incongruous.

'And Carole has taken over the job of prompter.'

'Carole?' Hester repeated vaguely.

'My friend Carole. Do you remember? She was with me when we met in the car park. You know, after you'd...'

'Yes.' Hester Winstone's face clouded. Perhaps she didn't want to be reminded of her 'cry for help'. 'I'm glad to hear all's going well,' she said with an attempt at insouciance.

'Though Olly Pinto's still having a bit of a problem with the lines...' Jude went on. No reaction. '...Having had to take over at such short notice...' Still nothing. '...From Ritchie Good.'

The name did produce a flicker in Hester Winstone's eyes. Quickly followed by a welling up of tears. Sobs were soon shuddering through her body.

Instantly Jude was up and cuddling the woman to her capacious bosom. 'Just lie down on the bed,' she said. Mutely, Hester obeyed. Jude ran her hands up and down the contours of

207

the body, not quite touching, as she concentrated her energy. The sobs subsided.

'What are you doing?' asked Hester drowsily.

'It's a kind of healing technique,' said Jude. She continued in silence for about twenty minutes, focusing where she felt the greatest tension, on the shoulders and the lower back. During that time Hester dropped into a half-doze, from which she emerged as Jude drew her hands away and collapsed, drained, into her chair.

'God, that feels better,' said Hester. 'Thank you.'

'My pleasure.'

'How do you do it?'

'I honestly don't know. It's just something I found I could do.' Jude looked into her client's hazel eyes. 'How're you feeling now?'

'As I said, better.'

'Is there anything you want to talk about?'

'Like what?'

'What's been bugging you. What's got you into this state.'

'Hm.' There was a long silence. Then, slowly, Hester Winstone began, 'It was Ritchie ... seeing Ritchie, that's what pushed me over the edge.'

'But what brought you up to the edge – that had been building for some time, hadn't it?'

Hester nodded. 'Most of my life, I sometimes think.' Jude offered no prompt, just let the woman take her own time. 'I think I've always had this sense of inadequacy. This feeling that when it came to the test – any kind of test – I'd be found wanting. And whereas I thought I'd grow out of it, in fact, as I've got older, it's got worse.'

'Was there anything particular that made it get worse – I mean, apart from what's happened the last few weeks?'

'I suppose when my father died, that hit me quite hard.'

'You were very close to him?'

Hester nodded. 'Yes. He probably spoiled me, actually. But he always, kind of, appreciated things I did. I was never particularly brilliant at anything – exams, sport, I was just kind of average. But Daddy seemed quite happy with that. He didn't want me to achieve more – or if he did I was never aware of him putting any pressure on me. So I, kind of, felt secure when Daddy was around.'

'How old were you when he died?'

'Nineteen. In my second year at catering college. My mother was disappointed – she said I ought to have gone to a proper university, but Daddy told me catering college was fine. I've always liked cooking and...' For a moment some memory clouded her focus.

'And then your father died...' Jude prompted gently.

'Yes, it was very sudden. I had a very bad time then. I couldn't finish my course, I dropped out.'

'Was it some kind of breakdown?'

'I suppose, in retrospect, that's what it was.'

'Did you have any treatment then?'

'No. Perhaps I should have done. I went back home and lived with my mother. And that wasn't good. Because she was in a pretty bad place too, and ... It was almost as if she was jealous of me.'

'Why?'

'I suppose because my father had found me easier to love than he had her.'

Hester looked shocked by her words, as though it was a thought that she'd had for a long time, but never before articulated.

'Anyway, then my mother remarried.'

'Did you get on with her new husband?'

'Yes, no worries there. He was fine. And I was quite grateful to him, actually. Because he kind of took my mother's focus away from me. And I got better and ... well, to say I blossomed might be overstating things, but I was OK. And then I did a course in sports marketing – not a university course, just a one-year diploma, but it was good. It was out of that I got a job with a company that was trying to raise the profile of cricket as a participant sport. They don't exist now, but it was quite fun back then. I mean, I'd only got a secretarial job, but the people I was working with were quite jolly.'

'And was it through your work there that you met Mike?'

'Yes. We went out a few times and I thought

210

it was just for laughs, but suddenly he's asking me to marry him.'

Classic syndrome, thought Jude. A girl who adored her father tries to replace him with another older man. But of course she didn't say anything.

'So we get married and suddenly we've got the two boys and ... so it goes.'

'And how have you been since that time?'

'What, you mean mentally?'

'Yes.'

'Fine. Quite honestly, bringing up two boys, you don't exactly have time to think about your own state of mind ... or anything else much.'

'So your feelings of inadequacy ... you didn't have any time for those?'

Hester grinned wryly. 'Oh no, they were still there. I think they were born with me, part of my DNA ... like red hair.' By instinct her hand found the hair at her temple before she said tellingly, 'And Mike does have very high standards.'

TWENTY-TWO

'You mean,' asked Jude, 'you feel under pressure to keep up with those standards?'

'I suppose so, yes. Mike likes things done a certain way. Not unreasonably,' she hastened to add, lest her words might sound like criticism. 'But he and the boys, well ... they're a lot more efficient and organized about things than I am.'

Her words confirmed the impression of the Winstones' marriage that had been forming for some time in Jude's mind: Hester cast in the role of the slightly daffy woman in a chauvinist household of practical men, her fragile confidence being worn away by the constant drip-drip of implied criticism. But again Jude didn't say anything about that.

'You once told me that you joined the SADOS because you had time on your hands.'

'Yes, well, with the boys both boarding at Charterhouse, there was so much less ferrying around to be done. I seem to have spent most of the last twelve years driving them somewhere or other, so yes, it did feel as if I had time on my hands.'

'And also it was doing something for you,

rather than for somebody else,' Jude observed shrewdly.

'I suppose that was part of the attraction.'

'And was Mike positively against the idea?'

'No, he wouldn't come out strongly against something like that. Not his style. But he'd sort of dismiss it as something silly that women do.'

And so the process of undermining would continue.

Jude wondered whether she should ask whether Hester minded the kind of gentle inter-rogation she was undergoing, but thought that might be unwise. The healing had created an intimacy between the two women that was too precious to break.

'And helping out with front of house on the pantomime was the first thing you'd done for SADOS?'

'Yes. I got in touch when Mike went off to New Zealand. In a rather pathetic fit of pique, I suppose.'

'Sounds to me like a fairly justifiable fit of pique.'

'I don't know about that. Anyway, I said I'd help out with the panto.'

'Did you actually become a member of SADOS?'

'You bet. I had Mimi Lassiter on to me straight away, demanding a subscription. She's like a terrier about ensuring everyone in SADOS is fully paid up. I think she regards it as her mission in life.'

Jude smiled. 'And it was then that you met Ritchie Good...?' She spoke the name gently, worried that it might once again set off the hysterics.

But Hester was calmer this time. The healing had done its work. 'Yes,' she replied.

'And you got the full chat-up routine from him?' She nodded. 'And were flattered by the attention?' Another slightly shamefaced nod. 'How far did he go?'

'What, in terms of what he wanted us to do?'

'Yes.'

'Well, he...' This was embarrassing too. 'He sort of implied he wanted us to go to bed together.'

'And were you shocked by that, or what?'

'Well, I was ... I don't know. I suppose I was attracted by the idea ... a bit. I mean, I was in a strange state, sort of vulnerable and ... And then Mike had just gone off to New Zealand – virtually without saying goodbye to me and ... I don't know,' she said again.

'And when Ritchie had virtually got you to agree to go to bed with him, he then went cold on the idea, saying that he couldn't cheat on his wife?'

Hester Winstone's eyes widened. 'Jude, how on earth do you know that? You weren't there in the Cricketers, were you?'

'No. Let's just say there seems to be a pattern in Ritchie Good's chatting-up technique.'

'Oh.' Hester still looked bewildered.

214

'And I dare say that left you feeling pretty bad?'

'Well, yes. I mean, the fact that I'd even gone along with the idea, that I'd even contemplated betraying Mike, it was ... It made me feel even worse about myself. It made me feel stupid and unattractive.'

'And weak when Neville Prideaux came on to you?'

'Yes.' Hester looked vague again. 'I told you about that, did I?' Jude nodded. 'Yes, Neville was much more practical about the whole business than Ritchie.'

'He really wanted you to succumb to his charms?'

'Mm.' She spoke with slight distaste. 'Though I don't know whether it was me he wanted, or just a woman. A conquest.'

'But you allowed him to ... conquer you?'

A quick nod. 'Really, once I'd agreed to go back to his flat ... well, he seemed to take it for granted that I'd agreed to everything else. And he kept saying he'd really fallen for me, and that I was beautiful and ... I suppose I behaved like a classic inexperienced teenager.'

'And Neville behaved like a classic experienced seducer?'

'Yes. I felt terrible afterwards. I mean, while I could convince myself there was some love involved, well, it was ... sort of all right. But when it had happened, and I realized he'd just taken advantage of me, and I'd done God

215

knows how much harm to my marriage and ... Neville didn't want to see me again. He didn't want to have any more to do with me, and at the read-through for *The Devil's Disciple* he behaved like nothing had happened between us.'

'And that's what made you feel so miserable that, in the car park, you took the nail scissors out of your bag and...?'

Hester nodded again. She looked very crumpled, very downcast. Jude let the silence last. Then she said, 'Can we talk now about the Sunday rehearsal when Gordon Blaine and Ritchie Good demonstrated the gallows?'

A shudder ran through the woman's body. 'That ... I don't ... That was what pushed me over the edge. I can't talk about it.'

'Don't you think talking about it might help?'

'No, it could only make things worse.'

'You must have talked to the police about it, Hester.'

'What makes you say that?'

'The fact that they released you.'

'How do you mean?'

'When I saw you that afternoon, you said that it was your fault, that you were the reason he was dead. By the way, I didn't tell the police you'd said that.'

'Why not?'

'Because, heard by the wrong people, it could sound as though you were confessing to having killed him.'

'What do you mean by "the wrong people"?'

'I mean people who thought Ritchie had been murdered, And, at least at first, the police must be included in that number. But you must have told them something which stopped them being suspicious of you, something that let you off the hook.'

'Yes, I suppose I did.'

'Are you happy to tell me what you told the police?'

There was a long silence. Then Hester said, 'I've tried to blank it out of my mind.'

'I'm sure you have.'

'I don't like going back there.'

'But you must know that your mind's going to have to come to terms with it at some point.'

'Mm.'

'And I think you'll feel better when you face it, face what actually happened.'

'Maybe.' But she didn't sound convinced.

Jude waited. She sensed that to push further at this point might break the confidential atmosphere between them.

The silence became threateningly long. Jude was just reconciling herself to having reached the end of any revelations she was going to get, when Hester said, in a thin, distracted voice, 'What I said to you was true. I was the reason why Ritchie was dead.'

'In what way?'

'If I hadn't been there, he still would have been alive.' Jude didn't prompt, just waited. 'I

217

wasn't in the hall when Gordon and Ritchie did their demonstration of the gallows for everyone. I'd gone to the loo. I was finding it increasingly awkward just hanging out with people during rehearsals. Because of Neville. He seemed so cold and unaffected by what had happened between us ... and also by then he seemed to be coming on to Janie Trotman. It was painful for me. So, as soon as the rehearsals finished, I tended to rush off to the loo, to avoid socializing. And I stopped going on to the Cricketers.

'But that Sunday afternoon I stayed in the loo until I thought everyone would have gone, but when I came out I found Ritchie was still there in the hall. And I was, kind of, a bit awkward with him – not as bad as with Neville – but not relaxed, anyway.

'He asked me what I'd thought of his escaping death by inches on the gallows. I had to confess that I hadn't seen the demonstration, and so he insisted that I must have a private showing of it. Ritchie was just a show-off, really. Like a little boy who won't allow anyone to miss the new conjuring trick he's just learnt.

'I thought it was a bit silly, but it couldn't do any harm to humour him. So Ritchie got himself up on stage and climbed on to the wooden cart underneath the gallows. And he put the noose round his neck – and told me to pull the cart away.

'He was being all silly and melodramatic,

saying, "You can be the one, Hester! You can be the person who sends me to my death!" But I'm sure he didn't mean it, he was just joking, just playing the scene for all it was worth, "showing off" again, I suppose I mean.

'So, anyway, I did as he told me to – I pulled away the cart. And there was quite a thump as he fell and the noose tightened around his neck. He was kicking out and gasping – and I thought that was just Ritchie playing up the drama and about to free himself. And his hands were up at his neck, trying to get a purchase on the rope, but it was too tight.

'Then finally I realized he wasn't play-acting, that he was being strangled for real. And I put the cart back and tried to get his feet on to it, but they were just hanging loose, with no strength in them. And I got up on the cart and tried to loosen the noose around his neck. But I couldn't, it was too tight.

'And then I realized that Ritchie was dead.'

TWENTY-THREE

'And what the hell are you doing here?'

Neither of them had noticed the door open, but they both looked up at the sound of Mike Winstone's voice. He was standing in the doorway, blazered and more red-faced than ever.

'I just came to visit Hester,' replied Jude, sounding cooler than she felt as she rose from her chair.

'Oh yes? And aren't you aware that she's meant to be having a course of rest and recuperation?'

'I don't think my presence will have delayed either her rest or her recuperation.'

'I'll have a strong word with the people downstairs. They shouldn't just let anyone wander in to a place like this.'

'I spoke to the Director. I'm here with his blessing.'

'Well, you're not here with my blessing.' As he spoke Mike Winstone's face grew redder still. He sat himself down with a proprietorial manner in the chair that Jude had just vacated.

'I'll be leaving shortly,' Jude said.

'I'm glad to hear it. And you're involved with

that "Saddoes" lot, are you?' He deliberately used the diminishing mispronunciation.

'Yes.'

'Well, if you value your life, don't you dare mention to any of them that Hester's in here, will you?'

'I had no plans to mention it.'

'Keep it that way.'

'So officially she's still "staying with a friend", is she?'

'Yes. And it's bloody inconvenient having her away from the house. There are only so many takeaways and pub meals I can put up with.'

'I'm sorry, Mike.' It was the first time Hester had spoken since his arrival.

'So you bloody should be. Have the quacks here given any indication of when they're going to let you out?'

'I'm afraid not.' Hester sounded very down. 'The psychiatrist says he can definitely see some improvement.' She offered this tentatively, a sop to her husband's anger.

He rolled his eyes in exasperation. 'Huh, it's all so bloody vague, isn't it? The whole business of "mental illness". Because ultimately, at some point the patient has to make the effort themselves. You know, snap out of it, stand on their own two feet, start to take responsibility for their life again.'

'I am trying to get better, Mike. Really.'

Hester sounded so reduced that Jude was tempted to say something in her defence, but it wasn't the moment to step in between husband and wife. Though she couldn't envisage much improvement in Hester's condition until Mike acknowledged that she was genuinely ill.

'Well, I hope you get sorted by the end of next week. The boys have got an exeat from school, and subjecting them to a whole weekend of my cooking comes under the definition of child abuse.'

'I'll do my best,' said Hester in a very thin voice.

'None of this would have happened,' Mike grumbled, 'if you hadn't got involved with that bunch of "Saddoes". God, what a load of posturing toss-pots they are. When I saw that idiot showing off his hanging on that gallows contraption...'

'Were you actually in Saint Mary's Hall for the demonstration?' asked Jude.

'Yes, came in to hurry Hest along a bit. She said the rehearsal finished at six, and it was easily ten past before—'

'And,' Jude interrupted, 'you knew that Ritchie Good was later strangled by the apparatus?'

'Oh certainly, I heard. Serve the bugger right, I thought. So end all show-offs, if I had my way. Good riddance. As I say, except for his bloody stupidity, my wife wouldn't have been traumatized – or whatever other fancy word the shrinks use for it – and she wouldn't be locked up here in a loony bin.' Clearly Mike Winstone was never going to score any points for political correctness. His bluff cricketing bonhomie had completely evaporated.

Jude didn't think there was a lot more she could do. She didn't want to create any further cause of discord between Hester and her husband. Sorting out what was already wrong with their relationship would involve going back many years into the past – and might only serve to make things worse – so she said she'd better be on her way. 'But I've got your mobile number, Hester, so I'll give you a call when—'

'My wife doesn't have her mobile phone with her,' Mike Winstone announced.

'Oh? Don't the authorities here at Casements allow clients to—'

'I don't allow it. Hest is here for rest and recuperation, not for chattering endlessly to all her women friends.'

'But surely talking to her friends—'

'Will you allow me to know what is right for my own wife!' The words were almost shouted.

Jude left. In spite of Mike Winstone's clear disapproval, she gave Hester a hug and a kiss. Then she went downstairs to Rob's office. He was interested to hear that Jude had done some healing on the patient, and wanted to know how it had gone. 'Maybe you could try some more with her?' he suggested.

Jude grimaced. 'I don't think I'd better until it's been cleared with her husband.'

'Ah yes. I saw him coming in. Apparently he

223

was just passing. Maybe I should try to persuade him of the efficacy of another healing session?'

'Good luck,' said Jude.

'Well, we have made one big advance,' said Carole when Jude had finished reporting her encounter with Hester Winstone.

'Hm?'

'Assuming that Hester was telling the truth – and there doesn't seem to be any reason why she shouldn't be – we know that Ritchie Good caused his own death. He just wanted to show off the gallows to her.'

'Yes.'

'Which is quite a relief, in a way.'

'In what way?'

'Well, trying to create a scenario in which someone actually persuaded him to put the noose round his neck, or manhandled him into doing it or made him do it at gunpoint ... well, none of those ever sounded very convincing, did they? But the idea that he put his head in the noose of his own volition, that makes a lot more sense.'

Jude nodded. 'And then there's only one thing we have to find out. Who switched the Velcroed noose for the real one.'

'Exactly.'

'And why they did it.'

TWENTY-FOUR

It was clear to Carole and Jude the moment they were admitted by Elizaveta Dalrymple on the Saturday evening that the seafront house in Smalting was a shrine to her late husband Freddie. The hall was dominated by a top-lit large portrait of him in the purple velvet doublet of some (undoubtedly Shakespearean) character. The pearl earring and the pointed goatee beard were presumably period props.

Except, as Elizaveta led them up a staircase lined with photographs of Freddie, it became clear that the beard at least was a permanent fixture. Whatever part he was playing, the presence of the goatee was a non-negotiable.

His wife's hair was the same. Jude remembered the scene reported by Storm Lavelle of Elizaveta not wanting to have her head covered by a shawl when she was still going to play Mrs Dudgeon. In some of the earlier photographs on the wall, before she'd needed recourse to dying, her natural hair did look wonderful, though not always of the same period as the costume that she was wearing. The flamenco dancer look was fine for proud Iberian peasants, but it didn't

225

look quite so good with Regency dresses or crinolines.

But clearly that was another unwritten law of SADOS. Freddie and Elizaveta Dalrymple had set up the society, so it was as if everyone else was playing with their ball. Whatever the play, Freddie and Elizaveta would play the leads, he with his pointed goatee and she with her long black hair.

There was further proof of this at the top of the stairs, in one of those large framed photographs which are textured to look like paintings on canvas. Their crowns, Freddie's dagger and the tartan scarf fixed by a brooch across Elizaveta's substantial bosom, left no doubt they were playing Macbeth and Lady Macbeth. With, of course, the goatee and the long black hair.

The space into which Carole and Jude were led showed exactly why the house's sitting room was on the first floor. It was still light that April evening and the floor-to-ceiling windows commanded a wonderful view over Smalting Beach to the far horizon of the sea.

The sitting room demonstrated the same decorative motif as the hall and stairs. Every surface, except for the wall with the windows in it, bore yet more stills from SADOS productions, again with the goatee and the black hair much in evidence. Presumably the plays in which Freddie and Elizaveta Dalrymple took part featured other actors in minor roles, but you'd never have known it from the photographs.

'Welcome,' Elizaveta said lavishly as she ushered Carole and Jude into the sitting room, 'to your first – but I hope not your last – visit to one of my "drinkies things". Now I'm sure you know everyone here...'

They did know everyone, except for a couple of elderly ladies who had 'retired from the stage, but as founder members were still massive supporters of SADOS'. Otherwise Carole and Jude greeted Olly Pinto, Storm Lavelle, Gordon Blaine and Mimi Lassiter. All had glasses of champagne in their hands. Storm's hair was now black and shoulder-length (hair extensions at work – there was no way it had had time to grow naturally to that length).

'Now,' said Elizaveta. 'Olly's in charge of drinks this evening, so you just tell him what you'd like.' On the wall facing the sea, space had been made among the encroaching photographs for a well-stocked bar. Olly apologized that there was no Chilean Chardonnay – he knew their tastes from the Cricketers – but wondered if they could force themselves to drink champagne. They could.

A lot of glass-raising and clinking went on, then Elizaveta said, 'Now, Carole and Jude, the agenda we have for my "drinkies things" is that we have no agenda. We're just a group of friends who talk about whatever we want to talk about ... though more often than not we do end up talking about the theatre.'

'In fact just before you arrived,' volunteered Olly Pinto, 'we were discussing the wonderful *Private Lives* the SADOS did a few years back, with Freddie and Elizaveta in the leads.'

'Oh, we're talking a horribly long time ago,' said Elizaveta coyly.

'Sadly I never saw it,' said Olly, 'but I did hear your Amanda was marvellous.'

'One did one's best.' This line was accompanied by an insouciant shrug. 'And of course I was so well supported by Freddie. So sad that Noel Coward was never able to see the SADOS production. He would have seen the absolutely perfect Elyot. The part could have been written for Freddie.'

'I think it was actually written for Noel Coward,' Carole ventured to point out. The information was something that had come up in a *Times* crossword clue. 'He played the part himself.'

Elizaveta Dalrymple was only a little put out by this. 'Yes, but Noel Coward was always so mannered. I'm sure Freddie brought more nuance to the role.'

Not to mention a goatee beard, thought Jude. And a barrel-load of impregnable self-esteem.

'It was a very fine performance,' said Gordon Blaine, as if he wanted to gain a few brownie points. 'And of course your Amanda was stunning.'

'Thank you, kind sir,' said Elizaveta with a

little curtsy. 'Freddie always had such a touch as a director too. Very subtle, he was. Not one of those bossy egotists. He let a play have space, let it evolve with the help of the actors. "A gentle hand on the tiller" – that's how Freddie described the business of directing.'

'Did he always direct the plays he was in?' asked Jude.

'Invariably. Freddie was always very diffident about it, said he'd be very happy for someone better to take on the role. But there never was anyone better, so yes, he directed all the shows we did together.'

Carole and Jude exchanged the most imperceptible of looks. Both of them were realizing to what extent the SADOS was the Dalrymples' private train set. Other children were allowed to play with it, but only under the owners' strict supervision. They also realized how painful relinquishing total control of the society must have been for Elizaveta.

'Freddie often designed the shows too,' Gordon chipped in. 'I mean, he didn't do elaborate drawings of what he wanted, but his ideas were very clear. I was more involved in building the sets when Freddie was around.' This was said in a slightly accusatory tone, as though there might be someone present who had caused the limiting of his involvement. 'And Freddie would always say to me, "I have this image in my mind, Gordon, and I'm sure you can turn that image into reality."'

'And did you build lots of stage machinery, special effects, that kind of thing?' asked Carole. 'Like the gallows for *The Devil's Disciple*?'

'Oh yes, that sort of thing was always my responsibility. Freddie would come up to me and he'd say, "Now I may be asking the impossible, Gordon, but it seems to me that the impossible has always rather appealed to you." And then he'd say what his latest fancy was. Do you remember, Elizaveta, when we were doing *As You Like It*, and Freddie asked me if I could make those thrones for the palace which were trees when they were turned round?'

'Oh, goodness me, yes, Gordon! Such a coup de théâtre they were. Suddenly, with just the turning of a few chairs, we were right there in the Forest of Arden. It got a round of applause every night. Wonderful, Gordon, wasn't it?'

He positively glowed beneath his ginger beard. 'All my own work. Yes, though I say it myself.'

But, from Elizaveta Dalrymple's point of view, Gordon was now taking too much credit on himself. 'Though, of course, it was Freddie's concept,' she said quite sharply.

'Oh yes,' a chastened Gordon Blaine agreed. 'It was very definitely Freddie's concept.'

'And the *Fethering Observer* gave a real rave of a review for my Rosalind. Which was rather one in the eye for those SADOS members who suggested I might be a bit old for the part.'

'I remember,' Mimi Lassiter chimed in. 'The *Fethering Observer* actually talked about you moving "with the coltish grace of a teenage girl".'

'But that's what acting's about,' Elizaveta enthused. 'You think yourself into the character you are playing, you become that person. Considerations like age and size and shape become totally irrelevant once you're caught up in the magic of the theatre. And, Gordon,' she said, feeling that the technician should now be thrown some kind of magnanimous sop, 'your chairs that turned into trees were part of the magic of that *As You Like It.*'

He grinned, his good humour instantly restored.

'Anyway, Gordon,' said Carole, eager to steer the conversation round to Ritchie Good's death, 'you've also done a splendid job on those gallows for *The Devil's Disciple.*'

'Oh, relatively straightforward, those were.' He started to laugh. 'Certainly compared to the palaver I had with that balcony on wheels Freddie wanted for *Romeo & Juliet*!'

Elizaveta Dalrymple laughed theatrically at the recollection, while Jude winced inwardly, visualizing a Juliet with flamenco hair and a Romeo with a pointed goatee beard.

'But the gallows,' Carole insisted. 'They seem to work very well. Possibly even *too* well,' she dared to add.

Her words did actually prompt a brief silence.

231

Then Gordon said, rather defensively, 'I created a set of gallows that were completely safe. Everyone saw that. If they'd been used properly, Ritchie Good'd be alive today. I can't be held responsible if people mess around with the equipment I've made.'

'By "messing around" you mean changing the doctored noose for the solid one?' suggested Carole.

'Exactly.'

'Can I ask something?' said Jude innocently. 'Why did you have a solid noose when the one that was going to be used would always be the one with Velcro?'

Gordon appeared pleased to have been asked the question, as it gave him an opportunity to provide a technical explanation. 'I was determined to make the gallows look real, so I needed to see what it would look like with a proper noose attached. Then I'd know what the doctored one had to look like.'

'But why did you bring it with you to St Mary's Hall that Sunday when you were demonstrating it?'

'Ah well.' He coloured slightly. 'The fact is, I had planned to have the stage curtains open during the rehearsal, with the gallows there with a proper noose. Then anyone in the company who had a look at it would see a real, businesslike noose there, and they'd be even more surprised when Ritchie appeared to have it round his neck.'

'What, and you would have switched the two nooses just before the demonstration?'

'Yes. We'd have drawn the curtains for a moment and done it. I thought that'd be more dramatic. But Ritchie didn't. He said we'd get the maximum effect if the curtains were closed right through the rehearsal, and then when we opened them we'd get a real coo ... what was that thing you said, Elizaveta?'

'Coup de théâtre,' she supplied.

'Exactly. One of those.' Gordon looked grumpy. 'I still think my way would have been better.'

'Well, it was quite dramatic,' said Jude. 'Of course, you weren't there, were you, Carole?'

'No, but you told me about it. So after the demonstration, Gordon, someone must have switched the two nooses round.'

'Yes.'

'But you don't know who?'

'I know it wasn't me,' he said huffily.

'I wasn't suggesting—'

'Mind you, I can think of one or two people in SADOS who might have—'

'I'm not sure,' Elizaveta Dalrymple interrupted magisterially, 'that I want my entire "drinkies thing" taken up with talk about that ill-mannered boor Ritchie Good.'

'I'm sorry,' said Jude meekly.

'But I've spent a lot of time,' Gordon continued, 'thinking how the two nooses got switched, and I've come to the conclusion that—'

233

'Nor,' Elizaveta steamrollered on, 'do we want to spend the whole time talking about your wretched gallows – particularly since you've already spent one entire evening telling us all about them.'

'Have I?' asked Gordon, puzzled.

'Yes,' said Olly Pinto. 'It was three weeks ago, the day before you were going to do the demonstration. We were all here for Elizaveta's "drinkies thing" and you couldn't talk about anything else. Goodness, by the time you'd finished we all knew enough about your gallows to have built a replica ourselves.'

Carole and Jude exchanged a quick look before the SADOS Mr Fixit said abjectly, 'Oh, I'm sorry. Was I a bore?'

'Yes, I'm afraid you were, Gordon darling,' Elizaveta replied. 'Let's just say that by the time the evening finished the gallows was a subject on which you had "delighted us long enough".'

Her coterie sniggered at the line, unaware that Elizaveta had filched it from Jane Austen. Then the star of the show vouchsafed a gracious smile to Carole and Jude. 'Now do tell me, you two, what's *The Devil's Disciple* going to be *like*?'

'I think it's coming together,' Jude replied cautiously.

'And is Olly keeping you busy as prompter?'

'Still a little ragged on the lines,' Carole was forced to admit.

234

Elizaveta smiled indulgently on the young man under discussion. 'Yes, you always go for the approximate approach, don't you, Olly? I remember you were all over the place as Lysander in Freddie's *Dream*.'

'It didn't matter,' said Olly gallantly. 'No one in the audience had eyes for anyone except your Titania.'

'And Freddie's Oberon,' said Elizaveta in gentle reproof.

'Oh yes, of course.'

'And our doubling, me also playing Hippolyta and Freddie giving his Theseus.'

'Yes, they were all splendid,' said Olly.

'There was a very good production of *A Midsummer Night's Dream* at the RSC last season,' Jude volunteered.

'Really?' Elizaveta Dalrymple dismissed the idea. For her theatre began and ended with the SADOS. No stage other than St Mary's Hall was of any significance. 'Anyway,' she went on, 'it doesn't matter so much, I suppose, if Olly's paraphrasing George Bernard Shaw's lines. They are at least in prose. But with Shakespeare's blank verse it was a complete disaster.'

Olly grinned winsomely, as if already enjoying the chastisement he was about to receive.

'"Doesn't the boy have any sense of rhythm?" Freddie kept asking. "How can anyone have such a tin ear for the beauties of blank verse?"'

Elizaveta laughed and the others joined in, Olly as heartily as anyone. 'He did try to help you, didn't he?'

'Oh yes,' Olly agreed. 'Freddie was always so generous with his time and his talent.'

'He was.' Elizaveta let out a nostalgic sigh. 'And of course Freddie was a wonderful verse speaker.' Everyone mumbled endorsements of this self-evident truth, as she focused a beady eye on Olly. 'So, will you know your *Devil's Disciple* lines by the first night?'

'Of course I will. Sheer terror will keep me going.'

'Oh yes. When a man knows he is to be hanged in a fortnight, it concentrates his mind wonderfully.'

The coterie greeted Elizaveta's latest bon mot with more laughter, unaware that she was quoting Dr Johnson. Then she turned sharply to Jude and asked, 'How's Davina doing?'

'Doing in what way?'

'As a director, of course.'

'Well, she seems to be ... fine.' Jude wasn't sure what kind of answer was expected. 'I mean, obviously her plans were all disrupted by what happened to Ritchie, but she seems to have managed to regroup and ... As I say, everything's fine.'

'Hm.' Elizaveta Dalrymple managed to invest the monosyllable with a great deal of doubt and suspicion. 'Of course, Freddie and I taught her everything she knows.'

'In the theatre?'

'Oh yes. Hadn't an idea in her head when she started in amdram. Freddie sort of took her under his wing. And she's developed into quite a nice little director. But I'm not sure how this *Devil's Disciple* is going to go.'

'As I said, I think it'll be fine.'

Another loaded 'Hm.' Elizaveta looked across to where Olly Pinto was deep in flirtatious chatter with Mimi Lassiter and the two old ladies. Then she moved closer to Jude and started to whisper.

Carole felt awkward. She wasn't quite near enough to hear and she didn't know whether she was meant to be included in the conversation. Rather than moving closer, she shifted nearer the window, as if suddenly fascinated by the movement of shipping beyond Smalting Beach.

'At least,' Elizaveta whispered fiercely at Jude, 'from Davina's point of view, she'll be better off with Olly as Dick Dudgeon than she would have been with Ritchie.'

'Oh?'

'Bit of bad blood between her and Ritchie. She thought he was keen on her, which he certainly appeared to be. But when she suggested taking the relationship further, he dropped her like a brick.'

Par for the course with Ritchie Good, thought Jude.

'And Davina didn't like that at all. Hell hath

no fury ... you know the quote. No, Davina would have done anything to remove Ritchie from her production of *The Devil's Disciple*.'

TWENTY-FIVE

As they walked to the Renault from Elizaveta Dalrymple's front door, Jude quickly told her neighbour what their hostess had whispered to her.

'Strange,' Carole observed. 'That's now two people who've pointed the finger at Davina.'

'Two?'

'Come on, Jude. Neville Prideaux. I told you what he said.'

'Oh yes.'

It was after eight and still just about light. They were suddenly aware of the spluttering sound of a car engine failing to fire. Then the slam of a door, a muttered curse and a bonnet being opened. They found themselves facing a very cross-looking Gordon Blaine in front of his ancient Land Rover.

'Trouble?' asked Jude.

'Bloody thing. It's got a new engine and ... not a sign of life.'

'Oh well, if it's a new engine,' said Carole, 'at

least you can bawl out whoever put it in for you.'

'I put it in,' said Gordon Blaine lugubriously. 'Ah. Oh. Well...'

'Bloody useless!' He slammed the bonnet down, disturbing the genteel Saturday evening quiet of Smalting, and looked around in frustration. 'Where the hell do you get a bloody cab in this place?'

'Can I give you a lift somewhere?' asked Carole. 'Where do you live?'

'Fethering,' came the grumpy response.

'What serendipity,' said Jude.

Gordon Blaine's house was a semi with a garage on the northern outskirts of the village. A couple of streets further along and he'd have been in Downside, regarded by people like Carole as the 'common' part of Fethering.

She had insisted he sat in the front seat of the Renault, 'because you've got longer legs than Jude'. As he got out he said, 'Can I invite you two ladies in for a drink?'

Anticipating Carole's refusal on the grounds that they'd already had plenty, Jude said quickly that it was very kind of him, they'd love that. Reflected in the rear-view mirror, she could see the tug of annoyance at her neighbour's mouth.

The interior of the house was strangely cramped, a tiny sitting room with an even tinier kitchen en suite. The furniture was old and dark and the décor gave the impression that the owner didn't notice his surroundings. There seemed no evidence that Gordon cohabited with anyone. Nor did their host give the impression that he was much used to having guests.

'Now, drinks...' he said rather helplessly. 'You were drinking champagne at Elizaveta's, weren't you? I'm afraid I don't have any of that. Or white wine, actually. I think I've got some red ... certainly beer. I'm going for the Scotch myself.'

'That would suit me perfectly,' said Jude.

'I'll just have water, because I'm driving.'

'It'll have to be from the tap,' Gordon apologized. 'I don't have any of that sparkling mineral stuff.'

'Tap is fine.'

The ease with which he found the bottle of Teacher's and the size of the measures he poured suggested that he might have quite a taste for the whisky, though he probably rarely had company to share it with. He raised his glass. 'Well, thanks very much for rescuing me.'

'No problem at all,' said Carole.

He sat down, shook his head and said, 'It doesn't seem right, Elizaveta not being involved in this *Devil's Disciple* production.'

'Really?'

'Well, you wouldn't know, Jude. Nor you, Carole, only just having joined the society.'

'And having paid my subscription, after what

240

almost amounted to harassment from Mimi Lassiter.'

'Oh yes.' Gordon chuckled. 'She does take her job a bit seriously. No, but what I was saying, you wouldn't know because you're new, but SADOS without the Dalrymples just doesn't seem right. I mean, it was bad enough when Freddie passed away, but now with Elizaveta not being involved ... well, it doesn't seem right.' He couldn't think of another way of saying it.

'I heard from Storm Lavelle,' said Jude, 'that Elizaveta walked out of *The Devil's Disciple* because Ritchie Good was so rude to her.'

'Well, I think that was part of it...'

'You mean there was something else?' demanded Carole, instantly alert. She had now caught on to Jude's reasons for agreeing to come in for a drink. It was an investigation opportunity.

'Well, she didn't seem to be getting on so well with Davina.'

'Oh?'

'They'd always seemed to be great mates. You know, Freddie took quite a shine to Davina when she first joined SADOS. He thought she had potential as a director, so he was very helpful to her, and gave her opportunities to get the directing going.'

'You don't mean,' asked Carole, 'that he "took a shine" to her in any other way?'

Gordon looked puzzled for a moment before

he understood what she meant. 'Oh, good heavens, no! There was never anything like that with Freddie. He and Elizaveta were always the most devoted couple. A lot of the younger actresses in the society kind of hero-worshipped him, but he was never the type to take advantage.'

He shook his head again. 'No, but something really seemed to have gone wrong between Elizaveta and Davina. I think that may have been the real reason Elizaveta wanted out of the production. Ritchie's rudeness just gave her a good excuse.'

'But you've no idea what the problem was?'

'No. Here, Jude, let me top you up.' She didn't need more, but he was drinking faster than her and wanted to justify refilling his own glass.

Gordon sat back down again and said gloomily, 'A rift like that could spell the end of SADOS.'

'Do you really think so?'

'Yes. Now Freddie's gone, Elizaveta is so much the dynamo of the society. Without her, it would be...' The prospect seemed too dreadful for him to put into words.

'You've been with SADOS for a long time, have you?' asked Jude gently.

He nodded. 'Since my mother died. Elizaveta and Freddie sort of took me in. They needed someone with engineering skills and, though I'd never had anything to do with the theatre, I have got quite a practical mind. Till I retired I worked for a firm that fitted kitchen cupboards, so I was quite used to building stuff and...' He looked very forlorn. 'If I hadn't got the SADOS, I don't know how I'd fill the time.'

'I was interested,' said Carole, moving the conversation along, 'in what you were saying at Elizaveta's about the two nooses on your gallows...'

'Oh yes?'

'...and how they got mixed up.'

There was a new caution in his expression as he said, 'What about it?'

'You said you had some thoughts of people who might have switched them round, but then Elizaveta interrupted you.'

Gordon Blaine was silent. He looked from one woman to the other. 'Are you thinking that what happened to Ritchie might not be an accident?'

'The thought had occurred to us, yes.'

'Hm. The police were very interested in that possibility when they talked to me.'

'But presumably they did come down on the side of accidental death?'

'What makes you say that?'

'Well, they've ended their investigation.'

'How do you know?'

'I've just assumed it,' said Carole. 'Jude told me there've been no more enquiries. And they released Ritchie's body for his funeral.'

'That's true.' Gordon spoke as if he hadn't

thought of it before.

'You sound relieved.'

'Well, I suppose I am in a way.'

'Why?'

'Because the gallows are my work. I built them. If there was anything unsafe about the design, it'd be my fault. And I've been worried about the police coming back to me at some point. So if their investigation is really over, that's quite a relief.'

'I don't think you need worry any more,' said Jude. Gordon looked pathetically grateful. Clearly the anxiety had been weighing on him. 'Where are the gallows now?' she asked.

'People seemed a bit spooked by having them still there in St Mary's Hall. So I brought them back to my workshop – that was in the brief period when my bloody Land Rover was working. I've been doing a bit of fine tuning on them.'

'Where is your workshop?' asked Carole.

'Would you like to see it?' The excitement in his voice showed that he very much hoped they would.

And indeed, when they assented, there was a trace of schoolboy glee in the way he led them through to the back of his tiny kitchen. And once through the door they could understand why the front two rooms of the house seemed so cramped. The house must originally have had a sitting room at the front with an equally large dining room and kitchen behind it. But this space had been opened out and the wall to the garage taken down to create an extended working area. The slightly makeshift black-painted plasterboard walls suggested that Gordon had done the conversion himself.

The bright overhead lights revealed something on the lines of a mad professor's lab. There had clearly been attempts to impose order on the chaos. On the walls were rows of neat racks, but the tools that should have been stowed there lay on the floor or on work benches, along with paint pots, piping, rolls of wire netting, offcuts of wood and plastic. There was a musty smell of sawdust, oil and paint.

The *Devil's Disciple* gallows were there, but in the midst of a huge selection of other stage props. Papier mâché rat masks had perhaps featured in a SADOS pantomime, plywood battlements adorned a Shakespeare production. And the chairs with cut-out trees on the back were probably the famous ones designed for *As You Like It*.

Also on the floor were car tyres, jacks and other automobile impedimenta. Clearly this was where Gordon had replaced the engine of his Land Rover. A procedure which, as Carole and Jude had cause to know, hadn't worked properly. There hung about the workshop the aura of a great many things that hadn't worked properly.

'Wow,' said Jude as they looked around the space. 'So this is where you work your magic.'

The beam on Gordon Blaine's face showed that it had been exactly the right thing to say. Carole recognized rather wistfully that it was the kind of thing she'd never have thought of saying in a million years.

'Would you mind showing us,' Jude went on, 'how the noose gets changed on the gallows?'

'It's very easy,' said Gordon, more confident in his own environment. 'Simple design. I always go for simple, no point in faffing around with stuff that's more complicated than it needs to be.'

He picked up a noose from a workbench, clattered a pair of metal stepladders over the floor to the side of the gallows and climbed up. There was already a noose in position hanging from the beam. 'This is the doctored one,' said Gordon, slicing down on to the loop with his hand and causing the Velcro joint to swing apart. 'You see, as soon as that takes any weight, it gives way ... greatly to the delight of the Health and Safety boyos.

'But what holds it up, you see,' he said, reaching to the top of the beam, 'is this hook ... from which the doctored noose can be simply removed –' he matched his actions to his words – 'and the real one hooked on ... threaded through ... and left to dangle ... ready for its next victim.'

'So the whole process,' said Carole, 'takes less than thirty seconds.'

'Yes,' Gordon agreed, as though accepting a

compliment.

'And anyone could work out how to do it?'

'I would think so. Certainly anyone who'd watched me do the switch.'

'Or someone who'd heard you describe how to do the switch,' said Jude.

'Sorry?' He looked down in puzzlement from the ladder. 'Don't know what you mean?'

'Well, we just heard, earlier this evening at Elizaveta's, how you described the working of your gallows in meticulous detail at another of her "drinkies things".'

'Oh yes, I remember that. Elizaveta seemed very interested in it. Which was unusual. Usually she shut me up when I got on to the details of the technical stuff. "Gordon darling," she'd say, "I'm an actress. I deal with the emotional side of putting on a play. I can't be expected to understand the nuts and bolts of the business."'

'And that particular "drinkies thing",' said Jude, 'was three weeks ago.'

'Was it really? I can't remember.'

'Three weeks to the day.'

'The day before Ritchie Good got strangled,' said Carole.

TWENTY-SIX

'Who is this speaking?' asked the elocuted voice at the other end of the line.

'Jude.'

'Jude? Oh yes, Jude!' said Elizaveta Dalrymple.

'I was just ringing to say thank you so much for the party last night.'

'Oh, hardly a party, Jude darling. Just one of my little "drinkies things".'

'Well, it was much appreciated, anyway. I really enjoyed it. And I'm sure Carole will be in touch soon to say thank you too.' Though, actually, knowing Carole, she was much more likely to post a graceful note of thanks than use the telephone.

'It was a pleasure to see you both. I do like to keep up with the new members of SADOS ... even though I'm not involved in the current production.'

'But presumably you'll be back for others,' suggested Jude, 'now that Ritchie Good's no longer around to insult you?'

'Oh, I don't know, darling. I'm not as young as I was.'

'You're still looking very good,' said Jude, shamelessly ingratiating.

'Yes, well, of course I am lucky to have the bone structure. If you have the bone structure, the ravages of time are not quite so devastating. But,' she concluded smugly, 'so few people do have the bone structure.'

Jude, whose face was too chubby for much bone structure to be discernible, made polite noises of agreement. Then she said, 'Carole and I took Gordon Blaine back to his place yesterday.'

'Really?' Elizaveta sounded affronted. She didn't like people in her coterie doing things she didn't know about. 'Why was that?'

'His Land Rover had broken down.'

'No surprise there. I must say, for someone who's supposed to have engineering skills, dear Gordon is astonishingly inept.'

'He showed us his workshop.'

'Oh, that glory hole. He used to keep dragging Freddie down there to show him the development of his latest bit of stage wizardry – frequently rather less than wizard, I'm afraid. At times Gordon has qualities of an overeager schoolboy.'

'Maybe. When he was talking yesterday he seemed to be worried about the future of SADOS.'

'Oh?'

'Well, if you were not involved, he thought there was a danger it might pack up.'

'Really? I hope not.' But Elizaveta's voice betrayed her attraction to the idea. 'SADOS is more than one person, just as it was more than two people while Freddie was still alive. I owe it to his memory to keep the society going.'

'Gordon seemed worried that, with you having walked out of *The Devil's Disciple*, there might be—'

'I did not *walk out* of *The Devil's Disciple*. Ritchie Good's behaviour put me in a position where I could no longer stay as part of the production.'

'Well, however you put it, Gordon seemed worried that you might be so angry that you wouldn't come back for another show.'

'Oh, he shouldn't have thought that. Of the many things I may be, Jude, vindictive is not one,' Elizaveta lied. 'If the right part comes up, and if I'm lucky enough to pass the audition, then I'm sure I'll be back for the next production.'

'And what is that? I haven't heard yet.'

'The autumn show's going to be *I Am A Camera*.'

'Isn't that the play on which the musical *Cabaret* is based?'

'I believe so.'

'Based on the book by Christopher Isherwood.'

'I've no idea who wrote it. I just know it wouldn't have been my choice, but now Neville Prideaux's on the Play Selection Committee all kinds of weird stuff's getting through. If there really is a threat to the future of SADOS, it's much more likely to be Neville Prideaux's choice of plays driving the audiences away.'

'But you will audition for it, Elizaveta?'

'Oh, I suppose I'll have to. I mean, Sally Bowles is meant to be quite a mature character.'

Jude only just stopped herself from voicing her disbelief and saying, Oh, for heaven's sake, there's *mature* and there's *far too old for the part*. But she didn't want to break the confidential mood between them.

'Last night Gordon was talking about his gallows and what had gone wrong with them.'

'Oh, I'm sure he was. Gordon can be a very tedious little man.'

'We were discussing how the two nooses might have got switched.'

'Incompetence on his part, I would imagine.'

'I wonder...'

'What do you mean by that, Jude?'

'Well...'

'Are you suggesting the nooses might have been switched deliberately?'

'It's a thought, isn't it? Which would have meant someone in the *Devil's Disciple* company really had it in for Ritchie Good.'

There was a silence. Jude could sense Elizaveta assessing her response. Then the older woman said, 'Well, if you're looking for that person, Jude, you might do a lot worse than remember what I said to you last night.'

'Davina?'

'You said it.'

Both Carole and Jude were required for the rehearsal that Sunday afternoon. Rather boldly, the director had announced that they were going to do the whole play for the first time, 'which, given the fact that we open in a month's time, should put the fear of God into all of you.'

If that was the sole aim of the exercise, it certainly worked. The unreadiness of the entire company was made manifest, and no one seemed less ready than Olly Pinto. His lines were still all over the place, and Carole as prompter had one of the busiest afternoons of her life.

Olly's incompetence seemed to infect the others like some quick-spreading plague. Even Jude, who'd always been rock solid on her lines, found herself stumbling and mumbling. And she was by no means the worst. By the time they got to the end of the play, the whole thing was a complete shambles. The final scene, the near-hanging of Dick Dudgeon, had never been rehearsed properly with all of the extras who were meant to populate the town square, and they milled around like sheep in search of a shepherd.

As Davina's mood grew increasingly frayed, Carole and Jude found themselves watching the director closely and trying to reconcile her with the suspicions raised by both Elizaveta Dalrymple and Neville Prideaux. What he had said did make a kind of sense. Until that Sunday afternoon Davina had been more relaxed in rehearsal without the presence of Ritchie Good. In Olly Pinto she'd got a much less convincing Dick Dudgeon, but a considerably more biddable actor. She seemed to revel in bawling him out, in a way she never would have done with Ritchie.

Davina was dressed that day in jeans and a bright coral jumper with a high collar. Jude observed that she always seemed to wear high collars. She wondered whether this was a vanity thing, disguising the age-induced stringiness of her neck.

And Jude tried, without success, to think of Davina Vere Smith as a murderer. It just didn't fit, didn't seem right.

When the last line of the play had finally been spoken, at just before six o'clock, the director indulged herself in a major tantrum. This was all the more effective for being unexpected. Up until then in rehearsal, except for her regular verbal assaults on Olly Pinto, Davina had been conciliatory and friendly to the rest of the cast. So they all looked shocked to hear her finally losing her rag.

'The whole thing was complete rubbish! I don't know why I've been wasting my time with you lot for the last three months! This afternoon was an example of absolutely no one showing any concentration at all! OK, this is just an amateur production, and if you've come along for the ride and don't care about the quality of the show and just want to have a giggle at rehearsals, then fair enough. I think you should leave now. We can very happily manage without you.

'But I have certain standards I want to maintain. SADOS has certain standards it wants to maintain, and on the evidence of what I've seen this afternoon, we aren't achieving any of them. But for the fact that the box office is already open and tickets have already been bought for *The Devil's Disciple*, I would pull the plugs on the whole production now!

'So...' Davina paused for a moment to gather her breath and her thoughts. The *Devil's Disciple* company were too shocked to say anything, as she continued, 'I know it's six o'clock and you're all gasping to go to the Cricketers, but I'm afraid I'm not going to let anyone go until we've had another look at the blocking of that last scene. It's a complete dog's dinner and we need to do a bit of basic work on it.

'So those of you who aren't involved can go. Jude, obviously, since Mrs Dudgeon is long dead. And Carole, you can go. I'll be concentrating on the movements not the words for this bit. But the rest of you ... will you please all pull your bloody socks up and concentrate for the next half-hour!'

It was a measure of the effect Davina's

unwonted outburst had had that nobody moaned about being kept from their liquid refreshment in the Cricketers. All of the company looked very chastened as Carole and Jude slipped out to the pub.

'I was idly thinking about Davina's neck,' said Jude, as they settled down with their large Chilean Chardonnays. The pub was virtually empty, just Len behind the bar reading the *Mail on Sunday*. Again she wondered how the Cricketers would keep going without the regular custom of SADOS members.

'Davina's neck? What on earth do you mean?' asked Carole.

'Well, every time I see her at rehearsal she's wearing these high collars. I assume it's because – as happens at our age – her neck is getting a bit stringy and her cleavage a bit wrinkled.'

'What do you mean – "as happens at our age"?' Carole was quite put out. 'I don't believe I'm getting either stringy or wrinkled.'

'No, but you're so thin no wrinkle would dare to sully your skin.'

Carole looked beadily at her neighbour, unsure whether she was being sent up or not. Eventually she decided that what she'd just heard was probably a compliment. 'As a matter of fact,' she said, 'Davina's cleavage is in very good condition.'

'Oh? When have you seen it?'

'First time I met her. First time I met her properly, that is. In the Crown and Anchor, when she tried to persuade me to take over as prompter.'

'She not only *tried* to persuade you. She *succeeded* in persuading you.'

'Well, all right. Anyway, on that occasion she was wearing a purple cardigan, unbuttoned to show quite a lot of cleavage. And, as I say, the cleavage in question was in very good condition.'

'I'm glad to hear it. Then I wonder why she always wears high collars at rehearsal?'

'Up to her, I would have thought.'

'Sure.'

'Incidentally, I don't want you to get the impression that I make a habit of staring at other women's cleavages.'

When Carole made remarks like that, Jude could never be quite sure whether she was serious or not. Deciding on this occasion she probably was, Jude said, 'Thought never occurred to me.'

'The reason I noticed it on that occasion was that Davina was wearing a rather distinctive pendant.'

'Oh?'

'Silver. Shaped like a star.'

This prompted a much less casual 'Oh.' Jude's brown eyes sparkled with excitement as she asked, 'Was it like the one Elizaveta wears?'

'I've never noticed Elizaveta wearing any particular jewellery.'

'But she showed it that first evening in here. After we'd delivered the chaise longue.'

'What? I've no idea what you're talking about, Jude.'

'Oh, of course you weren't in the group with Elizaveta, were you? You were being bored to death by Gordon Blaine.'

'I still don't understand a word you're saying. I just...'

But Jude was already out of her seat, crossing to the bar and snatching the landlord's attention away from his *Mail on Sunday*. 'Len, do you remember the silver pendant that got left here after a pantomime rehearsal?'

'Oh yes. What about it?'

'I remember, first time I ever came in here you asked Elizaveta Dalrymple if it was hers. And when she said it wasn't, you said you'd keep it behind the bar until someone claimed it.'

'Uh-huh,' he agreed.

'Well, did anyone ever claim it?'

'Yes. Only a few days later. I can't remember whether it was the Tuesday or the Thursday, but she came in early for rehearsal and said it was hers.'

'Who did?'

'Davina.'

'Are you sure?'

'Yes. I remember particularly because she

257

was the only person in the pub, and she very specifically asked me not to tell Elizaveta that she'd claimed it.'

'And so you didn't tell her?'

'No. Mind you, the wife might have done.'

'Why did your wife know about it?'

'Because I mentioned the engraving on the back of the pendant to her.'

'Engraving? What did it say?'

'"YOU'RE A STAR – WITH LOVE FROM FREDDIE".'

TWENTY-SEVEN

The members of the *Devil's Disciple* company who trickled over to the Cricketers round half past six looked very subdued. They were not used to Davina Vere Smith bawling them out and the rarity of such behaviour had had a powerful effect. As they bought their drinks and formed into little groups, the laughter was nervous rather than convivial. Facing the reality of *The Devil's Disciple*'s unpreparedness had wiped smiles off quite a few faces.

Davina herself stalked in last of all and there was a silence, not of unfriendliness but rather of trepidation. None of the cast dared to speak to her, afraid that they might again get their heads bitten off. She ordered 'a large G and T' from Len and stalked across the bar to sit at a table, studiedly alone. The actors shuffled around, talking in low voices, as though there was an unexploded bomb in the room.

This in fact suited Carole and Jude rather well. Since neither of them was involved in the play's final scene, they alone had not felt the wrath of Davina Vere Smith. They felt rather like the class goody-goodies as they picked up their glasses and went across to join the director at her solitary table.

'How was the second run of the last scene?' asked Jude tentatively.

'Terrible,' Davina replied. 'I didn't think anything could be worse than the first run at it, but that lot proved it was possible.' She didn't seem upset. The outburst seemed to have given her increased confidence. There was even a slight twinkle in her eye.

Catching this, Jude said, 'Did you stage it?'

'My tantrum? Yes, of course I did.' The twinkle had now become a grin, which Davina was having hard work suppressing. She didn't want her secret to be known to the rest of the company.

'It's a very effective tactic,' she went on. 'I know enough about acting to control when I do it. And because I'm normally sweet and chummy to everyone, the effect is devastating.'

'So you don't do it often?' said Carole.

'Ooh no. It wouldn't work if I did it often. I

ration myself to one tantrum per production – sometimes not even one. The longer I go without throwing my toys out of the pram, the more effective it is when I do. And everyone in *The Devil's Disciple* really did need a kick up the arse. They're all getting very lazy and lackadaisical.'

'I suppose that's the effect of the long rehearsal period,' suggested Jude.

Davina nodded. 'Yes, it can seem to drift on forever. Then suddenly you're within days of the Dress Rehearsal and it all gets very scary.'

'Yes,' said Carole, wanting to move the conversation into investigative mode. 'Do you think the production would have been in as bad a state if you still had Ritchie Good playing Dick Dudgeon?'

The director shrugged. 'We might not have to stop as often as we do when Olly cocks up another line, but I don't think it'd make a great difference. There's a kind of rhythm to a production, you know. About a month before the show actually opens, rehearsals always tend to get a bit ragged and chaotic. But the thing with Olly and his words, that is quite serious. I was wondering, Carole, if you wouldn't mind doing a bit of "one-on-one" with him.'

'I'm sorry?' said Carole stiffly. 'I don't know what you mean by "one-on-one".'

'Just line-bashing.'

'What?'

'A sort of extension of your job as prompter.

If you could spend an evening with Olly, one night when we're not rehearsing, just going through the text line by line. That might make some of them stick to the Teflon interior of his brain.'

'Oh. Well, I'd be prepared to have a go, I suppose ... if you think it might help.'

'I can guarantee it would help. I'll tell him to have a word with you. See if you can sort something out.'

'Very well.'

Jude, also keen to move on to what they really wanted to talk about, said, 'By the way, Carole and I were honoured yesterday.'

'Oh yes?'

'We got invited to one of Elizaveta's "drinkies things".'

'Did you? Maybe she's trying to keep up the numbers.'

'What do you mean?'

'You may have been invited to replace me.'

'Oh?'

'Yes, I used to be a regular at those, certainly always went when Freddie was alive. But recently I've become persona non grata, so far as Elizaveta's concerned.'

'Do you have any idea why?' asked Jude.

Davina grinned enigmatically. 'I have a few thoughts on the subject.'

Carole went for the bald and bold approach, asking, 'Do any of them have anything to do with the star pendant that Freddie Dalrymple gave you?'

There was a silence. Davina looked calculatingly from one woman to the other. 'What do you know about that?'

'You were wearing it when I met you in the Crown and Anchor.'

'Ah yes. So I was. Normally, if I'm doing anything to do with SADOS, I keep it covered.'

Jude chipped in, 'Len here told us what was engraved on the back of it.'

'Hm.'

'Just like, presumably, what is engraved on the back of the one he gave to Elizaveta?'

'Yes. And to who knows how many other of Freddie's "little friends".' Davina looked rueful, but she made no attempt to deny anything. 'Freddie Dalrymple was basically rather a dirty old man.'

'Was he?'

'He had a flat in Worthing, on the seafront. That was where he used to go, as he used to tell Elizaveta, to "plan his productions".'

'So she never went there?'

'No. Which was probably just as well.'

'But you did go there?'

Davina nodded. 'I, and, as I say, who knows how many others.'

'Elizaveta told us that, as a director, Freddie took you "under his wing".'

'Yes. Not just his wing. Also his duvet.'

'Oh.'

'I did love him.'

'Right.'

'My father died when I was in my early teens. I think the older man always...'

Just like Hester Winstone, thought Jude, a pattern of going for the older man.

'Presumably,' said Carole, 'Elizaveta had no idea anything was going on?'

'No, I really think she didn't. She was wedded, not only to Freddie, but to the image of the perfect marriage that she and Freddie shared. I think it suited her not to know what Freddie got up to in Worthing.'

'But when she saw your pendant...' said Jude.

'Yes. I realized I'd lost it, but I didn't know where. The clasp's loose – or it was, I've had it repaired. It must have slipped off in here during the post-pantomime cast party. And then when Len showed it to Elizaveta after the *Devil's Disciple* read-through...'

'I remember. You said you didn't wear that kind of jewellery.'

'Well, I couldn't claim it right then and there, could I? In front of Elizaveta?'

'But you came back a few days later to get it?' Davina nodded. 'And Len told Elizaveta who'd claimed it.'

'I think, Jude, to be fair to Len, it was his wife who told her.'

'And was that why she stormed out of the production?'

'Yes. The flare-up with Ritchie was something she staged. She provoked him into being so rude to her. It gave her an excuse to stomp out. But the real reason was that she couldn't stand being around me once she knew that Freddie and I had ... it must have hit her quite hard.'

'Do you think,' asked Carole, 'that she hoped her departure – and the departure of all her supporters – would totally screw up your production of *The Devil's Disciple*?'

'That may have been at the back of her mind. She doesn't think that anything can happen in SADOS if she's not involved. And whereas that might have been true while Freddie was still around, I don't think it is any longer. Thanks to you, Jude, for stepping in to play Mrs Dudgeon.'

'But of course,' said Carole stepping deeper into investigative mode, 'Elizaveta's departure wasn't the only disaster that struck your production, was it?'

'What? Oh, you mean what happened to Ritchie?'

'Yes. That was a big setback.'

'By the way,' said Jude, 'did Ritchie ever come on to you?'

'Oh, when we first met, yes, of course. He had a kind of knee-jerk reaction to chat up any woman he met. He didn't get far with me, though. Freddie was still alive, and I was far too caught up with him for anyone else to get a look-in.'

'And what about Ritchie's death?' asked

Carole.

'What about it?'

'Did you think it was an accident?'

'Well, of course it was. And entirely typical of Ritchie, the way it happened. Like most actors, he was a total show-off. He'd done his show for everyone at the end of rehearsal, but Hester Winstone hadn't been there, so he had to do a command performance for her. I mean, of course I don't want anyone to die, but it did serve Ritchie bloody right, didn't it?'

Carole saw a potential anomaly in Davina's explanation. 'How did you know he'd done a command performance for Hester Winstone?'

'She told me.'

'Oh? When?'

'A couple of days later. She rang to say that she couldn't continue as prompter, and she told me exactly what had happened.'

'Before she had her breakdown?' asked Jude.

'I didn't know she'd had a breakdown. Though she certainly sounded in a pretty bad way when she rang me.'

'But what about the noose?' Carole insisted. 'Someone had switched the noose between the first and second times Ritchie had done the routine.'

'Oh, I assumed Gordon had done that.'

'Why?'

Davina shrugged. 'Just so's his precious gallows would look good. Or because he was making some adjustment to them, I don't

265

know.'

'I detect you aren't part of the group within the company who believes Ritchie was murdered?'

'Good God, no, Carole. I know there are lots of feuds and back-stabbings in amdrams, but I don't think anyone takes it that far.' Davina let out a healthy chuckle and both Carole and Jude were struck by how *normal* she seemed. In fact, amidst all the posturing of the SADOS crowd, she was a veritable rock of sanity.

But there was still something that, to Jude's mind, required an explanation. 'Davina, you remember the evening Ritchie Good died...?'

'Hardly going to forget it in a hurry, am I?'

'No, nor me. I was just thinking, though ... I was the first person to find his body – that is, the first person after Hester Winstone, who'd actually witnessed his death. I went back because I'd left my bag in the hall. And then you came in.'

'Yes.'

'And moments before I'd seen you in the Cricketers working your way through a large gin and tonic.'

'Sounds like me, yes.'

'So I was just wondering why you had come back into the hall?'

'Oh, I suddenly remembered a note I'd meant to give one of the actors. Normally I write my notes down, but I hadn't and didn't want to forget it. I looked round, but couldn't see him in the pub, so I thought maybe he might still be in the hall.'

'Who're we talking about, Davina?'

'Olly Pinto.'

TWENTY-EIGHT

'Maybe he'd just gone home early,' suggested Carole in the Renault on the way back to Fethering. 'Decided to forego the session at the Cricketers.'

'It would have been out of character for him if he did. Anyway, I saw him afterwards while everyone was waiting around for the police to arrive.'

'So you're thinking that Olly switched the nooses?'

'It's a possibility, Carole. He very definitely stood to gain from Ritchie's absence.'

'Getting the part of Dick Dudgeon?'

'Exactly.'

'For which he still doesn't know the lines.'

'No, that's true.' An idea came to Jude. 'I think you should set up your "line-bashing" session with Olly as soon as possible.'

Davina Vere Smith's eruption at the Sunday rehearsal had had the desired effect of putting a rocket up at least one of the *Devil's Disciple* cast. When Carole rang Olly Pinto later that evening and suggested he might benefit from a run-through of his lines, he was almost pathetically eager to set up the encounter as soon as possible.

It was agreed that he would come round to High Tor the following day after work (he was employed in one of Fethering's many estate agencies). Carole said she thought it'd help to have Jude there too, so that she could read the other parts. The real reason for this proposal was that, given the way her suspicions were currently veering, Carole didn't want to be alone with Olly Pinto.

She had only just put the phone down after her conversation with Olly when it rang. Her son Stephen. Gaby was laid low with another stomach bug. Could Granny possibly drop everything and come to look after Lily in Fulham for a couple of days?

Carole apologized that she couldn't. She might be able to come up for a couple of hours during the day on the Monday, but time would be tight as she had to be back for a 'line-bashing' session in the early evening. And then of course she had a regular rehearsal on the Tuesday.

Stephen said not to worry, he'd sort out one of Gaby's friends to drop in. But he did sound a bit bewildered by his mother's reaction. Normally, if it was something to do with Lily, Carole in Granny mode would be in the Renault and on her way the minute the phone call had ended.

Carole herself was a bit surprised at her reaction. She didn't love Lily any the less, but she couldn't let SADOS down. It was a measure of how much she had come to embrace amateur dramatics.

Olly Pinto arrived at High Tor about quarter past six on the Monday, not wearing his customary rehearsal garb of jeans and a fleece, but in his work livery of pinstriped suit and something that looked like a club tie but probably wasn't.

Olly accepted Carole's offer of coffee and replied to her polite enquiry as to the state of the housing market, 'Maybe picking up a bit. We usually see an upsurge in enquiries round Easter time. This year's better than last year at the same stage, though we're still way off where we used to be before the financial crash.'

Jude was once again struck by the contrast in the lives of these people, plodding through monochrome jobs by day and transforming into the variegated butterflies of amateur dramatics in the evenings.

The sitting room at the front of High Tor was not actually cold, but the austerity of its furniture always made it feel chilly. The pictures had all been inherited from distant Seddon aunts and put up on the walls out of duty rather than enthusiasm. The only positive colour came from a bright photograph of Carole's beloved granddaughter Lily on the mantelpiece.

Still, the sober appearance of the room seemed to fit the seriousness of the evening's task in hand. Olly Pinto had brought his copy of *The Devil's Disciple* with him, but Carole very soon confiscated that. 'No cribbing,' she said in the voice that had silenced many committees at the Home Office. 'Jude'll give you the cues and I'll prompt you when you get things wrong.' Carole's lack of confidence in the actor's memory was emphasized by her use of the word 'when' rather than 'if'.

'Shall we start at the beginning?' asked Olly hopefully because, allowing for a bit of paraphrase, he knew Act One pretty well.

'No,' Carole replied implacably. 'It was Act Three you were worst on. We'll start there, then go back to the beginning.'

He didn't argue. As Jude patiently fed him the lines, it occurred to her that, beyond the fact of his working for an estate agent, she knew virtually nothing about Olly Pinto's private life. And maybe for some participants that was the appeal of amateur dramatics, the opportunity to be someone other than your mundane self . Rather like the appeal of acting itself.

The 'line-bashing' was a hard and tedious process, but it did work. The one-to-one concentration – and perhaps the embarrassment of showing himself up in front of the two women – actually improved Olly's grasp of George

Bernard Shaw's words. In rehearsal when he cocked up a line he could sometimes get a laugh about his incompetence from his fellow actors; no such levity was allowed in the sitting room of High Tor. The world did actually lose a good dominatrix when Carole Seddon decided to forge a career in the Home Office.

It took them an hour to get through Act Three to the end, and then Carole offered more coffee. 'I'd offer you a proper drink, Olly, but alcohol might affect your concentration. We'll have a proper drink when we've done the whole play.'

When Carole opened the door on her way to the kitchen, her Labrador Gulliver nosed his way in to inspect the visitor. After he'd been hustled out by his mistress, Jude asked Olly whether he had a dog.

'No. Did have. When I was married.'

'Oh?'

'Yes. Divorced – what? – three years ago.'

'Children?'

'Two. I don't see them as much as I should. My wife – ex-wife – is not very cooperative about access.'

'I'm sorry.' And Jude could see the appeal of SADOS as a displacement activity for someone like Olly Pinto.

Carole returned with the coffee pot and recharged their cups. 'Feeling a bit more confident now, are you, Olly?' she asked with surprising gentleness.

'Yes, I am a bit. It makes me realize that, if I

really do concentrate, I can drill the lines into my head.'

'Exactly.' When she had refilled the coffee cups, she announced, 'I think we should go back to Act Two now. You were shakier on that than Act One.'

'All right,' said Olly, not exactly welcoming his fate but reconciled to it.

'Then we'll rattle through Act One at the end.'

So Act Two it was. And the build-up of concentration in the one-to-one setting still seemed to be working. Olly got more of the lines right than he had on any previous occasion. And he didn't lose his temper when Carole patiently dragged him back out of the realms of paraphrase.

So there was unaccustomed cheer in the sitting room of High Tor when they'd finished the Act.

'I think,' said Jude, 'you should open a bottle now, Carole. Olly's earned it, and I'm gasping. And he knows Act One pretty well. Lubricated by a glass of wine, he'll rattle through it, no probs.'

Carole looked dubious. Her upbringing had set her resolutely against the idea of bringing forward a promised treat. But she acceded to Jude's suggestion. 'White wine all right for you, Olly?'

'Lovely. Thank you very much.'

While Carole was in the kitchen, Jude said,

'We were very honoured to be included in Elizaveta's "drinkies thing" on Saturday.'

'So you should be. That really puts you in the charmed circle. But I'd be a bit wary.'

'Oh?'

'There's no such thing as a free lunch – or a free drink with Elizaveta Dalrymple. The fact that she invited Carole and you means she wants something from you.'

'What could we possibly have that would be of any use to her?'

'Information, usually. Reports from the front line of *Devil's Disciple* rehearsals.'

'I thought she was getting those from you.'

'Someone like Elizaveta can never have too many sources.'

'Do you think she'll actually come to the production?'

'Come to see *The Devil's Disciple*? Tricky diplomatic one for her. It's a SADOS production and, now Freddie's gone, Elizaveta is the spiritual leader of SADOS. So she should support it. On the other hand, she's had this big bust-up. She stormed out of the show, apparently because of things Ritchie said to her – though in fact it was because she'd fallen out with Davina.'

Jude was surprised Olly was shrewd enough to have worked that out. In fact, she was surprised how much more intelligent and congenial he was that evening than he had ever been at rehearsals. When he wasn't showing off, he was actually rather nice.

'Anyway,' he resumed, 'the one thing Elizaveta wouldn't want to appear is churlish. The thought of a SADOS production going ahead without her seeing it would be anathema to her. Also, she'd want to be there to see how bad the production is.'

'Do you think it's that bad?'

'No, but Elizaveta would as a matter of principle. She'd also be convinced that she would have played Mrs Dudgeon infinitely better than you're playing it.'

Jude grinned. 'She might be right.'

'Well, who knows? All I do know is that Elizaveta will be there – almost definitely on the first night – and afterwards she'll say that the production was absolutely *mahvellous*, and your performance was particularly *mahvellous*.'

'So, what – she'll book a ticket for the first night?'

'Oh no, it won't be as straightforward as that. There'll be some drama involved. Elizaveta will let it be known through her grapevine that she won't be going to the show, that it'd be totally against her principles to go. And then a friend of one of her friends will drop out and she'll be offered the ticket at the last minute and – surprise, surprise – she'll be there. May not be exactly what'll happen, but something along those lines.'

'You seem to have a very good understanding

of how Elizaveta Dalrymple works.'

'I've observed her for a long time. And I know she can be a monster, but she's also lively and fun, and if I hadn't got my relationship with Elizaveta and SADOS, I wouldn't have any social life at all.'

The confession was so honest, so potentially sad, that Jude couldn't think of anything to say. She was quite relieved that Carole returned that moment with a bottle of Chilean Chardonnay, three glasses and a bowl of cashew nuts.

'Olly was just telling me about the deviousness of Elizaveta.'

Carole snorted. 'Well, I've only met her the once, at her "drinkies thing" on Saturday. But I don't think anything I heard about her would surprise me. She seems the archetypal Queen Bee.'

Olly nodded. 'That's about right.'

'Or,' suggested Jude, 'while Freddie was still alive, the archetypal Lady Macbeth.'

'Well, of course, she did play the part for SADOS,' said Olly.

'I know. I saw the photo at her house.'

'Of course you did.'

'I was just wondering, though,' Jude went on, 'whether she ever played Lady Macbeth in real life...?'

Carole looked across at her neighbour in some confusion. She couldn't understand the new direction in which the conversation was being taken.

Olly also looked a little uncomfortable, but for different reasons. 'Not sure I like this discussion of "The Scottish Play". Bad luck, you know.'

Characteristic of an amateur actor to know all the theatrical superstitions, thought Jude. But what she said was, 'Only bad luck inside a theatre, Olly. Fine everywhere else.'

'Ah.' He looked at his watch. 'Maybe we should get started on Act One.'

But Jude was not to be diverted. 'I was meaning – did Elizaveta ever act like Lady Macbeth, controlling her husband, getting him to do things she wanted done?'

Olly Pinto grinned and nodded. 'All the time. Freddie was nominally in charge of everything at SADOS, but Elizaveta was very definitely "the power behind the throne".'

The tension in Carole relaxed. Now she understood where Jude was going with this, she started to watch with interest.

'And how does she use that power now she hasn't got Freddie to wield it through?'

'You mean how does she get other people to do things for her?'

'Exactly.'

'Oh, she just becomes more Elizaveta than ever, really turns it on. She can be extremely persuasive. I mean, this business about whether or not she attends the *Devil's Disciple* first night, I wouldn't be surprised if I end up somehow being involved in that. I'll get one of

Elizaveta's "little phone calls".'

'That's how she organizes things, is it?'

'Oh yes, still the old-fashioned phone. I get quite a few calls from her, though fortunately she's taken on board the fact that she can't ring me at work. God knows what she'd be like if she ever started using email or texts.'

'And has Elizaveta ever asked you to do something you didn't want to do?'

'All the time.' Olly grinned ruefully. 'Mind you, I usually end up doing it. As I said, she can be very persuasive.'

Jude and Carole exchanged a look and there was instant understanding between them. As a result, it was Carole who said, 'We talked to Gordon Blaine after we left after Elizaveta's "drinkies thing" on Saturday.'

'Oh yes?'

'I gave him a lift. His car had broken down.'

'God, not again. I must say, for the engineering genius Gordon always claims himself to be, a surprising number of his projects fail to function.'

'But his gallows functioned,' said Carole. 'Almost too well.'

'Yes,' Olly agreed soberly.

'On Saturday he was talking to us about a previous "drinkies thing" of Elizaveta's. The one the night before Ritchie Good died.'

'Oh?'

'And he said he'd described to everyone exactly how his gallows were going to work.'

'I remember that. Elizaveta was very intrigued – again regretting that she wouldn't be at the next day's rehearsal and so miss the demonstration. She was quite incapable of being "hands off" with anything to do with SADOS.'

'And Gordon described how easily the noose could be switched, did he?'

'Certainly did.'

'So did Elizaveta make any comment on that?'

'Only a joking comment.'

'What?' asked Carole sharply.

'She said, "So if one wanted to get rid of a member of the *Devil's Disciple* company one would have the means readily to hand."'

'And that was a joke?'

'Well, I assumed so at the time,' replied Olly, starting to look a little uncomfortable.

'Did she say anything else?' asked Jude.

'Yes. She said, "I wouldn't be at all upset if someone were to engineer a little accident between Ritchie Good and those gallows."'

'Did she?' said Carole.

'Yes, but I mean, it was a joke. At least, everyone laughed. Elizaveta had been bad-mouthing Ritchie all evening, in her customary very bitchy, funny way. What she said about the gallows just continued in the same vein. Which was why we all laughed.'

'And you don't think anyone took it seriously?' asked Carole.

'Oh God, no.'

'"Who will rid me of this turbulent priest?"' murmured Carole.

'I'm sorry? What on earth are you talking about?'

'It's what King Henry II said about Thomas à Beckett. And some listening knights thought they saw a way of getting into the King's good books, so they went straight down to Canterbury and murdered Beckett.'

'Are you suggesting that's what Elizaveta was doing? She hoped someone would pick up the hint, swap the nooses on the gallows and cause Ritchie's death?'

'It's a possibility, wouldn't you say?'

'It's a possibility in one of those stage thrillers SADOS used to keep doing. I wouldn't have said it was a possibility in real life.'

Carole shrugged. 'Stranger things have happened.'

Olly let out a chuckle which stopped halfway. Then he looked anxiously from one woman to the other. 'You're not suggesting *I* followed through Elizaveta's suggestion, are you?'

'Well, you weren't around in the Cricketers after the rehearsal ended. Davina went back to St Mary's Hall to find you.'

'Yes, but—'

'And,' Jude chipped in, 'you did benefit quite directly from Ritchie's death. No other way you'd have got the part of Dick Dudgeon, was there?'

Again Olly Pinto looked from one to the other. Then, with considerable dignity, he said, 'Well, I can assure you I did not do what you're suggesting. I've allowed myself over the years to be manipulated in many ways by Elizaveta, and I've been persuaded into doing a good few things that I didn't want to do because of pressure from her, but I would never do anything criminal.'

'But do you think it's possible,' Carole persisted, 'that Elizaveta did plant the idea of switching the nooses, in the hope that someone, wishing to curry favour with her, might act on the suggestion?'

'The thought hadn't occurred to me but, though it seems pretty unlikely, I wouldn't put it past her. Elizaveta likes sort of giving tests to her supporters, always threatening them with the ultimate sanction – the withdrawal of her patronage.'

'So, Olly, who do you think might have wanted to curry favour that much?'

He was silent for a moment, then said, 'I don't think it would be one of the people who's been part of Elizaveta's circle for a long time. We're all fond of her and want to keep in her good books, but we're also quite realistic about her. We know she can be a bit of a monster, so we take quite a lot of what she says with a pinch of salt.'

'So one of the more recent additions to the charmed circle...?'

'Perhaps.'

'Who?'

'Well,' Olly replied slowly, 'the newest regular – and indeed the one who seems most eager to please – is Storm Lavelle.'

TWENTY-NINE

Jude rang Storm that evening, but got no reply from either her landline or the mobile. She left a message on each, calming herself so as not to sound alarmist and asking Storm to ring her back.

The reply came the next morning, the Tuesday, just as Jude was washing up her breakfast things. 'Hello?'

'Oh, it's Storm, returning your call. What is it? Have you got transport problems for rehearsal tonight, because I'll happily give you a lift.'

'No, it's not that.' Storm sounded so cheerful, so full of life, that Jude found it really difficult to bring up the subject she wanted to discuss. 'Actually, it's in relation to you and Ritchie Good.'

'Oh?' The caller's tone changed instantly, from open and enthusiastic to crabby and suspicious.

'And it also concerns Elizaveta Dalrymple.'

The call was instantly ended. Jude tried ringing back straight away, but the mobile had been switched off. And calls to the landline switched straight through to the answering machine.

Jude didn't finish tidying up breakfast. She went straight round to High Tor.

The two neighbours quickly agreed that it was time to confront Elizaveta Dalrymple. 'There was no way she could have done it herself,' said Carole, 'but if she set up Storm...'

'I'm still finding it difficult to cast Storm in that role.'

'Maybe, but that's just because she's a friend.'

'Yes, I know.'

'And from all the encounters with murderers you've had, you should know by now that appearances are very rarely other than deceptive.'

'I know all that too.'

'Come on,' said Carole brusquely, 'I think you should ring Elizaveta and find out when we can see her.'

'Why me?'

'Because you know her better than I do.'

It was only when she had dialled the number that Jude realized that the two of them had spent almost exactly the same amount of time in Elizaveta Dalrymple's company. Still, there were times when arguing with Carole just wasn't worth the effort.

* * *

The late April weather, particularly benign that morning and with a promise of summer, had brought a surprising influx of tourists to Smalting. All the parking on the road facing the sea was taken and Carole was annoyed to have to pay at the small car park at the end of Elizaveta's road.

'Will we be out within the hour?' she asked as she took her change purse out of her neat and nearly empty handbag.

'I'd pay for two,' said Jude. 'Never know how long something like this'll take.'

Huffily Carole paid for the requisite ticket, placed it prominently on the dashboard and locked the car. The two women were both rather tense as they walked along.

'I wonder if she'll be on her own...' Jude mused.

'Why shouldn't she be? Did she say there was anyone with her when you rang?'

'No, she didn't. But I'll bet from the moment I put the phone down she's been ringing round all her cronies to tell them about our visit.'

'Do you think so?'

'I'm sure so. Maybe some of them will have rushed round to give her support.'

'You don't think any of them will be armed, do you?' asked Carole.

Jude giggled. 'No, I don't think any of them will be armed.'

The doorbell was answered promptly. Dressed in another ample kaftan, Elizaveta once again led them to the upstairs sitting room. Once again they took in the memorabilia of past SADOS triumphs on the walls. Jude looked particularly at the 'canvas effect' print of the Macbeths.

The beauty of the day meant that the view over Smalting Beach was better than ever. One of the high windows was raised a little to let in a soft, salty breeze. On the sand they could see parents and grandparents playing with pre-school-age children. Both Carole and Jude found themselves instinctively looking over towards the rows of beach huts and remembering a previous investigation that had focused on one of them.

Elizaveta sat them down. They refused her offer of coffee and so she sat facing them. Her chair had pretensions to being a throne. There was another identical one in the room. Presumably 'His' and 'Hers' when Freddie had been alive. Elizaveta looked as if she expected some major confrontation, and it was a prospect that excited rather than frightened her.

'So,' she said rather grandly, 'to what do I owe the honour of your visit?'

They hadn't planned any particular approach, so Carole decided to open the proceedings. 'We're here to talk about Ritchie Good's death.'

'Are you really?' Elizaveta let out a long-suffering sigh. 'If you were listening when you were here on Saturday, you should have realized I do not particularly wish to talk about Ritchie Good.'

'But I think we have to talk about him.'

'Do you? I must say I think it's a bit rich that I should be being told what to talk about by a mere prompter.'

'The fact is,' said Jude, 'that we are not convinced the Ritchie Good's death was an accident.'

'I imagine that is a subject on which there has been a great deal of fevered conjecture amongst the SADOS members. Now I'm no longer with the society, I cannot obviously—'

'Oh, come on, Elizaveta, you get reports from your personal grapevine about everything that goes on there.'

'Perhaps I do. But I still can't see how the accidental or non-accidental death of Ritchie Good has anything to do with me.'

'You can't deny,' said Carole, 'that his death suited you very well.'

She shrugged. 'Sometimes the fates are generous. No, I can't pretend I shed many tears when I heard of his demise. Apart from being appallingly rude to me, he showed no respect for anything that Freddie and I had achieved in SADOS.'

'And the death was easily engineered,' Carole continued. 'All that was required was for somebody to change the doctored noose on the gallows to the real one.'

'I'm not quite sure what you're talking about.'

'I think you are. Because Gordon Blaine explained the workings of his gallows in exhaustive detail at your "drinkies thing" the night before Ritchie's death.'

'Goodness me. You have been doing your research, haven't you?'

'Do you deny it?'

'No, of course I don't. One thing I would like to know, though. If either of you think I was responsible for Ritchie's death, I'd love to know how I did it. The hanging – or strangulation – happened, I gather, in St Mary's Hall. Now I have not been in St Mary's Hall since I was forced to leave the production of *The Devil's Disciple*, neither to sabotage a gallows nor for any other reason. I'd be intrigued to know how I am supposed to have engineered this fatal accident.'

'You planned it,' said Jude. 'You got someone else to switch the nooses for you.'

'How remarkably clever of me. What, so I had a private meeting with someone, did I? I took them on one side and said, "I wonder if you'd be kind enough to bump off Ritchie Good for me?" And they said, "Terrific idea, Elizaveta. Regard it as done." Is that how it happened ... roughly?'

'No, it wasn't as overt as that,' said Carole. 'At that same party –' (she couldn't bring herself to say 'drinkies thing') – 'when Gordon

Blaine described the mechanism, you said to everyone how pleased you'd be if Ritchie Good was accidentally hanged.'

'Well, I may have said that, but only as a joke.'

'But did everyone present realize it was a joke?'

'I assumed so, but...' She seemed rather attracted to the idea as she articulated it. 'Do you think there really was someone who took what I said seriously enough ... who cared enough about me to take the hint and do what I'd asked for?'

'I think that was what you were hoping,' said Carole.

'Really?' Elizaveta was still intrigued. 'But who might have done it? A few years ago I would have thought it was Olly Pinto. When he first joined SADOS, he was, I have to say, totally besotted with little *moi*. Then he would have done anything for me. Now ... I don't know what's happened to him, but whatever he once felt for me has been ... well, to put it mildly, diluted. Now I think he only comes to see me because he's lonely.'

Jude was surprised to see a tear gleaming in Elizaveta Dalrymple's eye.

'I think that's why most of them stay around me...' the old woman went on. 'Because they're lonely. I think with most of them, it was Freddie they were really loyal to, not me. When Freddie was around, our "drinkies things" were legendary. Just had to mention we were having one and people'd be falling over themselves to get here. Now I have to ring round those who are left and virtually beg them to come along.'

The tears were really falling now, streaking mascara down on to Elizaveta's heavily made-up cheeks. 'My life really stopped,' she went on, 'when Freddie died. Oh, I've tried to maintain a front. I've acted hearty, bitchy, thick-skinned. It's been the toughest performance of my life ... and I don't know how much longer I can keep it up. The effort of preparing to see people, of being a hostess, it just gets harder and harder. And after everyone's gone, I just sink back into total black despair. I just can't go on like this.'

Carole and Jude exchanged looks. Though Elizaveta was, as ever, self-dramatizing, they could both recognize the core of genuine suffering. And both wondered how big a blow it had been to her when she had discovered that Davina Vere Smith had also been given a star-shaped pendant. It must have brought home – probably not for the first time – the knowledge that the much-vaunted marriage to Freddie had not been as perfect as its mythology might suggest.

But Elizaveta's personality was not one to stay down for too long. She perked up with her next thought. 'So you do really think that someone took what I said seriously enough to act on it? To switch the nooses? Somebody actually

288

cared for me enough to do that?'

Without commenting on the woman's strangely skewed sense of values, Carole replied, 'We think it's possible. But nobody said anything to you about having done it?'

'No. Why should they?'

Jude shrugged. 'To report back: Mission Accomplished?'

'No. Nobody has. And I think in a way that's rather splendid. Whoever it is did something purely out of love for me, and then didn't want to crow about it.'

They could see Elizaveta Dalrymple transforming before their eyes. A moment ago she had been the sad, neglected, wronged widow. Now she was moving into the role of charismatic inspirer of others. She was eternally recasting herself, but the scenarios in which she appeared all had one thing in common: Elizaveta Dalrymple was playing the lead in all of them.

'So,' she said, now rather magnificent after her grief, 'who do I have to thank for my revenge on Ritchie Good? What is the name of my guardian angel?'

'We think it was probably Storm Lavelle,' said Jude.

'Oh,' said Elizaveta, basking in glee. 'I always thought that young woman had something about her. She's very talented, too. You know, I can see in little Storm something of myself at the same age.'

THIRTY

'Well, we didn't exactly get confirmation, did we?' said Carole as they left the house.

'We got confirmation that Elizaveta did kind of "issue the challenge". Say she wanted Ritchie Good dead.'

'Which presumably was enough to prompt Storm to take action.'

Jude's full lips wrinkled with scepticism. 'It just seems out of character for her.'

'Again you're only saying that because she's your friend. From what I've seen of her, she's pretty volatile – not to say unstable.'

'I agree. She's passionate. I mean, OK, if Ritchie had done something directly to hurt her, I can see Storm taking revenge on him in a fit of fury. I can't see her in this sort of "one-remove" scenario, exacting vengeance on someone else's behalf. It's not in her nature to be so unspontaneous. I'm sure there's some other explanation.'

'Well, it's not an explanation you're about to hear, if Storm continues refusing to answer your phone calls, is it?'

'No,' Jude agreed limply. Then, suddenly,

noticing they were passing a little general store, 'Oh, I've just remembered I haven't got any eggs! Could you pick me up here when you've got the car?'

Carole watched her neighbour rush into the shop with some censure. Her own organized shopping routine would never allow High Tor to run out of eggs. Then she looked at her watch and realized sourly that they had only needed one hour's parking.

Jude got her eggs, then realized she needed soy sauce and noodles too. Which meant she had to buy another 'Bag For Life'. If all the similar ones she'd got in her kitchen were counted up, they'd provide her with more lives than a full cattery.

She stepped out between two parked vehicles and looked towards the car park. The white Renault was coming towards her. She stepped out a bit further, so that Carole could see where she was.

It was only when the car was almost upon her that Jude realized it wasn't going to stop. In fact it was accelerating and aiming straight for her.

She tried to leap backwards, but was too late. She felt a thump that shuddered through her whole body. Then she seemed to be lifted up in the air and smashed down.

Everything went dark.

THIRTY-ONE

When Jude came to, she looked up to find herself surrounded by a circle of curious holidaymakers. Amongst the concerned faces looking down at her was Carole's. A confusion of voices commented on what had happened.

'I think we should phone for an ambulance.'

'There's a doctor's surgery just along the road.'

'Should be the police we call for. That car was going way over the speed limit.'

But it was Carole's voice saying, 'How do you feel?' that cut through the others.

'Not too bad, I think,' said Jude, trying to assess the extent of her injuries. 'Give me a hand and I think I could try standing up.'

Ignoring opinions from the growing crowd that 'she shouldn't be moved until the ambulance is here', Carole's thin arms hooked themselves under Jude's chubby ones and got her, first to a sitting position, then upright on her two rather tottery legs.

'Are you all right?'

'Think so, Carole. Just a quick check for damage.'

There was quite a bit. The wing of the car had turned her escaping body and flung her face down on to the edge of the road. Her arms had taken the brunt of the impact. Though that had protected her face, the encounter with the tarmac had shredded the palms of her hands. Blood was just starting to well from rows of little scrapes there. Her knees were in a similar state. They were the kinds of wounds that were too recent to have started hurting, but would be agony when they began to heal.

'Let go of me, Carole. See if I can stand on my own.'

She could. Just about. Not confident, stable standing. More the wobbly, determined kind.

Another voice from the crowd expressed the opinion that an ambulance should be called.

'No,' said Carole firmly. 'Be quicker if I drive her to the hospital.'

Her Renault had stopped in the middle of the road, with the driver's door open. Carole must have stopped when she saw the crowd around the injured Jude.

Ignoring protests from people who all clearly saw themselves as 'good in a crisis', Carole collected up the 'Bag for Life' (the eggs inside it all sadly smashed). Then she man-handled Jude into the passenger seat of the car, ignoring her insistence that 'I'll bleed all over your upholstery.'

The fact that she said, 'That doesn't matter' was a measure of how seriously Carole viewed her neighbour's predicament. Normally nothing would be allowed to sully the pristine cleanliness of the Renault's interior.

They drove a little way in silence, till they had turned off the seafront road. Then the car drew to a sedate halt in a vacant parking space.

'We're not going to the hospital, are we, Carole?'

'No, of course we're not. We're just going to get you patched up a bit first.'

It was entirely in character the Carole Seddon would have a well-stocked first aid box in her car. And the efficiency with which she mopped up and dressed the grazes on Jude's hands and knees suggested that her Home Office training might at some point have included a course in first aid.

'Right,' she said. 'You'll do. Sure you didn't suffer any blows to the head?'

'No, I was lucky in that respect. Just the hands and knees ... and the general feeling of a rag doll who's just been thrown against the wall by a particularly belligerent toddler.'

'You'll survive,' was the unsentimental response from Carole.

'Yes, I've no doubt I'll survive. Now, who are we going to get the address from?'

'Elizaveta'd know it.'

'Undoubtedly, but I'm not sure how good our credit is there. What about Davina?'

'Do you have her number?'

'It's in the "Contacts" in my mobile. But

you'd better ring her. I don't think I can manage the keyboard with my hands like this.'

Carole got through to Davina and the required information was readily supplied.

'It's in Fethering,' she told Jude.

The house was one of the oldest in the village, in a row of small cottages whose original owners had worked in what was then the only industry, fishing. Once regarded as little more than hovels, they were now highly sought-after second homes for wealthy Londoners. Many of them had been refurbished to within an inch of their lives, but there were still a few that had been passed on within families for generations. On these there were fewer window boxes, hanging baskets and quaint cast-iron name-plates.

The house that matched the address Davina had supplied was one of the untarted-up variety. Carole drew up her white Renault behind the already parked white Renault and looked across at Jude. 'Ready for it?'

Her neighbour nodded and the two women got out of the car with, in Jude's case, some discomfort. Even in the short journey from Smalting, as the shock of the impact wore off her individual injuries were starting to give her a lot of pain.

Carole knocked on the door, which promptly opened. Mimi Lassiter looked unsurprised to see her visitors, though perhaps a bit disappointed that one of them was Jude.

'I think you know why we've come to see you,' said Carole, very Home Office.

'I think I probably do. Come in.'

The sitting room into which she led them reminded both women of Gordon Blaine's. It was not just the small dimensions – in this case due to the original builder rather than the owner's DIY conversion – but the furniture, the ornaments and the pictures on the walls were all from an earlier era. The house had been decorated in the time of Mimi's parents and she had either not wanted to – or not dared to – change a thing.

It wasn't an occasion for pleasantries or offers of coffee. Mimi Lassiter sat in a cracked leather armchair, set facing the television, and her guests in straight-backed chairs either side of the box.

'Rather rash of you this morning, wasn't it?' said Carole. 'Making a public attack on Jude by driving straight at her? There'd have been lots of witnesses on the seafront at Smalting. I'm sure someone would have taken note of your registration number.'

'I wasn't thinking very straight this morning,' said Mimi, sounding as ever like a rather per- nickety maiden aunt. 'I was upset.'

'Do you often get upset?' asked Jude.

'Not very often, but I do. My mother used to look after me when I got upset, but since she's passed, I've had to manage it on my own.'

'And,' said Carole, 'do you regard trying to run someone down in cold blood as "managing it on your own"?'

'It made sense. I couldn't see any other way out. And when I heard from Elizaveta that you two were actually investigating Ritchie Good's death ... as I say, I wasn't thinking very straight. It probably wasn't the most sensible thing to do.'

To Carole and Jude this seemed like something of an understatement.

'No,' said Mimi. 'I've been very foolish. My mother always used to say, "At times, Mimi, you can be very foolish." And she had ways of stopping me being foolish, but now she's gone...'

'How long ago did your mother die?' asked Jude.

'Nine years ago. It was just round the time when I was retiring from work.'

'What did you do when you were working?'

'I trained in Worthing as a shorthand typist. I was very good. I got a diploma. I could have got a job anywhere, even in London. But I didn't want to leave Fethering. Mummy needed help with Daddy. He was virtually bedridden for a long time. So I got a secretarial job at Hadleigh's. Do you know them?'

'No.'

'Big nursery, just between here and Worthing. Lots of glasshouses. Well, they were made of glass when I started there. Now they're mostly that polythene stuff. Still a very big company, though. I did very well at Hadleigh's. They very nearly made me office manager. But I wasn't as good on the computers as I had been on the typewriter, so they appointed someone else. I never really took to computers in the same way I took to the typewriter. So they kept me on at Hadleigh's, but there was never any more chance of promotion. Then they opened up a Farm Shop and they suggested I might work in there. But I didn't like it. Some members of the public can be very rude, you know.'

'So,' Jude recapitulated, 'your mother died around the time you retired. That must have been a very big double blow for you.'

'Oh, it was. Two days before I left Hadleigh's. And it wasn't real retirement. I mean, I hadn't served all the time that ... They gave me my full pension, but it was really...'

'Early retirement,' suggested Carole, whose experience of the same thing still rankled.

Mimi nodded. She looked shaken by the memory. 'I was in a very bad state round then, I remember. I know it's wrong, but at times I did think about ending it all. I just felt so isolated.'

'Are you saying you attempted suicide?'

'No, not quite. But I thought about it. I even started stockpiling paracetamol, but then things got better.'

'In what way?' asked Jude. 'Was it because you'd joined SADOS?'

Mimi nodded enthusiastically. 'Fortunately that happened fairly soon after Mummy passed. That's what really got me out of the terrible state I was in. Elizaveta Dalrymple used to come to the Farm Shop while I was still working there. And she said how the society was always looking for new members and she persuaded me to come along to a social meeting. She can be very persuasive, Elizaveta.'

'Yes,' Carole agreed drily.

'So that's how I started with SADOS. As a very humble new member ... little knowing that I would one day end up at the dizzy heights of Membership Secretary.' Clearly the appointment was one that meant a great deal to Mimi Lassiter.

'I'd never wanted to act,' she went on. 'I couldn't act to save my life, but they found things for me to do backstage. And occasionally I'm in crowd scenes ... like I am for *The Devil's Disciple*. Elizaveta always makes me feel part of the company, though, and she even started inviting me to parties at her home.'

'Her "drinkies things"?'

'Yes.'

'Of course. Where we saw you on Saturday.'

'Yes.'

'And what about Freddie? Did you have much to do with him?'

'Oh, Freddie.' An expression of sheer hero-worship took over her face. 'He was wonderful.

299

Did you ever meet him?'

'Didn't have that pleasure,' said Jude.

'Though we've heard so much about him,' said Carole, 'that we *feel* as though we've met him.'

'He was just a wonderful man. So talented. And so kind to everyone, particularly to new members of SADOS.'

A look was exchanged between Carole and Jude. Each knew the other was thinking, 'particularly to new, *young, pretty* members of the SADOS'. Who could benefit so much from Freddie's assistance when working on their parts in his flat in Worthing. Another look between the two also made a silent agreement that they weren't about to ask whether Mimi Lassiter had ever been the recipient of a star-shaped pendant. It just didn't seem likely.

'I gather,' said Carole, 'it was a great upheaval for the society when Freddie Dalrymple died.'

'Oh, it was terrible. For a long time nobody knew what would happen to SADOS. It seemed impossible that the society could continue without Freddie. But that's when Elizaveta really came into her own. She's such a strong woman, you know.'

Neither Carole nor Jude was about to argue with that.

'Could we come back to this morning?' Carole's question was not one that would have brooked the answer no.

'All right,' said Mimi, instantly subdued.

'And your attempt to kill Jude.' Mimi did not argue with the phrasing. 'You've told us you were in a bad state this morning, that you weren't thinking straight, but you haven't told us *why* you wanted Jude dead.'

'I wanted both of you dead,' said Mimi with refreshing honesty. 'I still do.'

An anxious look passed between the two women. Was their unwilling hostess about to produce a gun?

'But Elizaveta told me that's not the right way to proceed.'

'I'd go along with that,' Carole agreed. 'But when did Elizaveta say this?'

'Just now. The phone was ringing when I got back from Smalting.'

'And had she rung you earlier in the morning as well?'

'Yes. She told me you were both coming round. And she said you were coming because you thought Ritchie Good's death might not be an accident.'

'Which is why you were waiting for us in your Renault? To run us down?'

'Yes,' Mimi replied quietly.

Jude took over. 'Elizaveta said just now on the phone that what you'd done wasn't the right way to proceed. Did she tell you what *would* have been the right way?'

'Elizaveta had seen what had happened in the street outside her house. She knew that I had

301

tried to kill you, and she said that I shouldn't try to do things like that ever again.' She made it sound like a child being chastised by a parent for not making her bed. And Jude was struck by the fact that Mimi Lassiter was childlike. There was something emotionally undeveloped about her, the little girl who could not make her own decisions, who had to be directed by a stronger woman. Like her mother ... or Elizaveta Dalrymple.

'Tell us about Ritchie Good's death,' said Jude gently.

'What about it?'

'You switched the real noose for the doctored one, didn't you?'

'Yes.' Once again there was pride in her voice.

'And had you planned to do that,' asked Carole, 'after you'd heard Gordon Blaine describe the mechanism the previous day?'

'That planted the idea in my head, yes.'

'So what actually happened after the rehearsal that Sunday afternoon?'

'Well, it was very lucky, actually.' Mimi was now talking with enthusiasm, and clearly not a vestige of guilt. 'Most people had left St Mary's Hall, but I was gathering my bits together, my bag and what-have-you. I'd left them in the Green Room, so I was near the stage, and I heard some people come in, and I recognized Ritchie Good's voice, and Hester Winstone's. And he was saying how she'd missed a really good show when he used the gallows and she must have what he called "a command performance". Well, Hester didn't sound very interested, and Ritchie was trying to persuade her, and I thought, "I'm never going to get a better opportunity than this." So I went onstage, and the curtains were drawn and it was easy to get on to the cart and switch the two nooses around. And then I slipped out of the hall without them seeing me, and I went to the Cricketers.' She smiled beatifically. 'It all worked remarkably well, didn't it?'

There was a silence. Then Carole asked, 'And did you do it because the night before you heard Elizaveta say that she wanted Ritchie dead?'

Mimi looked at her curiously. 'No, it was nothing to do with Elizaveta.'

'Then why did you do it?' asked Jude.

'Well, obviously ... because Ritchie Good was in a SADOS production while not being a member of SADOS. He hadn't paid his subscription.'

THIRTY-TWO

'What do you think we do about her?' asked Carole, as she drove her white Renault the short distance back to High Tor.

'Do you mean, do we shop her to the police?'

'Yes, I suppose I do.' Her voice took on its Home Office tone. 'It would be the proper thing to do.'

Jude grimaced sceptically. 'Pretty difficult case for them to bring to court and secure a conviction. Also, what I always think in situations like this is: does a person like Mimi represent a danger to anyone else?'

'Might I remind you, Jude, that we're talking about someone who only this morning tried to kill you by running you over?'

'Yes, I know. I really do think she's got all that out of her system, though. She virtually said as much.'

'But do you believe her?'

'Yes, I do actually. What about you?'

Carole was forced unwillingly to admit that she couldn't see Mimi Lassiter as a public danger either.

'I'm more worried,' said Jude, 'about the

threat she might pose to herself.'

'Oh?'

'She told us she'd got near to suicide when her mother died – or "passed", as she insisted on saying.'

'Well, this morning she seemed far from suicidal. Positively gleeful at having got away with killing Ritchie Good.'

'Mm.'

'And, Jude, you made her fix that appointment with her GP to talk about her issues with depression.' Jude nodded. 'In the circumstances I don't think there was a lot more you could have done.'

Over the next few months Carole's words came back to haunt Jude. She felt an ugly tug of guilt. Perhaps there was a lot more she could have done. But during the run of *The Devil's Disciple* both she and Carole had kept a cautious eye on Mimi Lassiter, and neither had seen anything untoward.

They didn't think there was anything significant about her absence from the last night cast party. In fact, to be honest, in such a raucous scrum of posing thespians they didn't notice she wasn't there.

Every night during the run of *The Devil's Disciple,* Mimi had dutifully done her (again unnoticed) performances in the Westerfield crowd at the near-hanging of Dick Dudgeon. That duty discharged, on the Saturday night she had packed up her belongings in St Mary's Hall and driven in her white Renault back to her parents' house (it still felt like her parents' house) in Fethering. Once there she had run a hot bath, got into it, swallowed down about thirty paracetamol from the store she had stock-piled when previously feeling suicidal, and slit her wrists with her father's old cut-throat razor.

The reason she had killed herself had nothing to do with guilt about causing the death of Ritchie Good. That event, she thought, had been very just and appropriate. Mimi had almost as strong an aversion to 'showing-off' as Carole Seddon. Ritchie Good had always been a 'show-off' and it was 'showing-off' that had brought about his demise. Besides, he'd never paid his subscription to be a member of SADOS.

But what had really made Mimi suicidal was the suspension of patronage by Elizaveta Dalrymple. After the attempt to run over Jude, the grande dame of SADOS had decided that perhaps Mimi was no longer the sort of person she wished to have attending her 'drinkies things'. By long tradition Elizaveta issued her invitations to her regulars on the Friday for the Saturday eight days away. By the end of the Friday which saw the penultimate performance of *The Devil's Disciple,* Mimi Lassiter had received no such summons. And by the end of the Saturday she realized she wasn't going to receive one. Mimi had been cast into the outer darkness. She would never get another invitation to one of Elizaveta's 'drinkies things'.

Without her idol's support, patronage and validation Mimi Lassiter crumpled like a rag doll. To her mind suicide was the only available option for her.

Of course, at the cast party nobody knew of the gruesome event taking place in Fethering. It was afterwards they heard the news which caused Jude such disquiet.

But at the party itself there was a high level of good cheer. This was because people in amdrams always like to let their hair down at the end of a production, rather than because *The Devil's Disciple* had been a huge success. Neville Prideaux's conviction that a wordy minor work by George Bernard Shaw was what the good burghers of Smalting were craving for had been proved completely wrong. They had stayed away in droves, and those who had attended had been unimpressed. In spite of all Carole Seddon's assiduous one-to-one 'line-bashing' sessions, when faced by a live audience Olly Pinto's memory appeared to have been wiped completely. He had ensured that Carole, in her role as prompter, had had a very busy week. And the people in the front row of St Mary's Hall had heard more from her than they had from some of the actors.

Storm Lavelle, on the other hand, had really built her performance throughout the run. She did have genuine talent and Jude wondered whether her butterfly brain would allow her to concentrate sufficiently on trying to get work in the professional theatre. Secretly, Jude rather doubted it. Like many aspiring actors, her friend had the talent, but lacked the tenacity required to make a go of it.

Storm had had her hair done on the morning of *The Devil's Disciple*'s final performance and, on removing Judith Anderson's wig, revealed a fuschia-pink crop with a long jagged fringe. For the cast party she wore a diamanté top over silver leggings. She looked terrific, her sparkle increased by the knowledge of how well she had acted in the show.

Storm seemed in such a relaxed mood that Jude thought she could ask about the strange moment when her friend had put the phone down on her. 'Do you remember, I said it was something about Ritchie Good and Elizaveta...?'

Storm looked embarrassed. 'The fact is, I had a bit of history with Ritchie which I didn't want anyone to hear about. And when you said it concerned that old cow Elizaveta too, I thought she might spread the news around SADOS.'

'And what was this "history" you had with Ritchie? An affair?'

'No, it didn't quite get that far, but it still left me feeling pretty stupid.'

'May I put forward a theory of what might have happened?'

Storm looked puzzled, but shrugged and said, 'If you want to.'

'I suggest that Ritchie Good came on to you quite heavily, got you keen and interested, got you to the point where you'd agreed to go to bed with him, and then said he couldn't go through with it because of his loyalty to his wife.'

A thunderstruck expression took over Storm's face. 'How on earth did you know that?'

'Let's just say there was a pattern to Ritchie's behaviour.'

'Oh. Well, the thing that worried me was that, I suppose trying to curry favour with the old bat, I told Elizaveta what had happened. Which was very stupid, because it was a sure way of guaranteeing that everyone in SADOS would soon know. And there was one person I really didn't want to know I'd had any kind of relationship with Ritchie Good.'

'And who was that?'

Jude's question was immediately answered by the wide smile that came to Storm's lips as she saw someone approaching them. It was Olly Pinto, grinning broadly.

His disastrous showing as Dick Dudgeon during the week seemed not to have affected him one bit. Jude had noticed him earlier at the cast party, in extremely high spirits, downing beer after beer.

And now she realized from the way he was looking at Storm Lavelle that there was another

309

cause for his good cheer. Jude felt a bit silly for not having seen anything developing between the two of them earlier, because it was now clear that Olly Pinto was destined to be the next man to feel the full force of Storm's adoration. Jude didn't think it would do either of them any harm, and might in fact do them some good.

As a result of *The Devil's Disciple*'s failure to bring in the audiences, there was now a move among the younger members of the society to oust Neville Prideaux from the Play Selection Committee. His star had waned considerably. And some of this younger group at the party were arguing quite loudly that it wasn't too late to change the SADOS's next production from *I Am A Camera* to three episodes of *Fawlty Towers*. The mention of this led to a lot of the men going into comedy goose-stepping, as if auditioning for the part of Basil Fawlty.

Elizaveta Dalrymple, who had somehow got entangled with this group, proved not to be as averse to the idea of doing the three television episodes as some might have expected. The reason was, of course, that she didn't really think she was too old to play Basil's wife Sibyl.

Inevitably, Elizaveta had come back into the SADOS fold. As Olly Pinto had predicted, she had been at the first night ('someone dropped out at the last minute') and had met so many people there who were delighted to see her and urged her to attend the cast party on the Saturday night, that she couldn't really disappoint

310

them. This suited her very well, because she had really wanted to get back in ever since Ritchie Good's death. With the man who'd insulted her removed, there was no reason for her not to reclaim her rightful place, the spider at the centre of the SADOS web.

Her rift with Davina Vere Smith also seemed somehow to have been healed. Jude did not know how this had been achieved, but suspected some telephonic machinations on Elizaveta's part, some agreement whereby Davina would never mention her involvement with Freddie and would always wear high collars at SADOS rehearsals.

Of course, Hester Winstone was not at the cast party. Jude had been in touch with Rob at Casements about future healing work and heard that Hester had left the convalescent home. Where to, Rob couldn't be sure, but he thought she had returned to her family. Jude didn't envy Hester her reunion with Mike because, in her experience, cricketers remained the most misogynist of sportsmen. Maybe she'd try to give Hester a call to offer help, but she very much suspected that the carapace of middle-class respectability would once again have closed over, and the need for any assistance would be denied. Hester would assure her that 'We are all right as we are.' It was frustrating, but there was nothing Jude could do about it. She did definitely plan to do more work at Casements, though.

The wine was flowing and some people were dancing. To provide the music, one of the younger members had produced a portable CD player. (Gordon Blaine had earlier set up a huge system of amplifiers and speakers in one corner of the room, but unfortunately it didn't work.)

Jude didn't feel like dancing. Apart from anything else, her body was still wincing from the bruises caused by her encounter with Mimi Lassiter's Renault. And her body language must have indicated her unwillingness to dance, because nobody asked her. Had Carole been thus neglected, although she 'didn't like dancing', she would have taken it very personally indeed.

Jude didn't mind at all. She just wanted to go home.

But it would be a while yet. Her transport, Carole, who 'didn't like dancing', was in vigorous motion on the dance floor, mirroring the movements of the Heil-Hitlering young man in front of her (yes, it was a continuation of his Basil Fawlty impression).

Her neighbour, Jude concluded with an inward giggle, was actually a little bit pissed. Tired after the evening's concentration on trying to get Olly Pinto to deliver at least a few lines of genuine George Bernard Shaw, Carole had gulped down the first two glasses of wine quicker than she normally would. And now Jude found herself witnessing something she had longed for but never expected to see –

Carole Seddon casting off at least some of her inhibitions.

Jude didn't want any more to drink, and wondered mischievously how an offer that she, being the more sober, should drive the Renault back to Fethering would go down with her neighbour. No, probably not a good idea.

She looked around St Mary's Hall. The main sets of *The Devil's Disciple* had been dismantled with surprising speed. Jude could not keep out of her head Lysander's line from *A Midsummer Night's Dream*: 'So quick bright things come to confusion.' There was always a pleasing melancholy about the ending of a theatrical production. The stage crew, encouraged by copious draughts of beer, were still stripping away flats and props. Gordon Blaine was at the centre of the operation, clearly happier doing something useful than trying to be sociable.

And, moved from the wings to the body of the hall, stood the chaise longue. Almost unnoticed by audience and critics alike, it had delivered another sterling performance. Jude didn't think she'd suggest taking it home in the Renault that evening. Carole seemed to be enjoying herself too much for that. They could pick it up another day and take it back to Woodside Cottage. Where it could wait, draped with throws and cushions, till it received its next summons to become part of the magic of the theatre.

Eventually it was clear that Carole's programme of dancing had come to an end. When they stopped, the young man of the Basil Fawlty impressions wrapped her in a bear-hug and it was a rather flushed Carole Seddon who came across to join Jude.

'Promise me I'll see you on the next production, Carole!' the young man called after her.

'Oh well,' she said with a little giggle. 'Never say never.'

Carole had driven with intense concentration from St Mary's Hall back to Fethering. She had not infringed any speed limits or deviated from a line exactly parallel to the kerb of the road. But she had driven rather slowly.

And outside Woodside Cottage she had kissed and hugged Jude rather more effusively than she sometimes might have done. But it was only when she fumbled with the keys of High Tor and had difficulty getting the relevant one into the lock that it occurred to her she might be a little bit drunk.

'Cold water,' she thought. 'Drink lots of cold water.'

As she moved towards the kitchen, Gulliver rose from his favourite position beside the Aga to greet her. As the dog looked up, she wondered if she was being fanciful to see reproach in his large, melancholy eyes.

Then she noticed the single red digit on the answering machine. She fumbled for the playback button and pressed it.

'Mother,' said the rather formal voice of her son Stephen, 'I thought you might like to have some explanation of these stomach upsets Gaby's been getting. Well, we've had the twelve-week scan today and it's confirmed. We thought you'd like to know ... you're going to be a grandmother again.'

Chicken Coops
for the
SOUL

With love to my daughters

Chicken Coops
~ *for the* ~
SOUL
A henkeeper's story

JULIA HOLLANDER

guardianbooks

Published by Guardian Books 2010

2 4 6 8 10 9 7 5 3 1

First published in Great Britain in 2010 by
Guardian Books
Kings Place, 90 York Way
London N1 9GU

www.guardianbooks.co.uk

A CIP catalogue record for this book is available from the British Library

ISBN 978-0852652206

Typeset by seagulls.net

Printed and bound in Great Britain by Clays Ltd, St Ives PLC

'You must have heard of chickens; they're all the rage!'
Spike Milligan

Contents

Funky Chicken

I confess that I, like too many others before me, became a chicken-owner on a whim. It was five years ago and those few weeks before Christmas when presents urgently needed finalising. My eldest daughter Ellie was insisting that her one and only wish was for a bunny rabbit; she had been saying so since the previous Christmas. My objections revolved around the usual – you are not old enough; I know it's going to be me that has to look after it; I'm not sure keeping a pet in a cage is kind, especially without company … each time I came up with a fresh and valid argument, it crashed against a wall of five-year-old willpower.

A major weakness was that I couldn't remember how old I had been when I myself got a rabbit. It was possible I too had only just started school, was only just able to take responsibility for cleaning my teeth, let alone keeping another little creature alive. What

I did remember was the huge satisfaction of caring for Ravioli the rabbit: building him a cosy nest; the feeding and the watering; the delights of both cuddling and taunting him; the drama of protecting him from the ravenous family dog. Later Ravioli turned out to be a mere warm-up for my even greater dedication to ponies.

How was it possible that since starting a family, I had survived this long without any animals at all?

On a drizzly Saturday morning Ellie and I made our way through chaotic traffic, out into open countryside. I was happy that this shopping trip was taking us away from the dazzle and bluster of the crowds, happy not to be jostling over plastic toys and computer games.

We were heading towards the animal sanctuary where as a toddler Ellie had first clasped a real live bunny. I remembered the occasion well – the two of them perfectly matched in warmth and softness.

As we entered we spotted them, there in the big cage – a pair of bunnies snuggled against the wire. White with black points, they were; Himalayans; small enough for even a five year old to handle. And behind them, skittering around the logs and stones, was a matching pair of chickens. The combination was irresistible.

'You don't want them useless bantams,' said the old lady who ran the sanctuary, leaving Ellie to bond with the bunnies and taking me round the back of the building. 'What you need is a couple of Warrens.' Warren sounded like a nice, traditional breed. Though my first thought had been to provide the rabbit with a feathered companion or two, already I was moving into a more utilitarian mode – here was a pet that in return for its care might provide us with breakfast. I was mighty impressed when, from the flock of identical red hens in her shed, she selected the two that would lay the best; through long experience, I thought, she must have developed some profound intuition about their abilities.

By the time we returned, Ellie had chosen her Himalayan and christened him – Snowy. As the sanctuary lady lowered each of the Warrens into an empty sack, stapling shut the opening in case they tried to escape, Ellie begged for the opportunity to name them too. I wasn't sure. One of the few things I knew about chickens was that they were extremely attractive to foxes, and round our terraced town house we have foxes galore. Surely their snitching a hen with a name would feel much worse than one without. Quite rightly, Ellie argued that I had let her name her bunny even though the fox might try to steal him. So I gave in and let her call them 'Roxy' and 'Loxy'. She had no explanation for her choices, except that they rhymed with 'Foxy'.

Then slowly home we drove, a two-storey hutch strapped to the roof; the sacks of chicken wedged behind my seat and a couple more of feed on the passenger seat. In the back, Ellie sat bolt upright with Snowy in a box on her lap, a frown of solicitude on her face. This was the beginning of a whole new era.

'How long do you think the hens might live?' I had enquired as we departed.

'Ooh, ages,' the lady at the sanctuary assured me. '11, 12 years, if you look after them.'

Great, I thought – that's like a dog or a cat; Roxy and Loxy could just about be around until Ellie leaves home. She will be off, forging a life for herself, and meanwhile maybe I shall fill the child-space in my life with these kinds of companions. I smiled as my imagination fast-forwarded to a future self, nestled on the sofa with two perfectly house-trained old hens; in the background a veritable menagerie where canaries tweeted and parrots chattered, while outside in the garden a flock of geese and ducks waddled about. Maybe I could adopt a disabled raven or two.

Having assumed that I had zero experience of chickens other than the oven-ready variety, my new enthusiasm began to unearth memories to the contrary. The most potent was also the earliest. I must have been two or three when my grandparents left their large house in the Home Counties. I had thought I was too young to recall that place, but now I could summon to mind shadows of an orchard with gnarled and spreading trees, in the far corner a coop. My feelings were anxiety mingled with excitement – a dark, chaotic mass in the shade of the Pippins – how huge each hen had seemed, like something prehistoric, vicious and screeching. I remembered how gently my grandfather had treated them, even as he herded them away from me, his voice crooning 'all right, ladies, all right, my beauties.'

When I phoned my mother and asked her about this memory, she said yes, her father had always kept Rhode Island Reds. Even during the war when he was running a horticultural centre in East Africa, Grandpa had somehow managed to acquire some and kept them in amongst the avocados and acacia trees. In his retirement, he had expanded his collection to include ducks and geese.

Another memory was from only ten years previously. Pre-motherdom, I had lived alone in a top-storey flat in South London. It was when a relationship broke up that I decided the answer to loneliness was a pet. There wasn't a whole lot of choice – dogs: too much work; cats: no way for them to come and go; rodents: nasty, dirty creatures … I did my research, and discovered that what I truly desired in life was a bird. A sulphur-headed, red-cheeked one with a jaunty crest and elegant long tail – a cock-atiel. I planned on its roaming free in the flat, learning to whistle the odd tune and even indulging me with a bit of chick-chat. I went out and started getting to know other bird-lovers; I bought a beautiful Art Nouveau cage to hang in the window … Then I met Jay, and decided that a bloke was better company than a bird.

Since then, from bloke to babies, my life had taken a decidedly birdless path. Except that suddenly Roxy and Loxy offered the opportunity to backtrack. Jay could have been appalled, but he wasn't, he was intrigued. Especially if it meant freshly laid eggs and the wife did the mucky stuff. That was fine by me – I had ambitions; I was out to prove that my cockatiel plan had been a serious one – that birds can make excellent pets.

The larger of our two new hens was Loxy. With a body all round and red, she looked just like the Little Red Hen in the children's picture book. We knew the story well – how a feisty hen scatters her corn, then harvests and grinds it to make bread. She has to do it all alone because her animal friends are too lazy to help. But not our toddler Beatrice. Determined to demonstrate how good she was at helping, she would happily have spent all day, every day, scattering seed for Loxy. Perhaps 'scatter' is not strictly the term one should use for Bea's rummaging in the bucket, scooping up whatever would stick in her fist and thrusting the contents clat-tering across the patio. Loxy didn't mind – the closer her grain was clumped, the quicker she could gobble it up. The only prob-lem came when the bucket was empty and Beatrice had nothing to do – soon enough she would grab at the fan of Loxy's tail, crying 'my chick chick, my chick chick' as she fled.

Not that Loxy was averse to human company. If you were prepared to forego the tail-grabbing, she was only too happy to be your friend. An hour spent sitting on the garden bench, and Loxy was bound to join me, kindly snipping short the grass around my feet. If I had brought a handful of corn, she would sometimes dare to hop into my lap to eat it. Cuddling Loxy like this made me realise why many mothers, including me, use 'chicken' as a term of endearment for their children.

In many ways, Loxy's style was more feline than gallinaceous. On summer afternoons, I could always find her in the south-facing corner of the garden, snuggled into a patch of long grass, her wings outspread.

If Loxy was the cat in the family, then Roxy was the dog. The skinnier and noisier of the two, she didn't approve of lazing around and if she found her sister sunbathing she might give her a spiteful peck. She was definitely inclined to bully, but at the same time possessed a playful streak. For example, if for some reason I had to put the duo away before the end of the day, I always went to Loxy first because I knew she could be easily cornered. Once she was safely locked away, I was in for the long haul. Roxy saw any attempt to catch her as an opportunity for a game of tag.

Sometimes I would try to ambush her while she was foraging – in amongst the bamboo was a good place for that. But even when I managed to creep very close indeed, at the last minute she would flit under my arm and away. If I pursued her, ludicrously emulating her zig-zag path down our narrow garden, Roxy would chortle as if in mockery – 'you can't catch me, you can't catch me!'

Another of Roxy's amusements was to strut up and down outside the back door. At first I thought it was because she wanted to come in, but when I went to turn the handle she skittered away. Eventually I realised she was watching her own reflection in the glass – attacking it and seducing it, taunting and testing it,

'Mirror, mirror on the wall.'

Eventually I opened the door and the spell was broken.

Chickens round the kitchen door were part of an ideal family life I had once dreamt of. One Jay and I had even tried. When Ellie had been six months old, we moved from our noisy London flat to a cottage in the Cotswolds. For a couple of years we pretended that life in the countryside was all about the wildlife, the space, our close-knit community tending the land. We tried to ignore the quad bikes and the SUVs, the fact that we and most of our neighbours were commuting away each day. In the end we returned to the city, reconciled to the fact that a truly rural upbringing was something we might never be able to offer our children.

But at least they could have a chickeny one. Chickens and children seemed ideally suited to one another; the daily routine of caring for them perfectly compatible. Though by nature a late riser, I had been disciplined by my daughters to get up soon after sunrise, even in summer. There was nothing for it, however thick the lining on their bedroom curtains, the day began with the light and one or other of them shouting the house awake. Next stop – Roxy and Loxy, also fretting to be let out. I learnt to relish the cacophony of birdsong, the smell of the dew – surprising rewards for performing the first-chore-of-the-day.

Their bedtimes were similarly in synch, except that the children had a lot to learn from the hens. I was charmed to discover that Roxy and Loxy knew exactly when they were tired and needed to go to bed. As dusk began to fall, the two of them would cease their business and potter down the alleyway at the side of the house. There they would huddle, patiently, until someone came to shut them in.

Needless to say, the bunny rabbit's natural schedule contrasted unfavourably with the hens'. Ellie was disappointed to discover that when she wanted to play, Snowy was dopey; when she needed to sleep, he was tearing around his cage looking for company. This unfortunate truth persuaded me that an essential quality in truly domesticated animals is that they keep the same hours as their owner.

They should also provide entertainment. Sitting and watching our chooks was excellent downtime for little Bea and me. We giggled at their funny way of walking, heads jutting forward and back, as if on a spring, their feet as big as clowns'. If the weather was dry, around midday they could always be found in the corner by my peonies, taking it in turns to enjoy their dust bath. As Loxy rolled around, she expressed her pleasure in appropriately feline terms: by purring.

And then she could growl. Deep in the throat this sound sat, her beak kept closed. It was definitely an early warning signal – telling that bitch Roxy she was not coming out of the bath until she was finished.

Unfazed by this, Roxy had plenty more impressive effects in her own repertoire. First and foremost, a noise disarmingly similar to a cock's crow. At first I worried it was a sign that she was one of those weirdos that lay a couple of eggs before transmogrifying into a male. People think this happens because they get an infection that renders their reproductive system useless; rather than having to admit their barrenness they pretend they have had a sex change. It must be this kind of avian sexual politics that inspired the old saying, *'a nagging wife and a crowing hen do no good for God nor men.'*

Fortunately for me, my bird's crow remained a cry of triumph to let everyone know she was far from barren. One long, high note using the head voice followed by six short, low ones in the chest signalled that a brand new egg had been born. My daughters loved to copy it; with some sexual politics-inspired lyrics from me, it became –

'Bra – not, not, not, not, not, not; Bra – not, not, not, not, not, not!'

Research from Macquarie University in Australia has established that domestic chickens have 20 different calls, falling broadly into two groups – food calls and alarm calls (the ultimate alarm call, naturally, being the one you get from a cock at 5am, though Roxy's egg-declaration comes a close second).

Food calls are interesting – members of the *Gallus* genus are said to have the richest array of food-calling behaviours in any animal group. Broody hens will use one particular series of clucks to draw attention to a tasty morsel; her chicks come running in response. When a cock is around, he will use exactly the same call to get his hens to take the earthworm he has found. He will also use it as a courtship song, or duping her into a quick shag, depending on how you look at it.

Roxy was always surprising me with her vocal range, and the apparent meaning behind it. She was partial to gargling. In its loudest, open-beaked version, it was less like water bubbling in the throat than stones rattling in a jar. I have a friend who swears her chickens can gargle the tune of Rossini's *William Tell Overture;*

Roxy's version was rather more prosaic – signalling she was desperate to get out of her enclosure and have a run around.

She could also cackle with laughter, especially if she was excited by the prospect of a really good meal – '*What a bit of luck!*'. High-pitched shrieking she was very good at; almost as good as my children. When she and Loxy fought, they used the kind of resonance with which a soprano might break a wine glass. If they were very frightened, their scream was so shrill it could shatter a window pane. But generally they were contented to carry on their business with a perfectly conventional clucking.

Some researchers reckon clucking has developed as a way of keeping predators at bay – the constant stream of low-grade noise as the chickens flit about confuses that hawk hovering overhead. I would say the onomatopoeic suggestion in the word 'cluck' is less like the actual sound than a deep-throated '*bop*'.

'*Bop, bop, boppety bop,*' it has a subtly irregular beat. I think this is the sound Beatrix Potter intended to evoke with Sally Henny-penny's '*I go barefoot, barefoot, barefoot; I go barefoot, barefoot, barefoot.*'

I often thought Roxy and Loxy were clucking in order to keep in touch – even though they were each off in separate bits of the garden, finding their own tasty titbit. Other times they seemed to be chattering away independently, absent-mindedly, as I might have been doing were I still living alone in that one-bedroom flat. It could sound a bit grumpy but never suicidal. With their beaks closed it was similar to the squeak your fingers make when you rub a wet window. The open-beaked version was highly animated, full of tonal ups and downs, with hardly a break for breath. The underlying meaning was sure to be equally complex:

'So where are those lovely juicy daddy long legs? There was a nice crop of them yesterday, if I remember rightly. I dunno. What with this weather and all, I dunno …'

Having been so delighted by my pets' vocalisations, I was disappointed to find a dearth of them in my classical music collection. Haydn's *'Symphony number 83'* earned itself the nickname *'La poule'* because of the fiddles' playful *appoggiatura*, contrasting with the oboe's dotted rhythm on one note. This combination is meant to sound very much like clucking and pecking; but I wasn't convinced. A composer friend who is quite obsessed with birdsong pointed to a hyperactive chicken in the *'Sonata Representativa'* by Biber; he even bothered to come round and play me Rameau's charmingly quirky *'La poule'* on the piano. But neither of them was quite chickeny enough for me; not after the real thing.

So what about chickens on stage? In his 1920s opera *The Cunning Little Vixen*, the Czech composer Janáček has a flock whose pecking gets the usual mechanical string treatment; they also sing. Unfortunately the composer was so smitten by his heroine, the vixen, that he gave her all the good tunes. The hens she kills are depicted as workaholic masochists, so numbingly institutionalised that their vocal lines lack any hint of bravura.

Janáček had a point. By the time he was writing his opera, most chickens round his way lived on large-scale poultry farms, soon to become the mass-production units of today. They had indeed become horribly institutionalised.

And yet in the very same period, just as chickens' voices were disappearing from most people's daily lives, musicians had started waking up to them. While in Czechoslovakia Janáček turned to farms, American jazz musicians went straight to the dirt and mess of a backyard much like mine. Big-arsed and busy, scrabbling about in the dust at the door, a flock of feathered females was ideally suited to Slim Gaillard's subversive art. Other musicians of the period, most notably Cab Calloway and Louis Jordan, were also inspired to write hilariously cheeky chicken songs.

From the 60s onwards the Funky Chicken came into its own. Where classical musicians had heard only regular monotony, the likes of Charles Mingus, Rufus Thomas, bands like The Meters, The Eliminators and the Chili Peppers ... all were transported by the syncopation of sound and movement. James Brown's saxophonist, Pee Wee Ellis, created a funk number called 'The Chicken' and it passed down to 80s bass player Jaco Pastorius who made it his signature tune. With a jerky four-time beat, shrieks and stabs from brass and woodwind, and a skittering about on electric guitar strings, its love of *Gallus gallus domesticus* is clear.

Back in my humble garden, it never ceased to amaze me how good Roxy and Loxy were at communicating. Not with the garden birds – they didn't seem in the slightest bit interested in them; their interest was in what we humans were up to. Who was that moving back and forth in the kitchen? Was that *Teletubbies* on TV again? Was Jay about to come out into the garden? And if so, did he have anything edible to offer?

Whenever they sensed we had visitors, they rushed up to the house to check them out. Sometimes, if we left the back door open we would discover them bustling about in the kitchen like a couple of bossy housewives, come to see that everything is up to their standards. When they wriggled their bouffant tails and deposited a Walnut Whip bang in the middle of the floor, Jay was appalled, but I didn't particularly mind. I shovelled it up and flung it straight out on the flowerbed. Then I put on my strict-Mummy voice, shooing the culprits towards the door, in the hope that gradually they might learn more civilised ways.

Not that I had entirely succumbed to my fantasy of house-trained hens. I recognised that they were happiest outdoors and we humans indoors. Catch me on one of my least sentimental days, I will tell you that chickens are not very bright, that they might be picturesque and charmingly friendly and all that, but mainly their talents lie in one, specialist area – eggs. In terms of food production, keeping egg-producers in the garden makes a lot of sense.

I am not an economist; I would say I am a thrifty householder and hen-holder, but I don't count every penny. That's why in the following calculations I am going to round my figures to the nearest easy number.

Roxy and Loxy were £10 each; their feed cost around £40 a year; their house cost nothing; add on a tenner for worming treatments and suchlike and you have spent £70 on the two of them. They each laid about 330 eggs per annum; that's 55 dozen in total. If you bought that many free-range eggs in the shops, they would cost you £150 – more than twice as much as you have spent.

Even though I maintain that keeping hens is cheap, things do become complicated if you start adding on things like your hourly rate for the labour. If you are a banker, for example, then I suppose even five minutes a day can make your hens look really un-economic. But if you are an unwaged mother like me, then you are seriously quids in. As food prices soar and City salaries plummet, which real economists reckon they might, then henkeeping could even start to look cost-effective for bankers.

Last but not least, along with all the pet-and-egg satisfaction, my chooks have introduced me to a whole new social scene. I had no idea quite how many people kept them or had kept them in the past – old and young; male and female; rich and poor; it is one of the few activities in this country that still manages to transcend social barriers. I find conversations about chickens are great ice-breakers, whether out shopping, at a party or at the school gate. Finding that your companion is one of the chickeny crowd brings a conspiratorial smile to both your faces – a chance to share one another's delight in bustling, chattering egg-producers. And once you're talking, you start discovering all the things you really should have known already, but that somehow, so far, had passed you by.

Cock 'n' Roll

He was like a cock who thought the sun had risen to hear him crow.
George Eliot, *Adam Bede*

Gradually it dawned on me that I had been too impulsive. I might, at the very least, have taken the precaution of scouring the net before I went chicken shopping. That way, I could have armed myself with all sorts of important information before Roxy and Loxy entered my garden. I might have discovered the existence of alektorophobia, and then I could have researched my rights and responsibilities regarding alektorophobic neighbours. Seriously. A thoughtful and considerate citizen never embarks on a major pet project without first finding out the rules.

Better late than never, I got on the phone to the council. Lara from the animal health department sounded friendly. She didn't think I needed to concern myself with my neighbours' phobias, as long as the garden was secure. She made sure I owned my property – tenancy agreements can contain prohibitive small print. She made sure it wasn't ex-council – their freehold stipulations can sometimes be anti-chicken. She told me if I was keeping fewer than 50 hens then I didn't need to get a licence. If the coop was of modest dimensions (meaning smaller than a large summer house) then I didn't need planning permission. If it was mobile, all the better.

'Can I keep a cock?' I enquired brightly, trying to sound as though the whole thing was still hypothetical.

'As far as we're concerned, you can.'

'What if the neighbours object to the noise?'

'A cock crowing is not an offence against any particular Act of Parliament, but there may be local bylaws. They would have to get in touch with the town council if they wanted to file a complaint.'

'Which department?' I asked, extra-specially mindful that fore-warned was forearmed.

'Environmental health.'

'Is there anything else I need to know?'

'I can't think of anything. Most people just get on with it,' she chortled.

I couldn't believe it. Was this the same local authority that obliged me to have a new Criminal Records Bureau investigation every time I volunteered for an activity with my children – Sunday school, helping out with the school garden or a week-end's community camping? And every year insisted I renew them? This year for two daughters I had so far clocked up three CRBs, at £64 a shot. But for a flock of hens I needed nothing at all?

'I live in the centre of town,' I said. My greatest preoccupation since the Warrens' arrival had been whether I was providing them with enough space to qualify as 'free range'. 'My garden isn't big – only about 4 metres by 25 ... '

Lara patiently opened up her files and read out the rules on hen husbandry. According to EU agricultural policy (annex II, point c), I could keep 2500 per hectare. She got out her calculator ... that made 1 hen per 4 square metres. My garden had room for 25 free-range hens. Crikey – what would the neighbours say to that?

A few days later, Lara phoned again. I wondered if somehow the neighbours had got wind of my plans and environmental health was already filing their complaints.

'Just to let you know,' she said, 'that we are getting a lot of enquiries at the moment ...' Surely she was about to say 'so we've decided to licence everyone after all ... £64 per hen'.

'So I thought I should take your address down, and put you on our database. Then if there is an outbreak of bird flu or something, we can come round and show you what to do.'

My conversation with Lara had turned out to be quite a relief. Rather than doing something bad through ignorance, I was doing even better than good. From her calculations, it seemed I was already providing my chickens with more than enough room. Even housing them on a balcony would still have been within the rules. And what about that cock idea? I had spotted some beautiful fellows at the sanctuary, cheaper than the hens.

Even as I was purchasing Roxy and Loxy, it had occurred to me that they might require a male presence in order to lay eggs. When the sanctuary lady failed to mention it, I decided there must be some kind of additive in their feed that provided the necessary hormonal stimulus. But now I knew the council didn't mind me getting a real, live, testosterone package; surely that would be preferable. I could buy one for a fiver and then give Lara another quick call, just to make sure of the bylaws.

In the back of my mind, I recalled Mick Jagger telling me I needed a little red rooster in order for there to be peace in the farmyard. It made sense. Without a cock, Roxy and Loxy had spent a lot of time and effort scrapping. They were fine when out and about in the garden, but I had been shocked at the way they fought over food, or snapped at one another's tails.

God forbid that a human 'hen party' has something to do with this kind of all-female behaviour – the most significant characteristic of such a group being the absence of that one, longed-for and assertive male. In avian hen parties, one female (in our case, Roxy) eventually fights her way to the top. The bigger the flock and the tougher the breed, the more this alpha female will assert her leadership qualities. Some use the exact same tactics their male counterpart might have used – crowing, mating with the others and even growing small spurs on her heels. But unlike the sex-change types, they retain their reproductive abilities. The human equivalent that springs to mind is Margaret Thatcher, 80s shoulder pads and all.

Were I to plant a male in their midst, Roxy and Loxy would cease their scrapping. Roxy the leader would instantly kowtow. And then, in proud assertion of his status, the master would start crowing, quite possibly very loudly indeed.

Like his wild cousins, the male blackbirds and blue tits, a cock needs to make his regular challenge to the world – checking whether a territorial competitor has expired, or a predator is approaching, he is probably letting everyone know that he is bold and brave and prepared to protect his unborn offspring at any cost.

He is also bang on time. A cock's announcing of the dawn has iconic status in our culture, from that weather vane atop a medieval church to the Kellogg's corn flakes packet. The Talmud refers frequently to the virtues of a cock that crows neither too early nor too late: the idea is that we humans must emulate his alertness, that our consciousness should be equally wakeful. He's there in all the Gospels, most famously in the Passion story as told by Matthew (Matthew ch.26, vs.34) when Christ predicts that his old follower Peter will betray him three times before the cock crows. The irony is that although Peter regards himself as utterly alert and faithful, following Jesus to the high priest's palace and attending his night-time trial, it is only when he hears the crowing that he wakes up to the fact that he has indeed betrayed him; but it's too late to go back.

These days, according to the poultry websites you can quash a cock's crow by housing him overnight somewhere light-proof and soundproof: indoors in a dark box or outdoors in a well insu-lated shed.

Not that Jay and I fancied a cock in the kitchen, and we had no shed. A sleeping compartment with a low ceiling might do the trick – he wouldn't be able to crow without stretching up his handsome head. But whenever he was out and about, he was bound to need to show off his vocal abilities. Over time, it might be possible to damp down the noise with judicious planting of bamboo or conifers. Or else we might just have to live with the neighbours' dirty looks and the odd run-in with environmental health.

A friend of mine who wishes to remain nameless went through endless battles because of complaints about his cocks' calls. The council threatened to fine him thousands of pounds; they must have had those bylaws in place that Lara warned me

about; they also harked on a veritable smorgasbord of legislation that these days stands for good citizenship; he threatened to
retaliate under European laws that stipulate certain decibel levels
his cocks could not possibly have attained. Fortunately, the local
Tory MP turned out to be fond of farmyard noises and the case
was dropped.

On this basis, I wondered if we might get more than one.
Contrary to popular belief, this was perfectly possible, as long as
they were the right breed. Partridge Pekin bantams might have
equated well to those mild-mannered fellows Mrs Thatcher
controlled in her cabinet. My friend Sally has three of them; for
the record, she also has neighbours with cocks, which meant that
when they crow, no one can pinpoint the culprit. She didn't intend
to have so many, but someone asked her to hatch some eggs and
once the chicks arrived she let her emotions get the better of her
and failed to cull the males. Out into the garden they went; her
grandchildren christening them The Three Teds. One of them
always takes the lead and the others follow behind as submissive
as can be (clearly there is a pecking order between males too).
Glorious fellows they are, The Three Teds, all decked out in gold
and blue, strutting about the garden, upstaging the herbaceous
borders with their vibrancy.

In purely aesthetic terms, there is nothing more appealing than
a cock to upgrade your garden. Forget that reproduction Venus
de Milo, or even a kitschy gnome. Apart from their disappointing
lack of mobility, those artefacts tend to become submerged in
living, growing things like plants. In contrast, a cock always
makes sure he is noticed.

Of course, his cockiness is well celebrated in our language.
You can cock your hat or your gun; you can be half-cocked,

cock-a-hoop or cocksure; you can cock a snook, or simply cock up. There are cocktails and cockpits and cockneys; there are ball-cocks and stopcocks, weathercocks and peacocks (previously known as peak-cocks). If the word does not originate in the cock itself (for example, the 'cockpit' being the small enclosure where they fight; or 'cockney' being a pejorative meaning 'cock's egg'), it is sure to indicate an erectile nature.

And it is not just in English that the word for a male chicken also refers to the *membrum virile*. In old Hebrew, *gever* refers to the bird, to the phallus and even to 'man' himself.

Ironically, avian cocks may look erect on the outside, but between their legs they have a hole (called the 'vent'), just like hens. It was Annie who taught me this. She's ten.

When Annie and her mother (my friend Katharine) went to buy a couple of Warrens and some Pekin pullets, the breeder said they should take the male bantam as well, free of charge. To Katharine it sounded a bit like the hen market's version of 'three for the price of two'. She tried to resist, but the salesman knew how to tug at both her purse and heartstrings – with his companions gone, he said, the cockerel would be picked on by the rest of the flock. They would be bound to peck him, or maybe worse.

At home, Annie's dad said they should wring his neck and make soup of him, but no one could bring themselves to do it. Such a handsome fellow he was, petrol black with feathery feet and a proudly arching tail. So they named him Brendan and let him out in the garden with the others.

It turned out that Brendan was quite a gentleman – Annie was impressed by the way he called to the hens when he unearthed a tasty slug for them; the way he always let them go first when the corn arrived. Most impressive was the way he defended them from next-door's cocker spaniel when it broke into the garden one day.

Annie said it was horrible to watch – little Brendan fluffing himself up to try and look bigger than he really was; flapping his wings and squawking while the hens hid under a bush. She grabbed at the dog, but he had no collar and escaped from under her hands, lunging at the cock. She screamed and ran inside to warn her mother, but Katharine just told her to be quiet. She didn't believe her.

When Annie came outside again, all she could see was a cloud of soot in the sky – Brendan's feathers, whooshing about. Then she saw that the dog had caught him in his mouth where he lay stiff and motionless. She screamed again, and luckily that startled the spaniel, who dropped his prey and scarpered. It was only when Brendan scuttled into the bushes with the others that she knew he was alive. His tail feathers had all been plucked out, leaving his bum bald as the parson's nose. But at least he was alive.

Annie told me she loved having Brendan for a pet. She found the sound of his crowing 'really beautiful'. When he 'trod' the hens, he always managed to trap them behind the hen house so they had a bit of privacy, she said. She had observed this activity quite carefully and decided that the hens didn't really mind: 'They don't scream – they just get on with it.'

After hearing Annie's stories, I decided the main reason to acquire a cock was for my children's sake. Brendan had furnished her with knowledge otherwise hard to come by when you are only ten. I could imagine our cock serving Ellie and Bea in the same way, and saving me a load of hassle when it came to sex education. When Annie told me that 'cocks don't have willies, they have vents' I was mighty impressed. She blushed only slightly when I asked for more detail – 'Dad told me that when he is shaking her around, his vent meets hers ... the stuff ... the sperm goes into her ... into her egg ... it slides in ... and that's how she gets pregnant!'

It was my multiple-cock-owning friend Sally who disburdened me of the idea that hens need a male presence in order to lay eggs. They don't even need something extra in their feed. They lay perfectly well on their own, thank you very much. In fact, they probably lay better for not being hassled by a randy inseminator.

So there, Mick Jagger and your little red rooster, plus the whole cultural legacy that preceded you. It's not just the weathervanes and the corn flakes packets, Western culture has been confusing people like me right from the start. There he is in Aristophanes' satirical comedy *The Birds*, so grand that he is apparently King of Persia before the reign of Darius. In Plato's *Phaedo*, he flies in at the high-point of the drama where the great philosopher Socrates is committing suicide by hemlock poisoning:

'Crito, we owe a cock to Asclepius; please pay it; don't let it pass.'

There has been much discussion as to why such a wise man should have left the world with this particular statement. Scholars say his cock represents not simply material currency – that it embodies all sorts of moral and existential aspects of life. Personally, I am more inclined to regard the story as evidence that even great philosophers forget to prepare a good exit line.

Tactful as could be, Sally advised that it might be best to drop my plans for getting a cock. She warned that The Three Teds might be beautiful, but in general the male of the species do not make very good pets, sometimes becoming very aggressive, especially during the spring and summer breeding season. No fun at all, especially for small children.

That did it. No way was I having some overrated male icon flapping and clawing at my kids. I decided that, at least at this preliminary stage in my chicken-keeping career, a couple of hens would do.

And so to my cock-less flock. I had purchased two Warrens for my back garden, and from the council's point of view there was no problem in my having done so. Great. But I really did know very little about them. All I had thought when I bought them was that they would make excellent (egg-laying) companions for the bunny. I suppose I associated their name with his home. Or else I reckoned Warren was some antique family name … They looked just like hens in nursery stories, for goodness' sake.

It turns out that Warrens are the commonest commercial strain of laying hen, developed during the 1950s specifically for one thing – battery farming. These days their market name may also be ISA Brown or ISA Warren or Goldline. They must compete with all sorts of other battery birds with attractively bucolic titles – the Meadowsweet Ranger, the Bluebelle and the Speckledy. Goldline and the Heritage Skyline sound ever so posh, and there is real glamour in the Star varieties – Sussex Star, White Star, Black Star, Speckled Star and Amber Star. They are the result of laboratory-based cross-breeding and commonly known as commercial hybrids. There are currently estimated to be 40 billion of them in existence.

I say 'laboratory-based' because they derive from a very particular breeding process, meticulously controlled by scientists. Left to their own devices, chickens (or rather, cocks) tend not to be very discriminating in their choice of sexual partner. Most wild birds are choosy but these *Gallus* types, roaming free in jungles and villages, seem always to have been randomly promiscuous.

This proclivity came to the fore recently when Darwin's convictions about the origins of the domestic chicken were brought into question. Because chicken bones don't preserve well, no one can be certain of the period when she first got clucking. The best the paleontologists can come up with is that it was millions of years ago, somewhere in the tropical forests of South East and South Asia. Nevertheless, Darwin felt pretty certain that her one and only ancestor was the Red Junglefowl (*Gallus gallus*): a beauteous tropical pheasant still to be spotted hiding under trees in Malaysia and Indonesia.

In 2008, Swedish biologist Leif Andersson and his team posed the question – how come that ancestor over there has white legs when our domestic birds have yellow ones?

After extensive research and whatever ancient evidence they could uncover, Andersson's team concluded that an early *Gallus gallus* must have hooked up with a yellow-skinned bird in order for the domesticated one to evolve. The most likely culprit was the Grey Junglefowl (*Gallus sonneratii*): a lesser beauty with groovy yellow stockings, surviving well in many regions of India.

So – right from the start it seems, *Gallus gallus domesticus* was a hybrid, but not a commercial one. Here's an example of the difference: ISA Browns are often referred to as 'sex-linked'. This is to do with their strictly controlled origins, where different genes from their parents are used to determine gender-specific plumage colour. The ISA Brown hybridisation is said to have begun with two old traditional breeds – Rhode Island Red and Rhode Island White. The former possesses a 'gold' gene and the latter a 'silver' one. If you cross a Red mum with a White dad, all the chicks come out pale yellow. However, if you do it the other way around – dark dad and light mum, the boy babies are born yellow because of Mummy's silver gene, but the girls are buff coloured because of Daddy's gold one. This characteristic would be irrelevant in the wild, but is mighty convenient on a mass-production line, because the moment the chicks hatch we can keep the useful girls and chuck the useless boys in the grinding machine. Colour-coded chicks – what could be simpler.

The 'sex-linked' colour of their down is one of the few things we know about breeds like the ISA Brown. Huge commercial hatcheries produce tens of millions of them every year, but as to their exact genealogy – how much they contain of this breed or that, who their parents were and from whence they came … such information is never divulged. You can understand why: there is loads of money at stake. Imagine – if a hatchery creates a bird that can produce not 330, but 350 eggs a year, then all the poultry farms will be after her. A breeding cock, capable of fathering hundreds of thousands of mega-layers, will be kept under high security his whole life long.

Over the decades this lucrative and secretive business has become monopolised by a handful of multinationals. The 'ISA' bit of the ISA Brown, for example, comes from a French company founded in the 70s, merged with another big company called Hubbard in the 90s, merged again in the twenty-first century until it now has operational centres on four continents and produces 50 per cent of the world's hybrid layer population. Meanwhile, smaller operators have been priced out of the market.

Now, perhaps this would matter not one jot were the big corporations to follow the course of nature and keep expanding the gene pool. However, that's not how it works in business. To your average shareholder, a good chicken is not one that adapts to change, or ranges widely, or displays interesting quirks of nature. A good chicken is simply a machine that produces the maximum number of eggs with the minimum amount of fuss. Her qualities come down to things like sex-linking and 'efficient food-conversion' – in other words, not one penny wasted. She must have a docile enough temperament that she doesn't murder her fellows in the cage. In order for her to be fully focused on egg laying, she will have lost much of her mothering instinct. Using an increasingly narrow selection of birds, the hatcheries have gradually winnowed off the genetic codes that determine such characteristics, leaving the rest behind.

At the same time Leif Andersson was checking on the ancient genetic legacy, American geneticist Hans Cheng was doing the same for the contemporary one. For the US Department of Agriculture, he looked at a variety of genes in a few thousand hens. What Cheng discovered was that on average industrial hens lacked at least 50 per cent and sometimes 90 per cent of the diversity of their non-commercial cousins like the wild Junglefowl or the old Silkie breed. The genes they had left might be perfect for the demands of the battery farm, but there was nothing at all in reserve. Where were the rarities to help them survive when a nasty new virus came along? What about that mutating bacterial infection, those unforeseen changes to their diet or environment? What did commercial hybrids have on standby with which to adapt?

According to Cheng, chickens around the world are at increasing risk of something called 'disease shock'. Their lack of genetic diversity, fatally combined with their en masse living conditions, means a new sickness could wipe them out overnight.

I wish I had known this earlier. Had I done my research, I might have said no to Warrens and gone for a truly traditional breed whose precious gene pool needs supporting. There were probably quite a few of them hidden away at the sanctuary where I bought Roxy and Loxy, if only I had known to ask.

The American Rhode Island Red is the old breed my grand-father kept and most people have heard of. From the Netherlands came the Welsummer and the Barnevelder; from France the Maran; Leghorns arrived in the UK from the Italian port of Leghorn, Minorcas from Minorca, Hamburghs from … England. Also originating in England is the Poland. Then there are ones that actually sound like Brits – Old English Game, the Orpington, the Sussex …

Of the 150 registered breeds available in the UK, most were developed through careful cross-breeding during the nineteenth century. They may be referred to as 'pure breeds' but, as we now know, there was never such a thing in chickendom. The reason they were given this title is that during Darwin's period, breeders began the process of genetic control, preventing chickens from randomly interbreeding any more than they had already. Through a rigorous registration process, and the dedicated work of small-scale poultry keepers across the UK, they managed to segregate and protect their fine chicken creations against any more hybridization (natural or laboratorial). Many of these preserved breeds now have their own club and some even have their own heritage-rich website. They certainly look very pretty in the pictures, and would surely have enhanced the garden more than my Little Red Hens.

But they would not have been so easy to care for. As a beginner, I don't think I could have coped with one of those supermodel breeds, prone to all sorts of serious disorders. Marek's disease, infectious bronchitis, Salmonella, coccidiosis, Gumboro disease and epidemic tremor – I wouldn't have known how to recognise symptoms for any of these.

Fortunately, with Roxy and Loxy I didn't need to – they had been vaccinated against them at birth by large-scale spray-misting and, later, in their drinking water. They may have lacked the genes to combat future disaster, but they had taken plenty of medication to withstand quite a raft of present-day nasties. They were also less neurotic than most of their pure-bred cousins, less broody and less likely to escape from the garden by flying. It has to be said, their breeders knew what they were doing when they set about designing a low-maintenance layer.

I wanted my chooks to lay eggs – not just the three or four a week offered by the pure-breeds, but twice that, if possible. Between them, Roxy and Loxy produced at least a dozen a week; in my family's attempts to cut down on environmentally and financially extravagant meat, they met half our needs. I was contented with that. I had imagined that two happily free-ranging hens was all my garden had room for. Even after learning from Lara that I could have multiplied my stock tenfold, I still thought it had been safest to start small-scale.

And safest to shop close to home. From the pure breed websites, it is clear that most specialist keepers live hundreds or even thousands of miles away from my home in the south of England.

What would I have done if I had needed some specialist advice once I got them home? Or needed to re-stock?

Come to mention it, some of these birds are gob-smackingly expensive.

Meanwhile, a foray in the Yellow Pages uncovers various local hybrid agents – the middlemen of the commercial industry. They buy vaccinated one-day-old chicks from one of the gigantic hatcheries, feed them up for a few months (probably keeping them indoors all the while) and then sell them on at 'point of lay' (POL), at between 16 and 22 weeks. Instead of buying my POLs for a tenner from the sanctuary, I could have got them from one of these agents at half the price.

So there it is. Had I sat down and done all the research in advance, I feel that the outcome would most likely have been the same. I would have launched my henkeeping career in exactly the same way – with a pair of cheap and cheerful Warren pullets. I feel bad about Hans Cheng's research – the fact that the breeders have caused such dangerously low diversity. I worry about the potential 'disease shock'. Like so many products of the industrial age, from pesticides to the combustion engine, commercial hybrids may in future prove more destructive than they have been beneficial to life on planet earth. But in the meantime, people like me choose them because they so conveniently meet our needs.

There Ain't Nobody
Here But Us Chickens

...There ain't nobody here at all,
So quiet yourself and stop that fuss
There ain't nobody here but us
We chickens tryin' to sleep, and you butt in
And hobble, hobble, hobble, hobble,
It's a sin.
Louis Jordan

Whether hybrid or pure, a hen needs a house. Unlike her wilder friends and relations, she is unable to create a safe one of her own. Once she became *Gallus gallus domesticus*, she relinquished responsibility to her domesticators.

Bought from the local pet shop or even off the internet, a coop can easily set you back a few hundred quid. Then again, if you want to save that second mortgage for another occasion, it is possible to spend less. Roxy and Loxy's first home was a two-storey hutch which cost nothing because (as its name suggests) it was really the rabbit's

When I first got them home, they were terrified out of their wits after their journey behind me in the car, cramped inside dark and smelly bags. Had I bought them in the late afternoon, it might have been fine – they could have dozed through the whole transition from sanctuary to hutch. As it was, in through the front door I charged around lunchtime, my hen sacks worryingly motionless. Having peered into their depths and established from the pairs of blinking eyes that the contents had not died of fright, what should I have done? Kept them in the hot and noisy house until dark, with the children constantly pestering them, and their droppings piling up? I dumped them in the hutch.

Jay had positioned it in the alleyway down the side of our terraced house, up against a brick wall, easily spied from the kitchen window and heard from our bedroom above. By the next morning we were rather more familiar with our pets' routines than we had anticipated. Snowy the bunny had spent the night thumping his back leg in warning against potential predators, rushing up and down the ladder, in and out of all the rooms. At six in the morning, when at last he settled, the chickens started chattering.

I found Snowy upstairs in his sleeping compartment, as far away from the noise as he could get, and the hens billing and cooing together in the bottom of the hutch. It was like one of those ghastly sleepovers when the children have kept one another awake all night, and everyone is grumpy for days afterwards, especially the parents.

Poultry books advise that you leave your new hens shut away for 24 hours before introducing them to something as overwhelming as your garden. When eventually you open up, they sometimes don't want to come out. At least, not until hunger and thirst eventually compel them to take the plunge. In my case, it was quite the opposite. Gently tucking Roxy under one arm so she couldn't flap, I inserted my fingers between her legs to prevent her scrabbling, just as I had seen the sanctuary lady do. It felt easy, almost as if I might have learnt the technique at my grandfather's heels.

Once the two chooks were out on the lawn and merrily pecking, I left them alone to investigate their new terrain. Only that afternoon, when I went to return them to the hutch, did I wonder if I was quite so knowledgeable about hen handling after all.

As Grandpa had so memorably demonstrated, when it comes to herding chickens, it is no use imitating their rhythm – getting all uppity. You need to stay calm and authoritative and always move slowly. Across the lawn I launched myself, arms outspread, knees bent and feet rolling carefully from heel to toe, hoping I looked a bit like a t'ai chi master. Jay stood guard at the main escape route, garden broom aloft. Perhaps we would have achieved our end, had it not been for our children. Someone had told Ellie she should raise her arms up and down in a vertical plane (apparently it confuses a chicken's vision). This technique, applied with five-year-old enthusiasm and mirrored with sound effects by her little sister, terrified Roxy and Loxy out of their wits. Off they ran, shrieking and flapping – one of them eventually digging herself under the shed, the other sheltering beneath the prickliest, thickest bush.

The first few days the hens were out, it took the whole family a good ten minutes to corner them and carry them back to the hutch. We could have resorted to a big fishing net on the end of a rod, but I reckon that might have frightened them off for ever. Instead we took to scattering a little corn and, while they were scoffing, gently swooping down and catching them. Along with the scattering, I introduced my farmer's wife imitation – *'Here, chick, chick, chick, chick'* which meant that soon enough I was able to impress my friends by simply calling out of the back door and the hens would come running. The daily expectation of delicious seed meant it did not take long for them to learn that being handled was really quite fun.

But being cooped up with rabbit was not. Snowy and the bantams might have looked good together in the shop window, but frankly what did a nocturnal mammal and two diurnal birds have in common? The hens' sleep must surely be wrecked (as was ours) by the rabbit's sport. Eventually I decided they should be separated. On a visit to the local tip I managed to salvage a modest-sized cage (those were the days when health and safety had not yet stepped in to disallow such risk-taking). Plonked on top of the hutch, with a bowl of food and one of water, this became the hens' peaceful new sleeping quarters.

An alternative, were I the DIY type, would have been to imitate my friend Paul from Zimbabwe and make their home myself.

A couple of years ago, as the political situation in his home country worsened, Paul and his wife Sekai made plans to bring their daughters to live in the UK. The children had been staying with family in Zimbabwe since their parents fled eight years previously. During all that time, Paul and Sekai had been in a state of limbo, never knowing from one day to the next if the Home Office might make a decision about their asylum status. They lived in a rented house and had never furnished it nicely or tended the garden, just in case they suddenly had to leave.

Before their daughters Kitty and May were due, a friend offered Paul some hens for which she no longer had room. And he thought – Why not?

In his home village they build houses for chickens out of large stones. About halfway up on the inside they insert horizontal poles that make do as perches. At the top of the four walls they build a frame out of sticks to support a roof made from savannah grass. These African coops look just like mini thatched cottages, standing side by side with the man-sized ones.

For Paul's English version, an old tea chest took the place of stone walls and a piece of corrugated plastic instead of thatch. He stood the chest with the opening facing upwards and cut out parallel elongated triangles from two opposite sides and joined up the lower end of these triangles by removing a rectangular section from a third side. Then he fixed his corrugated plastic across the sloping sides so the rain could drain off. A square of wooden batons attached to the underside of the plastic meant it rested in place and could be lifted to collect eggs or clean the inside. To prevent foxes from nosing it open, the roof was weighed down with bricks.

Bricks also provided the solution for keeping the floor dry – because English ground is so damp, Paul stood his chest on four sturdy brick legs. He cut a little door at the bottom for the hens to come and go, and screwed on metal hinges. Back home, the door would be hinged using strips of rubber from old car tyres; Paul says these are very strong and will keep out all the killers – English foxes are nothing compared to jackals and wildcats and snakes.

In Zim villages, cocks and hens roam freely during the day. Maize is the villagers' staple diet and there are always cobs left over to give the hens; they also get the husks of sunflower seeds, squeezed for cooking oil, and plenty of wildlife from their foraging.

When Kitty and Mary arrived at their English home, the first thing they saw was the chickens, running to welcome them. Paul phoned his parents to say the children had arrived safely, and heard them laugh at the country-clucking noise in the background.

For children with no money for computers or outings, chickens provide some recompense – Kitty and May spend happy hours feeding them, herding them and searching in the undergrowth to find where they have hidden their eggs. Once the children discover that place, the birds always go and lay somewhere else, but it's still fun looking for the new hiding place. Just the other day, the hens found a little grass snake in a bush and tried to kill it. Kitty rescued the reptile and brought it inside, but the chickens weren't having that – they followed, strutting around the kitchen until she gave them back their snake.

Recycled cage or recycled tea chest, the ideal position for a chicken coop is not necessarily down an alleyway at the side of a terraced house. After a good ten months housing our hens there, we had a visit from the next door neighbour. He said they were keeping him awake.

'But they sleep when we do!' I protested.

'Only if you get up at five in the morning!' he retorted.

His proposal was that we send them out of earshot to the end of the garden. I didn't like it. A couple of dozen metres away from the house felt terribly far.

'I have nothing against keeping chickens,' my neighbour proffered. But I felt somehow he must. He probably thought they belonged in a faraway farmyard, not lovingly integrated into domestic life.

I said, 'What about the fox? He doesn't dare come right up to the house, but he's bound to visit them down there.'

'Most people consider it more hygienic to keep their livestock at a distance.'

He sounded like he'd done his research.

Eventually Jay persuaded me that moving Roxy and Loxy was not such a bad idea. And that keeping in with our neighbours was a very good one. In many ways, the rougher, messier nature of the bottom of the garden would suit them better than our patio. Ellie and Bea could think of them as our fairies down there. On a more practical note, the trees and shrubs would provide plenty of shade and wind protection. Being jungle natives, hens get a sense of security from having jungly stuff around them, and I reckoned they were unlikely to spot the difference between a buddleia and a palm.

Then I decided I might as well go the whole hog and splash out on a home designed for chickens rather than for rabbits.

In terms of housing design, chicken coops, like dog kennels, seem not to have advanced with the times. I don't know from which period Paul's stone cottages derive, but the traditional British coop looks decidedly Victorian. There is something just a bit too idyllic about it, reminding one how perfect country life once was compared to our nasty, industrialised cities. If expanded to a human scale, these folksy homes would be the perfect place for Red Riding Hood or Hansel and Gretel. These coops are made of timber which, as every fairytale character knows, needs a regular daubing with weather-treatment to keep it waterproof and prevent it from cracking and warping.

Or else you can forego that pleasure and spend your money on contemporary plastic. For Habitat fans, the eglu is an excellent lifestyle choice for hens. My friend Fiona has two. These smooth capsules, in a range of bright colours, look as though they just landed in her garden from outer space. If you are concerned about sustainability, the label says it is 'made from energy efficient polymers using modern construction techniques; the eglu will last for years and at the end of its life can be 100 per cent recycled.'

If you are really concerned about sustainability, then an even better bet is the Eco Hen House from award-winning Scottish company Solway Recycling. Built from 100 per cent recycled plastic (maybe it's an eglu that got thrown away), in design terms it sits somewhere between the modernist chic of the eglu and the earthiness of a traditional coop. It is quite a bit cheaper than its competitor.

Though not a fan of plastic, even recycled, I appreciated the fact that these contemporary creations were both chicken- and keeper-friendly, with good-sized doors and removable sections for easy cleaning. Fiona said the main advantage over traditional designs was their lack of nooks and crannies, those nailed-down felt-coverings and awkwardly pitched roofs where tiny chicken mite reside. A smooth surface means those mite can never get cosy.

But chickens can. Some people find plastic doesn't adapt to temperature change as well as wood, but Fiona considered her eglus versatile enough. On a really sunny summer's day she might put them in the shade of the trees, and on a horribly cold night she slung a blanket over the top, just in case.

Being a jungle creature, a hen's optimum environmental temperature tends to be that of an average British home – around 21 degrees Celsius. However, on a frosty night it is probably best not to bring her inside, as once she gets used to central heating it could be mighty troublesome getting her to re-acclimatise. Fiona's hens manage to keep their body temperature up during the winter by eating more during the day and huddling in their double-walled eglu at night. They get through the odd cold snap by chasing each other up and down the garden a couple of times a day. Apparently you can protect their combs and wattles from frostbite by daubing them with Vaseline, but Fiona has decided this is more relevant for Iceland than England. She trusts their plumage to do its job just as it would inside her duvet – fluffing up and trapping the body heat.

As long as it doesn't get wet: wet feathers mean chilly chicken. Which is why the coop roof is such an important feature to consider. To keep out the rain, it needs to be well-pitched and close-fitting, but not too close. Paul's square of corrugated plastic was perfect because it had gaps between the ridges to release stale hen-breath. Hens do a lot of breathing. Seriously – they need a lot more oxygen relative to their body-weight than we humans, which perhaps explains why the Victorians introduced good coop ventilation long before they got round to the same in hospitals; it wasn't just because they loved their hens so much. 'Good coop ventilation' means some sort of window, air hole or door, preferably high up, where the bird's breath sails away rather than condensing and creating the moisture that makes her chilly.

Good ventilation also prevents overheating. A hen's normal body temperature is high – around 41 degrees Celsius. Lucky her – it guards against infection. Towards the end of the nineteenth century, when Louis Pasteur was looking for ways to vaccinate against killers like rabies and cholera, he discovered it was this heat that gave chickens their immunity.

But during hot weather a hot body can be problematic. While a duck keeps cool by paddling in cold water, and a human perspires discreetly, a hen must open her beak and pant. Though her tongue is not soft and pink like a dog's, it still manages to do the job – the water vapour rising from its surface to cool her system. Inside a badly ventilated house it will condense, leaving the poor chook prematurely stewed.

Having considered the roof, you need to think about the door. The official term for a hen's front door is the pop-hole – according to the manuals, it should measure no more than an A4 piece of paper and be facing away from prevailing winds. It has either a sliding shutter or a drop-down ramp that opens and closes with the aid of an electric winch-system and a light-sensitive timer to tell it when to do so. One problem with such technology can be if it interprets glowering clouds as darkness and locks your hens outside just as a major storm is breaking. Then you have to go and buy a clock timer, and remember to alter the opening and closing times for British Summer Time.

Personally, I was not attracted to all this gadgetry. I rather enjoyed the old-fashioned ritual of shutting up my hens at night and letting them out first thing in the morning. My new coop required nothing fancier than what I had previously in the cage – a front door with a serviceable catch.

I did need to improve on the perching facilities. Though Roxy and Loxy had managed for a year without one, a rod of wood is pretty essential for happy hendom. Like all birds, a branch (however high) is where they feel safe from predators while they sleep. In conventional coops it is generally positioned at least ten centimetres from the floor and is four centimetres wide, slightly rounded at the sides for easy gripping. If you can find a branch of similar dimensions, hens apparently prefer it to the machine-made version – they like to exercise their toes around its nobbles and bends; their wild ancestry feels safest with something asymmetrical. Each bird needs about a span's length of rod or branch; give them much more and they will simply huddle together at one end. They do poo in their sleep, which is why the perch needs to be raised high enough for them not to be sitting all night in their own mess. It should also be easily removable for cleaning, with newspaper or a droppings tray underneath.

One essential my rabbit cage had not lacked was the sleeping compartment. Not that sleeping was what Roxy and Loxy used it for. It was where they deposited their eggs.

If you have ever taken children on a farm visit, you will have come across nesting boxes. They are the sticking-out bits at the back of the hen house where the children are encouraged to form an orderly queue. Have you seen the henkeepers' trick? Under the lid of the nesting box, little Jenny discovers a lovely warm egg; she lifts it out, proudly presents it to the keeper and turns away, satisfied her job is done. Just at that moment, and before little Jimmy shuffles to the front of the queue, the very same egg (freshly warmed by Jenny's hot little hand) slides back under the lid.

In essence, the nesting box is a convenient way for the henkeeper to collect his or her booty. If it is the darkest place the hens can find, then they feel compelled to lay there, foolishly assuming that darkness means privacy. Paul's tea chest did not have one, which is why his hens imitated their Junglefowl ancestors and laid their eggs under bushes.

The ideal nesting box should be neither too big nor too small – its dimensions are roughly what you need to store half a dozen bottles of wine. Like Goldilocks, a hen needs to feel just right in there. And like baby bear, she shouldn't mind sharing her facility, though some of the larger coops provide several boxes.

To stop a hen using her nesting box as a toilet, it's useful to have some sort of shutter to close it off. The floor needs to be lined with something to give the eggs a soft landing – shredded bank statements might suit the contemporary chic of the eglu. Of the more organic options, untreated wood shavings are the least mite- and mould-friendly, but straw gives it that real-nest look. Hay can contain fungal spores that give chickens respiratory problems.

As for the outdoor space, like Paul's chickens, mine used to run straight out of their sleeping quarters into the garden. However, if avian flu comes along and the Department for Environment, Food and Rural Affairs (DEFRA) gets its act together, this kind of free-ranging will become illegal. It is already so for people who mind about the lawn.

All hens, especially hybrids, get their kicks by scoffing grass and scratching up grubs – so much so that within a shockingly short amount of time Roxy and Loxy rendered our few square metres of grass post-Apocalyptic. Having made the decision to exile them to the bottom of the garden, the best damage limitation I could think of was to confine their foraging. Fortunately, that area was well-drained – boggy land is more easily infected with parasites and generally unpleasant underfoot.

The most conventional way to confine a flock is to fix a run to their coop. If DIY Paul had had more time, he might have knocked one up for me using timber and wire mesh. Jay did offer, but I decided instead to go internet shopping, and thereby discovered the amazing array available.

Some looked modest enough, with walls only a couple of feet high and a mesh roof so Mr Fox couldn't hop in and Roxy and

Loxy couldn't hop out. Some had no roof at all, which looked inviting to Foxy, unless you had Colditz-style fencing around your garden. Others were more of an aviary – totally enclosed and tall enough to walk around in. Some versions were interlocking, so you could expand or contract the space to suit your flock. Some came with a coop that had two pop-holes; you took it in turns to attach the run to whichever side you were using.

This last design is where the concept of rotation comes in. The idea is that after a certain amount of time being scratched and pecked and pooed-on, the limited area inside the run is wrecked. If by some miracle the grass has survived, it may well be singed by the burning effect of nitrates from the droppings; it possibly also harbours nasty parasites and infectious diseases. In winter, this patch could do with a break even though the grass won't grow back – an opportunity to give it a sprinkling of lime to help reduce the acidity of the soil created by the droppings. Hens should be kept away from the limed area for a good month afterwards, as lime is bad for their tummies. Strictly speaking, for the ground to fully recover, it needs a good few months' rest, which means rotating the run to four separate areas. Many people make do with two.

My problem was that even with a two-patch rotation, most of these coop-run-combos were too big to fit in the bottom of my garden. As every estate agent knows, in these crowded British Isles every metre counts. So how was I going to give Roxy and Loxy room to roam?

In his marvellous 1920s tome, *Fowls and How to Keep Them*, Rosslyn Mannering describes Londoners 'successfully managing and rearing' chickens on their roofs. One of my ambitions was to find a creative carpenter to build a coop-run combo for my friend

Esther who lives in a top-storey flat off the Marylebone Road. I was sure Esther's balcony was big enough for some sort of multi-storey structure where a couple of happy hens could run around and scratch, have perches and nest boxes and all the things they love. If land-dwelling *Homo sapiens* can live in vertical formation, then how much more easily should *Gallus gallus domesticus* manage it, with that urban jungle heritage.

In the meantime, the most high-rise accommodation I could come up with was on a mere two storeys – sleeping and nesting quarters above and a run below. Apart from its obvious space-saving features, a major asset was the way the upper room protected the run beneath. Neither rain nor frost nor blazing sun was going to hinder my hens' daytime activities. It was also the kind of cover my friend Lara and her bosses at DEFRA would be insisting on if avian flu came along.

Having inspected numerous two-storey arrangements, I eventually decided on a sturdy triangular structure called an Ark. At over £400, it was one of the most expensive on the market but after almost a year of henkeeping I felt confident I was in it for the long run; the time had come to invest in infrastructure. My Ark came with excellent credentials from a company with 30 years' experience, and the word 'Ark' reassuringly in their title – *Forsham Cottage Arks*.

The Boughton, as mine was named, looked like a mini mountain hut – rather than Red Riding Hood, it would make a perfect home for Heidi. Its steeply sloping sides were originally intended not for snow but to prevent sheep climbing up. A pair of smooth handles sticking out either end meant it could be carried between two adults, or dragged by one when the hens needed 'rotating'. The walls were mesh on the run downstairs turning to solid slats of red pine upstairs. One of the walls was fitted with handles so I could lift out the whole side to clean. A nesting box hidden under the eaves had a ventilation hole at the top and its own little door that slotted in and out – perfect for childish hands in search of eggs. At either end, the bottom section of wall slotted in and out and was held in place with a couple of revolving catches.

Many people recommend replacing simple catches like this with bolts and padlocks. If you don't believe me, take a look at the Poultry Websites and you will find numerous missives from devastated correspondents who pottered out one morning as usual, only to find someone had nicked their flock.

Living in a terraced house, I did not feel too vulnerable to the chicken thieves. Nevertheless, if my hens had been costly pure-breeds I think I would have invested in locks. The birds exhibited at poultry shows are apparently particularly vulnerable because thieves are on the prowl there, getting details of where to come and steal them; unless such birds are microchipped, they are quite easily sold on. If I had owned a charismatic gamefowl I might have gone for the whole security shebang – wireless infrared alarms or even CCTV. Though illegal for more than 150 years, cockfighting is still popular in the UK and the owners of the most vicious fighters make good money.

I think the name 'Ark' appealed to me on security grounds. I rather fancied it as an Ark of the Covenant, containing something precious and awe-inspiring. And like Noah's, it would surely protect its contents, if not from the flood then at least from the fox.

My modern-day Noah arrived from Worcestershire with his walls flat-packed in the back of the van. By the time his creation was erected, it was clearly never going to get back through the house again. Ah well. If ever Jay and I sold up, an extra hen-home at the end of the garden might prove an asset. It certainly looked good – like the beginnings of a miniature Alpine village, its pine walls melding with the surrounding tree trunks.

That evening, as Roxy and Loxy were nodding off in their cage, one by one I carried them gingerly to their new quarters. I wasn't sure how I was going to get them on to the perch if, after so many months in the cage, they had lost the skill. For all I knew, they might never have had it, as I hadn't noticed any perches at the sanctuary. With the side-wall of the Ark removed, I eased them on to their rod of wood and watched fascinated as their perching reflex curled each claw tight and each ruffled body found its balance.

Between the two storeys of their new home hinged a solid ladder that levered up and down from the outside by means of a cord fixed over a hook on the roof. I raised it to the closed position to keep out night-time draughts and perhaps even a predator or two. In the morning I went out to unhook it and watched my duo scramble downstairs to their daytime quarters. This seemed absolutely natural to them, just as it was natural to take themselves upstairs to bed at night – like all the other birds and even me.

In my opinion, whoever designed the Chicken Ark really worked hard to combine its inhabitant's needs with her keeper's. Accessible and mobile for me, it provided all that Roxy and Loxy could wish for, including a sheltered play-area.

By the end of the very first day, they had dug themselves a sand-pit and were playing at stuffing their bodies with dirt. Under their wings and between their feathers it went; once they could feel it close to their skin, they would scrabble themselves deeper and deeper into the trough formed by their bodies, sometimes rolling right on to their backs, legs absurdly akimbo. I loved to watch them curling and stretching, drawing the earth up under their arms and letting it fall away again like so many waves of imaginary water.

Historians tell us that when the Emperor Napoleon was on campaign and had nowhere to wash, a valet used a 'flesh-brush' to clean his bare skin. It is to this same practical end that a hen takes a dust bath. After much rolling and flailing, the grit falls away, carrying with it all the bits and pieces that have been itching her – especially mites and lice.

Of course, a mud bath is not the same thing at all. Which is why the British climate is not brilliant for hens, who would far prefer the Med if only they knew. Though the Ark run was sheltered, still the rain managed to angle itself to enter through the mesh, and seep in from surrounding land. When things got really soggy, I threw in some wood chips – they soaked up most of the mud. In autumn I raked up fallen leaves and bagged them for the same purpose. I know now that my original ruse of chucking in bark chips that would otherwise have mulched my allotment was not a good idea – they can carry a dangerous fungus.

In defiance of my nation's weather, I set about creating my own dust bath. Into an old plastic seed tray I shovelled a mixture of topsoil and silver sand (not builder's, the chemicals therein cause all sorts of bother), which was the grittiest combination I could come up with. This I placed against the solid end-wall of the run, to shelter it from the prevailing wind (and rain). If ever it got wet, I chucked the contents on the flowerbeds and refilled it. In winter, when we had wood fires indoors, I added cinders swept from my hearth. Chicken bliss.

The one and only EU stipulation with which I could not comply was the one given me by Lara from the council regarding space. To qualify as free-range hens, Roxy and Loxy were meant to have 8 square metres of run (4 per bird). Mine measured only half that. And they did look cramped in there, side-stepping along the mesh walls from morning till night.

My solution? After all that fuss about the lawn, I gave in and let them run free in the garden during the day. But this time I blocked off the bits I could not longer bear to see bald.

Chicken Feed

We got ground to dig
And worms to scratch
It takes a lot of sitting
Getting chicks to hatch
Louis Jordan

H aving splashed out on my Ark, it seemed only right and proper to acquire complimentary feeding kit. For a whole year Roxy and Loxy had made do with entirely inadequate facilities – an old bowl for drink, another for food; grain and water constantly spilling and mixing to a gruel under their feet. The next step on from this would be to acquire 'Grub and Glug' pots from the makers of the trendy eglu – a pair of hollow orbs, moulded together like some disembodied bosom. My friend Fiona recommended them, but I decided I needed a system where feeder and drinker were entirely separate. Attached to the wall of the run was a hopper for the hens' feed. To keep the water clean, I fancied a classic half-gallon water fountain.

I could have bought a cheap one made of white plastic that you fill (somewhat awkwardly) upside down, but it would soon have worn out and didn't have much aesthetic appeal. For my money, the one made of solid galvanised steel set much the highest standard in industrial chic. Shaped like a hurricane lantern, this prop would look great swinging from my hand on my daily trips down the garden.

It was also a clever piece of design technology. Near the bottom of the main cylindrical can was a little hole where water could trickle out into the surrounding trough. Over it slid an outer cylinder (with the handle at the top) that revolved a few degrees into slots to hold it in place. As the water rose high enough to cover the little hole, it created a vacuum, thereby halting the outward flow.

According to Rosslyn Mannering's *Fowls and How to Keep Them*, it is possible to make a simple home-made version of this on the same principles using a bottle, inverted and hung in a metal bracket over a shallow pan. Had I not been on a spending spree, I might have tried it. Instead, I decided that the half-gallon galvanised water fountain was an excellent investment that would last a lifetime (mine, not theirs).

The day it arrived, Roxy and Loxy somehow managed to kick dirt and poo into the trough, and continued to do so on a daily basis. My solution was to raise their drinker out of the firing line, on to a couple of bricks. Nevertheless, I found that every time I refilled it I needed to scrub out both inner and outer cylinder. For this purpose I posted an old washing-up brush by the outdoor tap, and on occasions even took the bottle of Fairy Liquid with me to knock back the algae.

Just like humans, hens thrive on clean water. If it is frozen over on a cold winter morn, I add boiling water from the kettle and watch it steam. For something even fancier, I sometimes add a tablespoon of cider vinegar to keep the poultry in tip-top condition. For a while I added a special tonic that gave it a pretty pink glow (the water, not the poultry) – a teaspoon-full for every couple of litres. The label on my bottle said the ingredients were 'water, sugar and minerals'. I was interested in its high iron content (1,000 mg per kg, apparently); it also contained phosphorus, manganese and copper – Cheers!

Watch carefully while a hen is drinking, and you will see how supple is her neck, slinking in and out as she scoops up water. Because her tongue is less malleable than ours, she cannot easily direct a mouthful of liquid towards her gullet. She needs the help of gravity. Back her head tosses, beak wide, allowing the water to slip down her open, upstretched throat like a Cossack quaffing vodka.

When it comes to her eating style, the similarity is with a less assertive sort of human being: as the proverb tells us – she is toothless. Or, to be more precise – her one and only tooth is for piercing her shell at birth; it falls off her beak after about a week.

According to the paleontologists, until about 80 million years ago hens' teeth were not so scarce, and more recently someone succeeded in reactivating the dormant tooth gene, stimulating some unhatched chicks to grow a full set of ivories. Unfortunately, all these little mutants died before they hatched, so for the next few million years the proverb will still hold. And the hen will continue to make do – firstly with a sharp beak that is extremely adept at slicing off whatever morsel of slug or grass she fancies; secondly, with her little pointy tongue that tilts that morsel down her slippery gullet.

And then what happens? One important characteristic a chicken does not share with a human is a stomach. Instead, she has a two-part mechanism: a storage sack called a crop, and a primitive food mixer called a gizzard. As she forages, the un-chewed food gathers in the crop positioned down her front where a bib might otherwise hang. Pick up a hen that has just eaten corn or pellets, and you will be able to feel the ball of grains she has accumulated there. Slowly (normally when she is asleep), the food passes from the crop into a glandular stomach where digestive acids and enzymes moisten it and start to break it down before continuing on to the gizzard. This horny bag the size of a golf ball functions with the help of a load of grit that she has swallowed on her rounds. Its muscles expand and contract, jiggling the grit around and thereby mashing her feed as her ancient teeth might once have done.

And if it's not slug or grass she is sending down there, then like as not it's something that her keeper supplied in her hopper. Chicken feed. In everyday English, this word may suggest something inconsequential and trifling, but for the dedicated chickenkeeper, that couldn't be further from the truth.

By the time Roxy and Loxy came to live with us, just like every hybrid POL before them, they had been weaned off their baby food and on to what is termed 'compound feed'. Produced in a factory and containing all the nutrients required by a hybrid layer, this is the most convenient form of chicken feed, used by farmers and small-holders alike. Basically, it is a man-made mega-fuel.

Compound feed comes in two forms – 'layers' pellets' and 'layers' mash'. The difference between pellets and mash is much the same as that between cubed or granulated sugar – the former has been squeezed by a machine into bite-sized chunks. Because of the work that has gone into shaping them, pellets are slightly more expensive, but considered by poultry farmers to be more convenient because the nutrition is at its most concentrated. Some people recommend mash for birds confined to a run because it takes them longer to eat, giving them less time to get bored, poor things. It needs to be stirred before placing in the hopper because the calcium content may have dropped to the bottom.

My first 20kg of pellets cost less than a tenner and came with Roxy and Loxy from the sanctuary. The lady there advised me not to bother weighing the feed when I gave it to them – just to top up the feeder whenever it became empty. I had bought it with an accompanying sack of corn, but when I scattered the mixture for the hens, they always picked out the tasty seeds and left the weird-looking pellets behind. If I could have been bothered, I would have given them pellets in the morning and corn as a treat in the afternoon. In the end I gave up the corn option – after all, 'compound feed' meant the pellets were designed to serve all their nutritional needs. I thought I might just take a look at the label and see what that entailed.

The first ingredients were *Lutein* and *Zeaxanthin* from marigold extracts and *Citranaxanthin* from citrus fruits. Talk about 'compound feed'! It's not the hen that benefits from these, but rather the person who eats her eggs. All three are versions of *Xanthophyll* – the chemical compound that gives yolks their yellow colour (and which free-range hens pick up from grass and other greens). In fact, they provide no nutritional value for either creator or eater, but they do make breakfast more aesthetically pleasing.

Then came the main ingredients – the filling carbs: barley, maize and wheat. Then 'non-GM soya' for much-needed protein, a 'vegetarian vitamin mineral pre-mix' (meaning the vitamins didn't have a gelatine coating), plus *dicalcium phosphate* (for general wellbeing, especially bones) and limestone (for good, strong egg shells).

The label also reassured me that my pellets contained 'no hexane-extracted ingredients'. Apparently, the solvent hexane is used to extract the goodness from the soya bean meal and may be carcinogenic. I think probably consumers are worrying about hexane getting into their own food rather than their pets', but I could be wrong.

For the hens' sake, a 'best before' label warned me when the pellets might start to give them a tummy ache. This tended to be around three months from the manufacturing date (and, with any luck, the date when I bought my sack), which was another reason not to supplement with corn as it took all that time for my two to use up one sack. I could have bought smaller bags, kindly filled by my local pet shop owner: that's if I wanted to pay twice the price. Instead, I tried to be organised about buying a new 20kg sack only when the previous one was finished and always checking the 'best before' label.

I stored my pellets outside in a steel bin. My plastic bin with clip fasteners was probably more airtight but a ravenous mouse or rat could have gnawed its way through the bottom, so instead I used that one for bedding. There they stood, my two bins, side by side outside the kitchen window, like a pair of sentinels keeping guard over my Good Life.

Except that when you look into it, soya-based feed is not such a good thing at all.

The first problem is that it has to be imported. Unfortunately, Great Britain does not have a suitable climate for growing soya, not even in poly-tunnels. The closest place is Italy, but the Italians can't produce nearly enough to fulfil our needs. UK companies that use soya, not just in processed animal feeds but in human ones too, have to go to faraway places like Canada or China and in the process give their products a socking great carbon footprint.

But it's worse than that. Over the past couple of decades, Europeans have got very worked up about the genetic modification of soya seed. Meantime, the Americans get along nicely with their fully modified version, exporting enough of it to satisfy 46 per cent of the world soya market (and, incidentally, raising the seed price extortionately). People who are passionately against GM may well be eating US soya unknowingly, hidden away in burgers and biscuits and breakfast cereals. But they are also driving an expansion in demand for non-GM soya by 10 per cent a year.

And how can this demand be met? If people like me want to pay less than a tenner for a sack of non-GM soya feed, we need it grown somewhere cheap, somewhere warm and somewhere big enough to continue expanding production. Where better than that vast tract of virgin land, the Amazon rainforest?

I have been there – a couple of weeks living in a hammock on a steamboat; never had I seen a place more teaming with life, more throbbing with fecundity. That rainforest is home to nearly a tenth of the world's mammal population and a staggering 15 per cent of the world's known land-based plant species. It is also home to the Amazonians themselves: my boat was their means of transport; a trip to market meant several days on board, often with all the family. Dressed in jeans and T-shirts, they brought with them sacks of firewood or fruit or turtle meat, returning home with computers and televisions. By day they hung about in the heat, playing cards and gossiping, often three or four to a hammock. By night they drank home-made *cachaça* and taught me to dance lambada on the roof of the boat. They were cheerful but life was hard in the face of the usual problems: poverty and HIV.

Then came the soya boom. Faced with some feed merchant's contract, my steamboat companions must have leapt at the opportunity. At last they would be able to afford medication; an education for their children. All they had to do was slash and burn the forest to make way for the crop. No one said anything about the longer-term effects of polluting the waterways and eroding the soil.

Just to add insult to injury, these soya plantations turn out to have a major impact on global warming. Forget ocean algae or oak woods or any other form of carbon capture – the Amazon rainforest absorbs carbon dioxide faster than anything. It is the carbon sink of the world. In destroying it, we are exacerbating the problem of climate change in a really big way.

Which is why that innocent bin of mine was not really a sign of the Good Life at all.

When I started telling my chicken-keeping friends about the bad, bad soya industry they were concerned. A few were appalled. But all of them told me there was no alternative.

'You don't want to mess with a hybrid's diet,' they said. 'She needs really good protein to produce all those eggs.'

I said, 'But couldn't we find some other source of protein?'

They said, 'Don't you remember BSE?!'

Before BSE, most of the protein in industrial animal feed (including layers' pellets) came from meat by-products like bone and fat. It took all those spongy brains to teach us that it is not such a great idea for animals to eat one another.

'But have you ever heard of mad-hen disease?' I asked.

'We need to look after the food chain,' said my friends, gravely.

'What about looking after the rainforest?'

'If you think about it,' said one, 'a daily egg is such a miraculous feat that it is bound to require some sort of sacrifice!'

Maybe I needed to try a different tack.

'This is industrially processed food,' said I. 'The amount of grief I get keeping my daughters away from that stuff because it's bad for the environment, bad for them, and not even as tasty as the food I can cook myself!'

No one could disagree with that. When you looked at those pellets, so rigidly uniform, so dusty and unappetising, you didn't even think McDonald's; you thought supplements. They were the sort of things astronauts took when stranded in outer space, not what any sane being would choose to eat in the comfort of her own home. For Roxy and Loxy, the equivalent of outer space might have been the anonymity of their destined battery farm, but they hadn't gone there; they had ended up living with me, in my home.

And I had ended up eating their eggs. When you taste something salmony in a shop-bought egg, it is probably because of something its mother has been eating. And that isn't salmon; it's soya. According to the latest research, there is a problem in the way some hens metabolise seeds like rape and soya – it seems to cause their intestinal microbes to form fishy-tastes in the eggs. Yuck.

My friends conceded that I had a strong case. They agreed that my home was not a production line; it was one place where I could positively eschew the evils of industrial agriculture. They agreed that Roxy and Loxy did not particularly like eating pellets, and that salmon-flavoured eggs were disgusting. They were unconvinced I would come up with an alternative. But I wasn't.

It didn't take much surfing to discover that, in fact, people in the agricultural industry were already trying to do something about our dependence on soya. In the US, the law allowed farmers to feed their poultry on pellets made from 'spent hens'. That did not feel like a solution for me, but an interesting challenge for the BSE/food-chain folk.

A bit more surfing and I discovered that tests were underway in Europe to try and establish how locally grown beans can provide sufficient protein for high-performers like Roxy and Loxy. One of the problems the researchers have come up against concerns herbicides and pesticides: where soya requires minimal use (that's GM for you), peas and beans need loads. On the plus side, their production is less energy-intensive than soya-bean meal, partly because the seed doesn't have to travel halfway round the world. Most importantly, we don't have to destroy our carbon sink for them.

Even closer to home, I found that the organic grocer Abel & Cole was successfully fattening up its 'rainforest-friendly chicken' on a mixture of peas and beans, wheat, rape and sunflower seed. I reckoned a small-scale urban henkeeper might take a tropical leaf out of their book.

Next stop – the feed merchants. The same company that supplied my pellets would happily sell me sacks of 'super mixed corn'. A kind of muesli, it contained whole grains like barley and wheat as well as peas, though its label did warn that it would NOT provide a 'nutritionally balanced diet'. What this meant was that my hens needed to supplement their breakfast cereal with extra amino acids. Additional forms of protein.

Of course, before either industrial animal-product or soya came along, a major source of protein for hens was the world around them. It was just as well Roxy and Loxy still had access to a large chunk of my garden – I loved to watch them as they ventured forth from their run, snatching at leaves, flitting their little heads all the while to keep an eye out for predators, just as their jungle ancestors must have done.

Most of their protein-rich food came from scratching away the surface of my flowerbeds. Scratching was a whole technique in itself – how each bird would lower her centre of gravity slightly in order to stay stable, her head still up and alert. Out those big feet shot behind her, one by one – sweep, sweep, she shifted the ground aside, exposing fresh earth beneath. Only then did she risk a look downwards – quick as a flash, that squirming grub was in her beak and her head was up again. Sweep, sweep; off she went again.

Each time they were out in the garden and caught a juicy worm or a centipede, their amino acid count must have soared. In summertime, they were picking up all sorts of bugs as well – daddy long legs were particularly popular. Foraging like this was excellent exercise, and probably my chickens' favourite form of entertainment. It was infinitely preferable to those pellets.

And there were ways to improve the foraging potential in the garden. For starters, Jay and I should leave the lawn un-mown; even bounded as it was by chicken wire, long grass was the perfect breeding place for bugs. The roses would be left to ramble, as would the clematis and hop and jasmine. When I pruned the buddleia or the fruit trees, instead of packing them laboriously into the council waste bag, I would henceforward leave branches and foliage stacked against the fence so that tasty beasts might gather there. It was a very attractive prospect knowing that the less I tended things, the more bountiful would they prove.

I also realised that behind every flowerpot and under every slab hid a delicious meal or two. I found gathering up slugs and snails and feeding them to the hens much more satisfying than scattering poison. I even endeared myself to my neighbours by inviting them to lob theirs over the fence. The children found great entertainment in herding the chickens towards the latest crop of molluscs and watching them tweezer them from their shells, or simply thrash them against the patio.

The other protein-packed delicacy on the menu was frogs. If the chickens were rummaging around near the pond and I heard a noise like a rubber bath toy being squeezed, I knew they had found one and were starting to torture it to death. I did try to intervene – I like frogs.

But hang on a moment. Was 100 square metres of city garden really enough space in which to forage all the protein they needed? If they were NOT getting that 'nutritionally balanced diet', how would I know? Might they even stop laying?

Back at my computer, I searched out the Eden Farm research centre not far from my home and put my question to their hen specialist. Her immediate response was that the likelihood of Roxy and Loxy stopping laying was very small. Hybrids are genetically predisposed to produce more than 300 eggs a year, she reminded me; if they are getting a poor diet, then it shows up not in a reduction in number but in the condition of the eggs. After a moment of deliberation she confirmed –

'I think all a lower-protein diet might cause is smaller eggs.'

'That's fine by me,' I said, 'my family rather likes them small'.

But then I had the idea of protein-rich milk products. Hens just love buttermilk, as any Victorian fattening up their Sunday roast will tell you. What I could offer was the remains of the children's breakfast cereal, doused in cow's milk. Plus the dregs of each bottle, washed around with a little water. This I poured over whatever leftovers were hanging around in the kitchen.

Ah, leftovers. Some people feel that they are not acceptable food for chickens. I have heard it said that hens 'are not rubbish bins'; that giving them scraps is somehow undignified and dirty. One book I read said no more than one fifth of your flock's diet should be made up of scraps, though weighing them to find out struck me as unnecessarily arduous.

I have always been keen on leftovers. Born in the 60s to a family not fully recovered from wartime frugality, I fell in happily with childhood diktats about not wasting food. As Great Britain entered a new era, where the average household threw away at least a third of its food, I was stubbornly reheating yesterday's pasta.

And then my children came along. Most mealtimes young Beatrice would change her mind several times about what brand of cereal she liked, whether she wanted pesto on her spaghetti after all, whether potatoes were actually quite disgusting ... Argh! Loxy and Roxy arrived just in time to save me from a tsunami of leftovers. As I scraped the food from my daughter's plate, a huge consolation was that at least my chooks would gobble it up. I even used this fact as an effective taunt – any hint of 'I don't like it,' being met with 'Great, the chickens will!' and miraculously the meal became acceptable after all.

But an invitation to other people's meals could be testing. I cringed at the sight of all that precious food being tipped into the bin; meanwhile Bea grinned – at last Mummy was facing the fact that she was seriously out of touch with the zeitgeist. I stood my ground: how could people donate £500 a year to the starving nations and yet chuck away food worth triple that? How could Bea's nursery school be making all that effort to raise funds for Save the Children when the slop bucket from dinnertime could feed a whole refugee camp?

Slop bucket. If you have ever read *Charlotte's Web*, you will recall an intelligent pig's point of view on slops: a veritable smorgasbord of pleasures. With BSE the bottom dropped out of the slops market, leaving Chinese takeaways drowning in oceans of wasted pig feed. Poultry farmers say they never really liked it because it does what it says on the label – it slops about. It also rots a lot quicker than dry feed.

But in the comfort of your own home, why not go sloppy? I would like to start a campaign to bring back slops. I would dearly like to keep a pig and feed it on all the food Bea's school throws out. My lesser achievement (so far) has been to give some to the hens. I took to presenting the teacher with an empty bucket twice a week, and the dinner ladies filled it for me with whatever scraps remained on the children's plates.

The quantity of food I carried home was far more than we could use. When I thought about it, the frugal bit of me was angered by the sheer profligacy of this generation who thought meals were for throwing away. The more tender-hearted bit thought such an excessive volume of leftovers might be my fault: early on in my campaign I had given the children a talk about chickens' favourite foods being exactly the same as theirs (Cheerios, raisins, cherry tomatoes, that sort of thing). I printed out some photos of Roxy and Loxy eating these treats and the teacher kindly posted them on the wall where everyone could enjoy them. Young Ben was so inspired he even took to bringing in what was left of his supper in a little plastic bag – noodles, rice, pizza … Perhaps it was generosity of spirit that motivated these children to leave their meals on their plates.

The teacher was ever so keen on the ritual; she typed up and laminated a list of foodstuffs that should stay OUT of the bucket – banana peel; rotten or dirty food; citrus (especially orange peel); and meat. She ruled that salty food was a bad idea for both chickens and children, so were whole raw potatoes, and so was too much acid all at once (like cooking-apple peelings).

As for the hens – they were in ecstasy. Normally, I would say they were dainty eaters, but served with nursery leftovers it was a different matter altogether. Suddenly each one transmogrified from gentle herbivore to vicious carnivore. Grabbing a chunk of food in her beak, she drew it away from the plate, blocking out that other vulture with her body so there was less chance of competition. Rip, thrash, gulp. Then back she came for more.

Only once she had finished off all the choicest delicacies did she wander away to wipe clean the blade of her beak. First the right side and then the left – Swipe, swipe, against a branch or a rock. Swipe, swipe again. Having indulged in such filthy feasting, she was meticulous about returning to her pristine form.

*

I must admit I did not keep to the school rules about leftovers. The no-meat rule was to show that the teacher and I were well aware of fears about BSE. However, having discovered that American hens were officially allowed to eat one another, at home I did let the odd bit of chicken meat fall into my slops bucket. Sausage-ends and lasagne often found their way there too. Though I did avoid feeding the hens whole raw potatoes, one of their favourite things was potato peelings zapped poison-free and soft with a few minutes in the microwave.

The most abundant foodstuff in the school bucket was carrot, chopped into unnaturally uniform orange sticks. I was keen to offer it to the hens in large amounts, aware that carrot is regarded as a natural way to purge their system of worms. Unfortunately, the sticks proved as inedible to Roxy and Loxy as they had done to the children.

They were much keener on discarded sandwiches. Some people say you should not feed chickens bread because it gives them a tummy ache, yet we all know from childhood how their duck cousins love it. I decided that mouldy bread was a bad idea, but a modest amount of stale sandwiches or cake soaked in milk was a delicacy I couldn't deny my birds. In fact, according to the Roman, Cicero, if fed on soft cake, a hen can be effectively consulted as an oracle (*de Divinatione* – *Concerning Divination,* Book Two). When you need a prediction, you open up her cage and feed her the cake. If she stays in her cage, makes noises, beats her wings or flies away, the omen is bad; if she eats greedily, it is good.

Of course, in this day and age we are more aware of the dangers of a carbohydrate-heavy diet. Frankly, no hen (even one offering a good omen) should stuff herself too full with it, or else she will miss out on more nutritious alternatives. I think this means offering things like bread and cake often enough that she never feels the need to be greedy. I once stayed with a peasant farmer on the island of Ischia who cooked up a huge vat of pasta every morning for himself, his dogs, his cats and his hens. After such a hearty all-Italian breakfast, the hens spent the rest of the day rooting out slugs and snails and other goodies from the surrounding fields. They were in noticeably excellent health, and their eggs were scrumptious.

I didn't keep pasta in my kitchen cupboard especially for my hens, but I did get a stash of porridge oats. When I first acquired Roxy and Loxy it was wintertime and a hen-loving friend recommended cheering them up by giving them a hot meal each morning. I remembered how my grandfather used to go to quite a bit of bother, putting yesterday's kitchen scraps in a saucepan and boiling them to a stinking gruel. Me, at breakfast time I did my twenty-first century thing and whacked some oats, water and a little milk in the microwave, along with whatever tasty morsels were hanging around from the night before. Often I delivered the dish so piping hot that my diners had to throw it all around to cool it down.

From a chef's point of view, hens are easy to cook for because, unlike children, they have very few tastebuds. Where the average child will have around 10,000, a chicken has only a couple of dozen, situated at the base of her tongue and down her pharynx. It seems that nature has granted her only enough taste awareness to avoid the bitterest of plants that might poison her. There is variation from hen to hen – for example, some are happy to down the spiciest of curries, while others would reject it. But generally speaking, potent foods can bypass her taste system with alarming ease.

It was intriguing what exactly Roxy and Loxy were getting out of their favourite foods. I suspected that the attraction of little treats like tomatoes and raisins was mainly in their size and texture. The oat porridge was warm and comforting in their gizzards. The poultry spice I added to their mixed corn for a treat when they were under the weather contained all sorts of stimulants – ginger, turmeric, aniseed and fenugreek. It cheered them up no end, probably because it improved their digestion. And though the olfactory sense in *Gallus gallus domesticus* is thought to be extremely limited, they must have been able to pick up its exotic aroma.

My only disappointment was that the spices failed to resurrect themselves in the hens' eggs. People had warned me that I would get interesting variations in egg flavour when I started feeding my chooks their exotic slops diet. At the weekend, we stood by for the fish pie from Friday's school dinner to make a second appearance at breakfast, but it never did. The same with garlic, at least as far as I was concerned. For several months, I was feeding the hens mashed garlic cloves because it was said to be good for their digestive systems. No one noticed. Only when Jay found out what I was doing did he detect something garlicky in his omelette and so ordered up a powdered version for the hens, guaranteed not to influence the taste of their eggs. Fortunately, an unanticipated side effect of feeding garlic powder to the hens was that it made their droppings less malodorous, for which our neighbours were most grateful.

We also ordered up a grit and oyster shell mixture, but Roxy and Loxy didn't seem to want it and it remained untouched in their hopper. Eventually a chicken-keeping friend said they were probably picking up quite enough grit for their gizzards as they ranged around the garden. Instead of oyster shell, she suggested that I could provide essential calcium in the form of their own eggshells, recycled.

I remembered my grandfather carefully baking his hens' eggshells in the oven, grinding them up with a pestle and mortar and feeding them back to his Rhode Island Reds. My more informal version of the same tradition was that when I used eggs in the kitchen, I dropped their shells on to a tray in the bottom of the oven where they happened to get baked whenever I cooked something in there. I just had to make sure I didn't let them have more than one sitting, otherwise it was carbonised-shell time.

Next on my menu were the all-important greens. It is not an old wives' tale – a dark yolk is a nutritionally superior egg, as long as the colour is the result of Mum's eating lots of greens. According to US research, the eggs of chickens roaming on pasture contain 34 per cent less cholesterol, 10 per cent less fat, 40 per cent more vitamin A, twice as much omega-6 fatty acid, and four times as much omega-3 fatty acid as eggs from industrially fed hens.

Once I got rid of those industrial pellets, I started to see the difference between a yolk coloured by marigold extract and one coloured by grass – the former has a psychedelic saffron glow, while the latter is sunshine yellow tending towards emerald. Now I could see whether they were getting enough greens; and much of the time, I am ashamed to say, I found they were not.

If I had had a half-acre field, I would have made sure I shifted my Ark across it daily, giving Roxy and Loxy the chance to gobble up large amounts of grass. As it was, at the bottom of my town garden I was shifting it roughly monthly, from one patch of bare earth to the other. In the meantime, on the hens' daily forays abroad, the lawn (though busily breeding insects) was out of bounds. The best greens on offer were geranium and honeysuckle, nasturtium and alchemilla. In winter there was little even of these.

The allotment proved far superior. An early ruse was to take an old rabbit run down there and whenever I went for a few hours' digging, I took one of the hens with me, hidden in a canvas bag out of sight of the local dogs. As long as I positioned the run in exactly the right place, it was entirely a win-win situation: while I dug, she got to peck up all those weeds I would otherwise be on my hands and knees pulling up. The only problem was that Roxy and Loxy soon began to regard this activity as not worth the unpleasant trip in the bottom of a bag. Before long, whenever they saw me approaching with it, they skedaddled.

They knew full well they wouldn't lose out; soon enough I would return bearing delicious offerings. Comfrey (especially the bocking 4 cultivar) was a particular favourite, as were the plants whose names suggest people have long known who likes eating them – chickweed and fat hen. If none of these could be found, it was always worth bringing home uprooted dandelions or chard that had gone to seed. During the summer, cow parsley was popular; in winter, cabbages.

I also boned up on which plants to avoid. In alphabetical order, but probably not comprehensive, they are: aconite, bracken, bryony, buttercup, daffodil, delphinium, dock (seed), foxglove, hellebore, hemlock, henbane, horseradish, horsetails, hyacinth, hydrangea, ivy, laburnum, larkspur, lily-of-the-valley, lupin, nightshade (including tomato and potato plants), oleander, privet, ragwort, rhododendron, rhubarb (leaves), St John's wort, yew.

Of course, it turned out that Roxy and Loxy had been surrounded by these plants in the garden, but had never touched them. Such was their survival instinct. But what if I had thrown old potato plants or rhubarb leaves into their run? They might have been bored enough to try a bite, if it wasn't already soiled and trampled underfoot.

In retrospect, it was not such a brilliant idea to throw any loose leaves from the allotment on to the floor of their run. It took only a matter of minutes for them to become entirely unappetising. My guru, Rosslyn Mannering, advises that we henkeepers string up our greens in a net, high enough that the hens have to jump to peck them. A great believer in exercise was Mannering. But that was the 1920s; after well-nigh a century's worth of genetic refinement, my chooks were no more likely to jump for their greens than my children were.

Their style was more snatch and grab. Once I cottoned on to this, my solution became to string up a garland of greens on the inside of the mesh of the run. Not so high that they needed to jump, but at beak-height and fixed tightly enough that they offered resistance. When Roxy and Loxy came to snatch off their morsel of leaf, the stems held fast.

I did the same thing with sunflowers. Since giving up soya, I reckoned that home-grown seeds might provide the chickens with just as high a level of energy. At last I had something to do with my thousands of pumpkin seeds – I took to drying them on the windowsill and adding them to the mixed grain. But sunflower was an even greater delicacy. From around October, November, just as the colder weather set in and the hens were getting hungrier, my plants had perfectly shrivelled heads, bursting with seeds. I cut each one with a good length of stalk and left it to desiccate in a basket by the back door: a bouquet of prickly black orbs, ready to be presented to Roxy and Loxy over the winter months. One by one I carefully wove each stalk through the mesh.

It was well worth the bother of growing and harvesting and weaving. Come the spring, my plump and healthy hens would return the favour with a glut of creamy, fresh eggs.

Eggs

*It has, I believe, been often remarked that
a hen is only an egg's way of making another egg.*
Samuel Butler, *Life and Habit*

From day one, eggs were a major focus in my henkeeping. Once installed in their cage near the house, there was little for Roxy and Loxy to do, thought I, but lay some. Every morning I would rush downstairs, fling open their door and rummage around in the wood shavings like a child at the lucky dip, sure that today my treasure would be there, hiding in the corner.

But nothing. A couple of days before Christmas, I was out carol singing with a group of friends and someone introduced me to a woman who kept chickens. She welcomed me to the sorority with such warmth that I decided to let on about my birds' fundamental shortcoming.

'Do you know how old they are?' she asked. I wasn't sure; had not thought to ask. 'They might not be ready, you know. Even if they're full grown, they could still be a month or two off laying … Some breeds take six months to get going.'

For all I knew (but did not say), I had been sold birds whose egg-laying days were already numbered.

'Perhaps the trauma of the move might have set them back,' I suggested, trying to stay positive.

'Maybe,' she agreed.

'Have you tried pot eggs?'

I had to admit I wasn't sure what she meant.

'You can buy them at Countrywide – eggs made of pottery. You put them in the nest and sometimes that encourages them to lay.'

'OK.'

'But of course your main problem is the season.'

'Of course.'

My new friend and I exchanged knowing smiles, as if both fully aware of the link between chickens and seasons.

Back home at my computer, it turned out that just like humans, chickens suffer from SAD (Seasonally Affective Disorder). They are super-sensitive to light and as the days get shorter they conserve their energy by reducing their egg-laying activities.

Commercial breeders have done everything they can to get rid of the SAD genes in hybrids, but they have not entirely succeeded. This is why poultry farmers use electric lighting through the winter months – it cheers the hens up enough to think it is worth their laying. If you want to try this trick at home, you can place your coop up against the house and leave the curtains open for the evening. The light from your living room may be enough to fool them. However, it is worth bearing in mind that each hen produces a finite number of eggs – either she strings these out over the year, with the help of your local power station, or she keeps her work seasonal.

I bought a couple of lovely white eggs made of clay, but it didn't seam to inspire Roxy and Loxy, so I gave them to the children for their cookery games and decided it was such an extraordinary thing to produce an egg at all that my chooks shouldn't be expected to lay out of season. It was right and proper that they should take a winter break. Little did I realise this break would last so long that I would forget the whole egg-laying plan entirely.

It was a fine morning in the middle of February, Shrove Tuesday to be precise, and I couldn't think why Roxy wasn't coming out of the sleeping compartment; she must be ill. I went to check – she looked in the rudest of health; when I stretched out a friendly hand she went at it with a peck. I retreated to finish the washing up, and there at the sink it started to occur to me that she might be broody. As I was starting to scroll through the poultry-breeding forum, she began to shout,

'Bra – not, not, not, not, not, not; Bra – not, not, not, not, not, not!'

At which point, without even going to retrieve the evidence from the wood shavings, I clicked straight out of nesting and over to recipes for pancakes.

Have you noticed the lack of 'small' chickens' eggs in the supermarket? As sure as eggs is … if ever you go searching for them you will find nothing between the incy wincy quail's and a great big 'medium' one. Large can look as though it came from a dinosaur. The only reason I can think for this is that, in keeping with packets of crisps and fizzy drinks and packs of butter, these days only the Behemoth will do. And because small eggs are no longer required in the supermarket, the commercial hybrid has been engineered not to produce them. Only when she is a young thing like Roxy, just starting out on her laying career, might she produce something of modest size. Which is how I remember that first egg – a golden colour with a smattering of speckles at the pointed end, small enough to nestle in my palm; it was so perfectly bijou it might have been fashioned by Fabergé. I cracked it in half and made celebratory pancakes.

A few days later, Loxy presented her offering: pinkish and even teenier, its contents were all white – no yolk at all. This kind of egg is called a 'wind' egg and is a sign that the pullet has not quite got her act together. We ate it all the same and rather hoped she would produce more. Alas – the next one was normal.

Of the two hens, Loxy was the slightly less reliable layer, preferring to wait until the afternoon to produce hers. Taking a leaf out of God's book, she would often give herself one day off in the week. In contrast, Roxy created one golden egg every morning without fail: her 24-hour cycle even more efficient than the most reliable battery hen's (who is expected to have one of 25.5).

In keeping with their differing productivity, they also had unique laying styles. To produce an egg, Roxy needed several hours' sitting in the sleeping compartment, while Loxy took far less time but required absolute peace and quiet. Any kind of disturbance (like her sister wanting to come in) and she would burst out, screaming her head off. Eventually she found herself a private spot underneath the acanthus bush where she could lay without disturbance. Until Roxy followed suit and laid her eggs in the same place. By the time I cottoned on, there was a good dozen sequestered there.

*

As soon as our hens got laying, egg collection became an essential part of the family routine. Each morning five-year-old Ellie would race outside to open their door, ignoring poor Snowy in the cage below. Not long after, she would appear in the kitchen with breakfast clutched between her palms. As official breakfast-maker in our house, Jay was the one who got to cook it, with little Bea in her high chair making sure she got her fair share. If Ellie brought only a single egg, Daddy must make a big thing of taking out the one Loxy had laid the day before and scrambling the two together so both sisters got absolutely equal shares of brand-new and nearly-new egg.

My great pride was that, unlike most of their peers, they were fully aware of where their breakfast came from. Meanwhile, I was starting to wonder about all our previous breakfasts: I really knew very little indeed about all those shop eggs I had bought and eaten over the decades.

I was aware that a code stamped on the egg identified its origins. I had also noticed a striking red lion indicating British Lion Quality. But I had never thought to investigate further.

Apparently, the lion indicates that the producer belongs to a national 'hygiene and traceability programme'. In the interests of food safety, this stamp gives a 'best before' date – 27 days from when it was laid. As for the code, working backwards: the long number at the end identifies the registered flock from whence it came, 'UK' refers to the country where the flock lives, and the lonesome number at the start dictates what sort of egg it is.

I had known to avoid the cheapest eggs in the supermarket, produced by miserable caged birds. I knew not to be attracted by words like 'farm fresh' on the box – the packing company had merely omitted the word 'battery' from in front. But what about 'barn eggs'? What exactly were they? Was there a dust bath in that barn and room to run around? And what exactly was the difference between an organic egg and a free-range one? I had already gathered from Lara in animal health that the official free-range space entailed a modest 4 square metres per bird – nothing like the acres of gently wooded pasture I had once imagined. But what about organic birds? Did they get more space, and even the odd daddy long legs?

'Organic' is signalled by a lonesome 'O'. The EU stipulates that these chickens require only the same space as free range which means they have no more chance of catching insects in summer. But they are likely to belong to a smaller flock, which means life is less chaotic and competitive. They eat food containing no laboratory-produced chemicals or ingredients that might harm the environment, but it doesn't mean they avoid soya-based feed or get enough greens to produce naturally yellow yolks.

Because of the high cost of farming organically, these eggs are the most expensive and according to DEFRA they attracted only 4 per cent of the market in 2009; that number is going down. In contrast, 'free range' is an increasingly popular choice. Providing 3,289 million eggs in 2009, it was 37 per cent of the market and that figure is rising fast (by nearly 20 per cent in a decade).

The number '1' indicates 'free range'. These flocks (however large) must be given continuous daytime access to the outdoors from the time they start laying, but whether they use their privilege is another matter. Hens are creatures of habit – having grown accustomed to communing around indoor feeders and drinkers, they may need to be encouraged towards an alternative. Another thing we henkeepers know is that their jungle nature means they are unlikely to want to go out if there is nowhere to shelter, no bush or tree.

Which is where the RSPCA's 'Freedom Food' scheme comes in. There it is on the box – a circular logo with an 'f' swinging across the middle (almost every single free-range egg producer in the UK is signed up to the label). This tells you that the farmer who produced these eggs was working with animal welfare advisors, constantly researching and reviewing practices. The provision of natural shelter such as woodland and hedgerows is exactly what they have been working on recently, so let's hope the hens will feel inspired to use their range.

Meanwhile barn hens (with a number '2' on the shell) don't get the chance. The RSPCA reckons barn hens don't have such a bad life, but people like me feel less sure, and their eggs therefore constitute only 4 per cent of the market (around 1 million hens). From the EU's point of view, the hens can belong to a gargantuan flock, but have space to run around, raised perches or platforms to sleep and some sort of dust bath. The barn floors are carpeted in 'deep litter', sometimes with mesh for droppings to fall through.

As for the number '3's – in 2009, there were 17 million battery hens in the UK and their produce formed around 55 per cent of the market. These eggs are not quite as simple to avoid as I had assumed. It was all very well my leaving the shelled eggs on the shelf, but what about all the unshelled ones? Take a peek in my fridge and you would find a large jar of mayonnaise without any mention of what kind of eggs went into it. In the larder sat custard powder and luxury egg pasta, both similarly minus the information. By default, this meant they were made with battery eggs.

Worse still, because egg products don't have strict labelling, I had no idea whether their ingredients came from countries with non-existent welfare standards. For all I knew, my custard powder was made with dried egg from some giant battery farm in India. And this problem is likely to get worse. With new EU legislation coming into force in 2012 to improve the welfare of hens, British eggs are likely to rise in price, thereby doubtless expanding demand for the cheaper imports, both shelled and unshelled.

Which all goes to show that things can never be as good as they are in your own backyard. Only there do you know exactly what food is going into your birds, exactly the amount of natural shelter and mud and dust they are getting from day to day. Without the use of a single stamp, our homegrown eggs were 100 per cent free range, fresh, happy, soya-free, Salmonella-free, E.coli-free, and very nearly free of charge.

Not that my children were aware of their breakfast having such superlative credentials. All they knew was that their pets had produced it, and this simple association pleased me immensely. To have fed them and stroked them and looked those birds in the eye seemed to me the essence of responsibility when it came to eating eggs.

What I wasn't prepared for was the rather more existential question that occurred because Ellie was so regularly burrowing under their bottoms.

'Mummy?'

'Yes, my sweet?'

'What exactly IS an egg?'

There we sat at 7.30 in the morning with our tea and toast and eggs, the news on the radio distracting me.

Mmm. Well. What a time to launch my sex education responsibilities.

Of the two cells that come together to make a baby, the egg and the sperm, the egg is the larger, less mobile one; all the growing and the feeding happens there. It is the same for snails; the same for Mummy mammals like me. The difference between my eggs and Roxy's is in what biologists call our 'reproductive effort' – mine is somewhere well under a millionth of my body weight; miniscule. Whereas each of hers is about 3 per cent. In a year of laying, Roxy will convert about nine times her own weight into eggs; a quarter of her total energy goes into the act.

'If it takes so much energy, why doesn't she have a rest?' asked Ellie.

Because you keep taking her eggs away! In the bird kingdom there are two styles of egg-laying – the 'determinate' layer and the 'indeterminate' layer. In the former group are the blackbirds and the sparrows and all those other garden birds we know so well. During the nesting season, they lay a set number of eggs at a time; if the magpies come along and steal some, they have to make do with a smaller family. In contrast, an 'indeterminate' layer like an Indian Junglefowl slowly accumulates eggs in her nest (in the Junglefowl's case, about 12 glossy brown ones, laid over two to three weeks); once that clutch is completed, if a predator removes one, she will happily lay another to replace it. Given as much food as she wants and a predatory human or two, she might go on for ever.

Which is exactly what Roxy and Loxy are doing. Of course, over the year a domestic hen will lay far more eggs than she could ever hatch. But she may remember to lay them in the same style as her jungle ancestors – in other words, having accumulated a clutch, she will take a break. That's what Loxy was doing when she stopped laying for a day – completing her clutch, before that five-year-old predator came along again ...

Phew. It's time for piano practice and school and for me to get researching for next time. By then I shall have my *Encyclopedia of Poultry* on hand, plus Rosslyn Mannering and my other chicken guides, plus my food science manual ... I'm ready.

'Mummy?'

'Yes, lovely.'

'How does Loxy make an egg?'

Well. When Loxy was born, just like you and me and most female animals, she had several thousand microscopic germ cells in the sack of her ovary. But her body did not grow symmetrically like yours and mine – while the left ovary developed, the right one shriveled up, leaving her lopsided. Gradually the germ cells reached a few millimeters in diameter, and after two or three months each one accumulated a primitive, white form of yolk inside the surrounding membrane. When she got to laying age they grew together, like a bunch of grapes hanging from the ovary.

The story of how each of these cells becomes an egg is quite exciting. One by one, each one grows larger and larger; when it is about ten weeks old, the hen's liver uses fats and proteins in her body to create a yellow yolk. This yolk then drops into the oviduct – a twisted tube, quite possibly 3 feet in length, like one of those things you slide down at the adventure playground.

If we had a cock and Loxy had recently mated with him, sperm would be waiting at the entrance to this tube, and one lucky fellow would get to join the yolk on the subsequent stages of its journey.

What happens over the next couple of hours is that the yolk (with or without sperm) spins down the slidy tube. Gradually it picks up a coating of albumen 'after the manner of a rolling snowball', as my encyclopedia describes it. Albumen is egg-white (from the Latin *albus* meaning 'white'). Once well-coated, the snowball then spins even more, twisting some particularly thick albumen into two coiled strands called *chalazae* (from the Greek for 'small lump'). The *chalazae* are to keep the yolk steady in the centre of the albumen, stretching out to either end of the shell. Like safety cords, they protect the growing chick from hitting hard shell walls before it is big and strong. Before the egg enters Loxy's womb, it wraps itself in two rough, protective membranes that stick to one another everywhere except at the wide end where they form a little air pocket.

The next stage of development is by far the longest – first the womb wall pumps water and salts into the albumen, and then when the membranes are taut like a big balloon, it slowly secretes calcium carbonate and protein to form the shell. This process takes around 17 hours. Finally, the fully formed egg goes to its waiting room at Loxy's back end where it positions itself blunt end down, biding its time until it feels ready to make its entrance into the world. It arrives from her vulva at the temperature of her body (around 41 degrees centigrade) which, as we already know, is lovely and warm.

Still with me? In truth, my five year old is beginning to lose interest, but I'm not. For me, the most interesting bits are still to come – what I want to know is, what exactly is this egg? Not from the reproductive point of view, but from a nutritional one. Over to the food science book.

Well, it turns out – surprise, surprise – that a chicken egg is an excellent thing for a human to eat. It contains about 70 per cent water, 10 per cent protein, 10 per cent fat and 10 per cent minerals. All amino acids essential to animal life are packed inside, plus vitamins A, B, D and E. It includes a plentiful supply of linoleic acid, a polyunsaturated fatty acid essential in the human diet, as well as plant pigments that are especially valuable antioxidants. The amount of protein in a single egg is equivalent to 14 per cent of a British adult's daily recommended intake; its calorific value is roughly 75 calories, three-quarters of which is contained in the yolk.

The yolk is the part we have learnt to worry about, because of its high cholesterol content. Though medics used to recommend limiting consumption in order not to increase the risk of heart disease, recent studies have shown this has little effect, probably because yolk fat is unsaturated and because other substances in the egg interfere with our absorption of the cholesterol.

Of course, keeping your own hens is one way to reduce cholesterol in your eggs, as long as you are prepared to sacrifice a lawn or two. As someone who would like not to give up all my grass, I could always get some Aracaunas whose startlingly azure eggs have the lowest cholesterol levels of all.

But they could never have no cholesterol at all. That's because the yolk is a concentrated food source for the growing chick. When you open up a hard-boiled egg, the bit that might have grown looks like a tiny white dot at the centre of the yolk's surface. This is the blastoderm, otherwise known as the germ cell. There it sits, un-coagulated, just wishing it had been allowed to become a baby chick. It is especially rich in iron.

While we are investigating the yolk, let's slice through it and examine its history. It's a bit like a tree trunk. The dark rings were created during the day, while the hen was feeding; the light ones grew during the night, while she was asleep. The general colour depends on what she has been eating over the previous 24 hours. As we know from our feed explorations, marigold-yellow yolks probably means she's been eating marigold extract; dark yellow tinged with green means she's had lots of grass and other greens; really green yolks might mean she has found a stash of acorns or the pasture weed shepherd's purse on which to forage. The greenest I have ever managed was from an excellent crop of cow parsley; it tasted a bit more earthy than usual; probably ever so good for me.

Meanwhile, the white might not have been.

Made up of 90 per cent water, with traces of minerals, fatty material, vitamins (riboflavin gives the raw white a slightly yellow-green cast) and glucose, the albumen looks innocent enough. It supplies the chick with essential food and drink; but it also plays a more malevolent role in its development. Within its unassuming form hide an array of proteins, there to protect the growing embryo. Some act like a shield against infection, inhibiting the production of viruses or digesting bacteria. Others bind tightly to vitamins and to iron, thereby preventing them from being useful to other creatures who might want to eat them.

From the eater's point of view, this makes life quite interesting. If you have ever counted your calories, then you might have considered a 'white omelette' where the fatty yolks have been removed. Little did you know that if you ate it raw, you might have lost weight at a cracking rate, as laboratory animals have done when fed raw albumen. This phenomenon seems to be to do with the most plentiful albumen protein, ovalbumin, which inhibits protein-digesting enzymes. Whatever proteins you are swallowing, it stops your body from making use of them.

Though this inhibitor seems to be deactivated when cooked, ovalbumin can still be a problem – some people's digestive systems mount a massive defence against it that takes the form of fatal shock. Which is why we are told to feed our babies the yolk, but not the white. Just in case they have an allergy.

And while we are peeling baby's egg, it's fun to examine the packaging. First, there is the air pocket between the two membranes at the blunt end. In a fresh egg it is about 2cm in diameter and set slightly to one side. If that egg is fertilised, then the membranes will loosen and the pocket expands as the chick grows, thereby maximising the amount of air available for it to breathe while it is chipping its way out of the egg, sometimes over several hours. Even in an unfertilised egg, the sack expands over time because the contents are shrinking by at least 4mg a day as water evaporates from the shell.

This is useful to us in two ways: firstly, an old egg with its loose membranes will be much, much easier to peel than younger models. Secondly, a bit like a witch trial in the seventeenth century, we can tell if an egg is rotten by dunking it in water. A fresh egg sinks; if modestly fresh its wide end will rise a little; if guilty of decay, the whole thing bobs around on the surface.

And if this test seems too unscientific, we can always get out a measuring tape and make sure the height of the air pocket is no more than the 6mm stipulated by the EU (if the space is any larger, a shop egg must be discarded). But for this we will need candling equipment.

Candling has long been the way to check what's going on inside an egg without breaking it – you place it in front of a bright light and inspect its contents, illuminated through the shell. These days commercial producers use the method to determine the quality of their eggs. Where once they would have used an expert eye and a candle, these days a scanner can do the looking and an electric bulb the lighting.

To determine the condition of the yolk and albumen, the egg is 'twirled'. The scanner is looking for a well-centred yolk, visible as a shadow only, without any discernible outline. If it can be clearly seen, its *chalazae* are not doing their job properly and it is too close to the shell, floating free, which means the egg is possibly of poor quality.

Other things sought during candling are blood spots, caused when a capillary in the ovary ruptures; 'meat spots' are similar– blood or tissue comes away from the ovary and gets incorporated into the albumen. Neither is a threat to the wellbeing of the eater, nor does it indicate that an egg is fertile. But because consumers think this might be the case, the packing companies search out the spots and discard millions of perfectly edible eggs.

There is nothing quite like the power of consumer opinion. When I was small the only eggs available in the shops were white because white-producing breeds were the best layers. But then the nutritionists came along to teach us that white bread was bad and brown bread was good. Having got that basic fact into our heads, we started applying it to other foodstuffs. Those white eggs we had been eating must be nutritionally inferior, we thought; rustic-looking brown ones would be a much healthier option.

Soon enough, the egg industry realised that the public was prepared to pay more for brown eggs. And rather than confuse us with any more complicated nutrition stuff, they decided to concentrate their efforts on producing hybrids that would lay one brown egg a day in a rustic battery farm.

Of course, the colour is entirely superficial; so much so that you can scratch it from the surface with a kitchen knife. Look – that lovely speckledy golden hue will always capitulate to white, given a good scraping. Inspect the coloured cuticle closely and you see it has a powdery bloom, there to protect the growing chick from bacterial infection. Tilt the scratched section towards the light and you will see thousands of tiny holes – those are up to 15,000 pores where gases pass in and out of the shell. As a chick grows inside, it requires increasing amounts of gas and the protective bloom will gradually break down in order to allow for this.

But if you are intending to eat the contents of the egg, you don't want that to happen. Which is why the EU stipulates that commercially produced eggs should not be washed, as washing destroys the bloom. The temptation at home is to run an egg under the tap before storing it away, but in the interests of hygiene I try not to. If it arrives covered in muck and I feel I really must wash it, then I use water that is warmer than the egg – this way, though the protective bloom is destroyed, bacteria are less likely to be drawn inwards through the pores in the shell.

Only once you are producing your own eggs do you realise the huge variety there could be on a supermarket shelf, had the industry not fallen in with consumer opinion. The genetic determination is surprisingly simple – my Warrens have a brown-egg gene; Araucanas have a blue-egg one; in a breed like the Leghorn, the absence of either blue or brown gene makes the chicken a white egg-layer.

These days there are hybrids producing all three colours of egg and variations thereof, and even a variety of sizes. You should be able to tell the general colour of the eggs by looking at the chicken – a white bird will produce a white egg; a brown a brown. If she has an odd plumage like lavender or cuckoo, then you can consult her earlobes – the little patch of skin down in the corner of her cheek, behind the beak. Sometimes the ears are hard to pinpoint, hidden under flaps of wattle. She tends to use them one at a time, so when she hears something familiar or startling – a child's cry, a dog's bark, she will stand stock still for a moment, working out from which direction it came. Then she stretches her neck and tilts her head to that side, all the better to catch the sound the next time it comes around. Watch closely and you will eventually locate the ear and its lobe. In most cases, the colour of the lobe indicates the colour of the egg.

If, like me, you stick to hens with the boring brown-egg genes, you will still discover over time the surprising variety in their shells. The most obvious variation can simply derive from the time of day it was formed. Shells are composed of 94 per cent chalk (calcium carbonate) that the hen picks up while foraging. An egg that arrives early in the morning is likely to have a thinner shell than one laid by the same bird later in the day because it was created while she was sleeping and therefore not accessing instant doses of chalk. Another cause of thin shells can be if the chicken has been doing too much breathing, either because she has a respiratory infection or because of very hot weather. As she pants she gives out extra carbon dioxide, thus reducing the amount of carbonates in her blood and leaving her without enough calcium carbonate to build a solid shell.

Eggs from old birds are the most characterful – sometimes the shell can be papery, sometimes nobbly with rough patches, sometimes misshapen. Many produce thin shells; this is because they are not managing to process enough calcium from their diet to supply the needs of their ageing bodies as well as those of the egg. Sometimes an old hen will compensate by drawing the calcium from her skeleton, leaving it brittle and weak. As they get older, they lay much less often and when they do, the egg may be very large. They can also produce double yolkers – the result of two eggs reaching the albumen producing area and the shell gland at the same time, these magnificent orbs have a ridge around the middle where they became fused.

Weird-shaped eggs or fragile ones can signal a stressed or diseased bird. Pesticides and certain drugs also have an influence (check what the neighbours have been spraying on their lawn; check the small-print on any medication the hens have been taking). If an egg arrives strangely elongated by a double band of shell at one end, it may come from a hen disturbed during the 17 long hours she was creating the shell. A helicopter, a dog barking, next door spraying the lawn … whatever it was, her response was for her body to contract, including the muscles in the wall of her uterus. The shell inside there was very fragile and weak; the muscle contraction squeezed it and might even have cracked it. When eventually she relaxed, the uterine wall secreted calcium carbonate with extra vigour, producing this double layer of toughness.

A similar effect can be caused by internal fat pressing on the reproductive organs. As a keeper of lean hybrids, I never came across this problem, but people who keep rounder, fatter breeds, like the Orpington, say they can get striated or ridged shells.

Finally, some eggs have no shell at all.

I remember Roxy and Loxy once producing a cream-coloured blob that looked a bit like a dried pear, all squidged up. Because it had no shell, I couldn't tell who had laid it. I rang a friend who had kept hens for more than forty years: John. He told me not to worry – it was a 'lash'; a bit like the contents of the hoover; the result of the hen clearing out her egg-laying tackle. Neither chook seemed in any distress. I decided they might even feel better for the spring clean.

But it was a shock to find my first shell-less egg. Lying there in the nesting box, it looked as though it had been lightly poached and liberally seasoned with wood-chippings. When I touched it, the membrane wobbled dramatically to show how very uncooked the contents were. I carried it inside to show Jay and we buried it ceremonially in the compost bin.

What did it mean? My first thought was that Roxy and Loxy must be deficient in calcium, and I hadn't been baking enough eggshells for them. My second was to phone John again; he said it could signal sickness. He wondered, might something have frightened the hens?

Frightened them? It must have been something truly terrifying to halt 17 hours of shell production. Something actively intimidating; perhaps continually so. Something I had known about but conveniently forgotten. Until now.

Mr Fox

And nothing more was ever seen
Of that foxy-whiskered gentleman.
Beatrix Potter, *The Tale of Jemima Puddle-Duck*

There is nothing nastier for an urban hen than an urban fox. Her country cousins may have other enemies – the most common being a kite or a badger. In the city there might be the odd feral cat or a visiting Rottweiler, but nothing is so fearless nor so ubiquitous as the fox.

Surrounded by street lighting and the constant buzz of human activity, traffic and machines, he long ago lost his shyness and his nocturnal nature. There he is in broad daylight, strutting down the middle of the street. I have seen one on a summer afternoon in south London, sunbathing on the bonnet of a car. He is not just wily; he is brazen.

Before we moved in and built our shed at the bottom of the garden, there was a fox den there. The neighbours said the cubs used to come and cavort on the lawn. Ahhh. People used to leave milk out for them; one friend described in ecstatic tones how a darling fox cub came over and licked his toes (or was it kissed?) as he performed his t'ai chi exercises one morning. Ahh.

Having erected the shed, we reckoned Mr Fox had taken his family far away. The first few weeks Roxy and Loxy were out in the garden, Jay and I were concerned he might show up. I spent as much time as I could in the garden, and when indoors, I regularly checked out of the window for signs of a visit. As the months passed and no one came, I decided he had been so traumatised by his eviction that he had crossed us off his list of food-finding venues.

It was almost a year before disaster struck. The morning after Guy Fawkes Night: I remember because I had been worrying that I should have brought my chooks indoors in case the fireworks frightened them. When I went to let them out in the morning, I was relieved to see them bustle out on to the frosted lawn, just as usual. At around eleven (a time all self-respecting foxes should be snuggled up in bed) I was in my study upstairs and glanced out of my window to admire the russet triangles of my hens' upturned tails against the green and silver of the undergrowth. And there, exactly the same colour as my birds, slinking thief-like across the ground …

Call it what you will, it felt like maternal instinct that spurred me from my desk. Before you could say 'Mr Fox', I was down the staircase, out of the back door and across the grass, clapping my hands and roaring – 'Get away!' The chickens were shrieking at the top of their coloratura range. Roxy came sprinting towards me on skinny yellow legs, wings propelling her faster than Roadrunner. But Loxy was already trapped between vulpine jaws, flailing in the final paroxysms of life. As I lunged at her killer, he hopped over the fence into next door's garden.

Trust an urban fox to exploit the trespass laws – he knew I wasn't going to follow him on to Pete and Janice's property. From there he turned to face me and, adjusting the position of my pet between his teeth, decapitated her. Her fulsome body dropped to the ground hardly bleeding, no longer moving. And away Foxy trotted to bury his trophy in the bushes.

Meanwhile, having placed Roxy safely in the old rabbit hutch next to the house, I began storming up and down the lawn. But what could I do? I watched with impotent fury as Mr Fox returned from his burying ritual to enjoy his elevenses in a flurry of red down. While he munched and crunched, he gazed at me as if to say 'Who are you, you hysterical female, flapping about? I'm master round here.'

I remember the rest of that day, and days to come, how my fury gradually turned to sadness. I remember gazing out at the empty garden and feeling that things would never be the same again, our period of hen-loving innocence was gone. The children wandered around looking mournful. People say that after a burglary they feel somehow violated. That's how it felt after Loxy was taken.

As for her sister, we worried that she might perish from her own terror. For a couple of days she shuddered in her cage, hardly eating or drinking, her great laying talents gone. On the third day Ellie took her out a bowl of hot porridge laced with poultry spice and she seemed to perk up. I held her close and tried to encourage her – 'Come on Roxy, my girl. You're safe now. We won't let him get near you again.' But I felt the faltering of my tone; I knew I could not be certain of my promise. As I placed her on the ground, the whole family assembled to watch her take a few tentative pecks at the grass. That was a good sign. If she got through this, we resolved never again to leave her outdoors alone.

I think it was about a week before she laid an egg. I remember the relief when I heard her announcing its arrival – Roxy was back to her normal self. And back to the Ark I carried her, but this time as its full-time resident. I was sad that she could no longer scratch around in the open, and even sadder that she had no companion with whom to pass her days. Each time I opened the door to feed her, she tried to force her way out – in the back of her bird-brain there must have been some residual memory of free-range pleasures. But I couldn't risk indulging her.

With Loxy's death, Mr Fox had become an all too vivid aspect of our lives. I started lying awake at night, listening out for his cry. I had not been aware of it before – like a colicky baby, rending the darkness. In the morning, traipsing down the garden to check that my solitary chook was still alive, I found his calling card of a stiff black stool. Sometimes during the day I would hear squawking and know that he had come a-visiting, slinking back and forth along Roxy's wire walls. When I strode out to defend her, his shadow sauntered away – 'I'll be back,' that saunter seemed to say.

That's the thing about thieves – they know not to give up. With sheer persistence they will get their way in the end. One day some-one will forget to lock the door, or leave a window open …

Approaching the Ark, I felt my gut tighten. I couldn't see Roxy's eager form flitting behind the mesh. As I got closer, I saw that the little door into the nesting box had fallen down, leaving a triangular black hole. Even now, I can't fathom how he did it, but my best guess is that I had not revolved the catch precisely enough to its vertical position, that somehow his snout had pushed it around and managed to dislodge the wood. I didn't want to go any closer; I knew Roxy would be gone. Eventually,

I summoned my courage to lift off the side that hid her sleeping compartment. A couple of long tail feathers clung to the ceiling, some softer plumage scattered across the floor. She must have put up quite a struggle.

And stuck to the raw edge of the nesting box was a fringe of red and white fur.

In mourning for my pets, I talked a lot about their murder. And soon discovered people in the area who have given up keeping poultry because of similar experiences. I also discovered that it was not only hens who were terrorised. Take, for example, the poor old cats round the corner; now that's a gory story. My friends Dan and Polly were clearing up the garden in the autumn when Polly picked up what she thought was a ball. It turned out to be a cat's head, severed in distinctively Foxy fashion. The eyes were still half-open, and not rotted, so it couldn't have been dead all that long. Scary. A month or so later they were woken by a growling and a yowling outside their bedroom window. The lady next door ran out screaming; she managed to chase off the fox who had abandoned his second feline victim, half-mauled. The cat, covered in bites, was nursed by owner and vet but eventually had to be put down.

And the locals' response? Well, there was one lady who phoned to accuse Dan and Polly of making up the whole story – such gentle creatures as foxes would never do such a thing. Because of this sort of opinion, other people kept their heads down, bringing their cats in at night just in case the same happened to them. Everyone brought in their shoes, otherwise the tasty leather might get mauled. One neighbour with a small baby would not leave her outside in the pram – having witnessed Loxy's murder, I thought it a wise precaution.

Not to be outdone by the fox-lovers, I began looking into ways to free us of their tyranny. I had country-living friends who depended on their chickens to earn a living. They had fox traps, and rifles to ensure a humane death. I knew I was not allowed to use a firearm in a built-up area, so I made a deal with my friend Tim to borrow a couple of traps and drive my catches over to his place, where they could be swiftly dispatched.

In the meantime, I looked into the best forms of fox-proofing.

The main thing henkeepers said, based on bitter experience, was always to be vigilant. Never assume Mr Fox is having the night off, let alone the day. You can bet your bottom dollar he is somewhere in the shadows, biding his time like the opportunist he is, just waiting for the moment when your concentration falters.

Another general recommendation was to try my darndest to think like a fox. One thing he is especially proud of is his pearly gnashers; and not only for inflicting decapitation. One morning my friend John found his garden strewn with shards of plywood – the fox had spent all night ripping the hen house to pieces.

He is also pretty nifty at climbing. Though not generally spring-loaded like a cat, he can get a long way with a messy scramble. With this in mind, I looked into anti-burglar devices. Movement-sensitive lights are meant to be a deterrent, though I doubt my savvy urban thieves would have been bothered. The Neighbourhood Watch website suggested planting prickly bushes around the perimeter of the garden or sticking spikes atop a six foot fence. I decided that rather than prune my overgrown trees and ivy, I would encourage them to clamber high and messy over the fence.

Many friends swore by electric mesh. At around £100 for 50 metres, it is cheaper than solid fencing. The reason it works is that Mr Fox always takes a sniff at a barrier before he clambers up it, and a sting to the nose should be enough to send him packing. A set of posts, 2 metres of mesh and a rechargeable battery unit is easy enough to find at the local agricultural supplier. If the posts and pegs are too weak, like my friend Elaine's, the mesh sags, sending the electric current into the ground and rendering the fence useless. Her husband went out and bought a set of treated timber which took him a few days to dig in really deep. It is now part of their regular anti-Fox strategy to make sure the top and bottom wires are taut, and the weeds are not growing up and shorting it out.

In order to prevent hedgehogs getting caught on the bottom wire and accidentally wrapping themselves around it, you might consider placing 6-inch board along the bottom of the electric fence. Once you have had Elaine's early-morning horror of finding a sweet bundle of spikes mortified on hers, you will definitely be putting one in.

Dogs are a good idea. One friend has a little terrier who polices her back garden very effectively – most foxes prefer to avoid confrontation with a member of the same order. And it is strange how dogs take it upon themselves to guard the family flock. Another friend has a Lurcher who wrecked relations with next-door when he got into their garden and finished off a couple of hybrids. Yet when my friend started keeping hens herself he became the sweetest godfather to them and later to their chicks.

Sliding further along the eccentricity scale, some people use lion or tiger droppings from the local zoo (they deter cats too).

Others find room for a pet llama. Me? First, I needed to improve on what I had.

With Roxy's theft had come the realisation that my Ark was not as secure as I had imagined. It turned out, of course, that the name 'Ark' refers to a quality not of safety but of mobility. Had I made the association not with Noah but with pigs, I would have remembered those things like Nissen huts you see stranded in the middle of muddy fields. Completely flimsy and insubstantial, they are unlikely to withstand either flood or fox.

Fortunately, my Ark was sturdy. Even so, there must be ways to make it more secure. Were I to replace all the catches with bolts, Foxy would find it much harder to enter; the addition of a padlock would also deter human thieves. However, such an upgrading would test my screwdriver skills, and henceforward my cleaning and feeding and daily egg collection would be much more time consuming. Instead, Jay offered to tighten each revolving catch – that would present a challenge for even the most persistent snout. He could also put a second catch on the little door into the nesting box so that at least next time Mr Fox came around he would have double the bother.

Then we applied our new safety-awareness to the run. We had read Roald Dahl's *Fantastic Mr Fox*; we knew our enemy was an admirable digger. To give the run that extra Fort Fox dimension, we inserted a 'scratch-mat' on the ground – a big square of wire mesh, jutting out a few centimetres beyond the walls. Though the hens' scratching would be thus inhibited, so would their killers' skulduggery.

In thinking like a fox, we tried to be equally cunning. Foxes (even urban ones) hate the smell of humans, so from now on I intended to clean out my daughters' hairbrushes in the garden, leaving fresh clumps floating about in surprising places. They could also join Jay in urinating regularly along our boundaries (Bea was particularly keen on this chore).

Or I could take a break from chicken keeping altogether. But now my fox-awareness had been raised, I was bound to find myself bumping into him.

It was 9am at the start of the Easter holidays and my neighbour Lisa was on the phone, sounding in a panic.

'I want you to solve a moral dilemma for me,' she said. 'There's a fox in the children's guinea pig cage. He must have dug his way into their run, got up the ladder, and now he's stuck.'

I saw no moral dilemma whatsoever in her news – a fox was caught; time to put my plan into action and phone Tim. But by the tone of Lisa's voice, I sensed things were not going to be quite so simple.

'He's so beautiful,' she sighed.

Uh oh. Now I knew which way this dilemma was swinging.

'In my opinion,' I spat, 'that fox would look even better hung around the neck of a beautiful woman.' She laughed; I could tell she was nervous.

The story of Jemima Puddle-Duck filtered into my mind – Beatrix Potter's broody duck, seduced by a long-tailed gentle-man with sandy whiskers. Lisa and I read that stuff to our children, and despite all our better judgements, couldn't help but empathise with Jemima's fancying a handsome bastard. My friend was about to confess the real-life consequence of her weakness.

'I've rung the RSPCA and they are coming to let him out.'

'He's killed your children's guinea pigs!' I cried. Surely this was the role she wanted me to play – reminding her it was our pets that needed saving, not the fox.

'Yes, and your hens. I know if he gets Ellie's bunny you're going to blame me!'

'Did you try phoning the council pest control?'

'Yes, but they have a 'no kill' policy.'

'A what?!'

'They say foxes are a nuisance, not a pest … government legislation; you know…'

'And what about a private company?'

'Rentokil can't come straight away. We're meant to be going to Wales in an hour. And anyway, I'm not sure I want him killed. He was only following his nature, Julia …'

Now I object to this argument. I know about 'nature red in tooth and claw'; I respect the need to kill in many species, including humans. But when it comes to urban living, that whole nature thing goes out of the window. Urban foxes don't flourish because they are good at killing, but because we are. It's we humans whose dead chickens and pigs generously deposited in bin-liners on the street provide their sustenance.

In my opinion, the life of Lisa's handsome captive was no more 'natural' than her guinea pigs'. His urge to kill might derive from some ancient legacy, just like a dog's or a pussy-cat's, or even the late Loxy's when you passed her a snail, but if any of them had to kill to survive, they wouldn't stand a chance.

Reg from the RSPCA arrived in a pristine white van, bang on time. The RSPCA is generously funded by millions of animal lovers up and down the country. Which comes first, I wondered, the furry or the feathered? I decided my best option was to take Reg into my confidence.

'The thing is,' I began, 'we have a real problem around here – the foxes are terrorising our pets. It's not just the guinea pigs …'

He nodded. I wondered how Noah faced this problem, during those forty long days and nights.

'Trouble is, it's breeding time,' he said. 'I saw a cub just yesterday – six weeks old or so. It would starve without its mother.'

'But if this one's a male, there's no problem,' I responded. In my mind, these terrorists must all be male – yes, I know it's sexist, but feelings were running high.

'True,' said Reg. He opened the back doors of the van and took out a white cage, lined with a comfy cloth, and a long pole with a noose at the end. 'I'll tell you what. If it's a male, I'll take him away for you.'

'Where?' I enquired, my tone more eager than I had intended.

'Somewhere beyond the ring-road; there are plenty of rabbits up there … ' Wild rather than pet ones, I assumed.

In the back garden, the fox filled up the whole of the guinea pigs' cage. Reg and I craned our necks to try and get a good look between his back legs. A little flick of his body, and there it was – his manliness. Good. Reg reckoned he was last year's cub – maybe the son of the criminal who took my chickens. He reminded me of a handsome hoodie, annoyed that I had the audacity to look him in the eye – his golden eye, glinting out through the wire. His ears were tipped with soft black fur, his paws were clean, teeth unbroken. I could see what Lisa meant – indeed, he was so beautiful.

Reg offered me protective gloves and I became his assistant, excited and rather proud to be honoured with the role. I eased open the door of the guinea pigs' cage, while he inserted the pole, talking in low tones to keep things calm. To him, this process was no different from any of his other work rescuing traumatised animals. The fox was sniffing at the noose, picking up the whiff of cats and bunnies and all sorts of delicious previous inhabitants. Slowly, gently Reg eased it up and over the furry ears. I was thinking of my daughter Beatrice's favourite story – the little gingerbread man who is persuaded by the fox to climb on to his head, from whence he gets snaffled.

Go for it Reg, you beat this one at his own game.

At his end of the pole, Reg drew up the string. The noose was tight around Foxy Junior's neck. I opened the door wide, and Reg lopped our catch niftily into his new cage. I slammed the lid shut, perhaps with a little more vigour than was absolutely necessary.

The prisoner growled, low and throaty. Reg from the RSPCA had found him guilty, exiling him to a foreign land in punishment for his father's crimes and now his own. Lonely and confused, if he tried to come home he would face the brutality of the ring-road.

With any luck it would be a really ruthless truck.

Take Two

Tomorrow is a busy day
We got things to do
We got eggs to lay
Louis Jordan

Even if Foxy Junior did perish, I knew there were plenty more like him out there. Getting hens again was sure to mean more harassment. When I couldn't bear the thought of it, I reminded myself what people say when there's been a terrorist attack. They say – get out and lead the life you want to lead; don't let the buggers get you down.

One consolation was that neighbours moving to Africa gave us their aged cat, Tigger, who might sometimes condescend to a cuddle. Unfortunately, this just made me miss Loxy's version all the more. I missed the hens' enthusiastic company in the garden; I missed their chatter round the kitchen door – *'Bop. Bop, bop, boppety bop…'* I missed the clever way they converted leftovers into eggs.

I had invested a lot of time and effort over the previous year; I couldn't let all my new-found husbandry skills go to waste. Perhaps most importantly, there was £400-worth of vacant Ark sitting at the bottom of the garden, crying out for new tenants.

After a suitable period of mourning I took advice from a wise henkeeping friend who recommended getting in touch with Mr Hodgkins, the local pullet rearer. No problem – he had a batch of POLs ready to go; £6 each.

On a sunny March morning, I drove Beatrice over to Hodgkins' place. He opened up the stable door and revealed the most marvellous sight – a hundred Roxys and Loxys jostling towards the light. Each one was sleek and beautiful, their eyes bright, chattering away to us – '*Take me, take me!*' He leant down and gently lifted the couple closest to him under his arms where they nestled happily for a moment before being lowered into their transportation sacks.

When Ellie got home from school, she christened our new pets Ruby and Scarlet and we drank to their future with elderflower cordial. The household was complete again. My pair of brand-new red hens would help me prove that henkeeping was possible, even in the same world as fox loving.

With Ruby and Scarlet came a new level of dedication in my husbandry. Like someone who has had a health scare, I now became the most fastidious of keepers.

My experience with Mr Fox meant that I didn't dare let them out without human company. Either the children would be playing in their Wendy house, or Jay in his shed at the end of the garden, the door open. Best of all, during the summer months I found time to join them in the garden nearly every day, weeding. The job was so much more fun when accompanied by the hens' chatter, or their cackle when they uncovered a grub. Between the three of us, the borders became cleaner and tidier than ever before. And at the end of a good working session, under my arms I slung them and back home to the Ark.

Having caught them, of course. With Roxy and Loxy this was not something I had had to do regularly – they found their own way home at the end of the day. But now, whenever I left the garden I would first step confidently towards each bird, hands descending. The strange thing was that, instead of making a run for it, they would cower to the ground, their feet treading back and forth nervously. It reminded me of all those 'chicken' words – chickening out, turning chicken, being chicken-hearted ... And it bothered me.

I don't think chickens are intrinsically cowardly creatures. After seeing Ruby jump on Tigger's back the one time the cat dared to aggress her, I would say they are the most courageous animals I know. I admit that the local police helicopter can send them into a huddle – their Junglefowl genes are telling them that thing wheeling in the sky is a hen-eating raptor. But I wouldn't call it chickening out. The association only seems relevant to me in this one instance of Ruby and Scarlet cowering. Apparently it is what they would have done were I a cock; I decided to take it as a compliment.

As far as handling the hens two at a time goes, my hot tip is to do it with the hens facing backwards, clenching their bodies with your elbows, their legs safely knitted between your fingers. When you carry chickens in this fashion, two tangles of claws fire out from under your arms, like some medieval torture instrument.

At markets in Mediterranean holiday destinations, the poultry keepers' style is even more extreme – they hang their birds upside down, three or four from one hand. This vertical position probably inhibits the birds' breathing and as a result they hang limp, as though their necks have already been wrung. But the general principle is worth emulating: with their bodies wedged under each arm, angle the hens so their heads are lower than their tails; even with a gentle tilt, they become pleasantly passive.

And back to Fort Fox willingly they return.

With its new scratch-mat and extra catch, plus all the family's daily deterrents, the Ark now seemed reliably fox-proof. The only problem was that the hens had to spend most of their lives inside it. Fearing they might die of boredom, I decided to treat the run as if it were a baby's playpen and introduce some amusements. The hanging ladder was already like something from a mini adventure playground, so I added a few sticks in the hope they might enjoy hopping from one to the next. Then, remembering Roxy's fascination with her own reflection, I hung some old CDs up on the mesh walls. The pigeons watched warily from the buddleia bush; they couldn't understand how those shiny things I hung all over the allotment to scare them off my cabbages were now being used to entertain their cousins.

Regular cleaning became a must for both the run and the sleeping quarters. As spring advanced and the weather got warmer, it was the best way to prevent farmyard odours percolating into the neighbours' gardens. Hens are poo-full creatures, even managing to defecate during their sleep, so it's good to have a quick and easy way of clearing up after them. Under their perch I left some pages from my weekend *Guardian*, into which I wrapped their droppings, and threw them in my canary-yellow plastic bucket, with an old dustbin lid on the top to keep off the flies. Those deposited on the scratch-mat in the run I trowelled away each week when I altered the position of the Ark.

Chicken shit is one of the most potent compost activators around; which is why garden centres charge extortionate prices for it. The chicken-keeper, of course, need pay nothing at all. Richer in phosphate, sulphate of ammonia and potash salts than any other animal manure, it is packed full of bacteria whose greatest desire in life is to break down your organic waste.

Some people put their hens' soiled wood-chippings straight on to the flowerbeds as a compost/mulch combo; apparently currants and gooseberries thrive on it. Personally, I didn't trust myself not to frazzle my plants by feeding them the fresh stuff. Instead, once a week I carried my yellow bucket down the road to the allotment, slinging its contents into the bin along with my kitchen waste. I soon noticed the improvement in my compost – even thick stems and roots began to decompose fast.

Chicken shit is not only the gardener's best friend, it is also the henkeeper's – inspected on a regular basis, it can be a good indicator of health. Fresh droppings should be firm and brown with a white surface; the brown bit is the poo and the white bit the wee. If you spot weird-coloured ones or splatty ones, if they smell acrid or mouldy, then it is time to worry.

Having familiarised myself with Ruby and Scarlet's excretions, I needed to get to know their bodies. And as every good stockman knows, the best way to do this is to sit and watch. I can highly recommend hen-watching; simply sitting with your pets in the garden is an excellent way to switch off from worries and stress. Their focused foraging, unhampered by phones and emails and all the other things that distract us humans, is an excellent lesson in life's essentials. And out of such philosophising more practical questions can arise: Does that movement look normal (no lameness or stiffness)? Is her plumage as glossy and full as usual? Are the scales on her legs clean and smooth?

At the end of a good watching session, I would try and encourage either Ruby or Scarlet to hop into my lap where, instead of my looking at her, she would look at me. And what a fascinating look it was: those perfectly circular eyes, bounded by ripples of rosy skin, the iris bright yellow rimmed with orange.

Like other aspects of her movement, a chicken's blink is extremely swift. You know it is happening but in that millisecond you can't work out quite how. Flick. The iris has been swept clean, but the folds of skin around it seem not to have moved. That's because she is using her nictitating membrane (from the Latin *nictare*, to blink). Present in birds and reptiles, this is a translucent third eyelid that enables the hen to moisten and protect her eye while retaining visibility. The rod system inside those eyes is poorly developed, so when darkness falls she can't see at all well and takes herself straight to bed. Watch her going to sleep and you get the opportunity to see the third eyelid slowly passing over the eyeball before the big ones close on top of it.

With all three eyelids open, a hen has an extremely well-developed sense of sight – strictly, her vision has only about a third of the acuity of a human's, but because of the nictitating membrane it is unhampered by those moments when we blink ourselves blind. Like all birds, she has a very wide field of view while also being able to see things right under her beak.

Having checked that my bird's eyes were bright and clear, I would continue my health check across the rest of her body – how fat was she? How full her crop? By handling her regularly,

I was in a good position to diagnose loss of weight, loss of feathers and so on. I also tried to have a good rummage around for the usual suspects – mites (around the neck) or worms (around the bum), wounds on her legs or dodgy feather loss (indicating possible bullying). And once in a blue moon, I unfolded her wing and made sure her feathers weren't getting too long.

You've seen *Chicken Run* – like the very first, primeval birds, hens cannot fly; not without the aid of a catapult. Though some of the lighter pure breeds are able to wing themselves impressively off the ground, hybrids generally don't develop the knack. Having said that, the first time Mr Fox came visiting, Roxy's full set of wing feathers probably saved her life – it was the extra propulsion of her flapping as she sprinted down the garden that got her away so fast. Of course, then I started to worry that she might improve her technique: get up enough wing power to flap over the fence, and another fence or two until she fell straight into Foxy's jaws. With Ruby and Scarlet, I didn't want to risk it, so I clipped their wings.

I knew not to worry – the quill is made of keratin, the same substance as human nails, and cutting it hurts no more than it would a baby's toes. I just had to make sure I cut the white bit, rather than the pink bit lower down where blood flows. With Jay holding on to her to stop her flapping around, I opened out one wing and used a sharp pair of kitchen scissors to cut back the ten primary feathers. I avoided the shorter feathers on the body of the wing – she needed them to keep warm. Clipping one wing only meant she was sufficiently unbalanced that even an escape attempt with a catapult would have sent her horribly askew.

Another, very particular feature of the hen's body is her comb – the wizened bit of red flesh on top of her head that looks like a discarded washing-up glove; similar bits around her eyes and below the beak are called wattles. There are human versions of both these appendages – the flesh under our chins that gradually becomes pendulous with age may be termed a wattle or else 'dewlap'. In *A Midsummer's Night Dream*, Puck mentions pouring ale down a gossip's dewlap, which some scholars reckon refers to flaps lower down her anatomy. Shakespeare is also familiar with the comb – the 'coxcomb' worn by a jester signals his wise form of foolishness.

Cocks are especially proud of their combs – they tend to be larger that the hens' and grow larger still when he is feeling aggressive or aroused. For the female, a lovely pink comb is a sign of good health; if it becomes pale then she may be ill; if floppy, she is overheated or dehydrated. A heightened reddening signals that she is going to lay. Once you know this, you need no longer be awed by people like my sanctuary lady recognising layers as if by magic. Instead, you can start impressing your friends by predicting which member of your flock is soon to produce an egg.

Ruby was a marvellous layer and to prove it she had permanently red wattles and comb. Viewed from behind, she showed other signs of laying ability: her back end had a distinctive V-shape, a wide tail area pointing sharply downwards like a super-efficient egg funnel. Her bottom was fluffier and fuller than other hens', with her tail carried jauntily, as if to draw attention to her talents.

I hope I never failed to appreciate them; neither the egg-laying nor the beauty. Certainly Ruby herself was proud of her well-feathered form. Like all birds, for maintaining her beauty she possessed a preen gland (or uropygial gland as it is more scientifically known) that produced oil to condition her feathers; the more it was stimulated, the more it produced.

A chook like Ruby knows exactly where her little sack of conditioner is stashed – turning her neck 180 degrees, she buries her face into the base of her tail. Once her beak has picked up a good supply, she strokes it back and forth across her wings, her breast and her tail. That slinky neck of hers enables her to distribute oil right down to her knickers and tight up to her collar, burrowing her face in deep to condition the roots. Discovering a louse or a flea, she pecks it swiftly from its hiding place as she goes. When eventually the preening is completed, she niftily rearranges her feathers with her beak, picking up the shafts and replacing them until they are in perfect alignment. A good shaking of her whole feathery mantle concludes her toilette.

It took some effort, but I eventually managed to persuade Ellie that the shampoo-and-blow-dry version of hen-husbandry was not necessary. It would only have upset the natural balance of oils on our hybrids' feathers. She was also wrong to think they might love us more if we gave them a hot bath. Some hens are so traumatised by water that they stop laying just because they got caught in a rain shower.

Which is why it was fine by me if once in a while my hens sheltered in the house. Just like their predecessors, Ruby and Scarlet felt drawn to our indoor life. If the back door was open, straight into the kitchen they came to have a good snoop around. One day when it was closed, Scarlet even managed to shove her way in through the cat flap and finish off Tigger's breakfast. Had I left the rest of the house available, soon enough she would have been up the stairs, finding tasty biscuit crumbs on the children's bedroom floor. I have heard of people who allow their hens to hop into bed with them – their blood temperature being a good four degrees hotter than an average human's, they could be useful on a cold winter's night. Now I am mighty fond of my chooks, but not that much.

And not so much that I forget to wash my hands after handling them. Each time the news reported children hospitalised from E.coli infection, farms closed, parents worried about ever going near farm animals again ... I got the chance to nag my daughters – THAT'S WHAT HAPPENS IF YOU DON'T WASH YOUR HANDS! Though much more likely to be present in large numbers in lambs and calves than sweet ickkle chikkies, nasty bacteria like E.coli are worth worrying about, especially if you have young children. So there I stood, soap in hand, the kitchen tap running, ready for the kids to return from feeding them or fetching their eggs. As everyone who has ever been into a hospital knows, however much you adore the thing you touch, this elementary precaution is a major factor in holding back disease.

It was my born-again fastidiousness that made me take a fresh look at all sorts of health and safety matters.

Rats, for example. A fact of life in any British city, their population well exceeds our human one. They live happily alongside us, feeding on our food, using our guttering and our cavity walls for their transport system, our lofts and our cupboards for their nests. As a result of cuddly rat films like *Ratatouille*, the Great British public has recently been turning rat-lover. At the same time, with local councils reducing their pest control services and refuse collection, infestation is becoming increasingly common. From an urban henkeeper's point of view, the main problem with an infestation is when the neighbours blame it on your dirty birds.

I admit to a phobia about rats. Fine with spiders; happy with snakes and even welcoming of field mice, but when it comes to rats I turn chicken. Which was another good reason to limit my hens' access to the outside world. With its Fort Fox accoutrements, the Ark was penetrable only by the tiniest rat. Were it to have achieved this feat, it would have done so at night when the hens were tucked up, asleep on their perch. I imagined its ugly form slinking around in the dark, nibbling at the woodwork, snaffling whatever was left of dinner and finally scoffing the eggs hidden in the nesting box. Though the risk of rodents spreading disease is apparently exaggerated, I still worried about my chooks catching something from an intruder; I had nightmares about tiny rats turning into huge ones and attacking them.

In my calmer waking hours, I tried to be scrupulous. When I put leftovers out in an open bowl, I made myself sweep up any debris before dark. The hens' regular feed was in a hopper specifically designed to be inaccessible to rats; I tried not to spill any when I was transferring it to the coop. Were rat droppings to have appeared anywhere in the garden, I would have had no qualms at all about getting an electric rat-zapper.

Talking of zapping, you may have come across modern-day Rasputins who boast of their ability to lure hens into a state of trance. Generally this is done by holding the bird down on the ground and catching her attention with a forefinger held in front of her nose. By repeatedly drawing out a straight line in the air, or on the ground ahead of her, she is mesmerised into unblinking stillness. Or you can try drawing an actual line on the ground with a piece of white chalk.

I have to admit that I tried both methods on Ruby and never achieved my end. Perhaps I didn't have conviction enough to assert supreme mastery over my pet. But I did discover how to lull her asleep.

The best way was to hold her firmly in my lap, or in a comfy place like a patch of long grass and ease her head under her wing. Though it could feel as though I was about to wring her neck, I never got anywhere near. Lifting the wing wide (the one I had not clipped) I gently wrapped it around her head and held it fast, rocking her gently from side to side. Sometimes I even tried singing 'Rock-a-bye Baby'. Hey presto – she must have assumed it was time for bed and fell instantly comatose.

My second method came from watching *Ice Age* with the children – that bit where the animals play dead. The playing-dead mechanism occurs in real life as well as movies, and in all sorts of animals from pigeons to alligators – when under attack, they go into a fake rigor mortis in the hope that the predator will give up on them because he assumes they are dead already.

If you want to amuse yourself with your pets' talents in this area, you simply turn her on to her back (holding her sharp claws in to her body), stroke her gently and whisper sweet nothings in her ear. Soon enough her nictitating lid sweeps across her eyes. Once she is absolutely relaxed you can release your hold and chuckle with satisfaction at the big warm bird lying blissfully prostrate before you.

A sudden movement or a clap will awaken her.

More Eggs

I've not had one since Easter
And now it's half past three,
So, chick, chick, chick, chick, chicken
Lay a little egg for me.
Traditional rhyme

Second time around, I had got the egg timing right. While their winter predecessors had taken a couple of months to start laying, my spring POLs were delivering breakfast within days of their arrival.

'Twas ever thus. Long before Christians appropriated the symbol for Easter, eggs already meant renewal and regeneration. By the month of March the days were getting longer, the sun was rising in the sky, yet what did the land have to show for it? The seeds were hardly yet in the ground; over-wintered root crops had become wizened and inedible. Only the hens had got their act together to feed mankind.

When I was about eight I read *The Good Master* by Kate Seredy – set in the Hungarian Steppe before World War I, it told the story

of a feisty city girl, Kate, going to live with her country cousin
Jancsi and gradually becoming part of his family. Being a lover of
animals and all things outdoors, I adored Seredy's descriptions of
bareback riding and sheep herding. Her soft-focus illustrations
depicted pert rabbits and ardent songbirds, children wearing
embroidered waistcoats and trousers as full as skirts. Everything
in Kate's world was decorative – the furniture painted with
spiralling tendrils, leaves and flowers; cooking pots covered with
dots and crosses. I was particularly struck by the illustration at the
end of the 'Easter Eggs' chapter – two dark eggs lying together,
their shells adorned with flowers, one with an athletic-looking
chick tripping off its side.

*The last days before Easter were busy and exciting ones. Father and
Jancsi whitewashed the house inside and out. They painted the
window-boxes and shutters in bright blue. Jancsi and Kate selected the
largest, most perfect eggs, and they were laid aside for decorating ...*

*Evenings mother got out her dye pots and the fascinating work of
making dozens and dozens of fancy Easter eggs kept the family busy.
There were two ways to decorate them. The plainer ones were dyed
first. When they dried, father and Jancsi scratched patterns on them
with penknives. The fancy ones were lots of work. Mother had a tiny
funnel with melted bees wax in it. With this she drew intricate patterns
on the white eggs. After the wax hardened, she dipped them in the dye.
Then she scratched off the wax and there was the beautiful design left
in white on the coloured egg. In this way she could make the most beautifully shaded designs by covering up parts of the pattern again with
wax before each dipping. The finished ones were placed in baskets and
put on a shelf until Easter morning.*

Kate Seredy, *The Good Master*

Fifteen years after I read this book, I went to do some research in the Czech capital Prague. The city was still under communist rule and had a melancholy grandeur, its rusty trams clanking, its boulevards grey and empty, as were its shops. Wandering in the narrow streets of Malá Strana in search of some memento to take home, I spotted a little boutique and made my way inside. There, piled high in baskets on the floor were delicate blown eggs just like the ones Kate Seredy had described. In dazzling colours – scarlet, indigo, saffron – were etched intricate patterns of hearts and flowers, acorns and bells. Some had pictures of couples dancing and children playing. I bought several dozen, wrapped them in layers of paper and carried them home precariously in my hand luggage.

And now, more than another 15 years later, it was time to share my treasures with my daughters. At least with the eldest, Ellie, who at six and a half must surely be old enough to be trusted with them. She and I unwrapped them together and hung them on branches of flowering japonica culled from the garden and standing in a large vase on the kitchen table. Just as we would have done were we living in Eastern Europe. And then it occurred to me that we should celebrate Ruby and Scarlet's arrival with our very own decorating ritual.

The simplest way to colour eggs is to boil them in hot-dye. Dyes can be purchased over the internet – one person I know goes to the bother of buying them from Germany; beautiful they are too. Ellie and I had not had such foresight, so we did the simplest thing and boiled Ruby and Scarlet's pale brown eggs with some onion skin. After about an hour, the shells had turned a rich burnt sienna. A rummage in the cupboard produced more dyes I never thought I had – turmeric powder made them vibrant yellow; coffee grounds, darkest brown.

Knowing that Kate Seredy's eggs had been white rather than brown, I got hold of some duck eggs from the local butcher and started to experiment with other ingredients. The bottle of cheap red wine left to go vinegary by the stove discovered its destiny as a dye that turned duck eggs stunningly violet. A handful of boiled red cabbage leaves showed up a gorgeous purply blue; spinach water made the eggs green; Ellie's favourite was the grated beetroot that came out as pink as her baby dolls' cheeks.

Natural dyes can be a bit hit-and-miss. The liquid looks much darker in the pan than on the egg, and the eventual tone of the dried shell is often a surprise. Had I been a stickler for perfection I should have boiled and strained the liquid before putting the eggs in – this way I could have controlled the intensity and the uniformity of the colour. As it was, I rather liked the mottles and blotches from leaving the onion skins in the water, and the coal-dust effect from the coffee grounds. We needed to watch over the eggs as they boiled, rolling them around in order for the whole surface to get an even chance. With some of the vegetable waters, we left the eggs bathing overnight so they could take up as much dye as possible.

In this way, Ellie and I produced a couple of dozen rainbow coloured eggs. Their surfaces were luxuriously matt in texture, and piled together in a bowl they were wonderful to behold. Our Easter holiday guests took on the challenge of eating them, dyed whites and all.

Which inspired us to turn our creativity to fancy ones. For a contemporary version of Kate's second technique – a sort of Hungarian egg batik – the simplest version is a white wax crayon and poster paint. Even Beatrice, now nearly two, was allowed a go. I experimented with wax candles instead of crayons which were OK, though for some reason beeswax worked much better than paraffin-wax. I didn't try Seredy's version using melted beeswax from a funnel – I suspect it produces the best results. If you want something more sophisticated than poster paint, you need to use cold dyes so the wax doesn't melt as you apply it. The best cold dyes I discovered were shoe dyes; some of them leave a metallic sheen when they dry. One more tip about these fancy eggs – if you want to stop people eating them after you have gone to all that bother, then make sure you leave nothing edible inside.

Blowing eggs may require a combination of a micro-surgeon's hands and a trumpeter's lungs, but it is not difficult. All you do is take a needle or a pin and carefully make a tiny hole in the narrow end and a bigger one in the wide end. You hold the egg vertically over a bowl with the wide end downwards and blow hard through the tiny hole. The contents of the egg should fall into the bowl. If they get stuck, I try sticking the needle in as far as it will go and jiggling it about – that breaks the yolk and allows it to escape.

Before I get down to decorating, the insides need washing under the tap, or else the smell of rotten egg might ruin everything. I dry them and stand them in an eggcup to do the wax drawing, and then the painting. Naturally, these eggs are extremely fragile and not suitable for the likes of little Bea (hard-boiled only for her). After I had decorated them, I threaded a string down through the middle of the egg using a big needle. With the string hanging out from the bottom, I tied off the end with a double knot and bunged up the hole with a blob of clear nail varnish. *Voilà* – another beauty for the Easter tree.

*

Despite the large consumption of eggs in our house, I never reckoned on having eggshells to spare. I needed them for my veg plot – crushed and sprinkled in circles around my plants, they kept the snails at bay; I needed them for Ruby and Scarlet – providing calcium for the next round of eggs. Apparently as I get older I may also be needing them for myself, powdered with lemon juice, to try and waylay osteoporosis. But before then, there is one other activity I use them for, because it is such fun – eggheads.

Basically, these are the empty shells of boiled eggs, the top bit removed. Wash them and dry them, return them to their eggcup and fill them three-quarters full with a screwed-up ball of paper towel, or some cotton wool. You can even try putting in some John Innes compost, which gives you the clue to what happens next: you sprinkle a little water inside the egg and then a teaspoon of alfalfa seed, or cress, or any other seed you fancy (some grow faster than others). Keep watering your mini-garden each day and soon enough you will have lovely green fronds poking from the top of the shell.

The reason they are called eggheads is that you can draw faces on the shells. You need to make sure the eggcup is small enough that most of the shell peeks over the top; or else make a little egghead pedestal with an old loo roll. Dare to use non-water-based felt-tips which are a danger to the children's clothes but ensure your egghead won't be weeping the next time you water him. Like the sugar-solution we used to use before the days of effective styling gel, his punk-rocker hairdo is also edible.

*

Before you start to worry that this is turning into a craft book, I want to move on to cookery. And before you close the pages because you have enough cookery books already, I just want to mention my grandmother's recipe book. Here it is before me, bound in linen, its spine a little torn and battered after seventy years hard labour in the kitchen. On the opening page, Granny lists the recipes by page number in her careful calligraphy, their names often referring to a friend or relation long-gone – 'Joyce's lemon pudding', 'Shouna's noodles', 'Betty's chicken dish'.

Inside, the pages are spattered and stained, the recipes squeezed up against one another as three generations have added notes and comments. Their common origin is the food culture of World War II, meaning Granny's rations plus garden produce plus fresh eggs from my grandfather's Rhode Island Reds. And once in a while, the meat from that same flock. Almost everything except chicken dishes seems to have egg in it – how to stretch your bacon? Eggs. How to make a meal out of a tin of consommé? Eggs. How to make something delectable out of yet more potatoes or spinach from the veg plot? Eggs.

It is not just defiance of wartime deprivation that pours from Granny's pages. There is also the distinctive quality of a cuisine uninhibited by calorie-counting and cholesterol misinformation. Her family expected steamed pudding for afters. They were regularly tucking in to raspberry soufflé and honey cheese pie, after they had finished off the savoury cod custard. I have a strong compulsion to set down all these recipes so that eggy pleasures once more find their place in the Great British kitchen. Pleasures that are even greater if the ingredients originate in one's own back garden. But as this is not a cookery book, I shall choose just two – one savoury and one sweet.

Mayonnaise

1 egg yolk
Pinch of salt
Half a pint of sunflower oil
1 tablespoon virgin olive oil
Lemon juice
Pepper

There is nothing so markedly home-made as home-made mayonnaise, especially when it is made with your own eggs. Because you know your hens are healthy and vaccinated, you have minimal worry about Salmonella from the raw egg. Because your egg is fresh (the fresher the better), it has only ever known temperatures between mother's body at 41 degrees and your kitchen – probably around 20. If the bowl, the whisk and the jug of oil are all nice and warm as well, then there is very little risk of curdling. Of course, Granny used a hand whisk and probably not a very fine vegetable oil. Sunflower is my light oil of choice, with a tablespoon or two of virgin olive oil at the end to give it flavour. I use a hand-held electric whisk.

I start off whisking the yolks on their own, then I add a pinch of salt, then the oil. Whisking all the time, the important thing is to add the oil very, very slowly – initially, just a drop at a time. Once the first drops seem to have bonded with the yolk, I try to get a fine, golden stream flowing from my jug. I remember my grandmother pouring from quite a height – she said the oil seeped in easier this way. Scientifically speaking, what she was creating was an emulsion of oil droplets suspended in a base of egg yolk. The water in the yolk is an essential element – the base into which the oil droplets emulsify.

Fresh egg yolk is just about the best emulsifier around because the yolk itself is a concentrated and complex emulsion of fat in water, and therefore filled with emulsifying molecules. Here we are talking lipoproteins (both low density and high density) – the sort whose levels they measure in your blood when searching for cholesterol. When raw yolk (warmish) gets beaten with oil, its lipoproteins burst out and coat the fat droplets.

All the ingredients and utensils need to be nice and warm because warmth speeds the transfer of the lipoproteins from the yolk to the oil. The salt is there from the start because it causes the yolk granules to fall apart into their component particles, making the yolk more viscous. This viscosity then helps to break the oil into ever-smaller droplets.

Eventually I am hoping for a thick mayonnaise into which I can whisk the tasty virgin olive oil, a few squeezes of lemon juice and a little pepper. The reason the result tastes so much better than shop-bought versions is that it contains no stabilisers – often carbohydrates; sometimes a kind of white sauce; check the label. A lack of stabilising agent means my emulsion may be delicious but is also vulnerable to damage from too much heat or too much cold. Up to 80 per cent of its volume is oil that can easily separate while in the fridge and will need beating back in, perhaps with a drop of warm water.

Oeufs à la Neige

> 2 fresh egg whites (at room temperature)
> 2 fresh egg yolks and one complete egg (ditto)
> 2 oz caster sugar
> 1 pint of milk
> 1-2 oz loaf sugar (Demerara)
> Vanilla essence

This is the eggiest of Granny's eggy puddings – a sort of inverted version of the egg itself, with whites floating inside yellows. I am not sure why it is called *oeufs à la neige* – I can think of many more snowy egg concoctions than this one. Some people call it Floating Islands. Bea calls it Froth Cakes. Whatever the name, mine often turns out craggier than I intended, but it always tastes amazing.

Loaf sugar is some ancient form of sugar, pre-war even – the nearest I know is unrefined cane sugar called Jaggery from my Bangladeshi grocer. It is rough and slightly damp and sold in a block (or loaf) that you cut up. An ounce of Demerara does just fine as an alternative. By the way, the eggs don't have to be super-fresh; a very fresh egg white can be difficult to foam, but then again foam made with an old egg is unstable; eggs a few days old are the best. The egg whites need to be beaten until they stand up in stiff peaks.

Which is odd, if you think about it. Normally, beating things vigorously without heat breaks them down – butter and sugar at the start of cake-making; your children when they have taxed your patience too far. Egg whites adhere to a more Wackford Squeers philosophy – a good beating builds them up. Or, as the great food scientist Harold McGee likes to put it, 'thanks to egg whites, we are able to harvest the air.'

In his hefty classic, *Food and Cooking: an Encyclopedia of Kitchen Science, History and Culture*, McGee explains that, just like the foam on your bath, egg foam is a mass of liquid bubbles filled with air. The reason they don't collapse, he says, is due to the protein in the albumen. As the whisk pulls at the compacted protein molecules they are unwrapped; also, as air enters the liquid it creates an imbalance that tugs the proteins out of their usual folded shape. These unfolded proteins gather where air and water meet, with the water-loving bits immersed in the water and water-hating bits projecting into the air. Having thus unfolded and accumulated on the surface of the bubbles, the proteins bond with one another, creating a solid network that holds everything in place.

Of course, we need an effective tool with which to beat our foams – which is why meringues and soufflés did not enter European cuisine until the middle of the seventeenth century, when some clever chap invented whisks made of bundles of straw.

Not long after the bundles came on the scene, cooks realised they could also do with copper bowls. To understand the need for copper bowls, you have to know about collapsing foams – this is when the whole thing starts to leak and crumble. It happens because the albumen proteins have embraced one another just that bit too tightly and squeezed out the water held between. What copper does is it eliminates the strongest protein bonds that can form – those between sulphurs. Another, cheaper trick is to add acid to your egg white (half a teaspoon of lemon juice per white). It boosts the number of free-floating hydrogen ions in the albumen, making it harder for sulphur-hydrogen compounds to break up and thereby liberating the sulphurs to go off and find one another.

Even with copper bowls or lemon juice, your egg may still fail to foam. In my case, that is bound to be because the bowl is dirty. Detergent or egg yolk, oil or fat can all contaminate the process by competing with the albumen proteins and interfering with their bonding process. Even sugar can be a problem. Which is why Granny adds her sugar at the end of the whisking; any earlier and it would delay the development of the foam quite considerably.

But before we get to the sugar-adding, there is this 'stiff peaks' business. 'Stiff peaks' is one stage on from 'soft peaks', but a stage before 'slip-and-streak' where things start to collapse. This is the fullest and firmest my foam is ever likely to be – its bubbles approaching 90 per cent air content. As McGee sees it 'the protein webs in adjacent bubbles begin to catch on each other and on the bowl surface. There's just enough lubrication left for the foam to be creamy and easily mixed with other ingredients'. In other words – it's just perfect.

At this point, Granny recommends that I gently fold in the caster sugar.

Meanwhile, at the stove I put the milk and sugar and vanilla essence into a wide, shallow saucepan and bring slowly to the boil, stirring to make sure the sugar has dissolved. Then I take a dessert-spoonful of my egg white mixture, lower it carefully into the boiling milk and watch it swell. I add as many spoonfuls as I think I can safely fit without them sticking together, letting them bob up and down in the milk for a minute, then turning them over and cooking the other side for the same amount of time. What I now have is a clutch of soft meringues that I remove with a long-handled sieve and set on one side.

In a separate bowl, I whisk the yolks with the one egg and add a little of the hot milk. Then I turn down the saucepan of sugary milk so it is just simmering, and pour in the beaten yellows which I must stir gently until the custard thickens.

McGee has lots of wisdom to impart about what is going on at this stage, now the egg proteins are distributed in the milk and sugar. The sugar is a particular problem as it surrounds each egg protein molecule with several thousand sucrose molecules. With this shield between them, the proteins have to work really hard to find one another, so the liquid needs to be pretty hot. At the same time, the 'protein network' is tenuous and fragile, so just a few degrees too hot and it collapses, forming water-filled tunnels through the custard.

What McGee is telling us is that we must be patient. He compares turning up the heat to hasten the custard's thickening to speeding up the car on a wet road when you are searching for an unfamiliar driveway. You get to your destination faster, but you may not be able to avoid skidding past it, straight into curdle-dom.

My solution is to have the electric whisk standing by with which to attack any signs of the eggs starting to scramble. Eventually, having stirred and stirred and whisked and stirred, resisting all temptation of raising the temperature, eventually I have something that resembles custard. Maybe not as thick as the Bird's variety, but definitely MY birds'. I pour into a serving dish, let it cool and then bung it in the fridge so it has the chance to become as firm as possible before I place my craggy islands on top and serve.

Having kept to my promise of providing only a couple of recipes, I can't resist the opportunity to point out the convenience of eggs as pure, edible matter. As long as you have some sort of cooking facility, you can eat them utterly unadulterated; *sans* oil, *sans* sugar, *sans* salt, *sans* everything. They are one of the few things that people who never read a recipe still manage to cook. Forget pot noodles or tins of beans, a shelled egg offers the simplest form of ready-made food. For many of us, it is the first thing we choose to eat each day.

Which is why it is worth considering how to give it its best chance of success. For example, should we really take it straight from the fridge (its temperature at 4 degrees or so) and plunge it into boiling water (at 100 degrees)? Isn't that just asking for the contents to seize up and form a white so rubbery and a yellow so grainy they are well-nigh inedible? Leaving it too long or at too high a temperature can have the same results. Or else a greenish residue forms around the yolk – ferrous sulphide, created by sulphur from the albumen mixing with iron from the yolk. It is harmless, but unappetising in colour and smell.

According to Harold McGee, cooking an egg in boiling water guarantees a cracked shell. Jay tends to be the one who cooks the breakfast eggs in our house, which means he's vulnerable to a bit of nagging when I appear halfway through the process. I tell him that McGee says pricking a tiny hole in the egg before you boil it is unlikely to help; it may release a little of the internal pressure as the contents expand, but it won't stop all that knocking about caused by the bubbling water. I helpfully turn the heat down and even find a lid for the saucepan. But is this intervention appreciated?

The answer to such problems is for couples like us to agree to eschew the great British tradition of boiled eggs and have simmered ones instead. In order to coagulate, the contents don't need anything so hot as boiling water; in fact, coagulation happens at much lower temperatures, between 65 and 80 degrees. Better still, for an intact shell, a tender white and creamy yellow, we should get out the steamer (otherwise reserved for veg). Because of the coagulation thing, timings for steaming or simmering are exactly the same as for boiled eggs – soft centres need about 4 minutes; hard-cooked between 10 and 15.

Or else we can go the whole hog and leave them overnight. In the Middle East they have a long and noble tradition of being gentle to eggs. The Hamine method of slow-cooking appeals to me especially because it combines both my egg-craft and my egg-cookery skills: set some onion skins boiling in your egg pan, then lower the heat to almost nothing, slip in a couple of eggs and a whoosh of oil (to reduce evaporation) and leave to simmer for six hours or even overnight. Chocolate-hued, they are deliciously creamy.

Another version of Hamine eggs is when we go camping and want to make use of the dying embers of our bonfire. We bury raw eggs in the ash and dig out smoke-flavoured, firm ones in the morning. Buried deep enough, they don't end up like Touchstone's in *As You Like It* – 'damned, like an ill-roasted egg, all on one side.' Nor will they be broken, which is invariably the case with eggs that I try to store overnight in a tent.

At home, most of us keep our eggs in the fridge – McGee advises that it is the best way to inhibit dangerous pathogens. Though it may seem perverse of me to contradict my food science master, I have to say that the conditions offered by an average family fridge like ours are not the best for eggs. Jay and I keep them there mainly out of habit, reassuring ourselves that it won't be for long.

There are numerous good reasons not to. Firstly, in its humid atmosphere water passes into the yolk, causing it to swell and the membrane to weaken. That means when it gets to the pan, however careful I am with my 'sunny side up', I am far more likely to get an omelette. Secondly, because of their porous shells, eggs pick up whatever flavours are knocking around in the fridge. This sort of storage problem has a much greater influence on the taste of an egg than ever its mother's diet will. The garlic flavour detected in Jay's omelette, for example, is far more likely to have come from that nearby bowl of hummus than from the mashed cloves I had added to the hens' slops. Thirdly, using that set of egg-holes in the door means the delicate eggs are subjected to a regular banging and a-crashing, along with a waft of warm air from the central heating. If they are not actually damaged, they sure are unsettled.

Then there is the problem of cold eggs which, as we have seen, are no good for emulsifying or foaming or boiling. In fact, for any kind of food preparation, eggs are best removed from the fridge well in advance. I try to remember to do this, even if it means delaying supper. One day I will get the same set of wooden egg-shelves as my friend Jane, fixed to the wall near the cooker. She also Blu-tacks a pen nearby so the moment the eggs arrive from the coop, she can write the date on the shell, then be sure to eat them in the right order.

Eggs kept at a coolish room temperature (around 12 degrees) should stay edible for exactly the same amount of time as they would in the fridge – 27 days is what the Salmonella-sensitive Lion Code people recommend. The only issue in keeping eggs out of the fridge is that harmful bacteria are able to multiply much faster than they would inside it. The only way to be sure you have got rid of them is to kill them – this means simmering the eggs at 60 degrees centigrade for five minutes, or even at 70 degrees for one, or something in between if you are after a standard, soft-boiled egg.

If you are concerned about Salmonella, you should probably do this for refrigerated eggs because there are loads of bacteria knocking around in the average fridge; Salmonella is not killed by being there.

Nor in the freezer. My friend Karen sometimes freezes her excess Easter eggs. She says you need to crack the shells open in advance, otherwise their expanding contents are likely to force the issue, bursting out all over the freezer. Yolks and whites are best separated into bags or boxes, with a little sugar or salt added to the yolks to stop them becoming gunky when defrosted.

Growing up in 60s Hemel Hempstead, another friend, Bruce, vividly remembers the pre-freezer method of preservation.

'Preserved eggs!' I hear you cry. 'Pickled ones? Like trying to eat rubber balls!'

Dried ones? Far too redolent of wartime rations for Bruce's mother. Her way of preserving eggs came from an even earlier period of self-sufficiency. The same culture in which everyone learnt to pickle fruit and veg, dry their onions and bury their carrots in sand. She used a yellow, syrupy liquid called 'water-glass' or sodium silicate – a benign chemical compound used these days in things like glues and soaps and toothpaste – purchased from the pharmacist or poultry supply men. Bruce and I have managed to find an account from an old home economics book:

These early summer months are when the thrifty housewife who has her own hens, or who can draw upon the surplus supply of a nearby neighbour, puts away in water glass eggs for next autumn and winter. To ensure success, care must be exercised in this operation. In the first place, the eggs must be fresh, preferably not more than two or three days old … Earthenware crocks are good containers. The crocks must be clean and sound. Scald them and let them cool completely before use. A crock holding six gallons will accommodate eighteen dozens of eggs and about twenty-two pints of solution. Too large crocks are not desirable, since they increase the liability of breaking some of the eggs, and spoiling the entire batch.

Water glass is diluted in the proportion of one part of silicate to nine parts of distilled water, rainwater, or other water. In any case, the water should be boiled and then allowed to cool. Half fill the vessel with this solution and place the eggs in it a few at a time till the container is filled. Be sure to keep about two inches of water glass above the eggs. Cover the crock and place it in the coolest place available from which the crock will not have to be moved. When the eggs are to be used, remove them as desired, rinse in clean, cold water and use immediately.

Eggs preserved in water glass can be used for soft boiling or poaching up to November. They are satisfactory for frying until about December. From that time until the end of the usual storage period – that is until March – they can be used for omelettes, scrambled eggs, custards, cakes and general cookery.

One day, I plan to find space for more chickens and for them to produce more eggs than I can use. Come the glut, I would love the opportunity to give away boxes of them or even make a bit of extra cash by selling them to my neighbours (this is perfectly legal, as long as I don't try to do it through a shop or similarly formal outlet). I look forward to having to write the date on the eggs, store them in their own shelving, in the freezer or a charmingly traditional crock by the back door.

In the meantime, I am more likely to find that the egg holes in my fridge are empty yet again. At which point I send Ellie down the garden, reminding her of the old adage – *'The best way to keep an egg fresh is to keep it in the chicken.'*

Sick Chick

'What ought we to do?' asked Ukridge.
'Well, my aunt, sir, when 'er fowls 'ad the roop, she gave them snuff.'
'Give them snuff, she did,' he repeated, with relish, 'every morning.'
'Snuff!' said Mrs. Ukridge.
'Yes, ma'am. She give 'em snuff till their eyes bubbled.'
Mrs. Ukridge uttered a faint squeak at this vivid piece of word-painting.
'And did it cure them?' asked Ukridge.
'No, sir,' responded the expert soothingly.
PG Wodehouse, *Love among the Chickens*

A couple of months after Ruby and Scarlet arrived, we went away on holiday, leaving them in the excellent care of our neighbours. It amazed me how many people I knew were longing to exercise their husbandry skills. When I left my children for an evening with a teenager, I paid her £20 and crossed my fingers nothing happened to test her knowledge of paediatrics, let alone emergency services. Yet for Ruby and Scarlet I could afford to be choosy, picking the most responsible adult for regular, attentive visits, someone who would ask nothing in return but the opportunity to gather fresh eggs.

I knew I should not to be surprised if Ruby and Scarlet acted strangely on our return. However good their hen-sitter, they were quite likely to be hunched up and grumpy, refusing to come near. Like most pets, hens quickly get used to a routine, and it only takes a weekend away for them to go into a sulk.

Just as I had anticipated, the morning we got back we found Scarlet, the plumpest and the perkiest of the two, huddled in the corner of the run. 'Typical,' I thought, presenting her with a conciliatory bowl of scraps. By the afternoon, she was looking decidedly peaky. When I picked her up, I discovered a white discharge coming from her bottom. Damn. I stood there beside the Ark, holding my mucky bird stiffly, at arm's length, and wondering what to do next. Ruby was dodging up and down behind the mesh, eager for a run in the garden; I had better get her sister away from her in case she spread any germs.

Ideally, I should have created a sick bay close by, so Ruby could see Scarlet was still around and wouldn't treat her like an unwanted stranger on her return. But I worried about schlepping the rickety spare cage down to the far end of the garden where the fox might break in. Outside my kitchen window I could keep a watchful eye on her.

The next morning she had taken no food or water and seemed much the same as the day before, her head lolling sadly. I wondered whether I should spend £25 on a consultation with the vet and probably the same again on a course of antibiotics. And then throw away the eggs for 28 days, in order to ensure the drugs didn't get into us. I couldn't help thinking how another one of Mr Hodgkins' happy, healthy hybrids would cost me only six quid.

I got out my poultry books. In her beginner's guide, *Starting with Chickens*, the great smallholder's guru Katie Thear declares – 'not many vets understand chickens'. Good. In that case, I wouldn't bother.

But what if Scarlet got sicker? How long was I prepared to watch her suffer? How long was it right to let her do so?

I phoned Mr Hodgkins. As I stood in front of the cage, trying to describe Scarlet's symptoms, I could see that she was stretching her head upwards in crooked, straining movements.

'Could she be bearing down?' Mr Hodgkins enquired.

As someone who has gone through a couple of labours, I felt qualified to confirm that yes, this might well be what she was doing.

'In that case she's probably egg bound. Have you been away?'

'Yes – we got back yesterday.'

'Ah. Things like this do happen when you go away … They don't like change, you know.'

'No.'

'Do you think the fox might have been round?'

'Very likely. There was nobody in the garden most of the day.'

'She seems very poorly, you say?'

'I'm afraid so.'

'Then what I think has happened is that your fox gave the hen a fright while she was laying. The egg broke inside her and now she's infected.'

'What do you think I should do, Mr Hodgkins?' There was a pensive pause.

'Have you any experience of wringing their necks?' Another pause.

'None.'

'I'm off on holiday myself in a couple of days, else I'd come round and give you a hand ...'

'Can't we get her some antibiotics?'

'Well, that'll set you back a few quid ... and it might not do any good anyway.'

I'll tell you what,' he said, 'give her another 24 hours. You never know – she might get better of her own accord.'

She didn't. Nor did she get worse. Next morning I watched from the kitchen window as her head sank towards the drinking dish, sleepy but somehow still hopeful. Ellie spent ages cooking up a special oatmeal porridge for her, with a generous topping of poultry spice for extra flavour, and set her dainty dish before her. By the time she got home from school, the whole lot was gone. I phoned Mr Hodgkins and he said hang on in there, you never know ... He was off for his annual holiday.

Next morning her head was tucked into her breast. The whole family went out to the cage after breakfast and the girls stroked her lovely golden back. We all felt wretched; I thought probably it was too late to call the vet. Only now did I realise that a hen's wellbeing is a fragile thing. That evening, Scarlet breathed her last.

What Scarlet had is not uncommon. It's called egg-binding, and once the system becomes infected it is called egg peritonitis. It is especially common in pullets – sometimes before the infection takes hold they produce a series of soft or shell-less eggs, but often the peritonitis just hits them. Once a hen starts to feel unwell from an infection like this, it takes only a very little time for her to want to give up the ghost.

Next time a chick gets sick, I will immediately diagnose the problem and turn on the kettle. Seriously. I shall have a look up her vent – is there an egg stuck there? If there is, then a cure is also within sight. Quick as a flash I will get out my tub of Vaseline, rub it around her vent then hold her over the steaming kettle (not too close – don't want to scald either of us). Or else, I shall try breaking the egg with a skewer or some such and remove the broken pieces, being careful not to leave any bits behind.

If I can't see the egg, then I have a problem. It might lie out of sight, broken (as Scarlet's probably was), and it might already be causing infection (as the white discharge indicated). Because the hen's abdomen is so close to her egg-production system, that becomes infected too. Sometimes there is no egg at all, merely a general infection of the reproductive system. Even contaminated dust entering her breathing system can be the cause, as the air sacs are very close to the ovaries.

Had I immediately taken Scarlet to see the vet, he might have prescribed a course of antibiotics and a few crossed fingers, or he might simply have offered to put her out of her misery. Poor Scarlet.

My only consolation was that at least she never lived to suffer the rest of that summer of discontent. It was on a particularly beautiful June afternoon that I noticed the next wave of trouble. My English garden was at its most glorious – clematis bells nodding from the trellis; roses rambling all over the place; yet Ruby was not in the slightest bit interested in joining me. Instead she lay in her dust tray, dipping and diving like a hippo in a swamp. I thought maybe she was trying to stay cool. She didn't look miserable exactly, and had not seemed to pine for Scarlet over the preceding weeks. I did wonder if her usually bright comb was looking paler.

Just before bedtime, I went to hook up the ladder door and found that instead of settling on her perch, she was still hanging around outside. It was then that I began to cotton on – Ruby would rather risk a night out in the cold than go upstairs to her sleeping compartment. There must be something really nasty going on in there; I went to get a torch and opened up the nesting box. There in the wood-chippings, shining scarlet in my beam of light, was a seething mass of red mite. They were crawling over one another like a pack of drunks.

I had no idea how they'd got in, these nasty little parasites, cousins of the so-much-cuddlier spider. Perhaps in the bag of wood chips, or more likely from wild birds that had scattered them amongst the geraniums where they bided their time until my unsuspecting hen came by. Like leeches, red mite can last for many months between one meal and the next.

Despite their name, they are not in fact red until they have fed, which is when they become easiest to spot. The pre-prandial version is grey and smaller because not yet tanked up, varying in size from a full-stop to a semi-colon. Mite tend to hang out in gangs, and can scuttle a few feet, but not much more. Newly hatched ones are white and frustratingly difficult to spot. If you are making regular checks for mite, as I should have been, there could well be a grey powdery frass around the edges of doors and floors, resembling ground white pepper. These are their droppings and often the first tell-tale sign that the blighters have arrived.

Their absolute favourite time of year is a humid summer because they like warm, damp conditions. Plastic houses seem less attractive to them because of their smooth surfaces and a dearth of hiding places. Wooden ones like Ruby's, with gaps between the boards (or, worse still, extra layers of roofing felt) offer plenty and have my eglu friend Fiona smirking 'I told you so …'

Though mite live in the house rather than on the hens, I should have been giving Ruby a regular search around her neck, wings and bottom. I had grown lax in my husbandry duties. Had I investigated her before I got to the nesting box, I might have found she had itched away her feathers during those long hours in the dust bath. Other signals are if the hens start to lay less, or the eggs have pale yolks and splashes of blood on their shells; some birds become sleepier and hungrier than usual. Eventually, a chronic infestation can literally suck a hen to death. Which is why it needs treating.

The question is with what? Unfortunately, most repellents merely repel; once the little buggers have invaded, you need something stronger. Grandparents who used to keep hens may recommend old-fashioned remedies that are guaranteed to work; sheep-dip amongst them. Whether they kill the hens as well as their parasites is worth considering.

Fortunately, there are effective new products coming on the market all the time, some of them '100 per cent natural' AND efficacious. At my Countrywide shop I found a canister of powder to apply to the hen herself. Made from Diatomaceous earth – the fossilised remains of plankton (or diatoms) – it works by breaking down the mites' waxy coats and dehydrating them to death.

The shop assistant recommended treating at dusk, when the vampires would be on the move, creeping out of hiding towards their prey, or simply creeping all over one another as they had been the previous evening. He also recommended that I don protective clothing – though red mite tend not to enjoy human blood nearly as much as avian, given the sort of attention I was planning, they might fancy escaping into my hair.

In spattered old decorating overalls, surgical gloves and a shower cap, I resembled nothing so much as a shabby chemical weapons inspector. Jay took charge of the canister while I held sleepy Ruby, opening one wing and then another, turning her around so not one bit of her body would be missed. With WMD all over me, my garden and my chook, I put her in a cardboard box and let her snooze there while I made my assault on her home.

If I had had a steam blaster, I would have used it to evict the intruders. Large amounts of concentrated washing-up liquid will apparently incapacitate them if you want to do that first. One old-fashioned product people risk (if they can get hold of it) is creosote. It may be illegal for domestic use but it is still very effective painted all over the coop, inside and out, and even kills the eggs (which nothing else seems to). Maybe there are some alternative wood treatments coming on the market, just as sticky and just as pungent. You have to find the hens an alternative dwelling for a few weeks, or they risk expiring from the fumes.

My weapon of choice was a spray can. The active ingredients were permethrin and pyrethrin/piperonyl butoxide, which are also in head-lice treatments; like the lice treatments, the exact balance of ingredients has to keep changing as the victims develop immunity to their powers. Pyrethrin is a derivative of the chrysanthemum flower; with piperonyl butoxide it acts on the mites' tiny nerve cell membranes, interrupting signals traveling between their brains and their muscles so they become paralyzed and die. Permethrin does the same thing and can also kill the eggs.

First I removed all the infested bedding and the perch, and swept out the inside of the Ark. Everything went in my yellow bucket to take down to the allotment where I hoped my bloodsuckers would starve to death before they discovered the blackbirds. A better option would have been to burn them – mite-infested bedding crackles most prettily – but bonfires are much frowned upon on our allotment site.

In order to reach all the mite in the Ark, Jay helped me turn it on its side and we sprayed up into the pitch of the ceiling. Like bed bugs, red mite are happy to hide up there and wait until night to drop down and feast. Well, I was not putting up with that. I sprayed all the walls where they might clamber, the perch slots where they had left an incriminating smudge of blood, every potential hiding place on floor and walls. I tried to shoot killer into every nook and cranny; I tried not to inhale. Once the whole coop was doused, I shut it up for half an hour, and meanwhile gave the perch a good going over.

Though the spray was expensive, I knew not to scrimp. On the label it said 'hazardous to bees', so I only sprayed it on the inside of the Ark and hoped no bee was foolish enough to go in there for a while. A cheaper option would have been to use poultry house disinfectant, but apparently that is even more of a threat to bees. Alluringly pink and smelling slightly of lavender, it comes in a bottle and needs to be watered down. Apart from permethrin and pyrethrin, it also contains tetramethrin (another, related insecticide), detergents and paraffin.

When the dirty deed was done I stuffed my inspector's uniform in the washing machine and took a shower. Meanwhile, Jay threw out Ruby's box and scrubbed the brushes and buckets under the garden tap to prevent the little buggers hanging out there for months to come, waiting to be reintroduced to their hosts. Despite our efforts, for several days after that first mite-massacre I found I suffered from imaginary prickly head and forearms. Out of the corner of my eye, I thought I saw red mite scuttling across the draining board or into my bed. I struggled to remind myself they were NOT immortal. They may have seemed it, but they weren't.

If you have ever treated children for head lice, you will know that persistence is of the essence. It is no good just spraying something around and then skedaddling. You can guarantee that even as you walk away more babies are happily hatching into the world, ready to take the place of the ones you have just killed. Just one survivor can become thousands very quickly indeed.

Which is why Jay and I had to do the same thing the next night, and the next, until after three days the killer contents of my can were used up. On day four we took a day off, and I went on the internet to bulk buy more spray. While I was waiting for it to arrive, I asked around for alternatives. Some friends said to try household disinfectant like Dettol and Jay's cleaning fluid (the commercial stuff, not my husband's home brand). The most convincing brew came from my henkeeping friend, Karen, who recommended Jay's fluid plus clove oil. The smell of public toilets mingled with Christmas was absolutely nauseating.

After day five's assault, I left a bit of newspaper under the perch as a mite indicator. The idea was to count the number of mite hiding in its folds each subsequent evening, but I found it simpler to open up the coop and start sweeping. If there were still red mite around, soon enough one of them would find its way on to a bare bit of forearm, crawl between the hairs and give me a nip. Horrid. And my heart sank because it meant Operation Mite was not yet over.

Which in a way it never would be. Though Ruby dared to enter her sleeping compartment even on day one of the mission, and was back to her usual, colourful self within a few days, I knew the invaders were not likely to leave completely. It was now part of my henkeeping to be fully mite-aware and make sure I always had a can of spray on hand. Though a winter freeze might shut them up and last year's infestation looked as though it had disappeared over Christmas, come the summer it could well return.

I tried to minimise mite-friendly regions. I kept fresh bedding to a minimum – just one layer of paper in the sleeping compartment and a handful of wood shavings in the nesting box. I got hold of a benign repellent powder whose active ingredient was a pungent mixture of tea tree oil and citronella and talc-ed both house and bird each week. Plus a good dose in the dust bath. And whenever the sun was shining in the right direction, I opened up the sleeping compartment – mite like things damp and dark; UV rays they cannot abide.

The reason mite are such a palaver to treat is that they nest in the house. Parasites that live on a hen's body are much easier and can, in fact, be killed en masse with anti-parasite medication. Administered through the skin, it is not licensed for sale to poultry keepers in the UK, but you can get some for pigeons from the odd website or from the vet for the cat. I had one that I squeezed on to the back of Tigger's neck to keep away fleas. The hens could have had a small dose of the same thing dabbed under their wings, and from what my online poultry fora say, this is an increasingly popular option. The price you pay (apart from the obvious expense of the medication in the first place) is you have to throw away the eggs for about a week afterwards. But for a whole three months you rest body-based-parasite free.

First and foremost, that means free from lice and fleas. The first sign of one of these common pests is likely to be a greasy clump of eggs in amongst the feathers, especially in the shelter of wings and combs. Keep searching and soon enough you find the parents running or hopping around, the size of a large sesame seed.

There is lice and flea repellent powder on the market that contains exactly the same ingredients as mite repellent, but ground less finely. A regular talc-ing should keep fleas, lice and mite at bay to some degree, but will entirely fail to combat scaly leg mite – mite that burrow their way under the scales on a chickens' legs. Some breeds of chicken like the Silkie are particularly prone to it. You know you have an infestation if the scales on her feet and legs are lifting and even falling off, with white crusts pushing up from underneath. The condition is extremely infectious and can permanently cripple the bird if left untreated. Some people recommend dipping legs in surgical spirit twice a week and then coating them with Vaseline until the parasites perish. Others recommend soaking with soapy water, drying them and then painting on the white liquid insecticide benzyl benzoate (available from vets and chemists).

Or else they save themselves the bother and give her some of the cat's flea killer, which is so powerful it kills not only all those external parasites but internal ones too. Even the ubiquitous intestinal worms.

Easy to pick up from dirty ground and from scoffing slugs and snails (damn it – I took the risk and lobbed them into the run all the same), these parasites of the digestive tract come in all shapes and sizes. Symptoms of a bad bout can mimic those for mite and peritonitis combined – the hens look scraggy and pale, their droppings may be weird colours and runny, and their bottoms mucky.

Fortunately, my hens needed nothing more virulent than a little worm powder sprinkled in their feed. The same dose a couple of times a year seemed to keep the wrigglies permanently at bay.

Until I found that I wanted wrigglies after all. My friend Paul from Zimbabwe recommends feeding hens maggots when they become crop bound. Crop binding is a very uncomfortable and quite common condition, often showing up on a summer's night, after a good day's guzzling. Sometimes the sufferer will do weird things with her head, like Scarlet with her egg binding – rolling it round to try and dislodge the offending mass. Looking carefully down the front of her body, you see something bulging out like a big breast. You have a feel – there is a lump of food stuck fast in there.

A crop bound chicken may feel miserable but still goes on feeding (after all, her tummy feels empty), which is not such a great idea. Let her go to bed as normal, but don't let her eat next morning before you have felt her crop again. If it is still in the same bulgy state, you need to try and do something about it. A common treatment is to syringe a teaspoon of vegetable oil down her throat and massage gently to loosen the lump. You can also try tipping her upside down and 'milking her' – holding her beak wide open with one hand, you knead the blockage out with the other, while being careful not to choke her. Simpler and safer than either is to find your local fishing shop and get some of Paul's maggots – down in the crop they chomp away until the lump disbands.

But they won't do much good if it's turned sour. A sour crop is when her breath starts to stink. It is probably because she has eaten some mouldy feed or too many scraps (in our case, too many sandwiches from the leftovers bucket). This time she is miserable but her crop is squashy rather than solid; she may well have diarrhoea. A teaspoon of Epsom salts dissolved in a glass of water is the traditional answer. Indeed, my *Encyclopedia of Poultry* says 'this cheap and simple physic ... clears the system of fowl more thoroughly and speedily than anything else.' If you don't happen to have any, Paul says to try yoghurt; it soothes digestive troubles in humans too. For a sick chick you make a porridge of yoghurt and oats and give it to them for a few days instead of all the other stuff. Until she is better, Paul says to avoid scraps and even greens.

But we can give her greens if she has a cold – it's the vitamin C, I suppose. If ever I noticed catarrh on Ruby's nostrils, and thought her eyes were watering, greens were a major element in my cold menu. Also, poultry spice in her seed mix; garlic squeezed into hot oats; a slice or two of fresh, raw onion in her water. Though aconite is on my list of plants poisonous to chickens, a drop of it in a teaspoon of milk used to be recommended as an effective cold cure.

Apart from the special food and drink, Ruby also got taken from her run and given a couple of days in sick bay (yes – that old bunny cage), snuggled up in a bed of straw and shredded paper. Had her symptoms worsened; had she started sneezing and wheezing as well, I would have jettisoned the folk remedies and called the vet. Chickens' respiratory systems are sensitive – you don't want them infected for long. Because she was vaccinated against bronchitis, the most likely illness would have been a bacterial infection called mycoplasma which is treated with prescribed antibiotics.

Fortunately, my birds never got anything worse than the snuffles. Which is why I never had cause to try the snuff. What Ukridge's advisor in *Love Among the Chickens* seems to be talking about with his 'roop' is a parasitic infection of the respiratory tracts. I have read that the fumes of carbolic acid, breathed in by the chicken 'to the point of suffocation' will draw the parasites out. I reckon the snuff was not quite powerful enough.

And then there are the illnesses that threaten not only *Gallus gallus domesticus* but also *Homo sapiens*. First off: chicken pox.

Just joking. Though a century ago a scrofulous condition in poultry did go by this title, these days it is known as Fowl Pox. More common in America and Africa than Europe, it is spread by mosquitoes and can be vaccinated against. As for why we call our version 'chicken pox', possibly it is because the skin of the human sufferer looks a bit like my favourite birds'. Unlike goose pimples, these ones seem to have been badly plucked. Samuel Johnson suggested an etymology I like less but feel I should mention – compared to the full-blown pox (smallpox), it was 'less dangerous' or cowardly and therefore 'chicken'. Thanks Sam.

What we are talking about here is serious stuff like Salmonella. According to the Ministry of Agriculture in France, if we all kept French Maran chickens with their glamorous dark brown eggs, we would never encounter Salmonella because the pores of their shells are so tiny that those nasty microbes can never get in.

Unfortunately, most of us don't. Instead, most of us remember Junior Health Minister Edwina Currie's gaffe in 1988 when she told the nation that 'most of the egg production in this country, sadly, is now affected with Salmonella'. It sparked outrage among farmers and egg producers, causing egg sales to plummet and Edwina to get the sack.

Ten years later the British Egg Industry Council got its act together and instituted a hygiene programme across the nation's flocks to try and eradicate the bug. In a Food Standards Agency survey published in 2004, they confirmed that out of their comprehensive sample of UK-produced eggs (tested in boxes of six), the level of contamination had dropped from one in 100 eight years previously to one in 290. This was considerably better than the figure for imported shell eggs, which can be as high as one in 30 boxes.

One major reason the Salmonella count has gone down in the UK is that commercial hatcheries mass-vaccinate their chicks against infection. Not that it has been eradicated; not by any means. It is true that vaccination considerably reduces the number of bacteria in the hens, and the damage they might consequently inflict on humans, but it doesn't get rid of them. With over 2,000 members of the Salmonella family at large (living in the intestinal tracts of most animals, including fish), they are quite likely to arrive via wild birds and their faeces. Just by pecking around her run, the average free-range hen is in danger of picking some up, and having done so she may show symptoms (diarrhoea; misery – the usual), or she may not.

The trouble is that the members of the Salmonella family that poison her don't poison us, and vice versa. So even a perfectly healthy hen has the potential to deliver a dodgy egg. Well, at least we get the chance to cook away the danger.

And then there's bird flu.

Bird flu (or avian influenza – AI) is scary. Whole books have been dedicated to its potential to wipe out the human race. Then swine flu (H1N1) came along and we all forgot about it.

In fact, the current H1N1 virus is derived from something that includes avian genes. All of the known human influenza pandemics before the advent of swine flu, in 1918, 1957 and 1968, were caused by viruses that had acquired genes of avian influenza origin: a major reason we need to keep monitoring it closely.

From a chicken's point of view, AI is one of those diseases that manifests itself in a variety of forms, many of them by no means deadly. In what are called 'low pathogenic' or LP flus, symptoms can go entirely undetected, though the annoying thing is they can mutate and become 'highly pathogenic' or HP. A duck flies into your pond carrying something unassumingly LP and next thing you know your chickens have managed to make it virulently HP.

Most likely you will know an HPAI has landed not because your birds get sick but because DEFRA gets in touch (quite possibly via someone like Lara from the council). The most likely time will be at the beginning or end of summer when migrating wildfowl are arriving in large numbers, or a shipload of infected pheasants has been imported for the beginning of the shooting season.

I have never seen a bird suffering from an HPAI, but I read that symptoms include breathlessness, a blue discoloration of the wattles and comb, oedema (head swelling) and diarrhoea. Basically, it attacks every part of a chicken's body. And having infected one bird, it will spread like wildfire through an intensive poultry farm, sometimes killing off all the inhabitants in a couple of days.

HPAIs have been around for a while. The first recorded attack was in Italy around 1878 when the disease earned itself the title 'fowl plague'. Striking the United States in 1924–25, and again in 1929, the plague was seemingly eradicated until it hit Pennsylvania during 1983–84. The twenty-first century had its first serious outbreak in the Netherlands in 2003, spreading to Belgium and Germany and leading to the slaughter of more than 28 million poultry in order to contain the virus.

'Fowl plague' is not to be confused with 'fowl pest' (otherwise known as Newcastle Disease) – a disease that used to cause havoc with domestic flocks. Like the plague, the pest attacked birds' gastric and respiratory systems; it was transmissible to humans. In recent decades it has been brought under control through mass vaccination programmes like the ones enjoyed by my hybrids.

But the plague has not. The one to worry about is H5N1, which surfaced in South East Asia in early 2004, and has led to the culling of millions of birds. Transfers to domestic poultry have occurred in France, Sweden, Denmark, Germany and Hungary … Most likely, spread through wild bird faeces or 'respiratory secretions'.

Though vaccines for H5N1 exist and have been tried in some countries, they are not simple to administer on a large scale because they require each bird to be individually injected. The vaccine can take up to three weeks for birds to develop optimum protective immunity, and some require two doses.

For those of us who would like to vaccinate, things will not be easy. The EU Council Directive points out that vaccinated birds can become infected but not display symptoms, thus making it much easier for the disease to spread. It says that were H5N1 to hit the UK, vaccinating our flocks would not be desirable as it would increase the time taken to detect and eradicate it. However, DEFRA does say on its website that it has five million vaccines stored away for an emergency and has secured access to another five million somewhere in Spain. Probably these would be used for what is termed 'ring vaccination' – when a circle of lucky recipients is created around a central, infected farm.

The official line for poultry keepers (and their worried neighbours) is that if an HPAI hits the British Isles, we will all fall in with strict biosecurity measures like scrupulous hygiene, controlled movement zones and solid roofs over our chicken runs so a pass-ing swan can't spit down its germs. Even for those of us possessing less than 50 birds (and therefore not on the Poultry Register), DEFRA will be instituting a strict control. And with any luck there won't be a culling frenzy.

Nor should people get in too much of a state about catching it. Virologists are interested in H5N1 – the fact that it can survive over time, in a wide variety of conditions and a wide variety of birds, means it is one of those viruses that could cause problems in future. *Homo sapiens* has not developed immunity to it. Yet according to the World Health Organisation, across the whole world there have only been 442 cases of H5N1 in humans since 2003, all in people who were practically exchanging body fluids with dead or sick poultry.

The top three countries were faraway Indonesia, Vietnam and Egypt; there were 12 cases in Turkey in 2006, but nowhere closer to Europe than this. More than half the people with H5N1 have died, though most seem to have been suffering what is termed 'co-infection' – in other words, they already had some-thing like malaria or HIV before they contracted the flu. None of the poultry products infected with H5N1 has infected those who ate them.

Most reassuring of all is that some scary mutation of bird flu into human flu is only what DEFRA term 'a potential threat'. Even for chicken-lovers there is a significant species barrier between them and us; the virus does not easily cross over.

I called it the summer of discontent – that time when Operation Mite began. It turns out that summertime is when lots of horrible things can happen to hens – bacteria, viruses, parasites, even AI. And then comes the moult.

I was making one of my forays in the nesting box, checking for signs of vampires around the door as well as my usual egg booty, when I noticed a clump of ruby red feathers. Shades of a long-ago, cruel eviction. In trepidation, I looked into the run – there was my chook, happily hopping about. I opened up the side of the sleeping compartment and saw that below her perch there was a veritable orgy of down, as if someone had been having a pillow fight.

When I took Ruby out and inspected her, I saw that most of her back and neck feathers had fallen out. I couldn't resist a gentle tug at the remaining few – they slid into my palm, leaving her with a perfect collar of scraggy skin. Over the following week the balding process extended down her breast and eventually even her fluffy tail was gone. Had not her neck feathers already started growing back in a soft pinkish down, she would have looked like a walking oven-ready.

The reason the moult happens to hens is the same as for wild birds – they need to renew their plumage, ready for winter. It normally happens to hybrids when they are about 14 months old. Depending on what time of year they were born, some get going as early as May, others like my friend Fiona's wait until November, when it really is rather chilly for undressing out of doors.

Feathers are made of much the same stuff as eggs – minerals and protein; a chicken should not be asked to produce both at once. This is the reason commercial farmers cull when flocks are only one year old – they can't afford to hang around, waiting for their birds to don new outfits.

Having said that, such was Ruby's dedication to laying that during her moult she hardly faltered. Given some TLC and a tonic or two in her drinking fountain, soon enough her pink down had turned russet. And well before the cold weather hit, her full plumage was back, even more warm and glossy than before.

007

Higgledy Piggledy my black hen,
She lays eggs for gentlemen.
Sometimes eight and sometimes ten.
Higgledy Piggledy, my black hen.
Traditional rhyme

When Scarlet died with a broken egg up her bottom, my daughters were absolutely fascinated. The way the corpse went from warm to cold; the way her eyes sealed over and her claws curled. There she was – a really stiff bird; absolutely dead.

Death – the last taboo – that great mystery we twenty-first century folk seldom speak of and seldom experience first-hand. Not until it's our own. What Scarlet offered the children was an introduction to this mysterious phenomenon from the safety of their own backyard.

But what to do with her? Strictly, the council don't allow burial of pets in the garden; they say put the body in a plastic bag and chuck it in the bin. Ellie wasn't having that. She wanted a proper burial; and I rather agreed with her, whatever the council's rules.

We didn't have a whole load of room in our garden, not with the deliberately untended trees and shrubs, and snail-bearing pots all around. In the end, we decided that the most appropriate site would be at the feet of her sister Ruby. In case there was any possibility of contaminating the ground, Jay dug a deep hole – more than a metre down. It looked like a real grave, especially towards the end when the gravedigger had to complete excavations from inside, with only his shoulders visible and showers of soil shooting up over the side.

In slid the body, off the blade of the shovel, into its vast burial chamber. And then came the funeral ceremony, complete with Ellie's poem inscribed on a piece of card cut from the Weetabix packet. She had spent ages embellishing her text with daisies and tendrils – a six and a half year old's version of an illuminated manuscript.

'*Our Scarlet, who art in Heaven, Hallowed be thy name …*' she recited, in high solemnity.

Then Bea and she ripped magenta petals from the rugosa bush and anointed Scarlet's corpse with them. When eventually their consecration was complete, Jay and I followed with handfuls of earth.

'Rest in Peace,' I said, my throat catching at the thought that I should have taken her to the vet.

It was Ellie's idea to sing a hymn, though she wasn't sure what. My suggestion seemed to fit the bill:

*'Our Poor Bird, stay thy flight
Far above the sorrows of this sad night.'*

Admittedly, the real-life Scarlet could never have flown even as high as the neighbours' fence, and our ceremony was taking place not at night but just before lunch. Nevertheless, a bird lament in a minor key felt absolutely appropriate. Up and up the scale it flies until on '*above*' the melody has risen as far as it can bear, only to meander its way sadly back to the tonic. We sang our dirge in a two-part canon, Jay and Ellie on one part and me on the second, closely echoed by an enthusiastic squeaking from Bea.

Not yet two years into our henkeeping and already we had lost three chooks. This one felt the worst – perhaps because it marked a humiliating hattrick, or perhaps because the body was uncomfortably still in sight, rather than making its way down a fox's alimentary canal.

The ceremony concluded with Jay's shovelling the soil back into the hole and all of us stamping it down in a merry death dance.

It is not good to get sentimental about hens; Mr Fox had taught me that. Scarlet had taught me that even the birds themselves have a tenuous hold on life – one egg awry in the daily production line, and a healthy pullet can become just another lump of chicken flesh. From now on, I resolved, I was going to be a much harder-hearted keeper.

Already my daughters' enthusiasm for henkeeping had begun to wane. Beatrice had grown out of the tail-grabbing and the '*chick chick*' chasing. More often than not these days I was scattering corn alone. And Ellie – well, it was as much as she could to do to fulfil her duties to the rabbit. As for egg-collecting, that had lost much of its charm when the hens moved to the bottom of the garden – just that bit too far to traipse in pyjamas.

So – the chickens might be good fun for a funeral, but they were not really the children's. They were Mummy's mini farmyard. They might be picturesque and charming; they might be affectionate and even surprisingly savvy, but they weren't pets. The reason I kept them was that they were good at transforming leftovers into eggs.

My friend Aly had given me some poultry magazines dating from her childhood enthusiasm for keeping chickens. Printed in the 1960s, they were full of black and white photos of smiling, besuited men wielding pipettes and microscopes, measuring tapes and weights. Their slogan, printed bold and red across the page, read 'Science is the answer for Poultry Profits'. Attributes under development were 'feed conversion and liveability'. Already they had managed to eliminate broodiness, to have 'minimised cannibalism' and to have created hens 'with a temperament suited to modern production methods'.

Aly's mags mark an interesting stage in industrialised chicken farming. It was during this period that fabulous Higgledy Piggledy in the nursery rhyme, able to produce eight or ten eggs at a time, had started to become a reality. In 1900, average commercial production in the UK had been 83 eggs per hen per year; in these magazines it had risen to around 260. As if they were designing a fast car or creating a computer system, the breeders were hugely excited about the possibility of ever-greater efficiency and productivity. And over the next half century they did pretty well, raising the average figure another 50, to over 300 eggs per bird per year.

Another interesting feature was that the hybrids in the magazines had names like 'the 606', 'the 505' and 'the 404'. They weren't called 'Bluebelle' or 'Speckledy', as they would be these days. Once you have faced the fact that she exists primarily to serve a factory production line, a name like that starts to seem a bit absurd. Next time, I was going to call mine 007.

When I told my experienced henkeeping friends I was planning to get another pullet, they said, 'Why bother? Why not leave Ruby on her own?'

I said 'But the Ark is big enough for two or even three. My family eats a lot of eggs ...'

They said, 'If you introduce a new hen, Ruby is bound to bully her.'

And somehow, at the mention of bullying, I found myself sucked into my old, sentimental ways again.

'Hens are sociable creatures,' I heard myself cry. 'I don't want Ruby to be lonely!'

The friends explained that an intrinsic characteristic of hendom is the strictness of her social structure. Even in a flock of only two, the pecking order can be immutable; a newcomer throws everything into disarray.

'Don't let people tell you hens are all sweet and sociable,' said my friend John, whose decades of henkeeping had taught him all there was to know, 'they're not; they're vicious!'

And whatever husbands may claim, no human version of hen-pecking will ever be as cruel as its avian original. It isn't necessarily a foreigner that the pecker picks on; sometimes she attacks her companions, yanking out their feathers, often at the tail. She may be doing it out of boredom, especially if the flock is confined to a small run or cage. She may be doing it because something has changed in her life and she is feeling stressed. She may be doing it because she is a natural-born bully.

Though not nearly so common as anti-social cocks, anti-social hens can attack not only their peers but also their owners. When you enter their territory, they peck at your legs, or, worse still, when your back is turned they fly at you, beaks and talons bared. There are various tactics for bringing them to heel (including holding them upside down; dunking their heads in cold water; giving them a good, firm kick into the air …) As someone who expects even the rabbit to show respect, I wouldn't be averse to the most brutal of these if my hybrids were attacking me. Fortunately, those clever 60s scientists got there first.

John said he once came across a flock of Black Leghorns who started heavy pecking during their moulting season; he thinks it was the natural shedding of feathers that first gave them the idea. Leghorns can be pretty aggressive. Previous to this they had nibbled at one another's neck feathers, but never a drama like this, yanking out tails and wings.

John thought perhaps it was a sign they weren't getting enough protein in their food so he recommended their keeper make up a deliciously nutritious meal with a bumper pack of cheap margarine and an old loaf of multi-seed bread. They wolfed it down and went straight back to their cannibal ways.

The keeper went back to the larder and got out a pot of English mustard. An old remedy – the sharp-tasting mustard goes on whichever parts of the victims' body are being mauled. He daubed the yellow goo all over their tail and wing feathers, which must have made them feel even more warlike. A week and two large pots later, they seemed to have frightened one another into submission, which was a great relief, as even in those days mustard wasn't cheap.

It was only when things had settled down again that John and his friend realised it might have been the hot weather. Apparently, a sudden heat wave can set hens a-pecking. These days, organised people buy in some 'anti-cannibalism spray' for the summer, just in case. It contains paraffin, ethanol and other nasties, so you must remember not to light a match near anyone that's wearing it.

With some flocks, and especially confined ones, a hen-pecking problem can reach grotesque proportions. They might be attacking a bird that is sick, or a newcomer to their pecking order. In my friend Jane's recent case, it was both.

She was very surprised when she found that Poppy was broody – she has kept half a dozen hybrids for a few years now and, like me, trusted their breeders. She tried all the usual tactics – forcing Poppy out into the run; locking her out of the coop until it got dark. But there was only one place her chook wanted to be – inside the nesting box, nesting.

Jane has two very young children, plus a dog, plus a husband who is out from 7am until 7pm every day. She really didn't have time to get hold of fertilised eggs, let alone look after Poppy and her chicks. Her modest garden was already bursting under the pressure of six busy hybrids, the kids and the dog; there was no room for more.

Just as Jane was getting to the end of her tether with Poppy, a friend phoned who happened to have a cock in her flock.

'You don't fancy borrowing my broody?' asked Jane. And lo and behold, the friend accepted.

Poppy was gone for nearly three months. When she came home she was skinny as anything, having forgotten to eat while she was sitting, but mighty chuffed to have performed her surrogacy so well. Jane was happy to have helped her friend create a brand new batch of pullets. What she had failed to anticipate was the hen-pecking. Three months is a long time in a chicken's memory; so long that the other members of the flock had forgotten all about Poppy. The moment she landed in the run they ran at her, screeching. Immediately, she turned tail, only to find the gang following close behind. Round and round they chased, pecking at her emaciated body. She was too weak to stand up for herself, and maybe a bit dazed after the bliss of all that mothering.

Having stepped in and rescued the poor bird, Jane brought her indoors for the night. Next day she tried putting Poppy in with them and they came at her, so instead she left her to peck on the lawn. She thought maybe the other chickens would see her through the mesh and start to get used to her.

That went on for a few days until one evening, busy with bedtime, Jane forgot to bring Poppy inside. The moment she heard the screeching she knew exactly what was going on and ran outside with a stick. The fox ran off, but Poppy's wing was drooping and her tail feathers were gone. Next morning, she seemed surprisingly perky; Jane reckoned she had survived her ordeal and thought it best to continue her attempts at reintegration.

That was her big mistake. In retrospect, she says, she can't think why she didn't stay and watch what the hens were up to. In her defence, I remind her she had the school run to do. She wasn't gone for long – an hour at most. When she came home she met the most horrible sight – Poppy with her guts hanging out. The flock had pecked her to death.

I did wonder whether it was worth getting a new hen, with or without a name. I tried to stop myself thinking soppy thoughts like – Ruby would never bully another chicken; I can't make her suffer a solitary life.

Eventually, my friend Karen came up with a solution that adhered to the concept of hens as anonymous egg-producers while still indulging my more sentimental nature: she suggested I adopt an ex-bat.

There is no creature quite so anonymous as a battery hen. In order to produce an average annual yield of 338 eggs, she is kept in unremittingly midsummer conditions – the heating turned up to 22 degrees centigrade, artificial 'sunrise and sunset' provided by electric light. Her gloomy shed is stuffed with 20,000 birds or more, sometimes up to 100,000, in cages six stacks high.

The trouble is, she is not just an egg-machine. Cooped up four or five to a cage with nothing to do, she takes out her frustrations on her fellows; she would peck them to death had not her beak been removed. If she doesn't die from disease (more than 10 per cent do) this angry, moth-eaten creature survives approximately 72 weeks before, crippled from confinement, she is regarded as 'spent'. At which point, people like Karen step in. Rather than becoming a stock cube, the hen is taken to a loving home and spends the rest of her days scratching around in someone's back garden.

There is a registered charity, the BHWT (Battery Hens' Welfare Trust), who organise a national network distributing ex-bats to new owners. There are also individuals who chat up battery farmers and procure them for themselves. That farm is never hard to find – just follow the pall of ammonia.

Karen lived near one such farm and had a deal with the farmer's wife to pass on the healthiest birds due for culling. She reckoned an ex-bat would be the perfect new companion for Ruby. Her theory was that someone who has spent her whole life in a chick-eat-chick world is bound to know how to stand up for herself. If she proved a less superlative layer than she had been in her cage, then I wouldn't mind – I felt compensated by the satisfaction of rescuing her.

I was aware that I would not necessarily have such an opportunity in the future. After more than half a century producing the majority of British eggs, the battery industry is in for a radical overhaul. In their wisdom, EU legislators have drawn up new rules and, as usual, the UK authorities are keen to institute them. As of January 1 2012, battery farmers will be investing in 'enriched' cage systems that provide larger, more comfortable spaces, nesting and roosting facilities and even dust baths. From the chickens' point of view, their prison will start to look more like a modest B&B, and they might not want rescuing at all.

When 007 arrived she resembled nothing more than an escapee from a concentration camp. She had no plumage on her breast and hardly any on her back; her beak was mangled like a bad hare lip. One of the most common things that happens when battery hens are removed from their cages is that their legs get knocked, and sometimes the wings. Arnica cream worked wonders. Occasionally (though fortunately not with 007) she might have a broken bone and then you have to ask the vet to set it – apparently wings and legs can be mended quite successfully.

The main issue on our ex-bat's arrival was where we should put her. Placing such a creature straight in with Ruby seemed like asking for trouble. Anyhow, the general rule is that a new bird should be kept in isolation for two or even three weeks in order to make sure they don't have anything nasty to pass on. I possessed the perfect quarantine – once a home, then everyone's sick bay: that cage I had salvaged from the dump. Where better to make an ex-bat feel at home? While she was there, I got the chance to discover red mite and douse her with killer, and she got the chance to rebuild her strength.

Karen had brought a small bag of layers' mash with her. The BHWT strongly advises feeding this to ex-bats at the beginning of the adoption process – it is what they ate throughout their caged life. They also advise that we resist the urge to spoil our refugees with treats – no more than a dessert-spoonful of Chee-rios each day, otherwise we run the risk of upsetting their tummies. From my feed supplier, I got hold of a sack of Ex-Bats' Crumbs that are even higher in protein, vitamins and minerals than the usual ones.

It was early September when 007 arrived; the nights were warm so I didn't need to worry about her adapting to the vicis-situdes of outdoor temperature. After living in a smelly sauna all her life, her comb was large and floppy (it had acted as a heat dissipater). Gradually over the first week she was with us, it reddened and shrank to its normal size.

She had been de-beaked – the top section burnt to a stump. I reminded myself that, like claws and feathers, the beak has no sensation at its far end. It was very satisfying to watch it grow into the sharp and symmetrical utensil it was always meant to be.

After a week in quarantine, her beak and feathers were already starting to grow and she had perked up enough to venture out of her cage. I carried her down to the end of the garden and let her practise her pecking skills in a corner beside the Ark. Having spent her whole life in a cage, she might have found the whole garden or even the run an overwhelming experience; this way, under my close supervision, I hoped that she would feel safe while Ruby got a reminder that she was not the only chicken in the coop. Not that Ruby seemed in the least bit interested. After too many non-introductions through the sides of the run, I decided the time had come for a real meeting.

There are various things you can do to minimise the trauma of introducing a new hen. One is to establish the low-status newcomer in one part of the garden and then bring the leader of the flock into her territory for a few days. Having made friends on the new hen's patch, the leader should forget to bully her when they go home together. Like Jane, my problem was lack of space – I had nowhere that my birds could fit together, except in high-status Ruby's run.

The recommendation I *could* put into practice was to sneak 007 into the nesting box after dark, when the lonesome Ruby was already fast asleep on her perch. Early next morning I let down the ladder from the sleeping compartment and opened up the sides of the run so they could escape if need be.

First came she whose territory it was, her hackles raised, strutting about and squawking,

'Get out of my house!'

007 proved just as feisty as Karen had anticipated. Stumbling downstairs with her bare breast high, she expanded what neck feathers she had into an impressive ruff, flapped her wings hard and screamed,

'It's mine too!'

Ruby shrieked off out of the run, pursued by her fearsome night guest. When Ruby turned around and tried to peck her, 007 made even nastier jabbing movements of her own. When she jumped on her, talons bared, the ex-bat retaliated in similar style.

Perhaps Ruby's being on her own rather than part of a gang was the reason things turned out so well. Definitely her foe's superior fighting skills were an important factor. After half a day of

Hitchcockian activity, they decided pecking at the lawn might be more fun.

The friendship that evolved was glorious to behold. Ruby must have realised from 007's scraggy looks that she needed lessons in basic life skills. Having been hothoused so literally, she had never learnt to perch, or to lay eggs in a nesting box or to eschew the cold, the wet and the wind. It was Ruby who demonstrated how to move away from the sides of the run during a rainstorm, how to clasp her feet around a wooden rod and balance there all night long, and how to drop her eggs in a pile of wood shavings rather than wherever she happened to be walking.

By the way, it doesn't tally that an abused bird develops an abusive personality – her feathers restored and her bones toughened, 007 proved herself an excellent weeding companion. Those cheery chaps in Aly's magazines did a good job – the genes they so carefully selected to withstand battery imprisonment are just the ones that make her a good gardening assistant.

I wish I could conclude 007's chapter with that satisfyingly happy ending. But I would not be telling the whole story. Though healthy and affable and generally a successful addition to our household, she did have one very nasty habit.

Egg-eating.

It took a while to realise what was going on, as she was very good at cleaning up after herself. I thought the lack of eggs in the nesting box was because she was giving herself a break after her period of slave labour, and that Ruby's productivity was going down as the days shortened. But then one day – a half-eaten mush. I was shocked. Such an unnatural activity, I felt; shades of infanticide – gobbling up the very thing to which you have just given birth.

I blamed myself; I thought probably the shells I was crumbling in the feed had received too little baking and the hens had developed a taste for raw egg. Then I blamed the battery farm – their cages have sloping sides and collecting bays where the eggs roll far out of reach; an ex-bat might turn infanticide because she was so excited to have access to them at last.

Back to my luxury cage 007 returned, plus a packet of mineral supplements just in case eating eggs was a sign that she needed even more vitamins and minerals than those provided in her feed.

My plan was to try to stymie her fun by rushing out and removing her eggs as soon as they were laid. But I had no idea what her laying pattern might be; probably it was far from regular, with days between one egg and the next. Anyway, even on the occasions when she produced something, I wasn't necessarily going to be around to whisk it away.

Someone recommended filling empty shells with chilli or mustard, taping them up again to look like normal ones and leaving them in the nest. It sounds revolting, but often the infanticide hen is so far gone that she eats them all the same. Someone else recommended my putting in rock-hard pot eggs instead. The ones I had bought for Roxy and Loxy were sitting, forever mid-boil, on Bea's toy cooker. I reclaimed them and stuck them in the cage – with any luck, a bruise to that newly-restored beak was exactly the lesson she needed.

Meanwhile back at the Ark, proof of Ruby's innocence arrived each day in the form of one untouched egg.

And then one morning, about a week into her confinement, I heard 007 calling,

'*Bra – not, not, not, not, not, not; Bra – not, not, not, not, not, not!*'

Out to the cage I rushed and there, lying in the chippings – three whole eggs. I couldn't tell whether she had tried to attack the false ones, but the presence of that extra real one, entirely uneaten, was proof enough that my ex-bat had relinquished her habit and should be allowed back into the Ark.

Headless Chickens

It was a dish for old Caesar,
Also King Henry the Third,
But Columbus was smart, said 'You can't fool me,
A chicken ain't nothin' but a bird.'
Cab Calloway

From the summer Ruby and 007 got together, life settled down to a regular routine of cleaning and feeding and laying. I tried to keep my husbandry to no more than five minutes a day. I tried not to fall into old sentimental habits like letting them into the kitchen or calling them by name. I tried to be vigilant about egg-eating and mite and never giving them the freedom of the garden unless I was present. My second season of henkeeping came and went without another visit from Mr Fox, as did my third and then my fourth.

At last, we seemed to be living a reasonably unchaotic version of the Good Life.

As the summer holidays came round again, we planned a few weeks away in Cornwall. My hen-sitters were keen to oblige, but we also had the cat and the rabbit to think of. For £9 a visit, Kylie from *Pets Plus* promised to cuddle the cat, and give the rabbit and the hens a good run in the garden. With that much activity going on, I thought, the fox might assume the whole family was still around and not bother harassing our animals.

Ellie (now nine) and Bea (five) were just landing their buckets on the beach when Kylie called. She was using that tender tone of voice commonly favoured by funeral directors … 007 had died peacefully in her sleep.

I was thinking, 'She was only four and a half!'

What I said was, 'Just chuck her in the bin!'

Kylie's silence suggested my response had not been appropriate.

'It's what the council recommends,' I added.

So now I knew. It turns out that most hybrids, especially those that have slaved in a battery farm, are unlikely to last more than five years. Roxy and Loxy would certainly never have survived the 12 years their sanctuary saleswoman predicted. The word 'spent' says it all – it's their hectic laying programme that kills them.

In fact, most laying hens in the UK (free range, battery, barn … whatever) are culled much earlier than that – at one year of age, before they become too susceptible to disease, let alone reduce their laying capacity. Even the happiest free-range birds are likely not to have a good death – packed into trucks, they travel hundreds of miles to one of a handful of abattoirs where they are gassed en masse. Their carcasses are not saleable as conventional meat, though some might recycle as stock cubes and cat food.

In contrast, outside the industry, traditional breeds live much longer. According to the *Guinness Book of Records*, it is an Old English Game Fowl that has so far enjoyed the longest chicken life. Matilda belonged to magicians Donna and Keith Barton from Birmingham, Alabama, and took part in their show for over a decade. Her job was to appear from under the lid of a pan into which Keith had cracked an egg. Ironically, she herself never laid one and it is probably this conservation of effort that allowed her such an extraordinarily lifespan: Matilda died in 2006 at the age of 16.

When we got home from the seaside, Ruby was scuttling up and down inside her run. She seemed as unperturbed by 007's departure as I was. But as the days shortened, her egg production went down. And down. By September, my reliable one-a-day bird was laying only three eggs a week, large and sometimes fragile. She looked happy enough, was eating and pooing and pecking perfectly normally, but I decided the reduction in eggs was a sign she was pining. Many keepers more seasoned than myself say that hens pine for their fellows; after three years of companionship it would be only natural. She had just taken a while to realise 007 wasn't coming back.

The prospect of getting a replacement was not good. Frankly, I couldn't be bothered going through the whole quarantine process again just for 007 Number Two to fall off her perch. Trying to integrate an autumn pullet (if Mr Hodgkins the rearer had one) would mean loads of hassle and possibly very few eggs for several months; better to wait until the spring. In which case Ruby would have to get through the cold, cold winter alone; with no companion to help keep her warm.

I did the maths. She was four years old; if she lived another year (which she might well, having not had 007's crummy start in life), at this rate she was going to produce a maximum of 150 eggs. Meanwhile, I would be spending about £40 on her feed and treatments – more than those eggs would cost at Sainsbury's. Add on the time spent cleaning, feeding and watering her and I was losing money.

The hardened keeper in me knew the solution – my lonesome bird should be culled.

My friend Elaine once told me that when her eleven year old learnt it might be necessary to kill one of their chickens, he burst into tears.

'Does he eat chicken meat?' I enquired.

'Yes,' she admitted.

'Then he should learn that it entails killing – if we're not prepared to kill, then we shouldn't be eating meat …'

She sighed and looked away. She was thinking what a ruthless bitch I was, or cow, or … is there a word for this that is not a female animal? She felt I did not appreciate that special emotional attachment between a person and a pet.

And now the pet thing had returned to haunt me. Long ago, after my mortality hattrick, I had decided that hens were not pets but egg-producers. With my last surviving hybrid beginning to lose her ability in that area, I was in a dilemma.

What if I accepted that she was my pet? People spend a lot of money on their pets; without an animal National Health Service, it sometimes proves more than they spend on themselves. Even when Ruby stopped laying completely, I might feel she was worth it because of all she had given me in the past. But for how long? As she became increasingly decrepit and in need of the vet, how much would I be prepared to spend? What if she ran out on the road and got hit by a car?

Here's an interesting fact that might have something to do with all those jokes about chickens crossing the road: *Gallus gallus domesticus* has no right of way on the public highway. Ducks and geese do, but she doesn't. If someone ran over my hen, he or she would not be obliged to pay any compensation at all. Even if the surgery cost thousands.

Enough. It was time to alter my perspective. I needed to concentrate not on my needs but on Ruby's, here and now. Was it kind to keep her on her own like this? Might it not be better to put her out of her misery?

My cowardly self was inclined to leave her out for the fox. He would dispatch her in a day or two, cleanly and efficiently, without my having to witness anything but the odd floating feather. My responsible hen-husbandry self said – No. Death by fox is seriously traumatic. I certainly wouldn't want to spend my final moments of life being chased by that ruthless bully, snapped between that set of fangs. Nor would I like to endure a trip to someone else's place for some sort of impersonal, professional death. The local abattoir was probably the Dignitas of the hen world, but if the death were mine I would prefer it safe at home, in the arms of my carer.

Which meant me. It was my garden where she had enjoyed a luxurious free-range life; a better one than a free-range commercial chicken, let alone her battery cousins. As the person who had granted it I felt I was obliged also to give her a better death.

I thought back over the years – had I ever killed an animal? Plenty of slugs and snails under my boot; the odd fish or two. I had held plenty of sick and dying birds and mammals in my arms, but had never actively brought about their death. Though I remembered firing a rifle at tin cans as a child, I had never aimed one at a pigeon. When a baby blackbird had recently been half-mauled by the cat, it was Jay who took responsibility for chopping off its head with a spade.

Now, in my 40s – already at the age when expert killers start losing their sangfroid – I was planning to dispatch Ruby. With my own bare hands.

'Argh!' Cried my daughters. Though fascinated by the slow demise of Scarlet, they were horrified at the thought of murdering her sister.

YouTube was chock-a-block with home videos demonstrating that the best way of killing a chicken was to chop off its head. I had even seen it in real life – my friend Fred who had been breeding happy meat-birds for half a century had an axe block just outside his back door. One of his flock had earned herself the name Anne Boleyn because she so often offered herself there.

I knew from Fred's set-up that the axe method could get very messy, with the dead bird flapping horribly. The prop he used to prevent it was a 'killing cone' which is basically a traffic cone with the pointed end removed. You lower the bird into the inverted cone; its head pokes out through the bottom, while its body stays snugly enclosed. Then you aim your weapon right to the raw edge of the cone …

Though bloody and distressing, a beheading can have miraculous consequences. The most famous headless chicken, an American cockerel by the name of Mike, was created by the slip of an axe. On September 10 1945, in Fruita, Colorado, as Farmer

Olsen took his weapon to Mike's neck, the blade missed the jugular. Although his head lay there on the farmyard floor, most of his brain stem and one ear was left intact; a clot formed, preventing him from bleeding to death.

Since most of a chicken's reflex actions are controlled by the brain stem, Mike was able to remain quite healthy, fed and watered with an eyedropper straight into his beak-free gullet. His intact voice-box also enabled him to keep crowing. Being an enterprising sort of a chap, Farmer Olsen took Mike on tour, introducing him to headless-chicken fanciers all over the Republic. Over the next 18 months, Mike visited New York, Atlantic City, Los Angeles, and San Diego where millions of patrons paid 25 cents to see him. He was valued at $10,000 and insured for the same.

Needless to say, over the more-than-sixty years since Mike's demise (on tour from choking), many have tried to emulate the miracle. So far, all they have got for their pains is a pile of corpses. Not that there haven't been loads of near-misses. Dianne who runs the local bakery remembers one well.

Growing up in my part of town in the 50s, Dianne's large family always had chickens. It was normal in those days – most people had a garden big enough to grow the family veg and have a shed for the birds. The children each ate two boiled eggs for breakfast every morning.

Dianne's dad was the one who looked after the chickens – he was often to be found outside in their pen, making sure they were clean and healthy; sorting out the cocks. They normally had four cocks – great big things, they were, and aggressive. Dianne thinks that's probably why the children weren't allowed in the pen. Whichever cock was fattest was the one they ate on Christmas Day. The kids had to do the plucking and the gutting; they never complained; they didn't know any different; they used to sit there on the concrete step outside the house, plucking away. And when they were done, they took the feathers to Dad for him to line the nesting boxes.

One Sunday morning, Dianne's big sister Carol was waiting on the step while Dad was in the chicken shed, decapitating dinner. Suddenly out rushed a bird, intact right up to its neck. Seven-year-old Carol turned tail and ran, with headless chicken in hot pursuit, flapping mightily. The girl ran screaming up the garden; once cornered at the end of the veg patch she rushed back towards the house. So did the gruesome beast. Up and down the garden they ran, Dianne and her siblings chuckling on the side-lines. It was particularly amusing, they thought, because Carol was usually such a goody-two-shoes; nothing had ever happened to her before. Eventually she could stand it no longer and took an almighty leap over the fence into Mrs Marchment's garden.

Dianne cannot remember how long it took her headless chicken to die – probably her father came out and gave it another going over with the axe. What she does know is that ever since then, Carol has suffered from an absolute terror of birds.

For me the thought of replicating such a horror was a major reason to forego the axe. Another was the fact that I didn't trust myself with a log, let alone a wriggling chicken in a traffic cone. Jay offered his services but I said no – it was my duty to see the whole thing through myself. I went off to research my method some more.

According to the charity Humane Slaughter Association, an axe is not a good idea because it too easily misses its mark. Also, after decapitation the brain may continue activity for up to 30 excruciating seconds. Poor Anne Boleyn.

So what were the alternatives? What about pliers? My friend Fred said if I didn't trust myself with an axe then try culling pliers, but the HSA website said absolutely not: the way pliers crush the neck is neither swift nor efficient, causing unacceptable pain.

What about neck-wringing – that classic way to dispatch a hen? Fred hated anything like neck-wringing; I think he felt it was too intimate a way to see them go. The HSA advised that for birds weighing less than 3kg (ie all the laying hens I had ever come across) careful neck-dislocation was definitely preferable to axes and pliers. Best of all, they said, was the electrical stunner – little tongs applied to the bird's head that zap their brains with a 130 volt charge, rendering them instantly unconscious.

You can purchase a stunner from a poultry supply shop. Remember to remove your bling, then set to work according to the instructions on the packet. Once the chicken is stunned, you need to cut off the blood flow to the brain as soon as possible. Get out your super-sharp knife and dig deep into her throat to sever both carotid arteries and both jugular veins. After a couple of minutes of blood-letting, you can be sure she will never run around your garden again.

I was happy with the idea of stunning my chicken. I have seen it on the TV – it looked a pretty humane way of doing things. My only problem was that the gadget would set me back around £700.

I gave the HSA a call. The young lady on the end of the line said if I really couldn't afford it (or it was an emergency), then I could go ahead and kill by hand. Not the way some barbarians do it, swinging the poor creature in circles around their head; just a simple click of the neck to dislocate the spine. She warned that this technique takes a certain amount of practice. She recommended I try it out on dead birds first. I didn't have any, but reckoned I could practice on my live one; I just had to remember to stop when I got to the point of no return.

I asked around, and found plenty of people who knew how to do chicken neck dislocation. If they were not currently a keeper, they had done it in the past, had learnt as a child or from a book now out of print. Many said the best time was first thing in the morning, before the bird had fed. It is common for it to defecate as it expires, and letting it feed up until the last minute makes this all the more likely. In my case, I could do it straight after the school run – by the time the children got home, the whole thing would be over. However, my friend John said when he was regularly culling, his preferred time was after dark, when the chicken was already half-dead with sleep. He said to offer only water for the whole day preceding, so the gut was as empty as possible.

As far as the technique went, it didn't seem to differ much from person to person. Tim had learnt from an organic poultry farmer friend whose flock failed to attain sufficient proportions to sell at the farmers' market. His expertise developed fast – 50 corpses in one afternoon. The most common problem, he felt, was that people let their emotions get the better of them – they weren't truly committed to going through with the job; didn't believe they were strong enough; just stopped when they felt resistance.

In the school playground, my friend Marie-Eve told me she had learnt dislocation and other methods as a child on the homestead in Canada. A crowd of children gathered round as their mums mimed out alternative chicken murders in intricate detail.

'When are you planning to do it?'

'This weekend.'

'Would you like a hand?' she asked.

'I feel I should do it myself.'

'Yes, yes. But I could be there – just for moral support.'

I thought for a moment. That might be a really good idea – a bit like a birth partner when you have a baby.

'Will you be my killing partner then?'

'I'd be honoured!'

Right. I can delay the moment no longer. My four-year-old happy hybrid is waiting. The time has come for her gentle dispatch, and you, dear reader, are welcome to join me. I am taking a deep breath.

By the way – don't believe the books that claim you can't learn to kill a chicken from a book; it's only because the authors are frightened that if they describe it, you are going to stop reading. Were you about to do exactly that? Then I suggest you try picking up the story again at the start of the next chapter.

OK. It is a cloudy winter evening, no stars to be seen; no frost nor wind; the garden is quiet except for the growl of distant traffic. The Ark's steeple stands black against the sodium glow of the sky.

Marie-Eve and I have knocked back half a bottle of wine, donned my muckiest allotment gear – wellies and macs, and left our husbands indoors with the children. We are searching around the garden for the best site – somewhere in the beam from the outdoor light, but not too close to the house in case things get noisy. If the dislocation doesn't work, we have agreed on Plan B – the axe. We also have a bucket standing by for blood, an old wooden pallet as a chopping block, and my sharpest kitchen knife.

I take hold of the handles of the Ark and gently ease out the side, expecting to discover my prey dozing on her perch. But no – she is snuggled up warm in the nesting box (take note – in preparation for her dispatch, I have wiped her name from my consciousness). As the cold air hits her she rises to welcome me; how trusting she is; she must be hungry. If it weren't for Marie-Eve hovering in the background, I think I might lose my nerve right now. Instead, I lift her big body under my arm and carry her to the centre of the lawn where the standby kit is posted.

With my right hand under her back, I tilt the body away from me and take a while to arrange the legs in my left hand (poultry keeper's fashion, fingers slotted between the ankles). It feels clumsy, but Marie-Eve is encouraging,

'That's good, that's good.'

I am familiar with the following series of manoeuvres, having been busy practicing them; the bird is familiar with them too and makes no objection.

I shift the position of my right hand round to the back, so the skull sits firm in my palm; it feels amazingly small and fragile. Of all things, the closest experience that comes to mind is of supporting a newborn baby.

Marie-Eve is crouching on the ground near the bird's head, checking on what I am doing.

'OK – I've got my first and second fingers slotted around the head,' I say.

'That's good, that's good.' These fingers will function in the same way as a hangman's noose. The rest of my hand is searching for the weakest point in the vertebrae, where the spine meets the skull. I think I have established where it is.

'I can feel her cheekbones.'

'That's it. Right up, tight against her face. Is your thumb on the top of her head?'

'Like that?'

'Good.'

I pull the legs upwards and the head down, stretching her neck as far as it seems comfortable to go. I turn the bird so her tummy is facing to the left, her back firm against my thigh.

On previous occasions, it was at this point that I released her and breathed a sigh of relief. But not now. Now I am focused on my new role as dispassionate killer. I lower my centre of gravity a little, stretching my toes inside my boots so my feet feel firm against the ground.

But the bird senses something. Suddenly this is not what she is used to. Her head strains upwards and the wings flap open – in the darkness they feel much bigger and more fearsome than I expected.

'It's OK, chicken – it's OK,' says Marie-Eve.

'It's all right, little one,' I croon. My daughters would be horrified that not only am I preparing to kill my pet, but that in her final moments I am telling her a fib.

The body relaxes and hangs vertically down again, as if reconciled to its fate.

I know the next move needs the greatest speed and determination to minimise any distress.

'I'm going to go for it.'

'You go.'

With my left hand pulling the legs up and my right hand around the head, I yank the body even longer (9 inches is what I am aiming for) and twist the head sharply back, against the curve of the spine. I know if I am too violent I will decapitate her, but decapitation is probably less painful than a wimpish strangling. I dig deep into the vertebrae, pushing the sections of bone against their natural direction. Can I hear a click of the bones dislocating? A gap at the base of the skull where they used to be connected? All I want is to know that the deed is done.

My hands are weak. The neck is strong; really strong. I yank and twist again – nothing. Now she is moving. Oh God – I haven't managed it. One more go – I grunt with the effort, pulling her legs awkwardly up in one direction, twisting the head down in the other. There is a crunching sound.

It that it?

The wings should be flapping. Flapping and flapping. The lady from the HSA said there is nothing conscious in the movement, just the nerves going AWOL. She said the bigger the convulsions the better – a sign that the body is well and truly disconnected from the brain. I had imagined holding the legs as this happened, her soul flying off, up and away from this winged body.

The wings *are* moving, but not out of control; more like an urgent objection to pain. She doesn't want to die. Argh!

'I think you've done it,' says Marie-Eve. I crouch down to her.

'I'm not sure – I'm really not sure …'

'OK – come here.'

I lay the writhing body against the wooden pallet and hold the feet fast; my friend takes the head.

'Wow – that head is throbbing.' The axe crunches.

'She's a tough old bird,' I say.

'God, she's tough,' says Marie-Eve, wielding the axe again – not high, just sharp and quick. As the wings flail, I grab the kitchen knife and sever the final artery. Released from Marie-Eve's hand, the head is twitching and the body is doing the same in exactly the same rhythm. How strange is this connection between being alive and being dead.

At last she is still. Probably it has only been 20 seconds since my first yank, but it felt like three times as much. Her comb is already turning pale and floppy; her eyes are tight closed. There is a small puddle of blood against the pale wood. I am glad it's dark and I can't see more.

Marie-Eve and I hug one another; we are shaking.

And then we hear Jay shouting from the back door.

'You done?'

Behind him huddle the children, dressed in fairy costumes from the dressing up box.

'Can we see, Mummy?'

As Marie-Eve and I scrub the pallet and sluice the lawn, Jay takes the kids down to the end of the garden and buries the head. Ellie gets them to hold hands and give Ruby a minute's silence.

'What did you do with the corpse?' asks Ellie the next day.

'It's hanging in the shed.'

'Ugh! What are you going to do with it?'

'Well, she wasn't ill; we shouldn't waste her.'

'You mean …?' Ellie grimaces.

'You're going to eat her!' declares Beatrice.

'I'm going to make chicken soup. Will you have some?'

'I can't – I knew her!' cries Ellie.

'You don't *have* to, you know, Mummy,' says Bea, diplomatically.

'That's like eating one of us!' wails Ellie.

'It's like eating chicken.' I counter, just a bit smugly.

'But Ruby wasn't just any old chicken!'

'No – she was a happy chicken.' I say. 'All the other chickens we have ever eaten were miserable.'

When my Granny was little, her Sunday roast was probably a happy-go-lucky 'spring chicken' – a tender young male, plucked from the flock because he couldn't lay eggs. The other kind of chicken meat came from stewing a retired farmyard hen like Ruby to soften her stringy flesh. However, by the middle of the century, when Granny was writing 'Betty's chicken dish' into her recipe book, these by-products of egg-production were fast disappearing. The meat and the egg industries were becoming completely independent. And that's where it all got so miserable.

During the past half century, the efficiency of production in the chicken meat industry has risen a startling 450 per cent. This is mainly due to the selection of birds with a phenomenal ability to grow meat on their bones. These days, a meat bird is a completely different breed from a laying hen – a heavy, large-breasted creature of either gender (it never reaches sexual maturity), its body has been genetically refined to contain little real muscle; apparently we consumers have demanded this – so pale and clean is their flesh that it seems hardly like a dead animal at all.

According to DEFRA, more than 80 per cent of the chicken meat we buy in the UK comes from bog-standard broilers. Their short lives are spent largely immobile, stuffing their faces with high-protein feed. They grow incredibly fast, thereby avoiding the risk of too much disease and quickly making way for the next generation. Even before their adult plumage has fully developed they are big enough to eat – at five or six weeks of age. If you try boiling their carcasses, they quickly become a mushy gloop – that's how unformed the bones are.

From the shopper's point of view, such efficiency of production means our meat is cheap. It's the chicks who pay the price: so breast-heavy they can hardly stand, let alone skit about like normal birds, they endure crippling leg problems, heart failure and tumours.

On top of all this, the broiler parents (for, despite the industry's best efforts, chicken meat cannot yet be bred solely in a test tube, at least not without it costing a bomb) must suffer starvation. Think about it – cockerels and pullets only reach sexual maturity at around 18 weeks, by which time these breeds should be on the supermarket shelves. Without being starved, an 18-week broiler would grow into some sort of monster, so huge and unhealthy it would be unable to produce eggs or sperm (the breeders have methods to save them the bother of copulation).

And just in case, as consumers, we thought spending more money would solve things – even the more expensive birds aren't necessarily having a brilliant time. A 'free-range' label (2 per cent of the market) means they ate the same 'growers' feed' as cheap broilers but had access to outdoors; their minimum slaughter age was eight weeks rather than five, so it is possible they were a slower-growing strain. But not necessarily – they might have been fast-growing but made to slow down, again through starvation. And even if they were given access to a run, a fast-growing breed probably didn't have the time or energy to make use of it.

Our best bet is definitely the 'organic' label. It indicates that the dead chick was fed the most sustainable kind of feed, kept free range and slaughtered at as old as 12 weeks. Ideally, it was one of the slower-growing breeds, with a bit of free time to walk around, and able to make it to three months without having a heart attack. Because of its diet and the length of time it lived, organic chicken is the most expensive, and therefore forms less than 0.5 per cent of the UK market.

And the market is vast. According to the RSPCA, in 2008 830 million broilers were slaughtered in the UK (roughly 14 birds per man, woman and child). Henocide. Of course, that figure excludes all the possibly-more-miserable broilers we imported, stuffing their meat into sandwiches and pies before anyone asked where it came from.

I feel wretched about Ruby's death but I feel even more wretched about the death of all the broilers I have eaten in my life. Merciful but not kind, it entails shackling them upside down and sending them struggling along a conveyor belt into a water bath where, with luck, they are electrocuted to death. I say 'with luck' because if that frightened creature happens to raise its head as it travels towards the bath (as Ruby raised hers as I approached the point of no return), it may well not receive the full voltage.

And what's worse than a dead broiler? A half-dead broiler.

Ruby's carcass hung in the garden shed for nearly 24 hours, the blood dripping into a bucket. I hoped the process might tenderise her meat; I also hoped that next time I held her she would be well and truly cold. The night before, I had found the warmth of her headless body really disturbing; no different from holding her when alive. Instead of plucking her while warm, as the old poultry books recommend, Marie-Eve and I hoisted her by the ankles and went inside to finish off the wine.

Next day, the body was reassuringly stiff as I filled the compost bin with her feathers. It was good she didn't have a head – it made her more anonymous. Plucking the body was not difficult; the tail took a bit more effort, but the wing feathers stuck hard. Jay took his penknife to them, and then set to work chopping off the feet and carefully prising out the crop (strangely full, after all my efforts at starving her). At the tail end, he made an incision between vent and breastbone, thrust thumb and forefinger inside and drew out streams of gut and reproductive tract. At this point I summoned our daughters for a live anatomy lesson. When the first bright yolk appeared, full-sized with a filigree of blood vessels across it, we were all amazed; then two more yolks descending in size, the second with a very evident germ cell sprouting from its surface. Behind these came a string of baby-eggs, at least a hundred of them, getting smaller and smaller along the stem of the ovary. Despite her slowing in productivity, her whole body cavity was still stuffed with potential.

After a good wash under the kitchen tap, Ruby lay on the chopping board like any other healthy piece of meat. I had expected her layer's body to be scrawny and was pleasantly surprised how very chicken-like it looked. I had anticipated the flesh being dark, like a pheasant's, but in fact the breast was quite pale and soft to the touch. The legs had good muscle-tone from all that running around.

Jay and I looked forward to an excellent meal.

One thing I should add in anticipation of eating our bird is that Jay is Jewish – not practising, you understand, but the bearer of plenty of cultural baggage, especially when it comes to Jewish Penicillin. His mother used to make soup when he was sick; it was always delicious and sometimes curative. He remembers the recipe exactly – the carcasses carefully frozen over many months; the juices from several roasts likewise … I should know it off by heart, for each time he is ill he reminds me, but somehow I always manage to blank it out. What I can offer instead is what happened to Ruby:

Ruby Soup

Put the whole chicken in the pressure cooker with about a litre and a half of water, along with carrots, celery sticks, a large onion (peeled and quartered), half a head of garlic (peeled), half a lemon, a couple of bay leaves, some stalks of parsley and coriander and three slices of fresh ginger.

Bring to boiling pressure, then leave to simmer for 20 minutes.

Open up the pot and fish out the solid stuff with a slotted spoon. Return the garlic and carrots to the stock, along with meat from one leg and a little breast. You can reserve the rest of the meat for another meal – mixed with home-made mayonnaise there's no better sandwich filling on earth.

Liquidise the soup. Add more lemon juice and salt and pepper to taste.

Jewish people have a tradition of poultry sacrifice called *Kapparot*. Still common among the ultra-Orthodox, especially Chasidic communities, it takes place during the autumn when, conveniently, chickens are likely to be coming to the end of their laying season. The idea is that every man in the family should sacrifice a cock and every woman a hen; pregnant women get one of each. If you are seriously into the ritual, you lift said fowl above your head and revolve it three times. Meanwhile you recite the following:

'This is my exchange, my substitute, my atonement; this hen/cock shall go to its death, but I shall go to a good, long life, and to peace.'

The bird is then slaughtered and given to the poor, or you can cook it according to one of the myriad of Jewish chicken soup recipes and share it in your community as part of the feast before Yom Kippur.

Some people object to the *Kapparot* ritual because the notion that a dead chicken frees us from sin is just too simplistic. Others say that the sacrifice is just the beginning of the process of atonement, inspiring you to *teshuvah* – a period of repentance in which God weighs up your sins. What I like about it is the acknowledgement that a hen and a woman (or a cock and a man – *gever* and *gever*) are interlinked, that the destruction of one arouses the destruction of something in the other. I think it fits nicely with that whole Jewish Penicillin thing.

According to my research, the University of Nebraska Medical Centre has *proved* once and for all that chicken soup has medicinal properties. They think it is something to do with the way a fragrant broth inhibits the clumping of white blood cells (neutrophils) that cause congestion and inflammation when you have a cold. If you have ever had a bowl of golden, clear and aromatic broth while you have been ill, you may well confer. Or you may prefer more metaphorical explanations; you might well feel that chicken soup is eaten not just with the digestive and olfactory systems, but also with the emotions.

Which in my family's case meant our twenty-first century children making a right fuss over supper. Ellie swore that from now on she was officially vegetarian, that eating animals was as bad as eating one's parents. Bea bravely nibbled some breast meat and declared it 'just like real chicken!' Jay and I agreed that the soup was far superior to any we had ever tasted, its rich flavour augmented by our sense of satisfaction at having grown it ourselves. Each mouthful was sweetened by thoughts of all those eggs Ruby had given us (almost £300's worth, we calculated), plus nearly four years of garden company, from POL to pot.

And even if my daughters never get to do *Kapparot*, even if (God forbid) they never learn my superlative method of cooking chicken soup, they may still recall the sacrifice we made with Ruby.

'Gross!' said Ellie.

But still she sat there, sharing our contemplation, if not our meal. Helping us atone for all those miserable broilers we had eaten so thoughtlessly in the past.

Birth Plans

When the rooster starts to crow
Grab your partner on the floor!
Slim Gaillard

As the late great gardening writer Christopher Lloyd used to say – every death is an opportunity. What my Ruby soup had done was to whet my appetite for more. For more soup, even. Having undergone such an important rite of passage, the challenge was on to improve my dislocation skills. If I could make friends with someone like Tim's poultry farmer, I could get in some serious practice before I had to sacrifice my own bird again. I felt quite excited at the prospect of killing more happy birds and thereby permanently shunning the evils of the broiler industry. Perhaps I could persuade the allotment membership to let me use a shady communal corner that was rapidly turning into a dump. Then I could keep a decent sized flock.

The Chair of the committee was out on his plot, putting his dahlias to bed for the winter. When I mentioned my plan he frowned.

'Oh dear. I don't think the other plot holders are going to like that.'

'Why not?'

'Well … what if they get out?' His face looked strangely animated at the thought.

'That shouldn't happen …'

'But if it did – they could really do some damage, couldn't they!'

'More likely, the fox would get them.'

That should have drawn a line under the matter. But no; the Chair was on a roll; perhaps he was an alektorophobe.

'And what about avian flu?'

'The UK has been officially free of it for nearly four years …'

'But what if it comes back?'

'Then I would do whatever DEFRA tells me – there's loads of advice already on their website.'

I wanted to say – what about the ducks? What are you going to do about all the ducks and geese from the river, flying over the allotments? But I resisted.

'Well, I'd talk to the council if I were you,' he concluded.

When I phoned the council's Parks and Leisure department, they said,

'Look at the deeds'.

I said, 'I have and there's nothing about chickens in there.'

The man on the end of the line sounded stressed.

'The site is owned by us?'

I said, 'That's why I'm phoning.'

He said, 'Hang on a moment.' After a good few minutes he asked me to phone back later. I phoned back later. He'd gone home. I phoned back next day, feeling a bit of a sucker for punishment.

'Hi,' I chirruped, trying to sound as though we were old mates. 'I was just wondering if you'd found out anything about the chickens?'

'Oh yes,' he said, shuffling papers. 'Here we are – it says 'No Livestock on City Land.'

'Are chickens livestock?' I enquired, in as mild-mannered a tone as I could muster.

'I'm afraid they are regarded as a ...'

'... a health and safety risk,' I said.

Well, at least I'd stolen his punchline.

In fact, the conversation did not end there. We went on to have a long and animated discussion about food production and allotments. I tried to argue that unused corners should be turned over to useful food production; he suggested they were better left for wildlife. I explained about the wretched meat industry and how we all needed to find ways to improve animal welfare ... I said the council should change its rules; he said I could write in and make my suggestions, but he couldn't promise a prompt response, Parks and Leisure was an overstretched department ...

Eventually I gave up. I was angry and upset. But a friend of mine was determined I should not be so easily defeated. She offered to get Googling, and soon enough she had found what she was looking for.

It turns out that if you get the idea of keeping chickens on your allotment, rest assured – according to the Allotments Act 1950 Section 12, you have a statutory right to do so; the consent of the appropriate municipal authority is not required and need not be sought. The Act advises that you 'erect or place and maintain such buildings or structures on the land as are reasonably necessary for that purpose.' The same goes for rabbits.

*

So this was my plan: come the spring, I would erect an aviary in the shady corner and adapt the children's old Wendy house as a cheap coop. Or if the committee couldn't bear the idea, then I would get a couple of Arks from Solway Recycling and offer my fellow allotment holders a free weeding and manuring service.

As far as the breed was concerned, I felt ready to move on from the commercial hybrids. I wanted something good for meat as well as eggs with not too wild a personality: what used to be termed the 'utility' or 'dual-purpose' bird. When I was little there were lots of kinds that fitted the bill, the best known being my grandfather's Rhode Island Reds.

Named after the place it was born – the Little Compton district of Rhode Island, the RIR was developed towards the end of the nineteenth century, originally a cross between the Brown Leghorn from Italy and the sturdy Shanghai – the best layer and the best meat bird. Pioneers of large-scale food production, the Americans understood that the most economic breed was going to be good to eat as well as good for eggs. It was logical enough – instead of throwing the boy-chicks in the grinder, why not bring them up to deliver a decent Sunday lunch?

In the days before mass production, RIRs became popular with people like Grandpa because of their strength, their reliable reproductive abilities and the determination of their publicists. With numerous supplementary breeds introduced into the stock, they arrived in the UK in 1903 and were standardised in 1904. These days, Rhode Island hens are a common ingredient for commercial hybrid layers; for those of us outside the commercial sector, there are exhibition strains with beautiful glossy, chocolate-coloured plumage. The trouble with these is that they are no longer 'utility' at all.

I wish I could have continued Grandpa's legacy, but I needed to be practical. If RIRs could no longer produce meat for the table, I should consider something else. My friend Karen suggested her still-chunky American breed, the Wyandotte. Named after a Native American tribe, this utility bird was developed by crossing pretty crested Polands and Hamburghs with the stately Brahma. Though Karen admitted that her cock was proving too aggressive to stay out of the pot much longer, I found his smooth-fitting partridge plumage and athletic body strikingly attractive. He wore his comb tight to his head like chain-mail, instead of high and spiked. The range of colours currently standardised in the UK totals 14, so I should be able to find something to match the Chair's dahlias. My only potential problem was that the Wyandotte's athleticism gave it excellent flying potential which meant it really might escape on to other people's plots, unless ruthlessly wing-clipped. It is also happiest with plenty of space, which I definitely wouldn't be able to offer with an Ark.

Regarding these limitations, I turned to one last useful American – the Plymouth Rock. This was the utility bird people used to keep in the UK before the hybrids took over; quite possibly it was the one Dianne's dad had in his garden up the road from mine. Developed in New England in the 1800s and registered in 1869, it is still often the basis for broilers around the world. Happy enough in a confined space, yellow skinned and tender-hearted, it would be perfect for keeping in a decent-sized Ark. It is also rather pretty, with lots of colours to choose from, though the black and white striped (known as 'barred') is most common.

My only problem was that it seemed impossible to buy a Plymouth Rock (or either of the other two, for that matter) for under £20. I knew that traditional breeds were not going to be as cheap as hybrids, but I had rather hoped that keeping them for meat would prove economic. I was going to be spending quite a sum fattening them up before they were ready for my dislocation skills. And all the time, in the back of my head, I wouldn't be able to forget that their cousins' corpses at the farmers' market cost under a tenner.

Central to the problem of money was the problem of egg production or rather, lack of. During the 1950s and 60s, as the hybrid industry was taking off, there were very organised laying trials across the UK to establish which traditional flocks were the ones to breed from. Doubtless the utility strains were in there. But gradually, as the commercial hybrids raced ahead down their own production line, breeders of the old strains lost interest in keeping such records. These days there is no quality control, no recording of the productivity of parents or offspring.

Sadly, traditional birds lay much less than they used to. While the Victorians could expect a Plymouth Rock to produce around 285 eggs a year, we have to make do with 200. A contemporary Wyandotte might offer a similar number, but probably less. And what about the RIRs? Grandpa had expected his to lay at least 250. From the websites, I could see that some in the US still boasted the same, but in the UK they seemed to have gone right down. To 150.

In my financial calculations I also had to factor in the mortality rate, though I hoped not the shocking commercial broiler statistic of 1 per cent a week. Down on the allotment I was in danger of losing more than I would in the garden. There would be less human activity, so more foxes; new predators in the form of badgers and perhaps birds of prey. Then there would be the hen-nappers. Though the site has a padlock on the gate and I'd have another on the pen, I knew what happened to another flock in the area – the local lads decided torturing a bunch of birds was good for a laugh.

One way to keep down the price would have been to get them as one-day-old chicks and fatten them up at home; cheaper still would be to breed them myself. What I could do was buy just a couple of Plymouth Rock pullets from the best stock, get in a cock and breed a whole new flock for my meat 'n' egg plot.

My friend Sally, who has bred chickens all her life, warned me I was embarking on a whole new enterprise here. I reassured her that I would avoid keeping a cock because I didn't want run-ins with my neighbours; I left that to my friends. I suggested borrowing one of her Three Teds but Sally said there was no use in that – their progeny would fail both my meat and egg targets. If I asked around amongst my poultry-keeping friends, someone was bound to know of a good cock to rent or borrow; or else I could get in touch with him via his club, once I had decided on the breed.

Right. I reminded myself that this was my first foray into cross-breeding; I mustn't be too ambitious. For example, I mustn't borrow a cock belonging to one of the aggressive breeds and risk him harassing the kids. The point about cross-breeding is to introduce new qualities – so, if the mum's breed was a Plymouth Rock and good for meat, then Dad might as well bring some laying abilities with him. Though breeders say egg laying capacity is not a matter of breed but of selection, it was worthwhile confining my searches to a breed that had not lost all its talents in that area.

I would love to have tried an Italian Leghorn, with its stylish looks and excellent egg laying reputation. My problem was its extrovert Mediterranean nature: the sound of the cock's crow would reach the other side of town, and his enthusiasm for roosting in trees struck me as foolhardy, regarding our local fox population.

My first choice would have to be the much milder-mannered Great British utility bird – the Light Sussex. This breed has a nice backstory: a century ago, the farmers of Lewes got together and realised they had only one flock of genuine Sussex hens left. Having formed a poultry club, they rescued the local breed from extinction and gradually established a range of colours, the light one always proving the most popular. Its striking features – a white body with a zig-zag black collar and black tail, mean that in the past half century the Light Sussex has become popular as an exhibition supermodel and in the process has lost much of its laying power. Fortunately, my friend John informed me, long ago a few flocks were exported across the Channel where French farmers preserved their usefulness. Someone in John's local poultry club might smuggle one back to Blighty for us.

In the meantime, I could go for the original French breed that John himself used to keep. The Maran has grace and poise, and can become very tame if handled frequently. Famed for its mahogany-tinted eggs, it was developed as long ago as the 1800s in Western France by crossing the Asiatic Langshan with the dominant gaming birds of the region. The Marans standardised in Britain are clean-legged strains, Dark and Silver Cuckoo; those bred from the original French stock have feathered legs – the most popular being Copper Black with its petrol-green plumage. If I could find a strain that had retained its laying abilities, this might well turn out to be the one for me.

*

John reminded me that introducing a cock could be tricky, what with the hens' uncompromising pecking order and all. Having only two potential mothers to choose from should be easier: at least there wouldn't be others left behind, feeling jealous. Penning birds in a *ménage à trois* is common practice in chicken circles, and even has its own, socially acceptable name – a trio.

Though ideally I would have put my trio on the allotment, the Allotments Act 1950 Section 12 said I couldn't have cocks there, so they would have to do their thing in the garden. A cock generally has a repertoire of tricks with which to impress, and my children were looking forward to the show. They wanted to see him strut his stuff, his large comb and long tail extended to their fullest potential.

We would recognise a less confident seducer if he resorted to using the call that is meant to draw attention to a tasty morsel of food. The more honest approach would be the John Travolta style of seduction: standing sideways on, he tilts his body in towards the female, showing her the beautiful plumage along his back and tail. Then he lowers his gorgeous wing to the ground and begins to circle her, to the accompaniment of his own, excited squawks. The downward thrust of his body is almost supplicatory, as if on bended knee. Round and round he staggers, round and round. If she shows no interest, he doesn't give up but turns and performs the same steps with the other wing lowered in the other direction. Perhaps she will fancy him better from this side.

Eventually, with any luck, he triggers a response: the hen cowers to the ground, making it a cinch for him to tread her.

The way a cock mates a hen is called treading rather than mounting because he literally treads on top of her. Ouch. Worse still, while his spurs are scrabbling on her back, he keeps his balance by holding on to her neck feathers with his beak.

Grab your partner on the floor!

A really randy cock treads as many times a day as he can. Of the two hens I would be offering him, he might prefer one to the other and end up shagging her featherless, poor dear. John said in that case give her the day off and make him make do with monogamy.

My neighbours would be relieved to hear that the cock did not need to be around for long. After about a week we could be pretty certain the eggs were fertile. The sperm then hung about inside the hen's body for a couple more weeks, so even when he had departed, we would still be collecting fertile eggs. For hatching, I needed to choose the ones that were perfectly smooth and clean.

Contrary to popular belief, fertilised eggs do not need to be kept warm, in fact they should stay cool to stop them developing prematurely – around 12 degrees Celsius is best, stored in an egg box (with their pointed end upwards) in a shed or larder. They can wait for a couple of weeks, if necessary – just as they would were she accumulating a clutch of her own.

Then I needed to decide what to do with them. The trouble with hens is that presented with a clutch of fertilised eggs, they don't necessarily want to sit on them. With commercial hybrids, that's because the nurturing genes have been bred out of them. Not surprising when you realise that all through the incubation and the first few weeks of the chicks' lives, the mother will lay not one single egg. Broodiness is absolutely the last thing a poultry farmer needs. Like many in the non-chicken world (in my experience, boyfriends), he has it down as a serious affliction.

The signs are obvious – she starts going gooey over other people's babies. Nearly. She refuses to come out of the nesting box; when the poultry farmer tries to pull her out, she attacks him; her breast is puffed up and feverish to the touch. In *Fowls and How to Keep Them,* Mannering says if you want to cool her ardour then plonk her in the run or some other airy place, or else pen her with 'a vigorous spare cockerel', though sometimes the broody hormones are too torrid even for that. John advises using a box with mesh on the floor, a bit like a battery cage – the draughts put her right off nesting.

Of course, my problem was going to be quite the opposite – how to get the hormones going. What if my hens waited until their fertilised eggs were addled before getting broody? Just because I now realised that the meaning of life lay in the next generation, it didn't mean my hens would. They might decide they preferred successful careers in egg production.

Which is why incubators were invented.

I have vivid memories of eggs in an incubator when I was at primary school – taking it in turns to press our faces against the murky window and check for signs of life. My daughter Beatrice's class recently borrowed the same system from an agricultural college.

I don't remember if my childhood incubator had an automatic egg-turning mechanism; certainly the contemporary one did – it saves a lot of bother as the eggs need turning at least three times a day for the first 18 days. The turning has to be in both directions, to prevent the yolk cords from twisting too tightly, and an odd number each day, so the eggs don't lie on the same side on consecutive nights. I don't remember adding water to the trays to increase humidity or opening and closing the air vents to control airflow, duties which Beatrice's teacher accomplished with utmost dedication.

I do remember 'candling' the eggs at the end of the first week – closing the classroom curtains and holding each one up against a bare light bulb to see whether a network of veins was beginning to form. Then the same a week later, checking for that little bean-shaped blob of an embryo. Seminal experiences these – almost as heart-stopping as thirty years later, lying in the radiographer's darkened room with my own foetus inside me.

The eggs need to be of similar size so they all incubate at the same rate. It doesn't matter if they have been collected over a period of a week or more – the important thing is that they all go into the box at the same time; that way they are most likely to hatch together. Come the time for hatching, the full-grown chicks manage to communicate with one another through their shells using a tiny clicking noise, as speedy as a vibration –

'Clickety click – fancy taking the plunge?'
'Click, clack, click – I'm up for it if you are.'
'Click, click – see you out there, guys.'

In an incubator this event is a charming little miracle, but in nature it can mean the difference between life and death. Because Junglefowl and their relations nest on the ground, their young are very vulnerable to predators; at least if they synchronise their birth they can abandon the nesting site together and have the best chance of survival.

Depending on the efficacy of antenatal communication, the hatching period may last as long as 24 hours. In the old days, this was the time we kids were jostling for a chance to look through the window. These days, the teacher's dexterity with her camera meant that Beatrice and 29 other five year olds had no such problems. In glorious Technicolor up on their whiteboard, they watched as one chick used its tooth (that's its one, special 'egg tooth', on the top of its beak) as a little pickaxe. A muscle called the pipping muscle on the back of its neck gave it the extra strength to hack its way out of the shell.

The birth accomplished, the children were desperate to hold the new baby. But the teacher forbade their opening the incubator until all its brothers and sisters had arrived. Like opening the oven when a soufflé is in there, you need to be sure your eggs are all fully cooked or else you risk serious disappointment.

At the end of the afternoon, their down dried and chirping noisily, the babies were moved into their 'brooder'. The school brooder (then and now) was a large cardboard box lined with wood shavings, sitting on the carpet with an infrared heat lamp hanging over it. That lamp keeps them at a constantly cosy 35 degrees Celcius and gives them a lovely pinkish glow. It is on a stand that you can raise every week in order to gradually lower the heat until the chicks are fully feathered and able to chirp at regular room temperature (any time between four and eight weeks).

Chicks are the most darling creatures to observe, tottering about, so full of determination and yet so vulnerable. When you pick them up they are light as a dandelion head, their bodies sending a tiny electric whirr into your hand. They are born with all sorts of communal instincts, like the urge to follow one another, to huddle up if they are cold or to spread out if they are too warm. Beatrice's class knelt entranced at the sides of the brooder; it was all their teacher could do not to climb in and give the cuties a cuddle.

One young chap stayed at the incubator, looking down through its window.

'Miss?' he called, 'What about these ones?'

'What about them, Sidney?' croaked the teacher, trying to remain unruffled.

'Are they dead then?'

'I'm afraid they probably are,' she said. And he gazed even harder through the glass as if therein lay some answer to the mystery.

I resisted the temptation to interrupt Sidney's musings with the line that had hopped into my head – '*Don't count your chickens before they hatch!*'

It originates in Aesop's fables – the one about the milkmaid and her pail. A young girl on her way to market carrying a pail of milk on her head, plans how she will sell it and buy some chickens. The chickens will lay eggs that she will sell and with the money she will buy a beautiful dress and hat. At the thought of displaying her lovely garb, she tosses her head and the pail falls to the ground. When she gets home, her mother admonishes her with that now-famous proverb.

The odd thing about it is that, at the time of writing, chickens had yet to be introduced into Greece; the Greco-Persian wars being still a good half century away. It therefore seems unlikely that Aesop chose the metaphor. I suspect the chicken bits were added ages later. Which begs the question, what was that milkmaid really planning?

Talking of planning – none of Beatrice's class enquired what was planned for the fluffies when they returned to agricultural college. Neither the teacher nor I dared spoil things for them. If Sally had been there, I think she might have done. Her Three

Teds were a reminder that unwanted boy chicks hatch out just as often as girls. Sally had planned to cull hers when they were born but discovered she was one of those people who loses their killing ability as they get older. My problem was that I wouldn't know how to identify them.

Sally said it certainly wasn't easy. Probably the first I would know would be at around 10 or 12 weeks, when the males started to crow. A little earlier than this, if I was looking carefully, I might see the cockerels grow their combs sooner than the pullets, and have thicker thighs. Some traditional breeds have differing feather growth – in heavier breeds, the girls get grown-up plumage earlier; in lighter breeds it is the boys who grow their tails first; in some hybrids the young females have longer wing pin feathers than the males … Which is all very well if you are experienced with whichever breed it is, but well-nigh useless for the rest of us.

Unless we know how to sex day-old chicks. It is called 'vent sexing'; this is how it's done:

The sexual organs of both male and female are hidden away in their vent, tiny because they are so young. Picking up that fluffy ball, the vent sexer squeezes its back end and takes a good look inside. He or she has studied the characteristics of chick bits in minute detail, committing to memory the fifteen basic patterns that manifest themselves in different breeds. Broadly speaking, whatever breed s/he is inspecting, s/he is looking for a bump that indicates the chick is male. Some females have very small bumps, but rarely do they have the large bumps of male chicks.

This highly specialised craft originated in Japan. During the 1920s, Professors Masui and Hashimoto from Tokyo started giving lectures about it, but no one took much notice. Then in 1933 they wrote a book and an English translation was published in Canada under the title *Sexing Baby Chicks*. Suddenly, poultry breeders throughout the US and Europe became interested, employing the protégés of Masui and Hashimoto on a seasonal basis via the Japanese Chick Sexing Association. At the Kibworth Hatchery in Leicestershire, a breeder called WP Blount learnt the technique from his Japanese employees and published his version of their book called *Sexing Day-Old Chicks*. In it he confessed that he was neither as dexterous nor as reliable as his teachers, who could sex 3,000 chicks a day with 99 per cent accuracy.

In 1941, after Pearl Harbor, seven of the seasonal vent sexers got stuck in Great Britain and interned on the Isle of Man. Having completed a particularly successful sexing season, they were flush and found that their cash made them the most popular internees in the camp. When they were eventually released, three of them decided to stay on permanently in the UK, passing on their specialism to those who wished to undertake the training.

Fortunately, thinking again about Bea's chicks, I realise now that they didn't need vent sexing. They fell clearly into two distinct kinds of plumage – yellow and tawny. Most likely the colour was directly linked to their gender, either because they were sex-linked hybrids like the ISA Brown, or because they came from an auto-sexing breed.

Autosexing was invented during the World War I by an English professor called Reginald Crundall Punnett. When he crossed a barred (stripy) Plymouth Rock with a brown Campine he found the boy chicks came out pale yellow and their sisters came out barred and buff coloured.

These days there are lots of autosexing breeds available – you can tell because in their name they have the suffix 'bar' – for example, 'Legbar' from an original Leghorn cross, and 'Brussbar' from a Sussex. It is extremely convenient for the breeder. Where sex-linking required parents that came from particular, separate breeds, the autosexing characteristic is there within the one breed and continues down the generations.

Their handy colour-coding proved a Godsend for a friend-of-a-friend when the eggs she had been incubating failed to hatch.

It was a very special clutch of eggs, bought from a reputable breeder – the first chicks the family would ever own. Mum had promised the children that they would watch the babies emerging from their shells, that they could each give one a name and welcome them as adorable new members of the family … She worried what exactly she would say if any of the chicks turned out to be male. She knew there would be a dreadful scene if suddenly at 10 or 12 weeks or whatever age their testosterone revealed itself, the pets had to be confiscated. She decided to put her worry on the back-burner.

Every morning, the children leapt out of bed and rushed downstairs to check the incubator. Day 20 went by, then Day 21, then Day 22. The children grew anxious. The friend-of-a-friend grew desperate – how was she going to confess to her kids that all these weeks of waiting and watching had come to nothing? That all they had was a clutch of rotten eggs. Day 23 – after a sleepless night, she phoned the breeder and together they hatched not a chick but a plot: after she had dropped the children at school she would zip over to the farm and pick up five brand new buff-coloured chicks, born that very morn. And the marvellous thing was – they were all, incontrovertibly, females.

*

Back in Bea's classroom, the first thing the children did once the chicks were settled under their lamp was to offer them something to eat and drink.

Water is safest delivered in a chick-sized water fount, the grown-up ones being dangerously large for a chick who has yet not learnt to swim.

The food they most appreciate is chopped hard-boiled egg. As everyone who has ever eaten breakfast knows, hard-boiled tastes totally different from raw, so we don't have to worry that this early experience might cause them to eat their own eggs later in life. Finely chopped chickweed and even grass get gobbled up, as do dandelions and clover.

Bea's chicks were given 'chick crumb' for their very first meal, mixed with a little warm water so it was swollen and porridgy. Gradually the dry version was introduced over the following days, and that became their staple for the next few weeks. Chick crumb is a high-protein feed containing medication to keep coccidiosis at bay.

This killer disease occurs mostly in chicks around three to six weeks old, often in warm, damp conditions. It is caused by coccidia protozoa (single-celled parasites) that breed in the chickens' intestine and spread through faeces. Large-scale breeders use spray vaccines to guard against it, but there is no such facility for us smallholders.

If the chick picks up some coccidia on its foraging rounds, it can get sick very quickly indeed, hunched and cheeping miserably in the corner. A well-known sign of infection is bloody droppings, but unfortunately not all forms of the disease produce this symptom, and anyway if you see blood the chick is probably too far gone to be treated. The parasites multiply speedily inside its body, so it needs to be removed from its fellows and taken to the vet FAST.

Treatments come in a bottle and are administered with a pipette into the crop.

Infected birds excrete the coccidia eggs in droppings, thereby contaminating their bedding and the ground for up to two years. If you think you have a sick chick, you need to change the bedding every few hours. For the ground, normal disinfectants do not kill the eggs, but ammonia does, as well as temperatures above 56 degrees centigrade. A blast from the midsummer sun, or a few days' dousing with boiling water and household ammonia should do the trick.

With any luck the chicks develop immunity to coccidiosis as they get older.

By the time they are six weeks old they are ready to be weaned on to something called 'growers feed' – lower in protein than the chick crumb and without the medication. They also need grit to get their gizzards working, especially if you are starting to introduce grain. This new diet can be mixed with the chick crumb for a few days so they don't get tummy aches from too rapid a change. Growers feed comes in both crumb and mini-pellet form. Layers crumb or pellets come on the menu when they reach POL-stage, around 16–18 weeks old.

Some people have hard-and-fast objections to starting their babies on such a path. As someone who tries to avoid industrial feed, I do sympathise. But it makes life much more expensive when you decide to feed your chicks on pin-head oatmeal and millet. It also makes life harder – for a few months, you are watching like a hawk for the tiniest signs of sickness. And because coccidiosis thrives in humid conditions, without the medication you must be absolutely fastidious about keeping the chicks' bedding dry and changing it regularly. Leading to the old rhyme – *'Dirty and dry, not much will die. Dirty and wet makes cash for the vet.'*

Not that my friend Dianne from the bakery remembers her chicks ever needing to go to the vet. Half a century ago, when she was growing up in my area, the family had a constant stream of pretty chicks. And it was her job to look after them.

Every Thursday her mother bundled together some old clothes and set them by the front door. Dianne remembers it was Thursdays because that was baking day – a warm, yeasty smell filling the house. When they heard the van hooting its horn outside, the kids would pick up their bundle and run out into the street to hand it over. A friendly chap he was, Mr White the rag 'n' bone man, with his soft white hair and such a gentle manner. In return for their clothes, he opened up the back of the van, revealing two big boxes: one was a tank of goldfish and the other a flock of little yellow chicks. The children were meant to choose between them, but in truth they weren't allowed a fish because it would have been useless. Anyway, Dianne always loved to take away a fluffy, chirruping ball in her hands.

They lived in the back room in a cardboard box, feeding on kitchen scraps boiled to a mush on the stove. One time she remembers Mr White had some sort of job-lot to get rid of and her mother agreed to take 100 at once. They had to let them run free in the room, there were so many of them, scuttling between the legs of the benches and the dining table. It was quite a sight, all those yellow pom-poms darting about the floor. Of course, they put newspaper down for their droppings, but they were so tiny it was no bother. Dianne thought it was a great treat, having so many babies to care for, and felt sad when their adult plumage arrived and they had to go outside to Dad's shed.

I fancied turning over my back room to a flock of chicks for a while. I reckoned I would probably give them the medicated crumb, but they would still be vulnerable to all the diseases against which hybrids are vaccinated. Marek's is especially bothersome – formally known as Fowl Paralysis, this herpes virus affects the nervous system, causing limb paralysis and blindness; if it doesn't kill, it permanently incapacitates. Though vaccinated, one of my hybrids might have carried Marek's and left traces around the garden. That meant extra special care and fingers crossed when the chicks went outside. An outdoor run would be good for when they were tiny (vulnerable to rats and even to our ancient cat) – I would leave it in sheltered spots and move it around regularly, giving them constant access to what I hoped was fresh, clean grass.

When they were a bit bigger, I looked forward to offering them my whole garden to hone their foraging skills. Unlike full-grown hens, chicks can do little harm to the lawn or the flowerbeds. New mother as I was going to be, I intended to be more fastidious than ever: I would make sure the ground was not wet – wet down can cause a nasty chill; I would mow the grass before they went on it to prevent my babies getting impacted crops or accidentally choking; I would watch them like a (vegetarian) hawk.

And what about the Allotment Act 1950's insistence that the cockerels stayed home (once I knew which ones they were)? Utility breeds are much slower growing than any of those commercial broiler types; the males might not be ready to eat before they were seven months old. That meant a lot of crowing for my neighbours to put up with. If I was lucky, they would take a long summer holiday; followed by an autumn of apologies. Come Christmas, I would try and make up for it by inviting them round to share my supremely delicious, home-grown coq au vin.

Brit Chicks

Oh! De Shanghai!
Don't bet your money on de Shanghai
Take a little chicken in de middle of de ring
But don't bet your money on de Shanghai
Stephen C Foster

When Julius Caesar and his army invaded Britain, they were surprised to discover that *Gallus gallus domesticus* had preceded them, probably in the company of the Phoenicians. What surprised them all the more was that the birds were kept not for food but for fighting.

Though the Brits did gradually come round to the idea of eating their chickens' meat and eggs, it took several hundred years for them to relinquish their taste for cockfighting. Between 1833 and 1845, various acts of Parliament were passed that eventually banned it. And having at last acknowledged that birds tearing one another apart was unacceptable entertainment, the Victorians discovered the joys of breeding them. As trade routes and transport systems opened up, amateur and professional breeders began importing all sorts of interesting new breeds to replace their fighting stock. The most important being big, docile birds from the East.

In 1842, when the port of Shanghai opened to international trade, ships were launched carrying specimens of exotic Chinese chickens previously unknown in Europe or the Americas. The biggest and most docile of these was imaginatively christened the Shanghai. She went first to the US (where Stephen C. Foster came across her), but when a Mr Burnham of Boston judged her fine enough for an Empress, she was soon on her way across the Atlantic.

Renamed Cochin on arrival in England, the breed was remark-able for possessing quite opposite characteristics from indigenous fighters like the Old English Game Fowl. Queen Vic is said to have adored them; she and her visitors found their huge, round bodies and genial temperaments absolutely beguiling. Perhaps they saw in them something as wholesome as the royal matriarch herself, with their ample rumps and ankles reassuringly hidden away under feathered legs.

Soon enough, people were searching all over China for similar novelties. The little Silkie is likely to have arrived during this period, as did the handsome, black Croad Langshan, launched in1872 by a Major FT Croad who said he had discovered it in the Langshan district, north of the Yangtse-Kiang River.

Meanwhile, back in the US, breeders crossed the Shanghai with Grey Chittagongs from India to create another exotic with an Indian name – the Brahma (from the 4-headed Hindu god of creation, via their sacred river the Brahmaputra). But it wasn't just exoticism they were after; breeders throughout the land were inspired to experiment with crossing these meaty Asian breeds with already established layers to find the perfect utility bird.

It is these sorts of combinations, crossing Asian imports with older ones (like the Italian Leghorn) that caused *Gallus gallus domesticus* greater evolutionary change than in the whole of her previous existence. Well done, you Victorians; I call that a triumph for East meets West.

Sadly, the forces of industrialisation ran counter to those of cultural exchange. It was in the Great British chicken psyche: having spent thousands of years watching them kill one another, within a century of banning the cockpit they were driving them into factories. All those colourful new breeds were all-too rapidly distilled into the egg and meat machines of today.

So here we are. The vast majority of chickens are now commercial hybrids. Contemporary geneticists like Hans Cheng may be concerned about these chickens' inability to cope with unforeseen circumstances, but his predecessors didn't think like that. Like their colleagues working for the car companies, they were doing a great job facilitating productivity. And when a disease like fowl pest happened to hamper their progress, they turned to the pharmaceutical companies who kindly provided the vaccines. It is much quicker and cheaper to spray a vaccine than it is to breed immunity over generations.

'But what if …?', cries the twenty-first century scientist. What if some pathogen arrives for which the manufacturers have not yet found a vaccine? It only takes one, and suddenly their equivalent to the Formula 1 racing car is crashing straight into one almighty chicken pile-up.

Step forward the Poultry Club of Great Britain. Established in 1877, the Poultry Club has a long tradition with a major and pivotal role in the conservation and preservation of pre-industrial stock. Amateurs all over the country keep all sorts of interesting breeds; for a modest membership fee they attend meetings at their local clubs, exchanging tips or even chickens. Many of them enter competitions up and down the country where their chooks are closely examined by expert Poultry Club judges. These people are potentially the keepers of that pool of rare genes that has disappeared from the commercial sector.

Every winter, the Club holds its annual shindig at the National Agricultural Centre in the Midlands. Over one weekend, breeders from all over the UK gather to show prime examples of traditional pure breeds and their eggs. At the opening in 1973, they hosted 1,367 entries; gradually they attracted more and more interest until, in November 2009, the number of entrants reached four times that. It was only just over an hour's drive away from where we live – an excellent family outing for a rainy Sunday.

As we followed the signs towards the entrance, through the warehouse doors came a screeching and a yelling – the sound of a thousand cocks asserting their territory. Even five-year-old Beatrice, who has attended many a children's party in her time, was shocked by the cacophony.

Inside stood rows and rows of cages with perfectly unsoiled wood-chippings on the bottom, a little pot of water and one of mixed grain attached to the door. Each cage contained a beauty contestant, his or her pristine winter plumage impressively displayed. Forget the home-keepers' rule about not washing your hen; these birds wouldn't contemplate going anywhere without a major wash 'n' blow-dry. The Great British Orpingtons were especially impressive: rows of caramel coloured giants, their plumage blown into the biggest bouffant you ever saw. Apparently the Queen Mother had several prize winners; of course, they couldn't be expected to lay much – far too posh to push.

Leaving Jay and the girls to gawp at the Orps, I went in search of the utility breeds. The row labelled 'Maran' was modest: just a few birds, all with Dark Cuckoo markings. Maybe I could arrange to borrow one of the cocks for a couple of weeks.

As I arrived, a shy young man was carrying one to the main table; how obedient that bird looked – just right for joining a trio in my backyard. His proud owner drew out the curve of his tail with his fingers; the cock tossed his red-hot comb and flashed a look at me. I flashed back. It was an oddly pleasurable sensation, flirting with a chicken.

An older chap in a flat cap was busily inserting green cards in the doors of the cages – 'I want everyone to see how I judged them,' he told me. 'They've already got their rosettes, but this gives them an idea of the detail.'

'Do you judge them for usefulness?' I asked.

'What do you mean?'

'Marans are meant to be utility birds, aren't they?'

'Well, yes – you'll see the way we judge them from the card.'

I made my way over to an empty cage with the first prize rosette on it. The winning bird had got 15 out of 15 for 'colour and marking', 5 out of 5 for 'legs and feet' but only 34 out of 40 for 'carriage and table merit'.

Oh dear. It seemed that even the best Maran in the country scored better on chicken beauty that on chicken dinner. It occurred to me that if a commercial hybrid was a racing car, then this star would be a vintage Bentley – beautiful but useless.

As I turned towards the exit, I spotted an interesting sign on top of the next-door row – 'Utility'. A man in official Poultry Club overalls was making his way past.

'Excuse me,' I interjected. 'Do you know anything about these?'

'I'm not sure I do,' he said, peering into the cages. Again, the row was short – not more than a dozen birds in total. I recognised a Barnevelder: a Dutch breed imported into the UK in the 1920s. I loved the look of him – his laced plumage, each feather with rings of greenish black on a nut-brown background. The female lays caramel brown eggs (at least 200 a year, they say).

Next door was a Plymouth Rock, her owner standing beside the cage.

'How come you've got a bird in this class?' I enquired.

'I didn't think she was in the running for her breed class, so I tried this one,' he said.

'And how do they judge her?' I asked, realising all of a sudden that it is much easier to judge a hen by her looks than by her productivity.

'They measure the pelvic bone,' said the man, raising his right hand with the fingers held tight together. 'Three fingers' width and she's a good layer.'

'And the meat?'

'That'll be the cockerels,' he said.

Come to think of it, that Barnevelder did have nice fat thighs.

'So why's it such a small class?'

'It only started a couple of years ago – Prince Charles is Patron of the Poultry Club, and he's quite serious about food, isn't he!'

Well, hurrah for Prince Charles. His grandmother may have gone for looks over productivity, but now he was making up for it.

This was exactly what I had been looking for, neither Formula 1 nor Bentley – the equivalent of a really reliable estate car.

I took the Plymouth Rock man's details and said I'd be in touch. It was time to find the rest of the family.

Jay had taken the girls down the end to the sales section. Beatrice was finding the competitive atmosphere all too much and had started to join in with the crowing. She was standing in front of a cage containing two large snowballs with blobs of black rubber on the top. Eventually, I managed to comprehend that she had an urgent need to take these things home; she wanted them for her Christmas present. I peered at the label – White Silkies.

They did look odd, with charcoal skin under white feathers so fragile they resembled that autumnal fuzz you find in country hedgerows – old man's beard. Come to think of it, the duo Bea desired looked more like Santas than snowballs. I knew they were one of the oldest breeds of hen: during his thirteenth century travels in Asia, Marco Polo wrote of a furry chicken that might well have been a Silkie. According to Hans Cheng and his team, it still has a full 100 per cent of the genes a chicken is meant to possess.

'Mummy,' announced Ellie, gravely. 'When I was five I got Snowy for Christmas.'

'But those aren't bunnies …' I started to protest. I had a vague feeling that Silkies were indeed once thought to be a cross between a rabbit and a hen … From Bea's point of view, that was exactly what they were. Bunny-chicks.

After all my confusions about keeping hens as pets, these were nothing but – terribly cute and easy to tame, apparently they don't damage the garden like other chickens; their life expectancy is a good nine years. The Silkie is neither utility bird nor hybrid, her flesh being unappetisingly dark and her egg-count no more than four a week. Her laying season starts over Christmas and finishes during the summer. The reason for this is uncertain – perhaps it is an acute sensitivity to light, stimulating her to start laying the moment the days get longer and to stop the moment they shorten. Or else, she stops because her Shanghai-original genes tell her the monsoon season has arrived and it is time to concentrate on keeping dry.

Her lack of meat and egg producing attributes doesn't mean she isn't useful: the Silkie's *raison d'être* is to bring up a family. Indeed, some say that the mere sight of an egg gets her mothering instincts going. Which makes me think how very unnatural our modern hybrids are. In the old days, maternal dedication was exactly what hens were celebrated for. The best-known allusion I can think of is in the Gospel according to St Matthew (Matthew 23:37), when Christ uses the hen as an example of selfless dedication to other people's children. She is the absolute opposite of the religious leaders with their brutality and their hypocrisy. At the high point of his diatribe, he cries – '*O Jerusalem, Jerusalem, you who kill the prophets and stone those sent to you, how often I have longed to gather your children together, as a hen gathers her chicks under her wings, but you were not willing.*'

Standing in front of the Silkies' cage, I was starting to think of another well-known piece of avian imagery – two birds with one stone. If I were to give in to Bea's pleas for a cuddly Christmas present, she would get the most adorable pets and I would get a couple of potential foster mothers for my allotment flock. I had been worried about my American Utility hens not becoming broody for their fertilised eggs, but, from her reputation, this

Chinese bird would always be there for them. A simple alternative to the incubator, the lamp and all those gizmos: just one fluffy bottom and a life of selfless dedication.

It's lovely how some breeds are prepared to look after foreign birds' babies. They are so satisfied by the experience of sitting and nurturing that they don't notice the breed. Come to think of it, the Orps with their huge bottoms have similar inclinations. Thank God Bea hadn't fallen in love with a couple of them – we would never have got them in through the front door.

A penchant for fostering was something we knew a bit about through ten-year-old Annie and her bantams.

One day Annie went out to the hen house to fetch the eggs and found Pong the Pekin refusing to leave the nesting box. When she tried to put her hand under her, the hen gave her an angry peck. That was weird, Annie thought, because Pong was usually so gentle. Her mum said she must be broody.

There was a moment of panic. Only now did the family realise that having Brendan the petrol-black cock meant all their eggs were fertilised and ready for a broody. All of a sudden, with no forward planning, they had shifted from simple egg-production straight into parenting. They borrowed a little broody house from a friend and moved Pong in there with all the eggs she was sitting on (five brown and one white). A week later, they found that she had pecked the white egg; red veins were leaking out on to the straw. Annie had an idea about this – she thought Pong was worried that this chick was going to be different, like its egg. Maybe she thought the others would bully it, so she got rid of it. Interestingly, this was the only one she could possibly have laid herself; the brown ones were from their hybrids and could only ever become her foster-chicks.

Anyway, Annie really liked looking after Pong while she was sitting on her foster-eggs. Every morning before school she took her a handful of corn and fed it to her while she sat on her nest. She ate and she ate – half a cup or more, sometimes.

After three weeks, Annie's brother was out one day and he had a look at the eggs: there was a hole in one of them. He came running to get her and when she had a look she could see a little yellow eye peaking through the hole. She thought maybe the chick had got stuck, so decided to take a bit of shell off. That must have helped, because in just a few minutes she was out, all wet and pale; in a flash she was hidden beneath her foster-mum, but not before Annie had decided to call her Snow White.

Unfortunately, none of the other eggs hatched, which may well be because the children had interfered in the process. Annie said she didn't mind – she was sure Snow White would always have been her favourite. She used to run away from everyone, but with Annie she was docile; she would let her stroke her and carry her about, which Annie was convinced was because she had been there at the birth.

Until Snow White started to crow. At which point he was rechristened Rocky and left to strut about the garden, a perfect compliment to his dad.

In our case, if this Silkie plan went ahead I intended to prevent my children helping with the birth. Young Beatrice would have to keep well away from her broody Silkie when the eggs were hatching. And if she went and fell in love with a boy chick, I would have to hark on local traditions of half a century ago, when Dianne and her siblings were forced to part with their beloved, and later to eat him.

And to speed things up, I might decide to circumvent the whole *ménage à trois* insemination thing. The gallinaceous equivalent of

IVF has a long and reliable history: you simply get hold of some fertilised eggs from a reputable hatchery or friend and pop them underneath your already broody Silkie. There are loads available on eBay – they should arrive safely in the post, as long as they didn't have too far to travel and the postman didn't shake his parcels around too much. It would be sad not to have something as handsome as that Maran to stay, but probably a lot less hassle. And soon enough, we might have our own such bird for the meat 'n' egg plot …

And just at that moment, just as I was reaching the decision that Silkies were indeed my family's future, who should arrive at my shoulder, as if from nowhere, but John Marfleet, our piano tuner. It was such an amazing coincidence, it could only happen in real life.

'Like them Silkies do you?' said John Marfleet. John breeds bantams.

'They make good pets?'

'I'd say so. Broodies is what people use them for … nice looking pair. How much are they?'

He shifted his specs and peered at the price tag.

'Fifty quid! You're not paying that!'

'I was thinking of getting them for the girls for Christmas.'

'You know, I've got some Silkies coming along.'

'Full size?'

''Course! 'Lot cheaper than these ones, I'm telling you.'

'How much, John?'

'I dunno – I'll probably let you have them for nothing. 'Round nine weeks, when their Mum comes off of 'em.'

'Will you know which are the cockerels by then?'

'Mmm. Not sure – I've never been that good at telling the Silkies … We'll have to see.'

I looked down at my daughters whose faces were wide with joy. John Marfleet had just made their Christmas.

On our way home through the winter darkness, Ellie and Bea chatter about what we are going to call their new pets. *Fluffy and Snowball … Barley and Corn … Acorn and Popcorn … Lola and Mabel …* The possibilities are endless. Jay is just happy that this year's Christmas present originates in China but is not the usual plastic variety. And I am busy fantasising about next year's brood.

If we want chicks by Easter, we'll need one of the Silkies to be broody by March. She'll need fattening up because once in charge of the eggs she is going to spend a good three weeks glued to them. I will also need to give her a good going over for lice and mites; the last thing an expectant mother wants is an infestation.

I'm going to need a peaceful place for her to nest. A tough cardboard box with holes will do, with lots of woodchips and straw on the bottom to keep things comfortable. If the weather is still chilly, I'll give her a corner at the end of the kitchen, behind the chest of drawers; if it is warm, I could probably give my rabbit cage one last reincarnation – the sleeping compartment is perfect for nesting and the little run area will be useful for the chicks when they make their first forays abroad.

John will advise me how many eggs I need to get – they say nine for an average sized hen; seven might be a good number for a Silkie, and a lucky one for me, just slightly superstitious about my new venture.

We'll transfer the broody to her box (or cage) and once we're sure she is there for the duration, I can ease the clutch under her one by one. Then it will just be a case of waiting.

And what about feeding her? I shall have to feel my way on that one. Probably my children will be like Annie and want to hand-feed her, but John says not to bother; his broodies have always been so fixated on their job that he just leaves them alone for the full three weeks' incubation. All they get is a little trough of water that they can reach through the bars of his broody coop. My pre-war mentor, Rosslyn Mannering, advises intervention. He says take the hen off the eggs once a day; if after 10 minutes or so she still has not defecated, Mannering says you should scoop her up by the wings, hold her for a moment suspended about a metre from the ground and then suddenly drop her. He says not to worry – it really is no worse than her hopping off the perch, and 'the expansion and contraction of the muscles engendered seldom fails to produce the desired result.'

Oh, and if the children promise to be really careful, Mannering says while she is out pooing they can moisten the eggs with a little tepid water. Day 19 is when this is particularly important, in preparation for hatching; John says his broodies did the job themselves, swooshing water with their beaks from the trough into their nest.

Come Day 21, fingers crossed, all seven little darlings will appear under their foster Mummy's tummy. And soon enough all our friends and relations will be crowding in to welcome them.

The traffic is dense; lights multiply in the raindrops across the windscreen – red ones streaming forward and white ones against us. Even on a Sunday, there is not room enough for all the cars. Drivers veer between lanes, nudging in and out of one another's path in order to get that little way ahead and closer to home. There are just too many of us; too many humans needing too

many cars; too many chickens and too many eggs. As every year
our number increases, how are we going to cope?

Struck by the impossibility of the twenty-first century lifestyle,
I am starting to have bold ambitions for my new chicks. I have
this idea that maybe, once we are up and breeding, we will get a
cock for the Silkies and breed from them. What I am thinking is
that when that 'disease shock' comes along and wipes out the
hybrids, our birds will call on their 100 per cent genetic reserves
and survive. Suddenly they will be the only chickens on the
planet – unappetisingly black, with modest laying abilities. All
that pappy white flesh and rows of pseudo-rustic brown eggs will
be gone; and, instead, a rare and cherished sight will be a little
Chinese chicken, pecking around somebody's back garden.

Glossary of Chicken Terms

Alektorophobia – a fear of chickens.

Bantam – a little chicken, often a miniature version of a larger breed, though bantam breeds exist in their own right, for example the Pekin (given the name of the Chinese capital city by the Victorians, but probably originating in Java like all true mini-hens).

Broiler – a chicken bred for its meat.

Chicken – The word 'chicken' used to describe not the adult but the baby – hence the term 'she's no spring chicken' and that seeming tautology of a pub, 'The Hen and Chickens'. 'Chick' is simply a shortened version, introduced (it is thought) around the fourteenth century.

Chook – All over the internet you come across this generic term covering all ages of chicken and both sexes; the word is said to originate in the Antipodes.

Cock – a sexually mature male chicken.

Cockerel – strictly speaking this word refers only to a male chicken under a year old. In the UK, Canada and Australia many people coyly use the term for the mature male.

Dual Purpose – breeds of chicken that used to provide both meat and eggs.

Gallus – Apart from the domestic chicken (in all its forms), this genus of bird includes four varieties of Junglefowl living wild in South and South East Asia.

Gallus gallus domesticus – the Latin name for a domestic chicken.

Gallinaceous–belonging to the genus *Gallus*.

Hen – a mature female chicken, probably over a year old.

Pullet – a female under a year old.

POL – a pullet 'at the point of lay' (normally between 16 and 20 weeks old).

Rooster – the American word for cock.

Utility bird – same as 'dual purpose' – 'utility' as in something useful.

Acknowledgments

Thank you to all my friends who helped create this book. It has been such fun talking chickens with you, and getting your ideas down on paper. I am only sorry there was not room for all your names and all your stories.

I would also like to thank the following organisations and individuals who went out of their way to share their expertise:

Phil Brooke at Compassion in World Farming
Anna Bassett from the Soil Association
Elm Farm Research Centre
Mike Gooding and colleagues at FAI
Greger Larson, dept. Archaeology, Durham University
Jane Howorth, BHWT
Alice Clark and Mark Cooper from RSPCA's Freedom Foods
Humane Slaughter Association
National Society of Allotment and Leisure Gardeners Ltd.
The Poultry Club of GB
Rabbi Eli Brackman
Rev. Andrew McKearney

Rev. David Barton

Fiona Tomley and colleagues at the Institute for Animal Health, Compton, Berkshire.

As for the publishing bit – thanks to Lisa Darnell for so dexterously overseeing the project, thanks to Nigel Wilcockson for his imagination and encouragement, and to Vanessa Neuling for fine-tuning.

Finally, a special thank you to my family – to my father and father-in-law for rigorous attention to my prose, and to Jay and the girls for putting up with yet another encroachment on family life.